Th

MW01673593

The Law Magazine and Law Review

Volume 17

SALZWASSER
VERLAG

The Law Magazine

The Law Magazine and Law Review

Volume 17

Reprint of the original, first published in 1864.

1st Edition 2022 | ISBN: 978-3-75259-306-8

Verlag (Publisher): Salzwasser Verlag GmbH, Zeilweg 44, 60439 Frankfurt, Deutschland
Vertretungsberechtigt (Authorized to represent): E. Roepke, Zeilweg 44, 60439 Frankfurt, Deutschland
Druck (Print): Books on Demand GmbH, In de Tarpen 42, 22848 Norderstedt, Deutschland

THE LAW MAGAZINE AND LAW REVIEW; OR, Quarterly Journal of Jurisprudence.

FEBRUARY TO AUGUST, 1864.

VOLUME XVII.

LONDON

1864.

INDEX TO VOL. XVII.

OF THE

Law Magazine and Law Review.

THE

Law Magazine and Law Review:

OR,

QUARTERLY JOURNAL OF JURISPRUDENCE.

No. XXXIII.

Art. I.—SUGGESTIONS FOR THE AMENDMENT OF THE LAW OF APPEAL IN CRIMINAL CASES.*

THE practice of granting new trials, though not altogether unknown, was seldom resorted to in this country before the middle of the seventeenth century. So long as jurors continued to be mere recognitors, their functions were testimonial as well as judicial, and their verdict was of course paramount and final. It would appear from a statement by Glanville that, at all events in the reign of Henry II., jurors of assize, and the ordinary *jurata patriæ* were empannelled for the finding of facts on their own personal knowledge, and not upon independent evidence laid before them.†

As to the character and particularity of the personal knowledge which each juror was bound to possess, the rule was not very strict or well-defined; it being understood that where direct evidence was unattainable, the jury were to give their verdict *ex credulitate* or *ex conscientia.*

* A Paper, by Mr. G. Harry Palmer, read at a Meeting of the Jurisprudence Department of the National Association for the Promotion of Social Science, February 1, 1864.

† Glanville, lib. 2, c. 7.

The practice of *enforcing* a jury naturally suggested itself as the best mode of carrying out the ideal infallibility, with which it was sought to invest this popular tribunal. It consisted in a careful elimination from the panel of recognitors of those who, from ignorance of the circumstances or other cause, turned out to be dissentients, and in the substitution of a corresponding number of competent jurors whose verdict would be unanimous. Here, then, was a tribunal, uniting in itself functions which were at once testimonial as well as judicial, and from which, if the conditions above alluded to could have been strictly carried out, appeals would have been useless and unnecessary.

Unfortunately, it was found that this tribunal, although theoretically faultless, had its drawbacks. Great difficulty was experienced in procuring twelve men who were witnesses to the facts, and whose verdict was unanimous. Sometimes direct evidence could only be obtained from women or children, who of course could not act as jurors; while in other instances the circumstances were witnessed by only one or two observers. Thus the practice of *enforcement* gradually fell into disuse, and new elements became incorporated with the original conception of a jury trial.

In the twenty-third year of Edward III. a most important innovation was solemnly sanctioned, viz., the *adjoinment* of witnesses to the jury, for the purpose of aiding them by their testimony, but having no voice in the verdict; and whose evidence might indeed have been entirely set aside by such verdict. The change thus introduced raised the responsibilities and status of jurors. They were no longer mere depositaries of knowledge, but the higher and more intellectual task of deducing conclusions from the testimony of others now devolved upon them. Hitherto an erroneous verdict logically implied corrupt perjury (for the jurors were sworn to decide upon their own knowledge), and their punishment was by *attaint.* But when they became judicial officers of the court, a wrong verdict implied only error of judgment, for which it would be obviously unjust to inflict a punishment. This naturally led to a great revolution in legal procedure, viz., to the establishment of Courts of Appeal, and the granting of new trials. This privilege—a tardy concession to the demands of a people no longer barbarous—was confined for centuries to civil procedure. Appeal by way of motion for a new trial, or writ of error, or by a bill of exceptions, gave the dissatisfied litigants ample opportunity to test the validity of judicial decisions respecting the existence of a debt, or the meaning of a contract; but the finality of a verdict upon an inquest by jury was scrupulously left undisturbed as regards all indictable offences. Within a recent period, and after a hard struggle, the legislature conferred the right of appeal even in criminal cases, where the subject of it was a question of law. This is the nearest approximation that has yet been made towards the complete assimilation of the Law of Appeal in civil and criminal proceedings.

And permit me, in this place, to call attention to one provision, in the present Law of Criminal Appeal, which has been severely criticised by those whose experience and learning bespeak for their opinions a respectful consideration. I refer to the discretion now vested in the judges with respect to points reserved. It cannot be denied that the manner in which this discretion has been exercised has not given satisfaction. The anticipation of Mr. Justice Coleridge, expressed in his evidence before the Select Committee of the House of Lords, appears to have been fully verified. "I am not so much afraid of the wholly unprofessional magistrate," observed Mr. Justice Coleridge, "who might perhaps *refer* improperly, as I am of the half-educated lawyer presiding (a case of not unfrequent occurrence), who might, I think, sometimes also *refuse* to refer improperly. I am inclined to think that if the prisoner's counsel will certify, under his hand, that he believes there is error of law in the decision objected to, and will undertake to argue the point, the chairman ought to be bound to state the case. . . . . In civil cases, it is remarkable how small a proportion those in *formâ pauperis* (where such certificate is necessary) bear to other cases, and how small upon the whole the abuse is of the permission to sue." The greater portion of the criminal business of the country is conducted before the inferior judges of Quarter Sessions, and it is worthy of observation that those judges appear to show more reluctance to reserve a question of law than the judges of the Superior Courts, although it may, without offence, be supposed that the former have not a more extensive or accurate knowledge of its principles than the learned judges who preside over the higher tribunals. This is very natural. A judge imperfectly informed as to the law, often hesitates to reserve a question which may be important and new, under a fear lest it turn out to be a well-established point with which he ought to have been familiar. It must also be admitted that many who are most anxious for the proper administration of justice, in their diffidence and anxiety sometimes consent to state cases for the consideration of the Court of Appeal which ought to have been peremptorily refused. The result is that the reservation of questions of law which are of importance and difficulty, is very much a matter of chance.* Upon this point the illustrations given by Sir Fitzroy Kelly, in his evidence before the Select Committee of the House of Lords, are very apposite.

"I have myself, within my own experience, known some such fearful instances of injustice on the refusal by judges of great eminence and learning, and of great humanity, to reserve points which have afterwards been determined to be fatal to the conviction which has taken place, that I think the people of this country are entitled to demand that an appeal should be matter of right and not matter of discretion with the judge."

The case of ***Russell***, the Huntingdon gaolor, bears out in a

* This subject is ably argued in a pamphlet addressed to Sir George Cornewall Lewis, then Home Secretary, by W. Ribton, Esq., Barrister-at-Law.

most convincing manner the statement which I have just quoted. The prisoner was indicted for causing the death of a woman, by administering medicines to procure abortion. The learned counsel for the prisoner, Sir F. Kelly, in the course of the trial raised a question of law, and requested the presiding judge to reserve the point. The request was refused, the prisoner was found guilty and sentenced to be executed. Feeling the momentous importance of the issue to the prisoner, the soundness of the objection taken, and evincing a zeal in the discharge of duty, happily not singular, though seldom surpassed in the annals of the English bar, the prisoner's counsel eventually succeeded in inducing the judge to communicate with Lord Tenterden and Lord Lyndhurst, and to ask their opinion whether the point should be reserved or not. Fortunately they advised that the point should be argued. The execution was postponed, and the twelve judges, after hearing the arguments, decided unanimously that the question raised was fatal to the conviction, whereupon the prisoner was discharged.

I am told on the authority of gentlemen now practising at the criminal law bar—gentlemen who are among the leaders of that bar—that the injustice arising from granting discretionary powers to the court with respect to reserving points of law in criminal cases, is very great.

The following returns give some idea of the actual working of the law of appeal on questions of law in criminal cases.

The returns for 1857 show that the total number of appeals in criminal cases were thirty-six, out of which thirteen came up from the Quarter Sessions, twenty from the Assizes, and three from the Central Criminal Court. In fifteen of the above appeals the judgments in the courts below were reversed.

From this it appears that there were positively more cases of points reserved by the superior judges at the Assizes, than by the chairmen of Quarter Sessions, although the amount of criminal business in the sessions is greater than at the Assizes.

If it be said that the offences tried at the Assizes are of a more difficult and intricate character than those tried at Sessions (and that therefore the occasions for appeal are more frequent and urgent), the answer will be found in this remarkable fact, that the offences which form the majority of the cases reserved are those which actually arise within the jurisdiction of the Quarter Sessions—*e.g.*, larceny and fraud.

In the year 1858, thirty-one appeals were heard in the Court for Crown Cases reserved; of which fifteen were referred from the Quarter Sessions, eleven from the Assizes, and five from the Central Criminal Court. Out of the above eight were reversed.

Cases of larceny and fraud formed the principal subjects of appeal.

In 1859, fifteen cases were referred to the superior court by way of appeal: of which six were from the Quarter Sessions, seven from the Assizes, and two from the Central Criminal Court.

In six of the above cases the original judgment was reversed. The cases heard on appeal chiefly related to larceny and fraud.

In the year 1860, nineteen cases were reserved at the Assizes and Sessions, for the consideration of the Court of Criminal Appeal; of those, fifteen were affirmed, three reversed, no judgment having been given in the remaining case; twelve came up from the Quarter Sessions, two form the Central Criminal Court, and five from the Assizes.

In the year ending September, 1861, twenty-two cases were brought to the Superior Court of Appeal, three of which were reversed. Thirteen of the above were from Quarter Sessions, seven from Assizes, and two from the Central Criminal Court; embezzlement and larceny form the subjects in which the greater number of appeals were granted.

These statistics appear to show:—1. That the offences in respect of which points of law are reserved are generally, and for the most part, those which come within the jurisdiction of the Sessions as well as of the Courts of Assize. 2. That by far the greater proportion of those offences are tried at sessions, and yet the greater proportion of the questions argued on appeal in respect of them are reserved by the superior judges of Assize. 3. That in general the points reserved have been quite deserving of the consideration of the Court of Appeal. 4. That the prisoners tried at Sessions (forming the great bulk of prisoners) are not in so good a position to have the charges preferred against them investigated and decided according to strict law.

To continue this outline of the law of appeal in criminal cases, permit me to observe further that the Court of Queen's Bench will even now, under certain circumstances, grant a new trial in all indictable offences, and that upon disputed questions of facts as well as of law. Where indictments are originally found in the Queen's Bench, or are removed thither by *certiorari*, the prisoner upon conviction is entitled, *ex debito justitiæ*, to move for a new trial. It was for a considerable time doubtful whether the appellate jurisdiction of the Court of Queen's Bench extended to felonies, as well as to misdemeanors. That question was set at rest in the case of the *Queen* v. *Scaife, Smith, & Rooke*, 17 Q.B., 238.

That was an indictment for robbery with violence, removed by *certiorari* from the Hull Borough Sessions, and tried before Mr. Justice Cresswell at the York Assizes. A rule *nisi* was obtained in the ensuing term for a new trial, on the grounds of improper reception of evidence and misdirection. The rule was made absolute, and the Master of the Crown Office was consulted by the court as to the form of the rule, it appearing that there was no precedent for a new trial in a case of felony. The subsequent history of this remarkable case is no less curious than instructive. The rule was made absolute in *Trinity Term* 1851, whereupon the case was sent to York for trial before Platt, B., at the Summer Assizes, 1851. The trial was postponed at the instance of the prosecutor till the next Assizes. At the Spring

Assizes the prisoners came up to be tried before Alderson, B., but the learned judge, upon finding that the record had not been sealed, refused to try. The prosecutor, without informing the prisoners, then applied to Pollock, C.B., at Chambers, and attained an order for a writ of *puredendo,* under which the case was sent back to the Hull Quarter Sessions, where a verdict was returned against the three prisoners, although on the original trial one of them had been acquitted.

It would appear, then, that the prisoner who may be fortunate enough to have the indictment preferred against him in the Queen's Bench, or who may have succeeded in obtaining a *certiorari,* enjoys the exceptional privilege of appeal against the verdict of a jury upon questions of law and fact. The objections to this form of proceeding are obvious. It applies to very few cases, and can scarcely be available to poor defendants. Questions of law frequently arise unexpectedly in the course of an inquiry, and the discovery comes too late for the purpose of obtaining a *certiorari;* and even when from the beginning it is seen that the result will turn upon mere legal subtleties, the preliminary expense of obtaining the writ compels the majority of prisoners to take their trials in the ordinary way.

There remains one other mode of appeal in criminal cases. A prisoner, as the law now stands, is not strictly and irrevocably bound by the refusal or omission of a judge to reserve a point in his favour. He has, indeed, a remedy, but it is, in point of fact, almost useless, on account of the difficulty and expense of procuring it. The relief I allude to, is the supreme appeal by petition to the Crown, which is referred to the Lord Chancellor. The Crown, through the Lord Chancellor, will, on a proper case made, direct the body of the judges to hear the point argued. In the case of *Wait* (11 Price, 518), the Lord Chancellor having considered a point referred to him, directed the twelve judges to hear the same argued. The same was done in Fauntleroy's case.

Having now considered what the law of appeal in criminal

cases actually is, I venture to submit that in several important particulars, besides that to which I have referred, it is capable of amendment.

Whether a criminal trial be regarded as a litigious proceeding, in which prosecutor and prisoner are the parties, or as an inquisitorial act on the part of the State against one of its members, I think it beyond all question or argument, that the accused is entitled of right to be tried in a manner best adapted to elicit the truth of the matter. He is entitled, by the mutual rights and obligations of citizenship, upon showing reasonable cause for being dissatisfied with the decision of one tribunal, to have his defence laid before another. This is a matter of right, not a concession, because justice, even at the cost of delay or inconvenience, is the first and paramount consideration. In civil proceedings, such as proceedings for enforcing a contract, where only a few pounds may be involved, this right is now freely admitted. Unless we assume the infallibility of our legal tribunals, it follows logically that reasonable facilities should be afforded for testing the soundness of their decisions. Does it not appear strange that while a defendant, dissatisfied with the verdict of a jury, where the controversy is about a few pounds, has the indubitable right of appealing against such a decision, he is practically prohibited from seeking a similar relief where his very life may be in jeopardy? In civil proceedings the objection as to the delays, expense, the waste of public time, &c., arising from protracted litigation, have long taken a place subordinate to the principal and supreme consideration—justice. On the one hand, frivolous litigation ought, by every prudent means, to be checked; on the other, every fair opportunity should be afforded to eliminate the truth and vindicate the innocent. As an abstract question of right, therefore, there can be no doubt that every citizen, having just reason for being dissatisfied with the decision against him, whether in civil or criminal matters, is entitled to an appeal upon questions of law and fact.

But it cannot for one moment be denied that serious

difficulties, disadvantages, and evils would accrue from enlarging the privilege of appeal which now obtains in criminal cases. I am anxious to state these fairly and fully, not only because of their intrinsic importance, but because of the conviction they have wrought in the minds of so many eminent jurists and statesmen.

The following are the principal objections which have been urged against extending the right of criminal appeal:—First, that in criminal cases the questions involved are generally so simple that new trials would be unnecessary. Mr. Baron Parke put this argument strongly in his evidence before the House of Lords' Committee,—"Disputes respecting civil rights—rights to property—are of a complicated nature, involving difficult propositions of law and fact, from which the administration of criminal justice is free; and upon the whole it is better to give an unlimited power of appeal on questions both of law and fact in civil, and to withhold it in criminal, cases."* There are two obvious answers to this objection. First, that as to questions of law, however seldom they may occur, the legislature has considered them of so much importance as to have established a special court for their consideration. Secondly, however simple the facts deposed to upon a criminal trial may be, the verdict may, notwithstanding, be against the weight of evidence, or returned under surprise, or in the absence of material facts which have transpired subsequent to the trial.

The next objection which I shall notice, refers to the delay in the execution of the criminal law which the exercise of the right of appeal would introduce. Lord Brougham has illustrated this in a very forcible manner—"The criminal law depends, for the effect, more or less, which it has in deterring from crime by example of punishments, upon the speediness with which the execution of the sentence follows the trial. But in this case you would have a prisoner found guilty at

* See Report of Select Committee of the House of Lords on the Administration of the Criminal Law, 1848, p. 8.

York in the first fortnight in July, but no sentence, even in the most flagrant case of murder, ever could be executed till the middle of the November following."* As to the deterrent force of punishment, his lordship has proved, in a remarkable dissertation to which I cannot here refer more particularly, that at best the influence of punishment in deterring others from crime has been greatly exaggerated. The delay of a few months, upon which his lordship laid so much emphasis, was satisfactorily anticipated in the scheme of Sir Fitzroy Kelly, which, among other things, provided that the Court of Appeal should sit a few days after the Summer Assizes.

Again, it is said that the number of appeals would be so great, that the present bench of judges would not be able to accomplish the work. It is probable that after the first few years, the result of an appeal in criminal cases would become so well understood, that the applications would not be very numerous. But even if they continued to be numerous, I contend that it is the first duty of a State to provide for the satisfactory administration of its laws.

Again, it has been asked, at whose cost are appeals to be conducted? If at the expense of the prisoner, an advantage is conferred upon the rich; but if the public are to bear the expense, the burden of litigation would be thrown upon those who have no direct personal interest in the result. It is better to grant a relief which may be open to all though available to a few, than to perpetuate a hardship from which rich and poor must alike suffer. When a question of law is now reserved, it is very seldom that the poverty of the prisoner is an effectual barrier against the prosecution of an appeal. And even under the present system, the rich have a decided advantage over the poor. In how many instances might the life of a pauper convict have been saved, if the funds were at his disposal to set in motion the machinery which would move the Home Office? It probably costs more to secure professional and

* *Ibid.* 49.

other assistance sufficiently powerful to promote an effectual representation to the Home Office, than it would cost to bring the case under the notice of a Court of Appeal. The best system of laws cannot raise the enjoyments of the poor to the level of the rich. The wealthy will always command a better literature, better medical aid, as well as better legal assistance. When it was proposed to enable all prisoners to be defended by counsel, the same objection was raised. The Prisoners' Counsel Act has, however, given much satisfaction, for the poor as well as the rich have gained by it.

Another objection is, that instances of improper convictions are rare. Let those who wish to obtain reliable information on this subject, consult the second report of the Criminal Law Commissioners. Mr. Wilde, who held the shrievalty of London, and was also an attorney by profession, stated, "I am perfectly satisfied that many persons have suffered punishments where they have been positively innocent of the crime with which they were charged, and which, if there had been any court of appeal, with of course proper officers appointed, to whom the parties accused might have stated the grounds of appeal, there would have been a reversal of their conviction or sentence." (p. 99.)

He stated further, "within the space of nine months during which he was one of the sheriffs of London, no fewer than six persons who had been capitally convicted at the Old Bailey, and left for execution, were saved from death in consequence of investigations showing that they had been improperly convicted. From the want of a proper appellate tribunal, the sheriffs and the officers of the prison, who, of course, are the only persons in constant communication with the prisoners, are often placed in a most painful situation, in having to judge how far, consistently with the discharge of their own duties, they ought to interfere." (Report, Vol. viii., p. 20.)

There are other objections which I cannot here stop to discuss. I shall only enumerate them:—First, that if new trials were granted, witnesses could in the meanwhile be tampered with, and the crime of perjury would very much increase. Secondly, that if appeals were to be granted in cases of a conviction, they ought also to be conceded to prosecutors in cases of an acquittal. Thirdly, that the right of appeal would open a door through which the guilty might escape. Fourthly, that jurors would shirk their responsibility and return ill-considered verdicts on the ground that their decisions might be reviewed and rectified by a superior court.

Let me, in the next place, briefly relate what attempts have been made by the legislature to amend this department of the law. The first, and indeed the most comprehensive measure that has hitherto been laid before Parliament, was the Bill of 1844, introduced to the House of Commons by our learned Chairman. I may perhaps be permitted to add, that the speech of Sir Fitzroy Kelly, upon bringing in the Bill, remains to this day among the most exhaustive and learned dissertations on Criminal Appeal. "The substantial object of the Bill," to use the language of its learned author, "was to enable all persons convicted of any criminal offence, whether at the Assizes, or at the Central Criminal Courts, or before Courts of Quarter Sessions, or other inferior Courts, to make the same application to set aside the verdict, to have a new trial, to enter a verdict of not guilty, or to arrest judgment, before any of the superior courts of Westminster Hall as may now be made in civil cases, and upon much the same system of practice; that is, upon an application in the first instance, for a rule *nisi;* and in the event of a rule *nisi* being granted, then, upon hearing counsel on both sides, to make the rule absolute or discharge it, and enter final judgment accordingly."

In point of fact the scheme of Sir Fitzroy Kelly, as embodied in the Bill of 1844, amounted almost to a complete assimilation of appellate procedure in civil and criminal cases. It extended to all indictable offences—felonies as well as misdemeanors—and the appeal was to be a matter of right, and not a concession dependent upon the will and pleasure of the judge. Beyond this it is impossible to go. I am afraid, however, that the legislature of 1864 would follow the example of the Parliament of 1844 in rejecting a bill which proposed changes so comprehensive and important. Our system of law making is empirical; we advance by short steps cautiously taken. Beginning with small experiments, which result sometimes in failure, sometimes in success, we hit upon a good principle, we mould and shape it to our existing laws. If it assimilates—well; if it proves a mistake, we throw it away, and proceed upon some other experiment. Whether this be philosophical or not, it is a fact—a fact of which every statesman must take due notice, and for which he must make due allowance.

The Bill of Sir Fitzroy Kelly passed the first reading, but was withdrawn in the month of July, 1844, at the request of Sir James Graham, who stated "that he wished it to be understood that, in so acting, he did not preclude the Government from taking up the subject, when they had examined it calmly and at leisure." Four years later, that is to say in February, 1848, Mr. Ewart brought in a measure on the subject of appeal in criminal cases. Its second reading was postponed in favour of Lord Campbell's Bill, for granting appeals on matters of law in criminal cases. The Act 11 & 12 Vict., c. 78, passed in pursuance of Lord Campbell's Bill, established a court of appeal for the consideration of Crown Cases reserved.

The last discussion in Parliament on the Law of Criminal Appeal took place on the 31st June, 1860, upon the second reading of Mr. M'Mahon's Bill. That Bill, which was lost in the second reading, proposed only a small extension of the right of appeal. To this extent only, that the writ of *certiorari* should issue from the Queen's Bench after conviction as well as before trial. Inasmuch as the Court of Queen's Bench has the power of ordering new trials on all requests formed there, and also in all cases removed thither by *certiorari*; the effect of Mr. M'Mahon's Bill would have been to constitute the Queen's Bench the only court of criminal appeal.

I may be permitted before concluding this review of the various schemes which have been proposed relating to the law of criminal appeal, to refer to the observations of Mr. Stephen, the Recorder of Newark-on-Trent, in his recently published work on the criminal law of England. The remedy which that learned author proposes is the following:—"To constitute a court of law charged with the duty of doing openly and judicially what the Home Secretary at present does in secret. It might be enacted that if it appeared to the Secretary of State for the Home Department, that after the conviction of any person for any crime, new evidence or new reason to doubt the truth or accuracy of the evidence actually given had been discovered; or if the judge who tried the cause were dissatisfied with the verdict, the Home Secretary might call together a court, to be composed of the judge who tried the cause, one other judge, and the Home Secretary himself; who should call before them any witnesses they pleased, and examine both them and the prisoner (if they thought fit) in open court; and also, if they thought fit, hear arguments by counsel, and finally deliver judgment, either confirming, quashing, or varying the verdict of a jury as they thought proper. In order to protect the constitutional authority of the jury, it would be necessary to provide expressly, as a condition precedent to the summoning of the court, that the Secretary of State should certify that new evidence had been discovered; or that the judge should certify that he was dissatisfied with the verdict."

It is understood that the establishment of a court of appeal in criminal cases would not in any way interfere with the exercise of the Royal prerogative of pardon. That prerogative belongs to the Crown of right, and is absolute. No appellate procedure ought to supersede it, first, because it forms an important element in the nice distribution of constitutional rights between the Crown and the subject; and, secondly, because the free interposition of the royal mercy in certain critical and exceptional cases, can alone give adequate relief against the injustice which a strict administration of the law might otherwise effect. It is now well understood that the exercise of this sovereign power depends altogether, in point of fact, upon the recommendation of the Home Secretary. Nothing can be more unsatisfactory than the present procedure at the Home Office in investigating the facts of a case after conviction. No doubt great pains are taken, and the most earnest endeavours are used for the purpose of obtaining the best information as to the intrinsic merits of the case, and of arriving at a just and proper conclusion. A great outcry was raised a few weeks ago against the Home Office, and it cannot be denied that the administration of justice was brought into great scandal. I do not propose to refer with any particularity to the convictions of Townley and Wright, or to make any comment upon the respite extended to the former or upon the execution of the latter. What is remarkable, and, indeed, deplorable, is this, that all the proceedings from beginning to end, in both instances, appear to have been conducted according to the strict requirements of the law, so that no blame can fairly attach to any one individual—and yet the result has caused a widespread dissatisfaction. We witness at this very moment the humiliating spectacle of a dissatisfied and angry public taunting the administration of justice with a servile leaning to the rich and a sullen indifference to the poor. I cannot join in the extravagant censure with which the Home Office has been recently aspersed: the mischief is to be attributed to the procedure and not to the functionary—for I take it that the same results, if they had been attained by a public, deliberate, judicial investigation, would have been received with a respectful acquiescence, if not approbation. The Home Office, which was originally only a medium of inquiry for the information of the Sovereign, has now grown into a Court of Review, without rules of procedure or well-defined powers. Its investigations are secret. Statements which would be rejected in a court of justice, on the ground of not being evidence, are received, and no opportunity is afforded to contradict or explain them. The inquiry is conducted by some person or persons who have no public responsibility. It is doubtful whether there is any jurisdiction to administer an oath on making an affidavit to be submitted to the Home Office. False statements may be made, and are in point of fact made with impunity; and, lastly, the whole investigation is *ex parte*, no notice of the application being ever given to the prosecutor. Statements are frequently sent to the Home Office relating to facts which are alleged to have occurred after the trial, which, if true, seem to change the whole complexion of the case. The truth of such statements are tested in a flimsy and imperfect manner, and yet upon those very statements the deliberate verdict of a jury may be cancelled. Instances have occurred where persons have been in court during a trial who have not ventured to give their evidence, and yet have afterwards made affidavits of facts which ought to have been properly inquired into in public court.

This state of things is anomalous, and cannot be tolerated much longer. There is no doubt that a time will come when the law of appeal in civil cases will be adopted as a model for the administration of the criminal law. To quote the eloquent and statesmanlike language of that great law reformer, Sir Samuel Romilly:—"It should be recollected that the great object of the penal laws is the protection of the innocent; the punishment of the guilty is resorted to only as the means of attaining that object. When the guilty escape, the law has merely failed; it has done no good, but it has done no harm. But when the innocent becomes the victim the law not merely fails, but it injures the persons it was meant to protect—it creates the evil it was to cure. Appeals are not to be advocated from mere motives of clemency, nor opposed for fear of the guilty escaping: they are to be supported by a far higher motive, the desire to make justice certain."

Art. II.—A USE UPON A USE.

LORD BACON gave to his intelligent readers the following judicious advice, which is by no means obsolete at the present day:—"Now let me advise you of this, that it is not a matter of subtlety or conceit to take the law right, when a man cometh in by the law in course of possession, and where he cometh in by the statute in course of possession; but it is material for the deciding of many causes and questions."

This important distinction is worthy of the most careful consideration. A few concise remarks are now offered to the attention of the diligent student.

The statutes of 1 Richard III. c. 1, and 27 Hen. VIII. c. 10, being *in pari materia* are to be construed jointly, and this mode of interpretation is consistent with the intention of the makers of these enactments. The motive which induced them to frame the statutes, whether it were for the preservation of uses or for their extirpation, is at best but a remote clue to the interpretation. In either event, the means taken to bring about the end designed, is undisputed. The makers of both enactments intended, whatever may have been their conjectures as to the effect of it, to bring the use within the jurisdiction of the common law, in other words, to convert it into a beneficial legal estate. The statute of Richard took the initiatory step by investing the *cestui que use* with concurrent power over the estate with the feoffee to his use, and thus transformed the equitable into a legal estate. This statute proved inadequate to the end proposed, in so far as it failed to give *cestui que use* exclusive ownership of the estate. It even left sufficient power in the feoffee to enable him to destroy the estate of *cestui que use.* The statute in fact created a division of the estate at law into two independent parts, the seisin and the use, which it was the object of the statute of uses, in furtherance of the original design to invest the *cestui que use* with the legal estate for his own exclusive benefit, to consolidate and make one.

Where, however, the use was limited to a person who already had the seisin, the purpose of the legislature was anticipated by the act of the parties, and as the two parts thus united made one whole estate no room was left for the operation of the statute. A use united to the seisin filled up the measure of the estate hence the maxim that a use cannot be limited upon a use. Lord St. Leonards denies the existence of any such prohibition prior to the statute of 27 Hen. VIII. Gilb. Uses, Sugden's ed. 347, n. (1) Sugden on Powers, 7th ed. 162, *et seq.*

His lordship ascribes the origin of the restriction to what he conceives to be an erroneous construction of the statute. But whether the interpretation given to the statute be right or wrong depends upon the question or issue; to wit, whether a use could or could not be limited upon a use prior to the statute. The signification of the term "use," which was employed, though not defined by the statute, must be sought in the pre-existing law. If the maxim did not obtain in the antecedent law the statute would have gone through the series of uses limited, and executed the final use, as Lord St. Leonards consistently contends that it should have done. If, on the other hand, the maxim did obtain, the statute would have been, as the judges held that it actually was, exhausted by the execution of the first use. This decision upon the statute, therefore, is an authoritative declaration of the ancient law upon this point, and this his lordship virtually admits by finding fault with the construction given to the statute.

His lordship does not seem to appreciate the fact that the use was the complement of the seisin, making by its junction with it one integral estate, into which another use could no more be put than three halves could be compressed into one whole. A use, it should be borne in mind, is the beneficial ownership of the estate. Now two several beneficial ownerships cannot by any possibility co-exist simultaneously in the same estate; they are necessarily exclusive and adverse to each other, and when one prevails the other is defeated. The first use, therefore, exhausts the beneficial ownership of the estate and leaves nothing over for the limitation of a second use.

His lordship's confident assertion that a use could have been limited upon a use previously to the statute of 27 Hen. VIII., is likewise contradicted by the opinion of Chief Justice Baldwin in Bokenham's case (Dyer, 28 Hen. VIII. 11, *et seq.*) which arose before, but was decided subsequently to the statute. The feoffee in this case, who was seized to the use of Bokenham and his heirs, made a feoffment to the use of Bokenham and his wife, and his heirs. Baldwin, C.J., considered the second use to Bokenham's heirs inconsistent with the first, and hence superfluous and void, and he quaintly gives the following excellent reason for his opinion,—"A doner l'use a cestui que ceo aver derant, *n'est bon.* Car est common ground que home ne poit doner a moy un chose *que jeo ay already: car ceo serra impertinent.*" And the Chief Justice gives an illustration which proves that there might as easily be two several fees simple in the same land as two several uses in the same estate. "Sicome tenant in taile enfeoffe le doner, ceo n'est *discontinuance,* entant que il ne poit doner a luy fee *simple, le quel ne fuit unque hors de luy.*" Fitzherbert and Shelley, Justices, who decided the case, far from denying that *cestui que use* who already had the right to the entire profits to the land could not be benefited by a superrogatory right to the same profits, held that there was a preliminary and additional reason why there could not be a double use in the *cestui que use.* There would then, according to them, be also a double seisin in fee of the same land, but "est un imponvenience et impossibility en lee que 11 (two) homes several merit avera several droits et fee simples in un meme terre gimul et gemel." To prevent such an anomaly they held that the feoffment of the feoffee to use was a total destruction of the primary uses.

His lordship's inference therefore, that a common law use is no obstruction to the execution of a superadded statutory use, is involved in the destruction of his position. For if the judges in their construction of the statute held that the first use exhausted the beneficial interest and left nothing over for the second use, they based their decision upon the character of a use, and their knowledge of its character was derived from the common law. It was therefore immaterial whether the first use was at common law or statutory; in either event it absorbed the entire beneficial interest, and a second use was necessarily void.

The law upon this point being thus clear and emphatic, the position taken by Mr. Sanders is vindicated, that a use is void after the limitation of a use, though the *cestui que use* be in by common law. This position, however, has been vehemently and persistently contested by Lord St. Leonards, though it is submitted without shaking its solid foundation. The arguments which his lordship employed are the same as those which were vainly urged by counsel in *Doe d. Lloyd* v. *Passingham* (6 Barn. & Cress. 305). This will account for the striking aptness of the judges' replies to his several points. The case is well stated in the margin, as follows: "When an estate was limited to A., to the use of A. in trust for B. Held that A. took the legal estate, and that although he took it by the common law, and not by force of the statute of uses, yet the second use could not be executed by force of the statute." In spite of this decision, when the point was directly before the court for adjudication, his lordship slurs over the well considered opinions of the judges and goes on to re-assert his own opinion thus: "If the party out of whose estate the use is to arise do 'take the legal estate at the common law,' he is not a *cestui que use;* and if the first use 'is not a use within the statute,' then it is not a use at all; and therefore the use over must be executed by the statute where it is said that the fine or conveyance is a common law conveyance by which both the legal estate and the *use* pass to the conusee without any declaration of uses, it is meant that the whole beneficial interest passes, and the instrument amounts to a limitation of the estate, and *not* a limitation of the *use* properly so called. Where no use is declared to any other person than the releasee or conusee, it is not an use divested from the estate, as where it is limited to a stranger, but the use and estate go together. In truth, if the supposed use which A. takes, is not a use under the statute, it is simply void." This assertion is well answered by Mr. Justice Bayley, as follows: "Now ever since I have belonged to the profession of law, I have invariably understood that a use cannot be limited upon a use. This is admitted to be so in general, but a distinction has been taken where the limitation is to A. to the use of A. in trust for B., and it said that then A. is in by the common law. This is true; but he is in of the estate *clothed with the use, which is not extinguished but remains in him.* In the case of *Meredith* v. *Jones,* cited in the argument to show that when an estate is limited to A. to the use of A. he is in by the common law, it is said, 'for it is not an use divided from the estate, as where it is limited to a stranger but the use and the estate go together.' That case, therefore, shows that although the trustees in this case might be in by the common law, yet they were in both of the estate *and the use.* Here are two cases expressly in point—*Lady Whetstone* v. *Bury* is a very clear case, and the words used are precisely those found in the deed in question, and it was there decided, and also in the *Attorney-General* v. *Scott,* which came before Lord Talbot, one of the greatest real property lawyers that ever filled the office of Lord Chancellor, that the legal estate vests in him to whom by the words of the instrument the use is limited. Upon the authority of these two cases I am of opinion that the use of the estate in question was executed in the trustees," *i.e.,* A. Mr. Justice Holroyd also, after admitting that he was struck with the ingenuity of the distinction when it was originally made by Mr. Taunton, proceeds to say that upon further consideration the argument was insufficient to warrant it, which he explains as follows; "The argument is, that as the trustees did not in the first instance take to the use of another, but of themselves, they were in by the common law and not by the statute; that the first use was, therefore, of no effect, and the case was to be considered as if the deed had merely contained the second limitation to uses. *But that was not so,* for although it be true that the trustees take the seisin by the common law and not by the statute, yet they take that seisin to the use of themselves and not to the use of another, in which case alone the use is executed by the statute. They are, therefore, seized in trust for another, and *the legal estate remains in them.*"

Lord St. Leonards second argument is, that whether A. takes by the common law or by the statute is a question of intention. He thus elaborates the point: "It may be conceded, that upon a conveyance to A., and his heirs, to the use of him and his heirs, A. would take in the course of possession by the common law, but that admission does not affect the question; for in the the case put, 'the conusee,' as Pratt, C.J., observed, 'did not want the help of the statute, and therefore it meddles not with him, but leaves him in at the common law. No case as ever been decided in which, under a conveyance to A. and his heirs to the use of A., and his heirs, to the use of B., and his heirs, A. has been held to be in at the common law. It is true that in such a case A. takes the legal estate, but that is in favour of the intention, and he must necessarily take it under the statute. The limitation *unto and to the use* has received a settled construction, which is not suffered to be disturbed by a subsequent limitation of the use from which a different intention might be inferred. But where a further use is declared, A. must necessarily take under the statute in order to prevent the statute from executing the use limited over. Where no use is limited over to a third person, the estate vests at the common law, and the aid of the statute is not required. The limitation of the use therefore is not called into action." This point is certainly a triumph of ingenuity. However flat-footed a case may be against his lordship, it can be explained away by this process. Thus, in the illustration given of a limitation to A. to the use of A. to the use of B., which is the very case of *Lady Whetstone* v. *Bury* (2 P. Wms. 146), although it is admitted that A. takes the estate and that the limitation over to B. is void, yet it is insisted upon nevertheless that A. takes by force of the statute. The intention is manifest, as his lordship truly says, that the use should be executed in A.; but there are stronger reasons than the intention to give the estate to A.:—First, the character of a use which invests the first *cestui que use* with the exclusive beneficial ownership of the estate; this characteristic cannot be affected by an intention, however distinctly it may be manifested. Second, the statute does not embrace such a case, and its terms could not be satisfied unless there was a seisin by one person to the use, at least joint or partial, of another and a different person. And, third, where an estate can vest either at the common law or by statute, the rule is that it shall vest at the common law.

If a deed is to be construed like a will by the intention, then the fact that a consideration by or a declaration of the use to the feoffee at the common law was necessary to invest him with the use, proves nothing either way, as it may be pertinently said to exhibit an intention to give him the beneficial ownership of the estate; but, leaving the intention out of view, it marks distinctly the difference between the conveyance of the legal title, and of the beneficial estate. Until the grantor has received a consideration, or made a declaration of the use, he retains his power over the estate; but the moment a consideration is given, or a declaration made, he parts with his control over the estate, which by that act becomes vested in the *cestui que use*, and cannot be taken away from him by any further act or declaration of the grantor, any more than the legal title can be taken by the grantor.

To return, however, to the case under inspection. This conceit of interpreting a deed by intention in opposition to its language, a mode of construction which one would hardly-expect to see advanced since Sir James Wigram's masterly essay upon interpretation, is thus decisively rejected by Holroyd, J.: "As to the question of intention, even if it were intended that the deed should operate in a different mode from that pointed out by the law, when the legal estate is given to trustees, *that intention cannot countervail the law.*" Littledale, J., adds:—"I am entirely of the same opinion. It is said, that by the construction now put upon the deed, the intent of the parties will be defeated. If we were not construing a deed I should feel disposed to give a liberal effect to the intention, but if all matters of convenience and inconvenience which raise a presumption of intention are to be taken into consideration as affording rules for the construction of deeds, and are to have the effect of over-ruling the plain words of such instruments, the law will very soon be thrown into utter confusion. I have never entertained a doubt that a second series of uses could not be executed. It is true, that certain cases show these trustees to have taken the estate by the common law, *but they took it coupled with the use.* The cases cited upon this point are perfectly clear."

It is to be regretted that the editors of Mr. Sanders have seen fit to abandon his position on the authority of a case which, it is respectfully submitted, by no means warrants their precipitate retreat. The case from Dyer, 13 Eliz. 30, was this:—A feoffment was made to A., and his heirs, for the use of A. and his heirs, until the feoffor should pay him or his heirs £100, and then to the feoffor. Because the court said that on the payment of the £100 the estate of A., and his heirs, would be divested and transferred to the feoffor, it is inferred that A. must have been in by force of the statute. This, however, does not follow: A. may very well have been in by the common law, until the payment was made, but upon that event the use which had up to that time been in him, would be divested and another use substituted for it. A. would now stand seised to the use of the feoffor, and the conditions of the statute being thus complied with; to wit, there being a seisin by one person to the use of another, and a different person, the statute would come into play and execute the use in the feoffor. This, it is needless to say, is not a use upon a use; it is the well-recognised shifting use, which upon a given contingency divests the antecedent use and takes its place as a substitute. The mistake, if the expression may be pardoned, of Mr. Sanders's editors, is in treating the use to A. as merged in his seisin. If this be granted, the whole position must be surrendered to Lord St. Leonards; for the common law use being out of the way and of no effect, the statutory use would inevitably be executed.

The distinction between such a case, and a use upon a use, perplexed Mr. Sanders, who put the two following cases as similar: A conveyance to and to the use of A., and his heirs, to the use of B. and his heirs, and a conveyance to and to the use of A., and his heirs, subject to a power of appointment reserved to B. Lord St. Leonards thus neatly clears up the distinction: "In the first case, the use being vested in A., the use to B. is a use upon a use, and therefore void; in the last case, A. takes a seisin and a use, but the use is subject to the power, and is during the existence of the power executed *sub modo* only; that is subject to open and let in the estate created under the power. When the power is executed, the use takes effect as if properly limited in the deed creating the power; therefore the use arises out of the original *seisin* of A., and defeats instead of deriving its essence from the *use* limited to A." This is the point decided by *Moreton* v. *Lees*, C. P. Lancaster, March Ass., 1819. It is but just, however, to acknowledge that Mr. Sanders's perplexity arose from the statement made by Lord Coke, that "in case of a feoffment or other conveyance whereby the feoffee or grantee, &c., is in by the common law, such a proviso (*i.e.*, a power of revocation) were merely repugnant and void." The antithesis here, however, is evidently between uses and legal estates; for Lord Coke says, "this proviso, *being coupled with an use*, is allowed to be good, *and not repugnant to the former estates.*" A legal estate in fee being once vested, cannot be defeated by a power of revocation, though such power were reserved at the time of the creation of the estate, the power being repugnant to the nature of the estate. In this respect a legal estate differs from a use, to which a power of revocation may be annexed without being deemed inconsistent with the previous limitations which vest subject to the liability of being afterwards divested in favour of the appointee under the power.

Mr. Cornish in his essay upon "Uses," pp. 31-2, by an inattention similar to that of Lord St. Leonards to the nature of a use, which, as has been said, is the beneficial ownership of the estate, makes a curious blunder. But, in order to avoid misrepresenting Mr. Cornish, his language shall speak for itself: "It has been supposed that the establishment of a solid distinction between them (*i.e.*, "the trust and use of ancient times") is a satisfactory negative to the question which has been recently agitated, whether the above mentioned statute of 1 Richard III. c. 1, has been virtually repealed by the statute of 27 Hen. VIII. The words of the statute of Richard are confined to *uses;* hence it has been supposed inapplicable to modern trusts, whether at common law or by statute. But, perhaps, the argument drawn from the original difference between uses and trusts proves too much: for if the statute was solely applicable to the primitive use, in consequence of its nature *substantially* varying from the *special trust,* why does it not embrace the *modern statutory trust,* which under another name is the identical use of our ancestors?" A modern trust, instead of being the identical use of our ancestors, is a trust superadded upon that ancient use. Mr. Cornish would do well to consult Whately's Logic in reference to the fallacy of employing the word "identical" when similarity alone can be predicated. By the use of this equivocal adjective he is mislead to assume not merely a resemblance between a modern trust and an ancient use, but likewise an actual identity. It is only necessary to compare the two estates in order to detect the blunder which Mr. Cornish has made. It may be shown in the ordinary illustration: A. is feoffee to the use of B. in trust for C. The statute of Richard converts B.'s use into a legal estate, and thus divides the estate at law into two independent parts with concurrent power over it in the feoffee and in the *cestui que use.* The statute of 27 Hen. VIII. re-unites these separated parts in one legal estate, and in this limited view (which is also imperfect as the parts are united, not in the original owner, the feoffee, but in the *cestui que use*) may be said to repeal the statute of Richard, though its general aim as well as its effect was to carry out more completely the design of that statute by transferring to the *cestui que use* the feoffee's legal estate. Now if the statute of Richard were to operate a second time, it would create a use (*i.e.*, turn a trust, an equitable estate into a use, a legal estate) upon the use which the statute of 27 Hen. VIII. had executed. All the authorities agree that such a use is void. Where the trust is not limited upon the use which the statute executes, but upon a common law use, it has been the object of this article to show that the same reason applies. The first use exhausts the beneficial ownership of the estate, and any second use is void at law.

Art. III.—JUDICIAL STATISTICS, 1862.—ANNALS OF THE CIVIL COURTS.

THE "Judicial Statistics" will in future constitute the main oracle of the legal reformer. "Full and minute details," as was well observed by Lord Brougham, at the International Statistical Congress, 1860, "are to the law-giver, as the chart, the compass, and the lead to the navigator." They are, perhaps, even more. At least they represent, under an abstract form, the very elements upon which legislation is to operate. The importance, therefore, of having a well-digested system of judicial statistics cannot be over-estimated, since they so clearly indicate the comparative constitution and anatomy of the various branches of our criminal and civil systems. The study of statistics ought to be especially congenial to the English mind, which has always shown a preference for the inductive and practical to the more attractive and ambitious paths of *à priori* speculation.

Although the present condition of the judicial statistics indicates a tolerably perfect realisation of the conceptions they were intended to carry out, yet there is no reason why, in so important a matter, we should not endeavour to accomplish still further improvements. To effect this, the systems in vogue on the Continent of Europe may be advantageously referred to. Every practical art is more readily improved by imitation than by original suggestion. Amongst foreign countries, Belgium deserves especial estimation in respect of its statistics. These emanate from a General Statistical Bureau, founded in 1841, in connexion with the *Ministère de l'Interieure,* and were brought to great perfection by the illustrious M. Quetelet during the period of his presidency. Condensation and apposite correlation of parts are, doubtless, two of the most essential requisites for a practical system of statistics. These ends, indeed, are very effectively sought to be attained in the present Blue Book. However, we sometimes notice in it an unnecessary waste of space, especially in Part II. This defect, indeed, is not very considerable; we allude to it merely to suggest that condensation ought to be a main object of the compiler of the statistics. He should certainly have the assistance of a practising lawyer familiar with the procedure of our courts and the relative importance of the various steps in a suit. Mr. Redgrave, although himself so eminently competent for the work, expressed an opinion to this effect, in his report for 1858.

Part II. of the Judicial Statistics for 1862, comprises the annals of our civil courts, just as Part I. related to the criminal returns. The following table gives a comparative sketch of the proceedings on the Crown side of the Court of

Queen's Bench, for the years 1861 and 1862, and the average for 1861-60-59:—

	1862.	1861.	Average. 1861-60-59.
On writs of mandamus, made absolute	21	25	23
On quo warrantos, informations filed	1	7	7
On writs of habeas corpus, applications	33	63	48
On writs of certiorari, writs issued	81	74	81
Judgments and executions	25	18	18
On grand jury bills	...	...	—
On informations *ex officio*	1	...	4
On orders of Sessions, removed into Queen's Bench	28	25	27
On special cases from Quarter Sessions (12 & 13 Vict. c. 45)	4	11	15
On special cases on proceedings before justices (20 & 21 Vict. c. 43)	40	45	55

The amount of the chief proceedings in each of the three superior courts on the plea side, for the years 1861 and 1862, is shown in the following summary. An increase had appeared in 1860, as compared with 1859, under every head, except those of writs of capias and causes referred to masters. The increase in 1861 in the number of writs of summons issued was 17·1 per cent. over the returns for 1860, and amounted to no less than 32·4 per cent. upon the number for 1859. There was a decrease in this item, however, for 1862 of 10·3, as compared with the corresponding return for 1861:—

Nature of the Proceedings.	1862.								1861.	
	Queen's Bench.		Common Pleas.		Exchequer.		Total.		Total	
	Process Issued.	Matters Heard.	Process Issued.	Matters Heard.	Process Issued.	Matters Heard.	Process Issued.	Matters Heard.	Process Issued.	Matters Heard.
Writs of summons issued	32,531	...	27,997	...	43,036	...	103,564	...	114,301	—
Writs of capias	197	...	184	...	201	...	582	...	549	—
Appearances entered	8,650	...	8,365	...	10,628	...	27,643	...	29,100	—
Judgments	11,404	...	8,826	...	15,936	...	36,166	...	41,297	—
Executions	8,031	...	6,273	...	11,423	...	25,737	...	30,523	—
Motions for new trials	...	172	...	206	...	181	...	559	...	605
Other special motions	...	252	...	292	...	270	...	814	...	814
Hand motions, and on Side Bar rules	1,152	...	1,024	...	1,351	...	3,527	...	3,813	—
Causes referred to masters	138	...	198	...	257	...	586	...	501	—
Total amount of fees	£24,271 17 0		£16,883 13 6		£26,495 13 0		£67,651 3 6		£74,761 5 0	

It is not a little strange that the Court of Exchequer still maintains its old ascendancy in the favour of the profession; the Court of Common Pleas, on the other hand, is still avoided. Formerly a higher scale of costs attracted the profession to the Court of Exchequer; while the Court of Common Pleas, being virtually a monopoly of the serjeants, was avoided, in consequence of the high fees it thus entailed. But at the present day, when no advantage is to be gained by a resort to any particular court, it is singular that the force of old habits continues to prevail to such an extent; and what is still more surprising is, that the proportion of judgments to the whole number of cases in each court, is highest in the Court of Exchequer, as if in very deed its old advantages, where a suit was fully litigated, existed at the present day. When estimating the relative merits of courts having a concurrent jurisdiction by the standard of their popularity (a case in which, above all others, one would naturally be disposed to rely on statistics), we should therefore take care that the manifold condition implied in the phrase *cæteris paribus*, is complied with before we institute an *experimentum crucis*. For we find that courts, the condition, government, administration, and circumstances of which in no material respect differ from each other, nevertheless meet with very unequal favour at the hands of the profession. A comparison of the real merits of co-ordinate courts taken with reference to their popularity, it thus appears, can be safely instituted only in cases where these courts were established on the same footing at the same date without having had any previous existence. If they had their respective originals prior to their induced uniformity, their antecedents may long continue to affect their career. In reasoning upon statistical data, therefore, if there be any discrepancy in the originals or circumstances of the things compared, we should take it into account, and make due allowance not only for these obvious disturbing influences, but also for the prejudices, habits, passions, and associations to which the discrepant elements may have given rise. The anomalies we have just noticed, must, indeed, gradually disappear. Else we should abandon all faith in statistical philosophy. Their continuance, however, shows that a reform in legal procedure, however ultimately beneficial, will not necessarily at once bear fruit. In the Irish courts we may observe a most unexceptionable course prevails, which was prescribed by the Irish Common Law Procedure Act, 1852. The writs are filed in batches of four in each court in rotation, so that no one court can have over its fellows a greater number of incipient cases than the number mentioned. We are disposed to recommend a similar improvement in our procedure.

The Judicial Statistics for 1862 contain an item not given in the Blue Books for preceding years, in the shape of the number of bills of costs taxed in the preceding twelvemonth. Those taxed in the Court of Queen's Bench were, as between party and party, 6,218; as between attorney and client, about 824. In the Court of Exchequer the number taxed, exclusive of bills taxed under the statute, was 8,324. No return under this head is given for the Court of Common Pleas.

The writs of summons issued in 1862 were less than those issued in 1861, by 10·3 per cent. The total number of causes entered for trial was, at Westminster 2,225, and at Nisi Prius 1,366. The total of trials was 1,025. These returns vary very slightly from the corresponding numbers for 1861.

We need extract only a few items regarding the nature of the suits. The most numerous class was on promissory notes, bills of exchange, &c., 185. Next in number were those for goods sold and delivered, 169. Next come those for breach of contract, 151. Next are actions for work and labour done, 100; for compensation for injuries under Lord Campbell's Act, 69; trover, 56; ejectment, 42; trespass, 35; assault, 24; infringement of patents, 14; slander, 27; libel, 20; life and fire policies, 13; for breach of promise of marriage, 4.

The number of suits tried on each circuit was:—Home Circuit, 240; Midland, 106; Norfolk, 43; Northern (excepting Lancashire and Durham), 125; Oxford, 122; Western, 121; North Wales, 42; South Wales, 23; County Palatine of Lancashire, 125; County Palatine of Durham, 20. Total, 1,059. This portion of the Judicial Statistics is not without its interest to a barrister in quest of a circuit.

The total number of judgments in 1862 was 36,166; in 1861 it was 41,297. Of the former number, not less than 15,936 were entered up in the Exchequer. Of the contested suits the plaintiff obtained a verdict in 1,515; the defendant in 370. The total of executions was 25,727. The number of motions for new trial, &c., was 579; in 1861 the corresponding return was 105.

It is necessary that we should here caution the reader against applying statistics to cases to which they are unsuited. Statistics are the data of general laws only. They are the elements on which averages are calculated, and are, indeed, the *sine quâ non* of all important cases of abstraction or generalisation. But they do not at all apply to individual cases. If the proportion of successful plaintiffs in past years has been considerably higher than that of successful defendants, this only proves that this proportion is likely to be maintained in future as regards *all* plaintiffs viewed collectively. But no particular plaintiff could, with any show of reason, estimate his chances of success according to this proportion. Such an application of statistics would imply that *every* plaintiff was more likely to succeed than his opponent. A like observation applies to the probable result of a particular motion for a new trial. No survey of the judicial statistics of past years could be of the least use in determining such a question. Particular cases bear no more intimate relation to the general averages of success in litigation than those qualities of a simple substance do to a compound, in which, though constituting part of its elements, they no longer appear.

To the 103,564 writs of summons issued there were only

37,654 appearances entered. Nearly three-fourths (73·4 per cent.) of the suits commenced were therefore uncontested. This proportion varies but little (the report observes) from year to year. Of the cases in which appearances were entered, only 3,621 were entered for trial; and further, of this number only 3,204 or 2·1 per cent. of the suits commenced were actually tried, and of these almost 9 per cent. were undefended.

The following are a few of the more important items relating to the business in judges' chambers for the last two years. The total of summonses in 1861, was 45,814; in 1862, it was 43,434; common orders, 38,876 in 1861, and 37,030 in 1862; special orders 12,820 in 1861, and 12,334 in 1862; affidavits filed, 22,065 in 1861, and 20,505 in 1862.

The proceedings in the Court of Error Exchequer Chamber complete the summary of the business of the superior courts of common law, and were as follows for the last two years. These returns are in a more simplified form than that in which they were issued in preceding years.

	Queen's Bench.	Common Pleas.	Exchequer.	Total.
Writs of error allowed	...	...	...	—
Memorials of error lodged	19	14	12	45
Notices of appeal lodged	15	31	14	60
	34	45	26	105

	Queen's Bench.	Common Pleas.	Exchequer.	Total.
Set down for argument—				
Errors	14	9	11	34
Appeals	4	8	7	19
Remanets from 1861	12	3	16	31
	30	20	34	84
How disposed of—				
Errors	...	...	...	—
Judgments affirmed	8	9	13	30
Reversed	3	1	...	4
Venire de novo	...	...	4	4
Struck out	2	1	2	5
	13	11	19	43

	Queen's Bench.	Common Pleas.	Exchequer.	Total.
Appeals—				
Judgments affirmed	6	1	9	16
" reversed	1	...	2	3
Venire de novo	...	2	...	2
Struck out	2	...	...	2
	9	3	11	23
Remanets and standing for judgment	8	6	4	18

In the county courts the total number of plaints in 1862 was 847,288; in 1861 it was 903,957; in 1860, it was 782,384; and in 1859, 714,623. The total amount for which plaints were entered, was £2,006,680. The total amount on judgments obtained by plaintiffs on original hearings was, for defendants, £1,000,223, and for costs, £40,037. The total amount of fees on all proceedings was £270,641. Although the average amount of each plaint does not exceed £2 7*s.* 11*d.*, so that the whole amount of fees must consequently be considerable, yet so excessive an impost as the amount of fees mentioned cannot be justified. An increase appears in the returns of these courts under every head for 1861. In the total number of plaints entered, the increase amounted in that year to 121,573, or 1·55 per cent. on the number for 1860. In 1862 there was a decrease of 6·6 per cent. under this head. A remarkable proof of the growing popularity of these courts appeared in the increase of the number of judgments obtained in 1861 for debts above £50. This number, in 1861, was 204; in 1860, it was only 17; and in 1859, only 16. In 1862, we were sorry to perceive that it again had fallen to 11. Under the Charitable Trusts Act, only one matter was heard; although this return was 16 in 1861, it was 137 in 1860, and 140 in 1859. Of the causes brought into Court, 99·8 per cent. were determined without a jury, both in 1861 and in 1862. This, however, is but slight if any evidence whatever of the general unpopularity of trial by jury. For besides costing a few shillings, it virtually entails the employment of advocates—an expense greater in most cases before these courts than the sum at issue.

In 5 of the 33 ancient Manorial Courts no proceedings took place in 1862. In several of this class, however, considerable business is transacted. In the Sheriffs' Court of London, 11,410 plaints were entered. The amount of costs and fees in this class of courts was 25 per cent. upon the amount of debt recovered. The ancient practice of approaching persons in authority only after the presentation of valuable gifts, would still appear to flourish in a modified form in this description of courts. The amalgamation of these courts, however, with the County Courts, would not, as we have seen, quite cure this evil. If there is any doctrine of political economy, the justice and expediency of realising which have been conclusively demonstrated, it is that law taxes ought to be abolished. This argument applies with especial force to courts that are resorted to chiefly by the less wealthy classes.

The Blue Book before us contains no returns from the Courts of Bankruptcy for the year 1862. The bankruptcy statistics for 1861, relate only to the proceedings that were transacted from the 1st of January to the 11th of October, 1861. In this period there were—

	1861.		1860.
Petitions for adjudications by creditors	725	...	848
Petitions for adjudications by traders against themselves	366	...	432
Number of such petitions prosecuted to adjudication	1,034	...	1,215
Petitions for private arrangement under the control of the Court upon which adjudications in Bankruptcy were made	49	...	56

Of the petitions presented in 1861, upwards of 5 per cent. were not prosecuted. The total number of bankrupts was 1,222. The total amount of the debts, was £3,894,322. In 1860, the amount was £4,478,037. The average for each case is £3,791. The expenses of administration, to lessen which so many remedies have been suggested, amounted to £310,722, or £32 9*s*. 11*d*. per cent. In 1860, the charges were £30 9*s*. 8*d*. per cent. on the amount administered. The amount ordered for dividend to the creditors, averaged £16 17*s*. 5*d*. per cent.

on the total debts in the balance sheets, and £68 14*s.* 5*d.* per cent. on the amount received by the official assignee for administration. These averages, in 1860, were respectively £16 11*s.* 5*d.* and £78 19*s.* 7*d.* In almost 30 per cent. of the cases the dividend was *nil,* while only in one in every 52 cases was the full amount of 20*s.* ordered. Under the new Bankruptcy Act the classification of certificates is abolished. We need not, therefore, give any averages respecting them. The abolition of their classification is of very questionable expediency. He who contemns small things errs quite as much as the stoic; nor is the confounding together of different degrees of culpability likely to have general good results. In 84·1 per cent. of the cases, the bankruptcies were attributable to the misconduct of the bankrupts. There were 33 appeals from the Commissioners; in 11 the judgments were affirmed, in 9 reversed, in 10 varied; 3 were left pending or abandoned. The proportion of the business transacted in each Court was as follows:—

The London Court	44.5	per cent.
The Birmingham Court	16.9	,,
The Leeds Court	11.6	,,
The Manchester Court	8.2	,,
The Liverpool Court	7.4	,,
The Bristol Court	6.1	,,
The Exeter Court	3.4	,,
The Newcastle-on-Tyne Court	1.9	,,

The number of petitions for private arrangement up to the 11th of October was much beyond the number in either of the complete preceding years. The total number of petitions was, in the period specified, 301; in 1860, it was 218; and in 1859, it was 123. The total amount of debts in the balance sheets, was £1,443,478.

Under the non-trader statutes 7 & 8 Vict. c. 70, and 23 & 24 Vict. c. 147, there were 31 petitions filed, 23 of which were by debtors not in custody. The expenses of administration were £18 11*s.* 2*d.* per cent. Under the Winding-up Acts, there were 17 petitions filed.

As to insolvents, the number of petitions filed in the cases of imprisoned debtors for the portion of the year 1861 specified was 3,129, of which 18 were filed by creditors. Of this number, 683 cases were within the exclusive jurisdiction of the Court in London. The returns for nine months of 1861 exceed the total return for 1860 by 309, or 10·0 per cent. Of 3,101 schedules filed, 666 were within the jurisdiction of the Court in London. The large number of petitions filed in 1861 (as is observed in the statistics) indicates a desire on the part of insolvents that their affairs should be settled under the provisions of the old law. There appeared 708 insolvents before the Insolvent Court, and 2,503 before the County Courts. The expenses of administration averaged, in the London Jurisdiction, £35 14*s.* 6*d.*; in the County Courts £23 14*s.* 3*d.* Whence this diversity of expenses?

Of the proceedings in the Court of Chancery in 1862, the following table gives the total in all the Courts, under the different heads:—

Nature of the Proceedings.	For hearing at the commencement of the year.	Set down during the year.	Heard during the year.	Otherwise disposed of.	Remanet at the end of the year.
Pleas	1	4	4	...	1
Demurrers	10	32	32	4	6
Exceptions to pleadings	6	24	26	3	1
Motions for decree	179	1,012	918	82	200
Causes	81	227	199	47	62
Claims	...	1	1	...	—
Special cases	13	24	23	5	9
Causes, claims, and causes and matters for further directions and further consideration	71	579	562	9	79
Re-hearings and appeals	25	90	85	2	28
Appeal motions	12	60	55	5	12
Appeal petitions	3	7	10	...	...
Total	401	2,069	1,915	157	398
Total, 1861	486	2,048	2,001	132	401
Average of totals, 1862-61-60	437	2,181	2,010	134	442

The following table comprises the total of all proceedings

originating in the chambers of the Master of the Rolls, and the three Vice-Chancellors for the three years.

	1862.	1861.	1860.	1859.
Summonses to originate proceedings—				
For the administration of estates	415	480	420	332
Under the Charitable Trusts Act	7	23	59	81
For appointment of guardians and maintenance of infants	124	144	143	146
For other purposes	135	134	142	91
	681	781	764	650
Other summonses	16,569	10,066	16,184	16,381
Orders made—				
Of the class drawn up by registrars...	6,468	6,320	6,390	6,772
Of the class drawn up in chambers ...	4,908	4,914	5,143	5,770
Orders brought into chambers for prosecution (including 9 for winding-up companies)	1,852	2,112	1,941	1,930
Number of advertisements issued.........	882	888	914	963
Debts claimed and adjudicated upon—				
Number of debts	8,132	8,243	8,106	4,020
Amount of debts proved	£1,329,969	873,120	727,362	1,288,389
Accounts passed (other than receivers' accounts)—				
Number of accounts	1,103	613	476	475
Receipts thereon.............................	£1,176,285	1,551,132	1,035,106	1,124,806
Disbursements and allowances therein	£992,379	1,267,629	858,701	909,803
Sales of estates under orders of Court—				
Number of sales	519	411	457	490
Amount realized	£1,205,171	1,243,663	1,598,157	1,745,840
Purchases of estates under orders of Court—			74	
Number of purchases	88	94		84

There were 95 winding-up cases pending in 1862. The return of the examiners shows that the number of witnesses whose evidence was taken down was 338; and that the amount of fees (received by stamps) was £223 8*s.* 0*d.* In 1861 the number of witnesses was 347; the amount of fees, £723. In 1860 and 1859 the number of witnesses was 415 respectively, and the amount of fees £245 and £233. This progressive decrease shows that the system of taking down evidence by the examiners is not giving satisfaction.

The following table gives a detailed account of the number of the suits instituted in the Rolls Courts and the Courts of the three Vice-Chancellors, as also of the different classes of suits:—

Suits instituted.	1862.	1861.	1860.	1859.
Bills or informations filed...	2,177	2,176	2,209	2,083
Claims filed under General Order of 1850	...	...	27	76
Special cases filed under Act 14 Vict. c. 35	18	29	21	43
Administration summonses filed	422	488	412	327
Other originating summonses filed	266	303	362	318
	2,883	2,996	3,031	2,847

The total of proceedings in the different classes of the suits was as follows in the four last years to which the statistics extend:—

	1862.	1861.	1860.	18 9.
Proceedings in suits by bill or information	18,557	17,291	17,326	17,769
,, on claim	...	3	97	228
,, on summonses	1,029	1,208	1,171	923
,, in special cases	41	37	36	83
General proceedings	50,761	50,469	50,014	51,147
	70,388	69,008	68,644	70,150
Fees collected in the office by stamps	£22,726	24,084	25,107	25,905

The petitions in 1862 were presented for hearing as follows: —Before the Lord Chancellor, 21; before the Lords Justices, 112; before Vice-Chancellor Kindersley, 478; Vice-Chancellor Stuart, 662; Vice-Chancellor Page Wood, 603.

The number of petitions presented for orders of course in 1862 was 3,443; in 1861, it was 3,617; in 1860, it was 3,736; and in 1859, 3,555. The return made by the chief clerk to the Masters in Lunacy informs us that in 1862 there were 56 orders of inquiry made in Commissions of Lunacy executed by Masters in Lunacy. The return under this head in 1861, was 39; in 1860 it was 70, and in 1859, it was 69. In 1862 there were 124 petitions presented for hearing in Lunacy; in 1861 the number was 143.

The returns of the Chancery Court of Lancashire show

that this court still transacts a considerable amount of business. The number of suits and matters originated within the year were 149—a number not much differing from the returns of the three preceding years. An insight into the working of this court must have considerable attractions for the numerous class of law reformers who desire that courts of equity should be as accessible as the tribunals of common law.

In the Admiralty Court the total number of causes pending at the commencement of the year 1861 was, for salvage, 35; for damage by collision, 94; for necessaries supplied to foreign ships, 2. The corresponding numbers for 1861 were 145; 230; and 63. No other item was above 14. The total number of causes in 1862 was 644, in 1861 it was 695, in 1860 it was 730, and in 1859 it was 688. The average amount in each cause was in 1861, £785; in 1860, £737; and in 1859 £731. There is no return under this head for 1862. The total number of judgments was 171 in 1862; 199 in 1861; and 172 in 1860. The total number of motions and summonses heard was 322 in 1862, and 280 in 1861. Under the head of references to registrar and merchants, 52 cases are given for 1862, and 37 for 1861. The total amount of submitted costs and charges in 1862, was £26,656 2*s.* 1*d.* The total amount of Admiralty Court stamps sold by the Commissioners of Inland Revenue was in 1862 £9,993 3*s.* 3*d.* This return in 1861, was £10,008 16*s.* 2*d.*; in 1860 it was only £8,530 3*s.* 0*d.* The difference between these returns for the two last mentioned years is probably owing to the increased jurisdiction conferred upon the Court of Admiralty by the statute 24 Vict. c. 10.

The following summary shows some of the more important proceedings in the Court for Divorce and Matrimonial Causes since its establishment:—

	1862.	1861.	1860.	1859.	1858.
Petitions filed—					
In formâ pauperis	2	5	2	3	5
For nullity of marriage	4	5	2	2	10
For dissolution of marriage	200	187	210	211	244
For judicial separation	48	49	62	80	82
For restitution of conjugal rights	13	11	13	9	11
For jactitation of marriage	1	...	...	...	—
For Declaratory Act	...	6	4	1	—
	268	263	293	306	352
Judgments given—					
By the full Court	1	13	114	154	52
By the Judge Ordinary	178	236	26	48	
Applications for new trial	6	4	1	2	—
Appeals to the House of Lords	...	...	1	...	—
Appeals from Judge Ordinary to the full Court	...	...	2	...	—

There appears, as was anticipated, a progressive decrease during the last four years in the chief business of this court. On its first establishment it was burdened with the causes of the previous generation. By the statute 23 & 24 Vict. c. 144, the Judge Ordinary has the powers of the full Court. This accounts for the great difference in the returns of his judgments for 1861 and 1862 compared with those for the preceding years. The returns omit to describe the effect of the judgments.

The following is a sketch of some of the proceedings of the Court of Probate and of the Principal Registries in each of the five years to which the returns extend:—

	1862.	1861.	1860.	1859.	1858.
Total number of probates granted	8,139	8,165	8,542	8,009	8,398
" of administrations	4,304	4,437	4,405	4,541	4,341
" of motions	556	609	613	595	445
Probates and administrations granted—					
On hearing of causes	35	38	54	54	24
On motions	266	291	318	288	253
On summonses	11	7	4	7	67
Questions referred to courts of law	8	9	7	...	—
Notices of appeal to the House of Lords	...	2	2	...	—

	1862.	1861.	1860.	1859.	1858.
Revocations of probate or administration	45	28	45	35	18
Total amount of fees in court and contentious business (estimated)	£1,574	£1,706	£1,868	£2,685	£2,484
Taxed costs	12,725	9,665	15,557	8,012	4,237

Of the total number of causes the majority were disposed of by motions in court, a few by orders and summonses, and the remainder by final order or summons.

In the 40 District Registries there were granted, in 1861, of probates in common form 13,339; of letters of administration 5,144, with will annexed 679; the number of probates granted under direction of judge was 15; of letters of administration 7, with will annexed 2; the number of caveats was 284; the number refused under direction of judge 2; the number of probates granted on decrees of County Courts 2. The total amount of fees received was £56,362; the amount levied on stamps on probates and administration £495,405. These returns, as might naturally be expected, do not differ much from the like statistics for the four preceding years.

Of the returns of suits in the Ecclesiastical Courts, the jurisdiction of which has been, since the year 1858, confined to ecclesiastical matters, we may observe that the only item worth mention is the number of suits in matters of church rates. This return is 15. Under no other head (except suits for faculties) has the number of suits in these courts exceeded 3; there were 79 suits for faculties. The total amount of court fees was £300.

	1862.	1861.	1860.	1859.
Number of appeals entered	51	78	67	59
Dismissed for non-prosecution	14	15	6	7
Heard and determined	48	45	42	32
Judgments affirmed	23	24	25	16
" varied	4	6	2	—
" reversed	21	15	15	16
Appeals (lodged since order of 13th June, 1858), which remained for hearing	94	99	81	66

The preceding abstract comprises the proceedings before the Judicial Committee of Privy Council for the last four years.

The total amount of council-office fees on appeals was, in 1862, £1,381, 11*s.* 0*d.*; in 1861, it was £788 11*s.* 6*d.*; in 1860, it was £803 2*s.* 0*d.*; and in 1859, £626 19*s.* 6*d.* In 10 of the appeals, in 1862, no costs were given; in 38 costs were given. The amount of costs in 34 cases (taxed on one side only), was £9,082 7*s.* 1*d.* This gives an average of £267 2*s.* 6*d.*; for each case. In 1862, 11 applications for extension or confirmation of letters patent were lodged; of these 1 was withdrawn; 3 were dismissed, and 1 was granted. The amount of council-office fees on patent cases was £166 10*s.* 10*d.*; in 1861, it was £101 3*s.* 0*d.* In addition to the foregoing matters, the Lords of the Judicial Committee of Privy Council heard 25 petitions in appeals (interlocutory) argued by counsel.

Lastly, we come to a summary of the appeals and causes in error before the House of Lords:—

	1862.	1861.	1860.	1859.	1858.
From the Court of Chancery—					
England	12	16	30	20	13
Ireland	2	10	16	5	2
From the Court of Exchequer Chamber—					
England	10	2	14	9	8
Ireland	...	2	4	1	4
From the Court of Session—					
Scotland	28	30	36	25	18
From the Court of Probate—					
England	...	3	4	1	1
Ireland	...	...	...	...	1
From the Court of Divorce—					
England	2	1	4	2	—
Total	49	64	108	63	47

This table comprises 14 appeals and causes in error in suits relating to real property; 28 in matters of personal property; 1 of real and personal property; and 6 miscellaneous causes: 5 were withdrawn; 14 were dismissed for want of prosecution;

30 were heard; 8 of these were simply affirmed; 1 was simply reversed; 12 were reversed with declarations; 35 causes remained for hearing. In 1861, 26 causes; in 1859 and in 1858 there remained 49 causes for hearing at the close of the session. The total amount of fees in 1861 was £1,737 6*s.* 0*d.*; in 1861 it was £2,528 18*s.* 0*d.*; in 1860 it was £2,493 2*s.* 6*d.*; in 1859 it was £2,023; and in 1858 the amount was £1,791 2*s.* 0*d.*

The first part of the report for 1861 concluded with the observation that under each of its three leading divisions—Police, Criminal Proceedings, and Prisons—"an increase of crime appears, although not to any great extent, as compared with the preceding year." This increase (404 or 0·8 per cent.) must be read in connexion with the statement in page 8 of the Report, that the number of "known thieves and depredators" have exhibited a decrease of 21·3 per cent. as compared with the preceding year. To an increase of crime in that year, we have thus a set-off of a decrease of criminals. This decrease is, perhaps, attributable to the change of the definition of "known thieves and depredators" adopted in that Report; and also partly to a desire on the part of the police, not to have their vigilance called in question by too high a return of the unconvicted portion of the population. But throughout all the returns for 1862 an increase of crime appears. In no year since 1857 has the number of convictions been so high. It appears that the least number of commitments to prison in any year for the last 20 years was in 1846, when this item amounted only to 89,932; and that the greatest number was in 1849, when it was 119,715. In 1862 this number was 113,177. The returns from the civil courts, on the other hand, of which we have just given an analysis, show a considerable falling-off from the figures for 1861. If these ratios become progressive for a few years, the prospects of the criminal lawyer will be considerably better than those of his brethren. The second part of the Report for 1861, likewise contained the statement that a "review of the proceedings seemed to indicate a considerable increase of litigation, and of the business of the courts generally." This increase, however, was really slight, and denoted an accidental impetus, rather than any progressive growth of litigation. Accordingly, this progression is not continued in the civil returns for 1862.

We know of no branch of Jurisprudence the study of which will not be aided by a perusal of the valuable returns contained in the annual issues of Judicial Statistics. They indicate with peculiar accuracy the comparative merits of courts having a concurrent jurisdiction, and supply a correct measure of the operation of every change in our legal system. Part 1 contains a variety of matter possessing great interest for the philanthropist, and exceedingly well arranged for testing the general efficacy of our establishments for the prevention or punishment of crime. Part 2 comprises, in a similar manner, records of the ebb and flow of civil litigation for two and (in some instances for five) four years. The tables under every head ought to contain in a simplified form the returns for at least four years. The value of statistics is in direct proportion to the number of years over which their comparative analysis extends. Compared with such a comprehensive sketch, statistics respecting the successive stages of suits are comparatively unimportant. On the whole, the compilation before us substantially serves all the purposes for which the Judicial Statistics were originally designed, and, though admitting of some further improvements, contains even in its present state the most valuable materials for the solution of every question of law reform.

Art. IV.—THE FOREIGN ENLISTMENT ACT, 59 Geo. III., Cap. 69.

"*The Alexandra Case*" (*Attorney-General* v. *Sillim and others*), *and* "*The Pampero Case.*"

THE "Alexandra Case," after having dragged its slow length along for a year, has now terminated in a premature and most unsatisfactory manner. Unsatisfactory, not in consequence of the ultimate result in point of fact, namely, that the ship has been released; but in consequence of there having been no result in point of law arrived at on a subject of so much moment, notwithstanding the great expenditure of time and money of which it has been the cause.

The whole civilized world has for a year past been looking forward to the result of this case, as settling what the law of this country is with respect to the rights of British subjects to build ships in Great Britain or her colonies, for a belligerent or belligerents, with whom we are at peace. We say "the law of this country," because there is no doubt whatever that, according to international law, there is no prohibition whatever against such a trade, whether the ship be armed or not; and the whole question turned on the construction of our own municipal law, developed, or rather we may say obscured by the statute of 59 Geo. III. chapter 69, commonly called "The Foreign Enlistment Act." The question mainly turned on the 7th section, "And be it further enacted, that if any person within any part of the United Kingdom, or in any part of His Majesty's dominions beyond the seas, shall without the leave and license of his Majesty for that purpose, first had and obtained, *equip, furnish, fit out, or arm*, or attempt to equip, furnish, fit out, or arm, or procure to be equipped, furnished, fitted out, or armed, or shall knowingly aid, assist, or be concerned in the equipping, furnishing, fitting out, or arming of any ship or vessel, *with intent or in order* that such ship or vessel shall be employed in the service of any foreign prince, state, or potentate, or of any foreign colony, province, or part of any province or people, or of any person or persons exercising or assuming to exercise any powers of government, in or over any foreign state, colony, province," &c., "as a transport or storeship, or with intent to cruise or commit hostilities against any prince, state, or potentate, or against the subjects or citizens . . . of any foreign colony, province, or part of any province, or country, with whom His Majesty shall not then be at war . . . Every such person so offending shall be deemed guilty of misdemeanor, and shall, upon conviction, upon any information or indictment, be punished by fine and imprisonment, or either of them, at the discretion of the court in which such offender shall be convicted; and every such ship or vessel, with the tackle, apparel, and furniture, together with all the materials, arms, ammunition, and stores, which may belong to, or be on board of any such ship or vessel, shall be forfeited . . . ." N.P. The 8th section was much referred to as bearing on the question; it is as follows:—"And be it further enacted, that if any person, in any part of the United Kingdom of Great Britain and Ireland, or any part of His Majesty's dominions beyond the seas, without the leave and license of His Majesty, for that purpose first had and obtained, as aforesaid, shall, by adding to the number of the guns of such vessel, or by changing those on board for other guns, by the addition of any equipment for war, increase or augment, or procure to be increased or augmented, or shall be knowingly concerned in increasing or augmenting, the warlike force of any ship or vessel of war or cruiser, or other armed vessel which at the time of her arrival in any part of the United Kingdom, or any of His Majesty's dominions, was a ship of war, cruiser, or armed vessel, in the service of any foreign prince, state, or potentate, &c. . . . every such person so offending shall be deemed guilty of a misdemeanor," &c. It will be observed that this latter section applies as well to the case of a ship in the service of a foreign government, whether that government be at peace or at war. In other words, it applies at all times, to all ships of war of a foreign government.

The ship Alexandra was built in the yard of Miller and Sons, ship-builders, at Liverpool. She was in length 127 feet, in the beam 21½ feet, and her gross tonnage was 150 tons. Her build was such as was not usual in merchantmen, and was easily convertible for warlike purposes; she had a cooking apparatus sufficient for 150 or 200 men, but no stowage for merchandise. In fact, for our present purposes, we may assume that she was built for the Confederate States of North America, but the evidence failed to show that there was any intention to fit her in this country with any implements of war. She was seized by the government of this country as forfeited under the 7th section of the above Act; and an information was filed by the Attorney-General against several persons charging them with equipping, with furnishing, with fitting out (but not with arming), the said ship, "with intent and in order that the ship should be employed in the service of certain foreign States, styling themselves the Confederate States of America, with intent to cruise and commit hostilities against the Republic of the United States of America, Her Majesty not being at war therewith, and without the leave and license of Her Majesty." The substance of this charge was varied through 96 counts (the 97th and 98th being addressed to the fact of her being a transport or storeship, but those counts were subsequently abandoned), the persons who came in and claimed as owners, pleaded in substance that the said ship, her furniture, &c., was not forfeited for the supposed causes in the information charged. Whereupon issue was joined, and the trial came on before Chief-Baron Pollock, at the Sittings after Trinity Term. The evidence on the part of the Crown amounted in substance to what we have before stated, as to the build, &c., of the ship. The claimants offered no evidence whatever. The Chief-Baron, in his summing up, pointed out to the jury that independently of the Act of 59 George III., c. 69, international law permitted the sale of contraband of war, including ships by a neutral to a belligerent. He told them, in substance, that the question for their consideration was whether the ship was built in obedience to an order, and in compliance with a contract, without any intention, in the port of Liverpool or any other port of Her Majesty's dominions, that she should be *equipped, fitted out, and furnished, or armed for the purpose of aggression*, and that if so there was no breach of the statute of George III., although the parties building her might have a knowledge that she was intended to be used for warlike purposes; expressing his opinion that there was no distinction between the mere building of a ship and the sale of her, and the manufacturing of arms and gunpowder and the sale of them, by a neutral to belligerents. The jury found for the claimants.

A bill of exceptions to the judge's direction to the jury was tendered by the Crown, and the case came before the Court of Exchequer in Hilary Term last, but the bill of exceptions was ultimately abandoned upon the Court of Exchequer making an order under the Queen's Remembrancer's Act, 22 & 23 Victoria, c. 21, extending the practice as to moving for new trials, &c., to cases on the revenue side of the Court of Exchequer.

A new trial was accordingly moved for by the Attorney-General, on the ground that the judge did not sufficiently explain to the jury the construction and effect of the 59 George III., c. 69; and that he misdirected them on the construction of the 7th section; and that he did not leave to them the question whether the ship was intended to be employed in the service of the Confederate States to cruise against the United States, or the question whether there was any attempt or endeavour to equip.

The case was most ably argued for six days, when it stood over for judgment. The court differing in opinion, the members of the court delivered separate judgments, and we purpose to give here, as concisely as possible, the substance of those judgments.

The Lord Chief-Baron, in remarking upon his charge to the jury, observed, "If the making, in pursuance of an agreement or order for that purpose, with intention to sell and deliver to one of the belligerents, the hull of a vessel suitable for war, but unarmed, and not equipped, furnished, or fitted out with anything that enabled her to cruise or commit hostilities, or to do any warlike act, be a violation of the Foreign Enlistment Act, my direction to the jury was wrong in point of law; the verdict ought to have been for the Crown, and there ought to be a new trial.

"But if the commerce of this country in ships, whether ultimately for peace or war, is to continue, and, provided a ship leaves the ports of this country in no condition to cruise or to commit hostilities, though she may be of a warlike character, there has been no violation of the statute, then the verdict was right."

His lordship then analysed the counts of the information; and then coming to the construction of the statute in question and its history, observed that "the act was a highly penal one, creating a new crime or misdemeanor, making those who commit it liable to fine and imprisonment, if found guilty, and the ship liable to forfeiture." He then emphatically denied the power of the court to call in aid to the construction of a criminal statute such as the present, the opinions of eminent statesmen, learned jurists, or the decisions of foreign courts; or to allow political consequences to have any weight whatever in the construction of the statute. Citing 1 Bl. Com., p. 92, "For the freedom of our constitution will not permit that in criminal cases a power should be lodged in any judge to construe the law otherwise than according to the letter."

His lordship then came to the construction of the statute itself; and he maintained that it was a perfectly correct mode of construing a prohibitory statute, to ascertain by the obviously designed omission of particular words or expressions, what the statute did not mean to prohibit; and that if what it did not mean to prohibit was perfectly clear, then, what by doubtful words is supposed to be prohibited, must be consistent with what it permits. That the building of ships, which formed so large a part of the trade of this country, could not have escaped the consideration of the legislature when passing this Act; and yet the Act does not contain the word "build," that therefore, it was obvious that the word was designedly omitted for the purpose of leaving the trade of ship-building unaffected by the Act. That in common honesty it could not be suggested that the legislature meant to suppress the mere building of ships for a belligerent by a side wind, as it would be to include "building" within the terms "equip, furnish, fit-out or arm," thereby suppressing to a great extent the trade of ship-builders, without exciting their alarm. That when it is once admitted, as it must be, that the construction of the statute is far from being free from difficulty, it is contrary to principle to put a construction upon the words which will *create* a crime. That all argument on the ground of reciprocity with the act of Congress in *pari materia,* if it were to be allowed on the construction of a penal statute, would be against extending the crime to the act of *building ships* for a belligerent, for that according to the decisions of the American courts it was permissible for American ship-builders not only to *build ships* for a belligerent, but even to equip and arm such ships. That by comparing the 7th section with the 2nd section it was clear that the object of the Act was to preserve the ports of this country from being made ports of hostile equipment, and not to prevent the act of hostile equipment of a ship by a British subject; for that although the 2nd section prohibited enlistment of a British subject in a foreign service, no matter where that British subject may be, yet it could not be contended that a British subject might not in a foreign country, with perfect immunity, embark his capital in the fitting out of armed ships for sale to belligerents with whom we were at peace. And that by the 8th section *increase of armament* to a foreign armed ship was alone prohibited; and repairs were permitted.

His lordship then examined the wording of the 7th section, "If any person within, &c., shall equip, &c., with intent, or in order that such ship or vessel shall be employed in the service of any foreign state or government as a transport or storeship, or with intent to cruise or commit hostilities against, &c.," and observed that two questions obviously arose upon those words—1st, whose intention is it that is meant by the act? and 2ndly, what is the meaning of the words "equip?" &c. His lordship then showed that all the counts of the information which were framed upon the principle of reading the above section as if both intents were combined, namely, the intent "that the vessel should be employed in the service," &c., *and* "with intent to cruise or commit hostilities," must fall to the ground, as there was no evidence to show that the parties committing the act complained of had any intent to cruise or commit hostilities; and that it was absurd to suppose that one intent should be attributed to the party accused of committing the violation of the statute, and the other intent attributed to the persons by whom the ship might be employed. That the meaning of the words "equip, furnish, fit out, or arm," were explained by the context, "with intent or in order that such ship or vessel shall be employed &c., to cruise or commit hostilities," to mean a warlike equipping, &c., for that the words "with intent *or in order*" meant as a means to an end, namely, an equipping, &c., to enable the ship to commit hostilities. That had the word "arm" alone been used there might have been some doubt as to what degree of arming would be required to constitute the offence; but that the degree was settled by taking the whole sentence, namely, the ship was not to be equipped, &c., in order to cruise or commit hostilities. And he held that the 7th section should be construed as if the words were, "If any person within, &c., shall, without the leave, &c., equip, &c., as a 'means,' any ship or vessel 'to the end' that such ship shall cruise or commit hostilities." And observed that if after all the equipping, furnishing, or fitting out, the ship is incapable of committing hostilities, there has been no such equipping, &c., as the statute was intended to prevent. His lordship stated the result of the arguments on the part of the Crown to be this:—A ship-builder may build a ship altogether of a warlike character, and may arm it completely to the latest and most mischievous invention for the destruction of human beings, and may then sell it to one of two belligerents with a perfect fitness for immediate cruising, provided there was no previous contract or agreement for it. But if there be any contract or agreement for it, it cannot be made to order with the slightest warlike character about it, though this be part of the accustomed and usual trade of this country, and though the ship leaves our shores a mere hull, utterly incapable of cruising or committing hostilities. And he then showed how simply such a law might be evaded, observing that such a construction would require us to believe that the legislature had exhausted all their wisdom in settling the language of the 7th section and had none left to perceive the enormous loophole they, upon such a construction, would have left; through which, as his lordship said, not only could a coach-and-six be driven through the Act, but a whole fleet could sail through it. His lordship wound up his very clear and ably reasoned judgment, by expressing his opinion that the Act was not framed in order to make any difference between ships and guns, ammunition, and other implements of war, but to prevent our shores from being made the points of departure of hostile expeditions, commissioned and equipped to commit hostilities against a belligerent not at war with us.

Mr. Baron Bramwell, in commenting upon the 7th section said that the second insertion of the word "intent" immediately before the words "to cruise or commence hostilities," put it beyond a doubt that the equipment must be fit for cruising or the commission of hostilities. But that even had the word "intent" been omitted from before the words "to cruise, &c.," the meaning would be the same. His lordship observed, " I think it cannot properly be said that a man does an act with intent, unless he intends the act to bring about the thing intended, or unless the act is particularly fitted to do so. Thus, if a man builds a ship in which *he* means to go a whaling voyage, he builds with intent the ship shall go a whaling voyage, though unfit for whaling. But if he builds her for another, he does not build her with an intent that she shall go a-whaling, unless he particularly adapts her to that service. In this case, if ' building ' with intent that the vessel should be employed to cruise had been forbidden, I think the forfeiture would have been incurred, for by her build she was particularly adapted for that purpose; but the word " equip " is used, and there is no forfeiture, unless there is equipment particularly fitting her for cruising, the equipper himself not intending to cruise in her." His lordship then referred to sections 2 and 8, and expressed his opinion that they supported the argument for the defendants, and said that upon the very words of the Act he was of opinion that the 7th section prohibits that equipment only which is itself such that by means of it the vessel can commit hostilities, and that no equipment which gives no means of attack and defence is within that section. His lordship, after commenting on the rights and obligations created by international law on the subject of a hostile expedition fitted out by the subjects of a state at peace, expressed his opinion (as the Lord Chief-Baron had previously done) that an unarmed ship was nothing more than ordinary contraband of war, and that there was no law against selling contraband of war to a belligerent. And he said, " I am aware of the consequences if this is the law. A ship may sail from a port ready to receive a warlike equipment; that equipment may leave in another vessel, and be transferred to her as soon as the neutral limit is passed, or at some not remote port, and thus the spirit of international law may be violated, and the letter of the municipal law evaded. But as the law stands, or, as both laws stand, I see no remedy. I do not see what line can be drawn but the sharp line." His lordship agreed, therefore, with the Lord Chief-Baron that the direction was right, and that the verdict for the defendants was right on the evidence, and that the rule for a new trial should be discharged.

Mr. Baron Channell, in his construction of the 7th section, agreed with the Lord Chief-Baron and Mr. Baron Bramwell in considering that the mere building of a ship was not within the section, that the equipping, fitting out, and furnishing, are all acts subsequent in their nature to the building, and that the equipment, &c., must be an equipment for war; that an equipment which could not be used, and is not useful, for war, will not bring the case within this section. But then his lordship held that the equipment need not be of that manifestly warlike nature which the Lord Chief-Baron and Mr. Baron Bramwell considered necessary. And he said, "suppose there is evidence of some equipment or other, either completed or attempted, but that it does not, in itself, show whether it is an equipment for war or not, may we not take into consideration evidence of the intent, to prove that it is actually, and in point of fact, an equipment for war?" And he answered the question in the affirmative. Contending that as in the case of a "store ship" there was no equipment specially suited for it which could be distinguished from the equipment of an ordinary trader, other evidence of intent would be absolutely requisite and therefore admissible. So, in the case of certain equipments as to which it is doubtful whether they are for warlike purposes or not, he was of opinion that the jury might look at evidence of intent, "provided that the equipments as to which the doubt exists are such as can be directly used for war without further addition."

His lordship then examined the summing-up of the Lord Chief-Baron to the jury, and pointed out various objections to which he considered it open; but mainly on the following point, "That the Lord Chief-Baron did not direct the attention of the jury to the point whether there was an equipment (completed or attempted) of a character doubtful in itself, but still capable of being used for war, which was, to their satisfaction, established to be an equipment for war by the evidence of the intent of the parties." And he expressed his opinion that a new trial should be granted on the ground of misdirection, &c. His lordship said that he agreed with the Lord Chief-Baron and Mr. Baron Bramwell, in thinking that what the statute forbids is an equipment for war; and that the main object of the statute was to prevent our ports being made stations of hostilities. "Our difference appears to be this (he observed), that they think the equipment must be intended to be completed, so that the vessel, when it leaves our port shall be in a condition at once to commence hostilities; while it seems to me that in the fair and reasonable meaning of the words used, another case is included, viz., where the equipment not being complete to that extent, is yet capable of being used for war, and the intent is clear that it is to be used for war."

Mr. Baron Pigott, after stating that "the material facts disclosed in evidence on the trial were, that the vessel, the Alexandra, was built by Messrs. Miller, who stated that she was for Messrs. Fraser, Trenholme, and Co., agents of the Southern Confederacy; that she was launched in March, and at the time of the seizure, on the 5th of April, the defendant's workmen were variously engaged in fitting her with stanchions for hammock-nettings; her three masts were up, and had lightning conductors on them; she was provided with a cooking apparatus sufficient for 150 or 200 people; her build was apparently for a gun-boat, with low bulwarks over which pivot guns could play, and her hatches were too small for merchandise; in fact, she was not qualified for mercantile purposes," referred to the international obligations existing at the time of the passing of the Act. His lordship then referred to the preamble of the Act 59 Geo. III., c. 69, "Whereas the enlistment . . . . and the fitting out and equipping and arming of vessels by his Majesty's subjects, without his Majesty's license, for warlike operations in or against, &c.,

may be prejudicial to, and tend to endanger the peace and welfare of this kingdom; And, whereas, the laws in force are not sufficiently effectual for preventing the same," and observed that the enacting clause was studiously varied and extended by the introduction of the words "furnish," and the substitution of the disjunctive "or," for the copulative "and;" and further, by extending the forfeiture to an *attempt* to commit, or to aiding or assisting in the commission of the principal offence; and that effect must be given to the larger words of the clause. His lordship then examined the words of the 7th section, and expressed his opinion that the Act was not directed against the building a hull or vessel. "But," his lordship observed, "I am of opinion that any act of equipping, furnishing, or fitting out done to a hull or vessel of whatever nature or character that act may be, if done with the prohibited intent, is expressly within the plain language, and also within the evident spirit of the statute. This *intent* I take to mean an intent of the principal (who has the control of the ship) having directly for its object the employment of the vessel by a foreign state, or in the equipper a like intent, and with such intent contributing equipments of some kind necessary to such employment; and it is evident that the intents need not be derived solely from the nature of the equipments, but may be proved *aliunde*." And his lordship's reasons were shortly these. He felt bound, where the legislature used the four words "equip, furnish, fit-out, or arm," not to treat them all as signifying the same thing, and a mere redundancy, particularly as it was clear that the three first applied to a peaceful equipment in the case of a transport or storeship; and that he could not agree with the argument *reddendo singula singulis*, and refuse to apply the like meaning to equipments of a ship intended to commit hostilities. The argument that with reference to ships intended to commit hostilities, the statute only meant to prohibit warlike equipments, which would enable the ship at once to commit hostilities, proved too much, for then a ship with all her guns in her, but no ammunition, would be useless for actual hostilities, and, therefore, according to that argument the 7th section would not be violated; although it was admitted in the argument, that a complete equipment was not necessary to bring it within the prohibition. He could not hold that the intent must be evidenced by a *distinctive* equipment, for in the case of a store ship there would be none such; then why should it be required in the case of a cruiser? His lordship said that in his view the prohibited intent is the main ingredient, and that any act of equipping done in furtherance of that intent constituted the whole offence; and that the jury should have been distinctly told that the intent being established to their satisfaction, any act of equipping in furtherence of such intention would be unlawful within the meaning of the statute. And, further, that assuming that equipment of a distinctively warlike character was necessary, there was sufficient evidence of such distinctive equipment—fitting stanchions for hammock racks, and the cooking apparatus—and that, therefore, on the ground of insufficient direction, there ought to be a new trial.

In consequence of the equal division of the Court, the junior, Mr. Baron Pigott, withdrew his judgment, and the rule for a new trial was discharged.

The judicial history of this case may be completed in a few more lines. The Crown appealed to the Exchequer Chamber from the above decision, but that Court dismissed the appeal, upon the ground of want of jurisdiction, the Court considering that the Chief and other Barons of the Exchequer had not the power which they had assumed, under the 22 & 23 Vict., c. 21, of extending the practice as to moving for new trials, so as to give an appeal to the Exchequer Chamber which did not previously exist. The Crown appealed from that decision to the House of Lords, and their lordships affirmed it; but of course with no expression of their opinions upon the important question of construction above discussed, the Lord Chancellor expressing his regret of the empty result of the proceedings in these words, "The result is, that the efforts made to settle a question of the gravest importance, and most essential for the guidance of the Government of the country, and regarded with great expectation, have been rendered abortive, or rather, to speak more correctly, the *mons parturiens* of this great cause, raised with so much labour and expense, will produce nothing but the ridiculous issue of some discordant opinions on the meaning of the word 'practice.'"

Thus ludicrously terminated this case, on which—it is not too much to say—the eyes of Europe and America had been fixed for months past, involving a point of vast, of mighty interest to the world at large; the only result being, that one more Parliamentary monstrosity has been brought to light; holding us up to ridicule as incompetent of putting together in our own language a few simple sentences in an intelligible, not to say logical form, although from the nature of the subject, it being of world-wide importance, the greatest care and precision would have been presumed to have been bestowed upon it. When shall we awaken to a sense of the propriety and economy of having a responsible minister, to see to the proper grammatical and logical construction of our Acts of Parliament? It would be interesting to ascertain, approximately at least, what amount annually is expended in litigation, solely turning on vexed constructions of Acts of Parliament, and which would never have come into court had the intention of the legislature been embodied in careful, grammatical, and logical language; but we would venture to say that the sum would amount to six figures.

But now let us shortly examine the agreement and divergence in the opinions of those of our judges who have been called upon to express an opinion on this very obscure statute. And, first, all four agree in this, that there is nothing prohibitory in the statute against the mere act of building the hull of a ship for a belligerent, no matter what the intent may be as to its application. And further, that what is prohibited in the 7th section by the words, "equip, furnish, and fit out," are acts occurring subsequent to the completion of the hull.

They also seem to be agreed upon this, that the main object of the legislature in passing the Act was to prevent our ports being made ports of departure of hostile expeditions against a nation with which we are at peace. The great difference of opinion arises as to what must be the nature of the equipment, furnishing, or fitting out, which will create a forfeiture under the Act. The Lord Chief-Baron and Mr. Baron Bramwell hold that it must be such as, in fact, to render the ship immediately available for warlike purposes. (The case of a transport and store-ship was excluded, except as a matter of argument, those counts having been abandoned). Mr. Baron Channell and Mr. Baron Pigott held, that though the equipments, to bring the case within the penal clause, must to some extent be for warlike purposes, yet that it is not necessary that they should be *manifestly* so, but that the nature and object of the equipments and the intent with which they have been put in, may be made out by evidence *aliunde.*

For our own part, we should incline to a middle course between these two opinions, could we but find a safe one; but we much fear that it is impossible *ex tenebris dare lucem.* We see considerable difficulties in giving our adhesion to either opinion. We think that the proposition, that to create the forfeiture it is necessary that the arming must be such as to enable the commission of hostilities, is too general, and that it is answered by Mr. Baron Pigott's observation, that if that were so, every warlike equipment might be completed with the exception of, say, gunpowder or men, and the case would not be brought within the prohibition. At the same time we strongly incline to the opinion that the true key to the construction of this 7th section is given by the rule *reddendo singula singulis,* and that the word "arm" is used in it as a necessary part of the equipment to create a forfeiture of a ship intended to be used as a cruiser, or in commission of hostilities; we fail to discover any answer to the Chief-Baron's and Mr. Baron Bramwell's argument on the effect of the words "with intent or *in order* that," &c.; and we think that the extended construction put upon the Act by Mr. Baron Channell and Mr. Baron Pigott, founded as it is upon doubtful and ambiguous words, is far too lax a construction of a strictly penal statute. We incline to think that any equipment, &c., being in its character undoubtedly what may fairly be called "arming," though by no means complete, and with the intent mentioned in the 7th section is sufficient to create the misdemeanour, and to work the forfeiture; but that the crime of misdemeanour cannot be created and forfeiture effected by acts of doubtful or arguable meaning, patched up by evidence *aliunde* of the purposes for which the equipment is intended.

In truth, it is very far from clear what use such evidence of intent could be; for, if *armament* to some extent be necessary, no amount of evidence of the intent of the equipper, that a peaceful equipment should be used hostilely, could render that equipment warlike.

We must not conclude our notice of "The Alexandra Case" without referring to the case of "The Pampero," which has lately been the subject of discussion in the Court of Session in Scotland; the case, so far as we can collect from the sources of information at present available, seems on all fours with that of the "Alexandra," and is likely to be the subject of discussion in the House of Lords during the present session. The case was brought before the First Division of the Court of Session, during the last month, on a reclaiming note of the defenders', objecting to an interlocutor pronounced by Lord Ormidale, sitting as Lord Ordinary in Exchequer Causes, by which he overruled certain objections of the defenders taken to the relevancy of the charges contained in the information filed by the Crown after the seizure of the Pampero; the defenders contending that as the charges, assuming them to be true, did not bring the case within the penal effect of the 7th section of 59 George III., c. 69, it would be useless to go to trial upon them. Lord Ormidale overruled the objection, considering that the more proper time for discussing those questions would be after trial. The defenders appealed from that decision, and the Court of Session being of opinion that it would be more proper to discuss some of those questions before trial, the question of relevancy was discussed and decided.

The information seemed in its material allegations identical with that in the case of the Alexandra, in its charges and its number of counts. The first count will be sufficient for our purpose. It charged that the defenders "without any leave or license of Her Majesty, did equip the said ship or vessel with intent and in order that such ship or vessel should be employed in the service of certain foreign states, styling themselves the Confederate States of America, with intent to cruise and commit hostilities against a certain foreign state with which Her Majesty was not then at war, to wit, the Republic of the United States of America, contrary to the form of the statute, &c., whereby and by force of the statute, &c., the said ship or vessel, together with the said tackle, apparel, and furniture became and was forfeited." It is to be observed that none of the counts of the information charged the defenders with "arming" the said ship, they were confined to charges infinitely varied of "equipping," or "furnishing," or "fitting out," or intending to "equip," or "furnish," or "fit out," "with intent," &c. And the counts relating to the equipping as a store ship or transport were, as in the case of the Alexandra, abandoned.

The Lord President, in delivering his judgment, said, "The objection in substance is, that the statute is not directed against equipping a vessel to be used as a cruiser, unless the parties equipping the vessel do so with intent by themselves or others under their control, to cruise or commit hostilities. In my opinion the statute is not so limited. I think it is directed against fitting out a vessel with intent that such vessel should be employed to cruise or commit hostilities, whether such employment be by the equippers or persons under their control, or by others in the service of a foreign state. One result of the opposite construction would be, that the statute would be more carefully preventive of fitting out store ships, or transports, than of fitting out vessels to commit hostilities. The other objection was of this nature, that the information does not contain any allegation that the vessel was "armed," or intended to be "armed;" and it was said in the first place, that in regard to a cruiser or vessel to commit hostilities, the words "equip, fit out, and furnish," were not applicable, and that according to the true reading of the statute, these words were intended to apply to the case of a transport or store ship, and that the word "arm" in the statute was alone intended to apply to the case of a cruiser. I think that is a very strained interpretation, and I cannot adopt it. Another contention of the defenders was that in those counts having reference to a vessel intended to cruise or commit hostilities, "armed" should have been specially introduced *in terminis* to the allegation, and that this not having been done, those counts are defective. I cannot adopt that contention, I think that the words "equip, furnish, and fit out," are sufficient, and that these words will cover a greater or less extent of "arming." I am of opinion that both of these objections should be repelled, and that this should be done by express decision. which may be made the subject of appeal at a future stage."

The Lord President then glanced at other questions which had been argued; amongst others, as to what progress must be made towards bringing the ship into the condition in which she must be before she can be held to be equipped as a cruiser; but said that these were not objections to *relevancy*, which could then be properly discussed, and therefore gave no opinion upon them. The rest of the court, consisting of Lords Curriehill, Deas, and Ardmillan, concurred in the judgment of the Lord President.

We necessarily infer from this decision that the Scotch judges did not feel themselves bound in any manner by the result of the "Alexandra Case" in the Court of Exchequer.

And undoubtedly they were in no manner bound by it, it having been a judgment of two against two; but, had they agreed with the Lord Chief-Baron and Baron Bramwell, they must have held that the counts were insufficient as they did not contain a charge of "arming." This is all we can at present with certainty predicate of the opinions of the Scotch judges; but we shall probably not have to wait long before we shall have some more light thrown upon this most obscure and ill-worded Act of Parliament.

Art. V.—MR. J. G. PHILLIMORE'S LAST WORK.

Private Law among the Romans, from the Pandects. By John George Phillimore, Q.C., London and Cambridge. Macmillan & Co. 1863.

WE never met with a book more difficult to read, comprehend, or review, than this. It must lie in Mr. Phillimore's breast and conscience to explain why it has been written and printed; and we hope that such an explanation would not suggest that it owes its conception to the author's absolute contempt for all other writers and thinkers on the Roman law. On any other rational or intelligible theory of professional motive, it is not easy to account for its publication. We have waded through it without having discovered that in the present state of our legal literature it was in the slightest degree called for. Nor, as a legal work, is it in itself well done. It is not well arranged, and it wants a lawyer-like system or plan. The book—if book by courtesy it may be called—is little more than a selected compilation from the Pandects, with a few notes, a sort of hash of unnecessary learning, a queer stirabout of black letter oddities and crudities, which we verily believe no other man but the author could have seriously and deliberately offered to the public and profession Mr. Phillimore has doubtless been a diligent student of the Pandects, and his notes and comments on that profound but confused composition would no doubt, on proper occasions, be valuable. But their appearance in the form of this work we are unable to appreciate; nor, we say again, can we understand why it has seen the light, unless it has been for the pleasure and satisfaction of writing the bilious preface, and for the sake of those flings of idiosyncrasy and strong language which may be found in the foot notes. In his character of author, Mr. Phillimore does not hesitate to announce himself as follows:—"My belief that some knowledge of the Roman system of Municipal Law will contribute to improve our own, has induced me to prepare the work I now offer to the public." *Some knowledge of the Roman system of Municipal Law*, indeed! We have hitherto been without such knowledge (!) and we are, forsooth, to ignore the stream of legal publication before and since the grand work of Pothier, which (with the exception of the work under review) has flown so copiously and admirably down to the present day! Why, a year has not elapsed since we had the pleasure to notice, with the comfort and satisfaction we endeavoured to express, Lord Mackenzie's excellent work, a work infinitely superior in every respect to this one of Mr. Phillimore's, but to which, from beginning to end, he makes not the least allusion, although he indulges in the most extravagant eulogy on some very ordinary and commonplace topics; for instance, the judgment in Entick *v.* Carrington, in which it was in the quietest manner possible decided that a search warrant by a Secretary of State for the discovery of evidence of a libel against the Government, was illegal. The judgment is in language and argument of the most commonplace character, and with no marks whatever of particular legal enlightenment, except in being right, sound, and constitutional, and yet Mr. Phillimore describes it as "one of the *few* judgments on a great question in our Reports that a *Jurist* may read *without a blush!*" a sentiment which may serve to show the spirit in which our author applied himself to his unnecessary task. We can only say we hope Mr. Phillimore approves of the judgment as thoroughly as we do, when, in conclusion it states, "We (the court) are no advocates for libels; all Governments must set their faces against them, and whenever they come before us and a jury, we shall set our faces against them; and if juries do not prevent them, they may prove fatal to liberty, destroy government, and introduce anarchy; but tyranny is better than anarchy, and the worst government than none at all." To be sure, he tells us, when covering with contempt and scorn that "coacervation of absurdities under the name of law in our books," which he imagines to be the condition of the law of England, that he "desires particularly to be understood throughout the work as never speaking of his contemporaries except when he alludes to them directly;" and we cannot doubt that Mr. Phillimore's knowledge of the law with reference to any such allusion is consistent with his feelings as a gentleman. But such a caveat does not relieve him from the ordinary obligations of scholarship, or entitle him to profess to ignore the accessible learning of his professional brethren. And there is another consideration which Mr. Phillimore might with propriety have kept in view before committing himself to the self-ascription touching "some knowledge of Roman Law," viz., that he is one of the four readers of the Inns of Court, but that he is *not* the one whose particular duty it is to instruct us in that knowledge—that duty being rather within the province of another department, in which "Jurisprudence and the Civil Law" are exclusively treated. We have not the personal acquaintance of Mr. Sharpe, the present reader in the department referred to, but we are not aware that he has showed any unfitness for his office, and we rather think if Mr. Maine had been still among us here, he would have considered Mr. Phillimore's suggestion more obtrusive than discreet.

We should not forget to notice, and to some extent except from the objection we feel to the whole work, a tabular synopsis of the whole Roman Law, "taken in part from the French and German tables," and which, on the assumption of its accuracy, may not be without some convenience to the student; but with that exception, and also with the exception of the preface and the preliminary chapter (which, however, treats of matters which are far more satisfactorily considered in Lord Mackenzie's work) the book is simply a selection from and translation of portions of the Pandects, which were as well known to and at least as accessible to the body of the profession, as to Mr. Phillimore himself.

As for the preface, it, perhaps, deserves some attention. Its style is characteristic of the author's powers of sarcasm, invective, and denunciation; but it would be a mistake to describe it as a tissue of nonsense, for it contains some truth, and we confess to a certain amount of sympathy with it. And we are the more anxious that it should not escape observation, because, as we have hinted, we are seriously of opinion that it was for the sake of being able to publish the preface that this strange work was undertaken. It commences with the modest sentence to which we have already referred, in the following style:—"My belief that some knowledge of the Roman system of Municipal Law will contribute to improve our own, has induced me to prepare the work I now offer to the public. * * * As the diligent study of Homer and Euripides, of Cicero and Livy, of Dante and Bossuet, of Milton and of Shakespeare, would do more to refine the public taste and to correct our antipathy to what is elevated and generous, whether in active life or in speculative study, than any metaphysical inquiry into the principles of eloquence and poetry, so a familiarity with the works that formed Cujas and Doneau, Du Moulin, Pothier, and Montesquieu, a knowledge of that social wisdom among Europeans unequalled, which has bound together so many successive generations by ties that neither the sword of barbarous conquest could sever, nor the fraud of sacerdotal hypocrisy dissolve, would do more to open the eyes of those whom habit or the desire of gain *have* (sic) not absolutely blinded to the deformities of our law, than any general or abstract dissertation on jurisprudence. We built our Chalcedon with Byzantium before our eyes. This, however, is not the place to enter upon the reasons which alone among the nations of the West prevented England from sharing in the benefits of the Roman law, and which have made every attempt to cultivate it among us, as if it had been the seed of some plant blown by the wind on an unfavourable soil, sterile and abortive."

Grammatical inaccuracy does not, of course, frequently distinguish the composition of so stern a dogmatist as Mr. Phillimore, and therefore we pass over the little mistake which we have sufficiently indicated by italics; but we seriously ask Mr. Phillimore what he means by contrasting what he calls the social wisdom of the continent with the liberty and free system of government we have the happiness to live under in this country? The foreign lawyers he names, no doubt, were great jurists, and we could wish that such works as those of Pothier were more studied than they are among us; but we are not so sure that such exercises would infallibly lead, in the minds of the educated and professional public of this country, to Mr. Phillimore's sweeping conclusion respecting "the deformities" of our law. Nor is Mr. Phillimore happy in his historical metaphor. He says, "We built our Chalcedon with Byzantium before our eyes." Of course "Chalcedon" is the law of England, while "Byzantium" is that of Rome. But the allusion altogether fails. It does not even indicate the geographical fact; for while it suggests that Byzantium was built first and was staring us in the face all the time we were building our Chalcedon, the truth is, as well-read historians know, that Byzantium did not come into existence till some seventeen years after the building of Chalcedon. The dates commonly given are, as regards Chalcedon, 675 B.C., and as regards Byzantium 658 B.C. Then, as regards the original formation of our law, can it be fairly said that the Roman law was before our eyes? No doubt the ecclesiastics of the period were familiar with the *Corpus Juris,* and had embodied its leading principles and precepts in their Canon Law, and the Statute of *Merton* serves to show their willingness to incorporate the legal doctrines of the Pandects with the legal system of this country; but the old Barons were differently minded, and with great deference to Mr. Phillimore and his pitiless works, they were not far wrong. It was not till the 12th century that the study of the Roman law was revived throughout Europe; and in fact it does not appear that a scientific knowledge of it generally prevailed till towards the beginning of the 16th century. On the other hand, the work of legislation, or of the composition of laws, had made considerable progress in England at the periods referred to; and Magna Charta, which was passed in the beginning of the 13th century, sufficiently proves that, even without the assistance of the Roman Jurisprudence, the people of England could take good care of their liberties, their government, and their laws.

But the preface is distinguished by better things than little mistakes in grammar and history. Mr. Phillimore calls to mind, and quotes evidently with great gusto, a sentence from Lord Bolingbroke, in which the legal profession of the time in England is described in language of the deepest contempt. "I might instance," says Lord Bolingbroke, "in other professions the obligations men lie under of applying themselves to certain parts of history, and I can hardly forbear doing it in that of the law, in its nature the noblest and most beneficial to mankind, in its abuse and debasement the most sordid and the most pernicious : a lawyer now is nothing more —I speak of ninety-nine in a hundred, at least—to use some of Tully's words, 'nisi leguleius quidem cautus, et acutus, prœco actionum, cantor formularum, auceps syllabarum.' But there have been lawyers who were orators, philosophers, historians; there have been Bacons and Clarendons. There will be none such any more till in some better age true ambition, or the love of fame, prevails over avarice, and till men find leisure and encouragement to prepare themselves for the exercise of this profession, by climbing up to the vantage-ground as Lord Bacon calls it, of science, instead of grovelling all their lives below in a painful application to all the little arts of chicane; till this happen, the profession of the law will scarcely deserve to be ranked among the learned professions." Now, although we must differ from Mr. Phillimore if he means to apply such language to the legal profession, or, we should rather say, to the English Bar, of the present day, we are not sorry, notwithstanding any apparent injustice by which it may be characterised, that such opinions should be put forth, even in the strongest language. Their expression may be useful in the way of discipline, and as a warning against the shortcomings of a former period. But what chiefly moves us in refraining from any protest against, or objection to, the quotation from Lord Bolingbroke, is the reflection that it is calculated to rouse the spirit of our forensic body to an animating sense of their great calling, so that by their studies, their professional conduct, their performance of their juridical duties, and their bearing and demeanour as learned men, they may dignify, not only themselves and their class, but the administration, in all departments of the state, of our system of jurisprudence. If, indeed, there was a period in our professional annals when it might with justice have been said of the law that it was abused and debased sordidly and perniciously, and that a lawyer in ninety-nine cases out of a hundred was nothing more "nisi prœco actionum, cantor formularum, auceps syllabarum," let it be our endeavour, in these better times, to rise above such a miserable platform, and to show that our law is a science and philosophy, and not merely that which falls from the lips of our judges, and finds its way into Acts of Parliament. But, alas! in this course of thought there is a *check*, and we fully appreciate and sympathise with the association of ideas which led Mr. Phillimore to remark on the quotation from Bolingbroke in the following just terms: "Such was the language of Bolingbroke; that of Swift is still more pointed. Burke, almost on his death-bed, says, in a letter to Lawrence, 'our Courts of Justice seem in a league with villains of every description.' *And this state of things will last so long as attorneys are allowed to possess the exorbitant power they now enjoy, and instead of being subordinate to a class superior, or that society assumes to be superior, to them in education, are allowed to hold it in a state of comparative dependence, and a service that certainly is not perfect freedom.*" It is too true. The barrister who is the mere "prœco actionum" and "cantor formularum," and whose success is not only a scandal in itself, but is at the same time a gross injustice to others, who, while more able and learned, will not stoop to artifice—we say that the barrister who may be so described is the degenerate creation of attorneydom. It is the attorneys who find it for their interest and class profit to bring such practitioners into existence. And let us tell the honest truth. The attorneys are but too well and too frequently assisted in this matter by the jury element, and what may be called the popular platform, in our courts. We are aware that it is extremely difficult to define our objections against the existing practice before juries without appearing to tamper with the institution itself,—but we will not allow even our admiration of the trial by jury to prevent us from protesting against that unmeasured appeal to it which is too often made, and which has mainly been the cause of the low standard in point of learning and tone of practice to which the Common Law Bar has been reduced. But as for the attorneys, they are unfortunately all-powerful, and Mr. Phillimore gives an extraordinary instance of the unscrupulous manner in which they have been known to exercise their power. "No stronger proof of their influence," Mr. Phillimore remarks, "can be given than the fact that they actually threatened to ruin Mr. Brougham if he persevered in bringing forward his schemes of Law Reform. Mr. Brougham, indeed, said publicly, in answer to the threat, that if it was executed he would sit in his chamber and take briefs without them. But though Mr. Brougham, then in the zenith of his reputation, and the leader of a great party in the House of Commons, was beyond the reach of that powerful body, such is not the condition common ὀϊζυροῖσι βροτοῖσιν, who tread the rugged paths of professional life; and so long as such power is vested in such a class, the attempts to pluck up the tares sown in the field of English law, during the night of the dark ages and long afterwards, by the enemies of all reason and all right, will be languid and unavailing." For this plain speaking, Mr. Phillimore expects his punishment. "I say this, perfectly well knowing to what misrepresentation and abuse it will expose me, because the study of many years has satisfied me that I do well to be angry at the absurdities and abuses which contribute so largely to the profit of a handful of men, and to the moral and intellectual detriment of that class of the profession to which I belong." We hope Mr. Phillimore need not mind "misrepresentation and abuse" in so just a cause, although he himself would be a more successful and acceptable instructor in the qualifications for "great works on jurisprudence" if he exhibited in his writings more of the spirit of calm and erudite inquiry, and less of the precipitate temper which shows itself with its foregone conclusion. In regard to this expectation, however, we receive but scanty encouragement from the following self-pronouncement: "But if ever the time shall come in the history of this country, when all men in a certain station are ashamed of haranguing in favour of the servile empiricism which has made so many fit, it may be, for better things, mechanics instead of jurists, masons instead of architects, and the law a profitable trade instead of a noble science; which has given us Wrights, Norths, Wedderburnes, and Eldons, instead of De Thous, Hôpitals, Molès, and Lamoignons; and when incapacity to comprehend a principle is not looked on as a mark of practical sense; if ever that time shall come, I shall be rewarded far beyond my hopes, if my name is remembered with kindness by those who trace the progress of our institutions, not as that of one holding lucrative office, and opposing education because the system under which he obtained the patronage of an inferior and comparatively illiterate body must be perfect, but as that of one who, according to the measure of his abilities, and without regard to immediate interest, which he was not too stupid to perceive, was the first and ultimately the successful assailant of special pleading." Mr. Phillimore is therefore pleased with himself and his performances, and he expects posterity to be grateful. That it will approve his attacks on special pleading (which he has never appeared to us to understand) or his depreciation of the illustrious Englishmen he names, we have no desire to believe. At their expense he appears to compliment the present Lord Chancellor—although rather equivocally—for it is possible to hold the "highest rank" (alluding to the Chancellor) in such a profession as the author describes the legal one in this country to be, and yet not to be a De Thou, Hôpital, Molè, or Lamoignon. The truth is, Mr. Phillimore's literary and intellectual food is too strong to be nourishing, and with whatever kindness posterity may regard him, we are quite sure it will concur in our opinion that he ought not to have published the present work.

But let us give him a parting hint, and point to a field where his energy and industry might operate serviceably. We refer to a work with which no doubt he is familiar, Pothier's Pandects, "Pandectæ Justinianeæ in novum ordinem digestæ."

"Sensible," says Lord Mackenzie, "of the great imperfections of Justinian's collection in point of arrangement, Pothier resolved to throw light upon this chaos of Roman law, and to do for it what Tribonian and his associates ought to have done—that is to say, to collect together the texts which were scattered through those immense books, to elucidate these texts one by the other, and that solely by the manner in which they were placed and connected; in a word, by substituting order for confusion, to render almost useless the innumerable commentaries under which the buried texts had groaned for ages. Nothing could exceed the boldness of this design; it seemed to surpass the resources of any single man, and to require time exceeding the ordinary duration of human life. And how was this herculean task accomplished? After twelve years of continuous labour, Pothier produced a work written in Latin, in which he preserved the ancient division of the books and titles of the Pandects, but re-arranged the texts under each title according to their natural order, so that each title forms a complete treatise on the subject indicated in the rubric. Immediately after the exposition of the subject, are placed the texts containing definitions and general principles. Methodical divisions and subdivisions facilitate the classification and understanding of the other texts. The ancient law is explained and illustrated, and great care is taken to show how far its provisions have been confirmed, interpreted, modified, or repealed by the Institutes, the Code, and the Novels. Antinomies are either reconciled or explained, and obscure texts are elucidated in notes of remarkable clearness and brevity. Whatever is the work of the author, the transitions by which he has so skilfully connected the laws so as to show their relation to each other, the notes, equally learned and concise, with which he has illustrated them, are all clearly distinguished by being printed in italics, and by this ingenious device the texts are presented in their original purity." Now, if our learned author would apply himself to the following task, he would do great service to the law of England, and secure, we believe, the grateful acknowledgments of future generations. Let him with all necessary modifications and omissions, publish an edition of Pothier's great work, applicable to the state of jurisprudence in the present day, and in an English dress, everything but the text of the Pandects being in the English language, with notes for analogous or illustrative reference in the law of England. It would even be desirable if the text itself were translated into good English, and given along with the original Latin. Let him do all this calmly, steadily, and modestly. If so, we are very sure he will do it well, and, in the result, he would produce a work better calculated to diffuse "some knowledge of the Roman law," than a score of such books as we have felt it our duty to make the subject of this article.

Art. VI.—WHAT IS THE VALUE OF A SHIP?

By Laurence R. Baily.

AN answer to this question is necessary when a vessel is insured, when, by the fault of the crew of one vessel, another vessel is sunk in a collision, when the expediency of repairing or condemning her must be determined, when the shares of part owners of a ship are transferred, and when there is a general average. Consequently it is of great importance that the question should be answered correctly.

In the above cases, the values differ to some extent, because the time at which they are taken is not the same in all; but, in other respects, the value is the same in all. In the first, the value is the value at the time at which the risk under the policy begins. In the second, at the moment immediately before the collision. In the third, at the time when the repairs, if executed, will be completed. In the fourth, at the time when the transfer is made; and in the last, at the time when the ship becomes liable for the general average.

All will probably agree that her value to her owner is the value required; but, on the question—What is her value to her owner?—there will, probably, be much difference of opinion.

The *dictum* that "the value of a thing is what it will fetch," is treated generally as an axiom applicable to everything, and is applied to ships, even by some of the courts of law.

As an axiom, applicable to everything that can be sold, it is clearly erroneous: for instance—If a man sold his new coat, or his new wig, for which he had paid his tailor, and his wigmaker, fair prices only, he could not reasonably expect to realise the cost price of them. If he had worn either the coat or the wig, the proceeds of them would still less be a true test of their value to him, although there may have been no alteration whatever in the fashions since he purchased them.

It is correct, in most cases, to apply it to an article which, from its nature, the owner acquires only to sell again. The amount that article will sell for is, in most cases, a fair test of its real value to that owner. Thus, the selling value at the place of destination is, in most cases, a correct criterion, at any time, of the value of cotton and sugar to the merchant at that time; but, as a test of the value of an article which is built or made for use only, like the above-mentioned coat and wig, it is no test at all.

Is it a proper test to apply to a ship?

Most people will probably admit that the price for which an English ship will sell at a foreign port, is not in many cases a proper test of her value to her owner, since the foreign port, in most cases, is not even a market for English ships. The same with foreign ships in an English port, or in any port foreign to them. Most people will probably admit further that the value of each ship must be determined by her value in the country in which she is owned. Probably they will also admit that the time at which that value is to be taken, is the time to which the question applies—*i. e.*, When the value, on the 1st of January, of an English ship in a foreign port is required, that value is her value to her owner in her own country on that date, and in the state in which she is on that date.

Some may doubt whether a deduction should not be made from that value for the wear and tear that must result from her subsequent passage home; but, in determining a general principle to be applied to all cases—those of ships which go straight home from the foreign port, those which go from one foreign port to another, those which go home in ballast, and those which, on the passage home, earn freight sufficient to cover the wear and tear on that passage—even those who hold that such a deduction should be made, will probably agree, in the expediency at least, of ignoring that wear and tear, and of taking the value she would have on the 1st of January in her own country, on that date in the state in which she then is.

The question is thus narrowed to—What is the value of a ship to her owner in her own country on a given date?

There are two values which find numerous supporters,—

1st. The price for which she can be sold.

2nd. The price for which a similar ship can be bought.

Is either of these the true test of the value of the ship to her owner?

1st. As to the price for which she can be sold.

Probably all will admit that when, in the size or build of a ship, there is any peculiarity which makes her, although of great value to her owner, for whom she was purposely so built, worthless, or of but small value, to other people, the price she will realise if sold is not her real value to her owner; but when she is a handy ship which, under ordinary circumstances, can be readily bought and readily sold, most people will hold that the price for which she can be sold is her real value to her owner.

When the rates of freight, current at the date of sale, afford a fair return and no more on the shipowner's capital, and the rate of interest for money current at the date of sale is no more and no less than the average or standard rate of interest, the price for which she can be sold is the same as her real value to her owner; not because her real value to her owner is the price for which she can be sold, but because the two values happen to coincide: but, when the circumstances, in any country, affecting the selling price at the time of sale, are extraordinary and temporary—for instance, when an accidental scarcity of ships and glut of employment for shipping in that country, send freights up, and the selling value of ships rises in consequence; or when the rate of interest is 2½ per cent., instead of 5 per cent., so that a ship which, under ordinary circumstances, would have realised £5 only per ton, will, under those extraordinary circumstances, realise £6—is the selling price a true test of the value of a ship to an owner, who, it must be assumed, does not intend to sell? Is the value of that ship to her owner at that time

£6 per ton? And when the circumstances are reversed—*i.e.*, when there is a glut of ships, and a scarcity of employment, and the rate of interest is 10 per cent., so that the ship will sell for £4 only—is £4 per ton her real value to such an owner?

It must be admitted that a trading ship has no value in herself apart from employment; that a ship which never can be used is worthless; that her value depends on the income she returns to her owner; that freight is the proper test of that return; that the real value of a ship to her owner is greater when freights are high than when freights are low, and greater, therefore, when the selling value of the ship advances, and less when that selling value falls; but all this may be admitted, and yet the selling value may not be her real value to her owner.

It is not her real value; and for this reason,—a temporary rise or fall in freight, and a low or a high rate of interest for money, have a much greater temporary effect on the selling value of a ship than they ought to have. They do affect also the value of a ship to her owner, but their effect on the selling value is greater than their effect on the value to the owner. As, therefore, their effect on the former is greater than it ought to be, the price at which a vessel can be sold, is not, as a rule, a true test of her value to her owner.

2nd. As to the price for which a similar ship can be bought?

When the circumstances are such that the selling value and the value to the owner are the same, the sum for which the ship can be replaced is the same as her value to her owner; but, when the circumstances are temporary and exceptional at the time—like those mentioned above, for instance—the value for which she can be replaced is not the same as her value to her owner, and for the same reasons that her selling value is not her value to her owner. Under such circumstances the value at which she can be replaced is nearly as far from her real value to her owner, as the sum she will produce if sold.

The only difference between the buying and the selling price, is the difference which always exists between the price that a man wishing to buy a ship must give for her, and the price which a man wishing to sell the same ship can obtain for her; a difference which is no part of the value of the ship, but rather the value of the necessities of the purchaser or seller.

Since neither the price for which a ship can be sold, nor the price for which she can be bought is, as a rule, her value to her owner, the question still remains unanswered—What is the value of a ship to her owner?

Her real value at any time, including future interest on capital, is the money that the owner can make out of her, after that time, whilst she exists as a ship. This, as a rule, is the value she will ultimately have to break up, plus her nett earnings from the time when the question arises, up to the time when she will be broken up. The profit the owner may have made, or the loss he may have sustained, on her career previous to the time when her value is to be determined, must be entirely disregarded; for her previous earnings on exceptional rates of freight do not justify the assumption for the unknown future of similar rates, or of any rates but the average rates in the long run. Her future earnings cannot be affected by her past profits or losses. Her value is exactly the same, whether she has, looking at those causes only which are unconnected with her merits as a ship—for instance, the previous rates of freight &c.—been up to that time a profitable or an unprofitable ship.

The money she will produce when broken up at the end of her natural life, will not vary sufficiently to prevent a tolerably correct estimate of it being made in all cases.

The nett earnings she will make for the future, depend, as a rule, on the freights the owner is justified in expecting, *i.e.*, on the current rates of freight for the next voyage, and on the average rates of freights for such a ship for the remainder of her life, *i.e.*, the freights she can make in the long run.

The difference between the profit which a ship can make on a voyage on which the freights are exceptionally high, or exceptionally low, and the profit which she can make when freight is at a fair average rate, can easily be estimated.

The profit she can make for the remainder of her life is composed of two items, capital, and future interest on capital; the latter is no part of the present value of a ship. It is necessary, therefore, to separate the two.

A new ship fairly and economically built will, at fair average rates of freight, return, under ordinary circumstances, her cost price and a fair rate of interest on that cost, because the ordinary average rates of freight do not give any more or any less in the long run than a fair interest on capital, taking into consideration the duties and liabilities of the shipowner.

They may, for a time, give more or less, but it is for a time only. A higher rate of interest stimulates building, and with the consequent increase of tonnage freights fall. A lower rate of interest discourages building, and the consequent decrease of tonnage causes freights to rise. In the long run freights give a fair interest and no more; consequently freights may be disregarded, save in exceptional cases, in determining the true value of a ship to her owner. The amount of capital, *i.e.*, the value of a new ship fairly and economically built, is, therefore, under ordinary circumstances, her cost price.

If she is three years old and as good as new * and the prices of materials and labour are the same as when she was built, she is, when the freights are at average rates, and the rate of interest is the standard rate, worth the price she cost to build. But, if the prices of materials and labour, and the rates of freights, have risen since, and the rate of interest has fallen since the vessel was built, so that a similar ship built at the end of the three years would cost more to build than

* This cannot be strictly correct in fact, but it is assumed to be correct, so as to prevent confusion in the argument, and to illustrate the effect of a change in the cost of building ships between the date when the ship was built, and the date when the question of her value arises.

she cost—she is worth the sum that she would have cost if built at the date at which the question arises; and, if the cost of materials and labour, and the rates of freight, have fallen, and the rate of interest is higher, when the question arises, than when she was built, she is worth less than the sum which she cost to build, and her value to her owner is no more than the cost of a similar ship built at the date when the question arises.

It may be argued that no comparison can be made between the cost of a ship built three years ago and the cost of a ship contracted for at the date in question, because building a ship occupies time. That fact does not, however, really affect the value of a ship to her owner, for he does not pay for her until she is built.

Time does not affect the capital invested in a ship, save when that capital is idle. On average rates of freight and interest—*i.e.*, the circumstances now under consideration—the capital invested in a ship returns a fair rate of interest, and a fair rate of interest only, looking to the risks and liabilities of the shipowner. When his capital is not invested in the ship, he does not get, and ought not to expect to get, that return on it. When it is he does get it, but the capital is the same in both cases. Even the instalments which it is customary for shipowners to pay in the progress of the building, and before the ship is finished, do not affect her real value, for the capital in the ship when she is finished is the same whether the purchaser pays the cost by instalments, or in one amount when she is finished. When he pays by instalments before the ship is finished, the price of the ship is nominally smaller, but nominally smaller only. The instalments are not really unproductive. They nominally reduce the cost of building the ship, but nominally only, for, adding interest on the instalments, the price in both cases is about the same.

Other circumstances—as, for instance, an increase between the two dates in the necessity for a certain class of ships, or the reverse, to carry on a particular trade—will, in the same way, increase or diminish the value of the ship to her owner; and the extraordinary profit or loss which the rates of freight current for the following voyage, but for the following voyage only, will produce, will, in the same way, improve or decrease her value.

We thus have, as a standard, that the value at any given date of a new ship, or of a ship as good as new, is the cost price of a similar ship at that date, plus the extra profit, or minus the extra loss, which the rates of freight current at the time yield for one voyage for such a ship.

There remains only to consider—What deduction should be made from that value when the ship is not new?

The peculiarities of the past do not affect her present or future value to her owner, and do not, therefore, affect this deduction; consequently the deduction is the same, whether the past has been profitable or the reverse.

The length of time during which such a ship exists as a ship, the length of time remaining of that life when the question arises, and the probable proceeds of her materials when she is broken up on the close of that life, are all material elements in estimating the deduction.

The profits she will make during the remainder of her life, on average freights, may be disregarded when those rates will not, by reason of her age, be less than those for a similar ship of a less age—for such rates of freight return capital and a fair interest on capital only—but when, by reason of her age, those rates will be less than the rates for a similar ship of a less age, that fact does affect her present value. On these principles, when a ship lasts five years as a ship and her cost to build was £5,000, and her proceeds when she is ultimately broken up will be £500, and her earnings per annum on the last three years of her life will be at the rate of two-thirds only of those per annum of the first two years by reason of her age, the deductions for age are on (£5,000 cost less £500 proceeds) £4,500, 25 per cent. for the first year; 50 per cent. for the second year; 66⅔ per cent. the third year; 83⅓ per cent. for the fourth year; 100 per cent.

for the fifth year; making her value to the owner, when there has not been any alteration in the cost of building such a ship since she was built, and freights are at average rates. At the end of the first year £5,000 less 25 per cent. on £4,500, *i.e.*, £3,875. At the end of the second year £5,000 less 50 per cent. on £4,500, *i.e.*, £2,750. At the end of the third year £5,000 less 66⅔ per cent. on £4,500, *i.e.*, £2,000. At the end of the fourth year £5,000 less 83⅓ per cent. on £4,500, *i.e.*, £1,250. And at the end of the fifth year £5,000 less 100 per cent. on £4,500, *i.e.*, £500—*i.e.*, her value to break up.

If at the end of the third year the cost of building a similar ship has increased to £6,000, and the rate of freight current at that time gives a nett profit, for the next voyage, £300 above what average rates of freight would give, her value at the end of the third year is £6,000

Less 66⅔ per cent. on £5,500 (£6,000 less proceeds to break up) 3,666

2,334

Add exceptional profit on freight . . . 300

£2,634

If the cost at which a similar ship can be built has decreased to £4,500, and the rate of freight current at the end of the third year gives a nett profit, for the next voyage, £200 less than average rates of freight would give, her value at the end of the third year is £4,500

Less 66⅔ per cent on £4,000 (£4,500 less proceeds to break up) 2,667

1,833

Deduct exceptional loss on freight . . . 200

£1,633

Some, even of those who may agree in the correctness of the above principles, will think that the value of a ship to her owner could not, practically, be ascertained in this way. Are they correct in that opinion?

The data for ascertaining her value on the above principles are:—

1. The cost of building a similar ship at the time when the question arises.

2. The length of such a ship's life.

3. The date when she was built.

4. The difference between the nett freight she will earn for one voyage on current rates of freight and on average rates of freight. And,

5. The falling off per annum in her receipts at the latter part of her life by reason of her age,—when there is such a falling off.

Every one of these data is well known to every man competent to judge of the value of a ship, and must be considered by every judicious man before he can determine whether it is expedient to buy or sell a ship, as those data also really determine the market value of a ship, to the extent that her market value is her value to her owner; consequently, there is not even so much difficulty, in practice, in determining the value to her owner on the above principles as there is in determining it by her market value; for the latter involves the consideration of all the data included in the former, and, in addition, the extraordinary temporary effect of the high or low price of money, &c. Theoretically, and practically also, therefore, the value of a ship to her owner should be determined on the above principles.

Art. VII.—POLITICAL EQUALITY.*

IT is a favourite doctrine of the so-called advanced school of modern politicians, that government which interferes equally with the liberty of all, ought to be equally under the control of all. But not only is the assertion on which the claim is based, erroneous, but even its truth would not support the claim. Though the office of government were to restrain liberty, the pressure would bear more hardly on the strong than on the feeble spirit. The argument, therefore, which, resting on the restraint to freedom, supports the claim of the weaker citizen to a share of political power, favours the demand on the part of the more energetic citizen of a greater share of that power. But it is altogether ineffectual to support the doctrine either of equality or inequality of political power. Though of negative force in limiting the number of those from whom the governing body is to be selected, to those who are subject to the government, it is of no positive force in supporting the claim of those who are incapable of discharging political duties. No argument, in truth, can sustain a claim to attempt that which the claimants are unable to perform.

And, while the argument drawn from the supposed functions of government is invalid, that function itself is the reverse of the true office of government. So far is the restraint of liberty from forming the duty of government, that its one end is to secure for its subjects the greatest amount of liberty on the whole. Without directly interfering with their efforts under the name of advancing their progress, its great office is to remove the restraints on individual activity, and secure for its subjects a fair start in the work of their own self-improvement.

The whole argument, therefore, of the advocates of political equality is, both in its reason and its consequent, erroneous.

* We insert this article, which contains some ingenious and original ideas on the subject, without committing ourselves to the opinions of the author.—Ed. L. M. & R.

In asserting that error we have, in a general way, referred to the quality in the citizen which both founds his right to political power, and determines the extent of that power, and we have alluded to the functions of government to which that power corresponds. In proceeding, therefore, to a fuller inquiry into the nature of that power and of those functions, it will be proper to state the question in a form which raises both points.

Does there exist in man a special power of which political influence is the object, and is that power and the right which corresponds to it equal in all men?

I. *The right.*—Right may be defined as a relation between a subject and an object,—a relation of power on the one hand, and subjection on the other. The only subjects of rights are persons, and the only objects of rights are things; whether external objects, or such qualities of mind as respect, obedience, gratitude. As to the varieties and the origin and measure of rights, they are of two kinds, one absolute, the gift of nature or the result of culture, the other relative, conventional, the gift of other men.

The powers of the subjects of those rights, differ essentially as the rights themselves. With regard to the powers corresponding to absolute rights, they are bestowed on men for some purpose, they have relations to other things. Power has two relations. Subjectively it is related to the necessities and wants of its possessor and of other men, and gives him the right, and lays him under the obligation of supplying those necessities: objectively it is related to the objects fitted to supply those necessities, and gives its possessor the right to appropriate those objects for the benefit of himself and others. But absolute or real power exists independently of those relations. Though the supposition would imply a deficiency or redundancy in the arrangements of providence, it is conceivable that absolute power should exist without any want to be relieved or any objects to be appropriated, and, therefore, without any rights attached to the power.

But the powers which correspond to conventional rights do not form part of the absolute character of the subject of the rights. They have no independent existence. Instead of creating the rights, they are created by the rights, and exist only so long as the rights exist. They are logical as distinguished from real powers.

II. *The object of the right.*—We come now to the more important inquiry into the sphere and functions of government. The word government has two meanings. Viewed as the governing body it is society, through its representatives, speaking in a tone of command; viewed as an organisation, it is the machine employed by society for furthering a considerable number of its ends. What is the portion of the social field which government occupies?

There are two great ends to which all the endeavours of man should be directed, one negative, the other positive. All his energy, so far as it respects himself, ought to be directed either towards the prevention of self-deterioration, or towards the accomplishment of self-development. And society, which supports and strengthens all the aspirations and strivings of men, necessarily finds its efforts directed towards those two great goals of all human endeavour. Society, in its lower and negative function, as a government, employing force either in its pure form or in the shape of compulsory assistance, strives to preserve the objects of its care from deterioration; and in its higher and positive function, as a friend, endeavours by encouragement and the offer of aid, to secure for those objects the highest development of which they are capable.

And government, in turn, has its negative and positive functions. Corresponding to those duties respectively, are the two great motives which prompt and guide all the actions of a good government—justice and charity. Both seek to preserve men from deterioration. In its negative function, government, as a judge, prevents one man from developing himself at the expense of his neighbour's deterioration. In its positive function, as a reformer, it endeavours to raise that portion of society which has fallen below the common level, moral, intellectual, and physical, of the mass of its members; or, as a friend, affords support to those who through weakness are ready to sink. Justice is the foundation of government, but charity is its superstructure. In both its functions government is essentially conservative.

The duties of government, therefore, are not to be determined by directing attention merely to actions themselves, and choosing such as it may seem right for a government to undertake, but also to the persons subject to the government, and selecting those whose condition makes them the fit objects of the authoritative interference of society. The positive work of government is directed to the cases of those who are unable or unwilling to contend with nature, external or internal, and its tone of command is equally authoritative, whether it affords aid or employs force alone. Those who have fallen below the common level of society are presumed to have lost, and those who remain at or above that level are presumed to have retained, command of themselves and of external nature. And government assumes the command where it has been lost or relinquished.

Liberty, therefore, is the great end of government. In its negative function, it endeavours to protect men from the injustice of their fellows; in its positive function, it strives to liberate men from the overpowering pressure of external nature, or of the lower part of their own internal nature.

But property also is one of the objects of government, and the duties of government in regard to it are analogous to those which relate to persons. Government preserves the property under its control from disorder and deterioration. An example of the legislation which provides for the preservation of persons is the poor law; and of that which provides for the preservation of property—the legislation on salmon fishings. But government endeavours to maintain the excellence of property as a whole, and pays no attention to special cases of deterioration; whereas, in the case of persons, its efforts are directed to the individual and isolated cases of those who have fallen below the common level of society, leaving the maintenance of that standard as a whole, the ebb and flow of the tide, to the case of society in its positive function.

But has government rights in as well as duties to its objects, beyond the right to discharge those duties? It has been maintained by those who desire to make the possession of property the foundation of a direct claim to political power, that government disposes of property. But government has no right to the property of which it is loosely said to dispose, just as it has no right to the persons of those who are in certain respects under its control. For government does not legislate in the strict sense of that word. That is the privilege of God alone. The governing body merely secures that the laws which God has established, shall be ascertained and translated into the laws of the realm. It applies the law already fixed to the general case, as the ordinary judge applies it to the special case. The function of government, therefore, is judicial.

III. *The power which creates the right.*—Is there any absolute power in man which gives him an absolute right to a share of political influence proportioned to that power? Or are the right and the power which correspond to it created by contract?

An express social contract is out of the question. But does the mere fact of social life raise the presumption of an implied contract? Duty and interest are the primary motives of social life, and it is as certain that that duty and that interest are universal, as that the ability to direct wisely the operations of government is only partial among men. All are, therefore, bound to enter into society, but no one would dream of asserting that children have political ability. Society therefore existed before there was either the power or the right in some of its members to take part in its government. The mere existence of society, then, does not raise the presumption of an implied contract that political power should be shared either equally or unequally by all.

If on the other hand, the arrangements of Providence are complete, there must be a power existing in nature corresponding to the social want or necessity which the maintenance of order and justice supplies. An absolute power and absolute right and duty to exercise political functions must, therefore, exist, and that power must have a character corresponding to the nature of the functions which it is fitted to fulfil. The functions of government are judicial, intellectual. The power, therefore, which corresponds to those functions must be an intellectual one. Political intelligence, then, is the grand principle on which any claim of distribution of political power should be founded, and the extent of the power should be proportioned to the strength of the intellect.

But what if the possessors of the intelligence should use their power for their own selfish ends. May a better result be anticipated from other arrangements than from those of Providence? Will the representation of all the interests of society in just proportion secure legislation perfectly impartial? Let us compare the competing claims of interest and intelligence, as founded, not on right primarily, but on expediency.

The objections to the theory of interests lie on the surface:—

1. To try to secure a body politic and legislative, with evenly balanced interests, is to attempt an impossibility.

2. Suppose this impossibility got over, the laws, in order to be impartial, must be passed unanimously. And, as the theory of interests demands that each legislator shall give expression solely to the interests which he represents, all the laws would serve the interests of the majority.

3. The laws would be not only one sided but confused, because there is no disturbing element like the passion of self-interest.

4. The controlling influence of elevated public opinion on such a legislature would be much weaker than on a refined and intelligent one.

5. The practice of such a theory would lower the standard

of morality, not only of the legislature, but of the constituencies which elected it.

The advantages of the theory of intelligence exactly correspond to the disadvantages of the other theory.

1. There is no such impossibility as in the former case.

2. Chosen on account of their ability to ascertain the truth, the governing body and the legislature would feel the trust imposed on them to found their laws on truth, which is impartial.

3. Symmetry of legislation would be secured when the laws were passed by a legislature capable of working according to a plan.

4. Intelligence is peculiarly sensitive to the influence of elevated public opinion.

5. The standard of political morality in both the legislature and the constituencies would be raised.

But apart from this detail, there is a presumption that the theory which, asserting that a legislature chosen on the principle of intelligence will legislate on the principle of self-interest, proposes to elect that legislature on the principle of self-interest in order to secure legislation based on pure intelligence and truth, is a false theory.

IV. *Tests of the power.*—Political power and political intellect ought, then, to be in the same ratio. How is the presence of this intellect to be ascertained, and its strength measured? From the theoretical we here pass to the practical part of the subject.

The negative test of the presence of political intellect is, that the claimant of political power must be at the stage of advancement to which the mass of society has reached, and be, therefore, beyond the sphere of government aid. That social position is necessary and sufficient as a security that the citizen shall clearly apprehend and dispassionately judge the political questions which he will have a share in deciding. If the citizen has clearly before him the negative and subordinate functions which belong to government, and acquiesces in their completeness as functions of government, he will not use his influence to turn the material power attached to the executive to other and selfish purposes. A qualified universal suffrage, therefore, if such an expression may be used, is the true foundation of the scheme of distribution of political power.

The positive tests which measure the strength of the intellect, and determine the extent of the right, are the subject of a more important and difficult inquiry. Those tests imply the existence of disparities in the strength of individual intellects. Any proof of that inequality is unnecessary. He who asserts that any real power which forms part of the independent character of a man, and specially intellectual power, is equal in all, must consider himself more intelligent on this point than the man who controverts him. Setting aside, therefore, an opinion which contradicts itself, we may assume that the political knowledge of the statesman is greater than that of the peasant.

What then are the positive tests? Omitting the test of examination, which tests the intelligence, not of the answerer but of the author whose books he has read, three leading tests have been proposed:—

1. Property, which, as a test of the presence of the intellect, not of the extent of the power, is the test at present in use.
2. A man's engagements or profession.
3. Social position.

Those are all, of course, indirect and most imperfect tests of political intelligence. But the first and the last qualifications are supposed to found a direct claim to political power. The claim is founded on the fact that government disposes of property. But it has been shown that the functions of government in regard to its objects are entirely judicial. The proprietors of possessions of every kind are equal before the law, and therefore, with the single exception of political intellect as corresponding to the social want, they are equal before the government. For in regard to such profession, government has but one function, itself reverently to receive the eternal laws which regulate the relations of persons and property, and to dispense those laws. The poet and the philosopher and the man of science or literature are entitled to high consideration and power in society engaged in its higher work of advancing humanity, but government or society in its lower function must be indifferent to them. To maintain, therefore, that social power should be translated into political power involves the erroneous assertion that political work is co-extensive with social work.

Taken as tests of political intelligence, however, all three are true though imperfect tests. But there is an insuperable objection to the third test, the social one, which does not apply to the others. The first two are definite, they are in fact measures, but the third is no measure at all. How is social position itself to be measured? But apart from this objection, it so happens that in our constitution ample provision has been already made for giving political expression to the political capacity which is considered to be implied in the possession of the first and last qualifications, namely, wealth, birth, and high character. One entire chamber, the House of Lords, is reserved for the wealthy, the high-born, and the noble. With nearly one-half of the political power of the country placed in such hands on a mere presumption, it would be unfair to demand additional influence.

We are, therefore, restricted to the test of profession, or of those attainments to which definite marks, such as academical degrees, have been given by society, together with any other tests which can be proposed with acceptance. No single test ought to be applied. If the tests are real and workable, the more numerous they are, the better will be the result.

Besides the test of profession and academical degrees, another may be proposed, namely, age, extending our measure up to a fixed and by no means advanced period of life. It has been found necessary to adopt tests of general intelligence as political tests, because, with the exclusion, for the reason already stated, of examinations on the particular subject of political science, it appeared that we possessed no direct test of political intelligence. But here we have a test comparatively direct. Life in a society which is self-governing, forces political knowledge not merely into the memory, but into the very nature of the citizen. The education of circumstances is, in a practical knowledge like politics, better than the education of books. Moreover, fast governments are bad governments: all true political progress is slow progress. Experience, therefore, not energy, is the primary requisite in the citizen. A man at thirty years is probably a much better politician, in the right sense of that word, than a man at twenty or twenty-one. If the unit of political power in the case of this particular test were fixed as at the twentieth year, and if each decade up to the fiftieth year brought to the citizen an additional vote, it would bring also to the State additional political knowledge. The advantages of this test are,—

1. That it is a true test.
2. That it is a definite one.
3. That it includes all citizens justly.

While all the other tests have a certain character of invidiousness, the test of age would be highly grateful to those who are at the bottom of the social scale. Among millions, a few may reach the House of Lords; not many, compared with the mass of society, are engaged in high professions; but all, without exception, whom death does not overtake, must reach the years which, with political experience, bring political power. The young voter who, in his heat, desired, with the aid of others of like influence and years, to alter the whole political frame, would more contentedly await the season of increased political power, which would bring a change of opinions as well as of influence.

It will not be out of place in an article which advocates a suffrage almost universal, to refer to a scheme of representation, which, with such a suffrage, would secure in the legislature the most perfect representation of the body politic, but which, with the present distribution of political power, would be simply a plan to facilitate bribery. We refer to Mr. Hare's proposal to represent numbers rather than local constituencies.

Large constituencies of, say, ten thousand voters with, say, forty thousand votes, would be created by universal suffrage, and the decrease in the number of the legislature of which Mr. Hare's plan would afford an opportunity. Bribery, therefore, which would find willing objects, principally among single voters, would become a moral impossibility. And the harmless result of the representation of a few crotchets in the House of Commons would signalise the perfection of the representation. The advantages of Mr. Hare's plan are, among others—

1. That the representation is perfect; an advantage which includes most of the others.

2. That not only minorities, but individual citizens are represented: no vote is lost.

3. That advanced opinions are represented.

4. That a greater responsibility would rest on citizens who voted, not in herds, but as individuals.

5. That all but the most apathetic citizens would take part in national affairs, when not restricted to local candidates to whom they are indifferent.

6. That men of the highest intellect and the most elevated moral character would present themselves as candidates.

But whatever be the details of the plan which is to perfect the political constitution, two general conclusions may be drawn from the consideration of the whole subject.

1. That the franchise must be extended to every man of full age who is beyond the sphere of government assistance.

2. That the suffrage must be graduated according to the political intelligence of the citizen.

Art. VIII.—THE TRIAL OF ARMAND.

MR. STEPHEN, in his recent work on English Criminal Law, concludes his sketch of the French system with the just observation that its peculiarities can only be understood by following the course of a French criminal trial. The trial which has lately taken place at Aix, in the south of France, offers an excellent opportunity for making such an examination. The unusual circumstances under which it occurred; the strange conduct of the presiding judge; the exercise by the prosecuting official of his powers in a most arbitrary manner; the presence of two distinguished Paris counsel to protest against the course pursued by the prosecution; bring out in strong relief the defects of the procedure, and have naturally drawn upon the whole system a good deal of adverse criticism. It appears to us, however, that this criticism has failed to be just, because it has not carefully made the distinction between defects of principle and defects arising from the excessive or improper application of a principle. It does not follow that because undue discretion has been assumed by, or even given to, the French prosecutor, the principle of Crown prosecution is essentially vicious; or that the principle of making the accused an instrument for proving his own innocence or guilt is unjust, because in France it has been exclusively extended in one direction, until it has issued in a secret inquisitorial instrument for ensuring conviction. No study of this singular example of French criminal procedure can be of any use, unless it serve to distinguish the defects in those principles on which the system is based from such defects in the procedure as may be traced to independent causes or influences, such as the social or political condition of the country. It is with a view to establish this distinction that we draw attention to the trial of Armand.

At this trial, the accused, Mons. Armand, a wealthy merchant and old inhabitant of Montpellier, was charged with having attempted to murder a man, named Roux, who had been for some time in his service as a coachman. The character of Armand, as deposed to by witnesses of position and respectability, was that of a highly honourable and estimable man. The character of Roux, as deposed to by many witnesses at the trial, was most unfavourable. He was stated to have led a dissolute life; and his demeanour on his examination at the trial tended strongly to confirm the evidence against him. The bare facts on which the prosecution rested were these. On the 7th of July last, Roux was found by a fellow-servant lying in the cellar of his master's house, with his hands bound behind his back, and a cord loosely tied about his neck. His feet were fastened together with a handkerchief, marked with the prisoner's initials. To all appearance he was senseless. He could not answer any of the questions put to him; and, when taken to the hospital, his state seemed so serious that the last sacraments were administered to him. Suddenly, however, he rallied and regained speech and consciousness. Whereupon he at once charged his master with having followed him to the cellar, struck him down, bound him hand and foot, and left him there to die. He renewed, at the time of taking the sacrament, his declaration that the outrage had been committed by his master. No sooner, however, had extreme unction been afforded to him, than he grew well with marvellous rapidity. The reason alleged for the assault, namely, that he had once called his master's house "a poor hovel," was quite inadequate to supply a motive for such a crime. Mons. Armand was, however, arrested. After having been examined by the Juge d'Instruction, he reported on the subject to the "Chambre de Conseil." The Chambre de Conseil is a court composed of not less than three judges of the correctional tribunal for each arrondissement. Of these judges the Juge d'Instruction is always one. Its functions are to sit, at least once a week, for the purpose of deciding all criminal matters which have been brought under the notice of the Juge d'Instruction. This court is always attended by the

"Procureur du Roi," or the official Crown prosecutor, who is attached to each correctional tribunal, and whose special function it is to search out and pursue all offenders in the arrondissement to which he belongs.

As soon as it was known that Mons. Armand, the wealthy merchant, had been arrested, after examination by the Juge d'Instruction, on a charge of great gravity, the town of Montpellier was in a ferment. The accuser was in a humble, the accused in a conspicuous position, a fact quite sufficient to account for the strong feeling which at once arose amongst a populace whose ancestors burnt and tortured the Camisards, and refused Christian burial to the adopted daughter of the poet Young, because she was a Protestant. Reports of all kinds were put in circulation, imputing every evil to the master, and making him out to be a monster of wickedness. It was said that a skeleton had been found in his cellar; that this was the last of a long series of crimes and outrages which the accused had only been able to conceal through the overpowering influence of his great wealth. That this report was quite groundless, did not of course affect its credence with the vulgar. In the midst of the excitement, which would seem to have been artfully inflamed by Roux, the accuser, the Juge d'Instruction brought the affair before the Chambre de Conseil. We shall see in a subsequent stage of the trial that this officer had been influenced by the general rumour when he was making his private examination (interrogation) of the accused. It was plain that he came to meet his colleagues strongly impressed with the belief that the accused was guilty. The result of the discussion was that the *procès verbal,* or statement of the accusation, and a statement of the matters tending to a conviction, were forwarded to the Procureur-General of the Cour Imperiale, to which the department of Herault belonged, for reference to the Chambre des Mises en Accusation. The Chambre des Mises en Accusation is a special department in each of the twenty-seven cours imperiales, which sit as courts of appeal in civil cases from the tribunals of première instance. Before this court the Procureur-General, once at least in every week, must bring up all matters which have been submitted to him since the previous sitting. The judges examine the papers and decide whether there are any indicia of an act having been committed which would constitute a crime, and if these indicia are sufficiently strong, to justify a remission of the charge (*mise en accusation*) to the court of assize. At these proceedings neither the person aggrieved, the accused, nor the witnesses, are allowed to be present. The Procureur-General alone attends and explains the charge. If the court sees no trace of an offence against law, or thinks the proofs too weak to support the charge, it orders the immediate release of the prisoner. If it considers that it is a case which, if established, would only constitute an offence cognisable either by a tribunal of simple police, or by a tribunal of correctional police, the charge is sent to the proper tribunal. If, however, the offence would amount to a crime, and if the evidence in support of the charge be thought sufficient, the court orders the accused to be sent to the assizes.

In the present instance the offence charged was a crime of a grave nature, subject to the severest class of punishment (*peine afflictive et infamante*), and the Court decided that the depositions made before the Juge d'Instruction, taken together with his report and that of their own officer, justified them in sending the accused to be tried at the assizes.

A court of assize is held in each department every three months. The judges at each sitting are three in number, one of them being president, the others apparently acting merely as his assessors. The questions of fact are in these courts submitted to a jury of twelve. But whether for or against the accused, the verdict of a simple majority prevails. It is a peculiarity of the French as contrasted with the English law that it treats all offences as constituting two distinct wrongs; the one penal, or public against the community; the other, civil, or private, against the person aggrieved. Independently, therefore, of the action taken by the Ministère Public, or ministry of public justice, for the detection and punishment of offenders, it allows the person aggrieved, concurrently with the criminal, to commence civil proceedings for damages, whereupon the complainant becomes what is called a *partie civile.* In this capacity, he stands quite apart from the public procedure, and his claim is decided not by the jury, which deals only with the criminal aspect of the charge, but by the judge. Roux of course availed himself of this civil privilege, and preferred a claim of 50,000 francs as compensation for the injuries he had sustained at the hands of the accused. The latter was consigned to prison to await his trial; for the offence which was imputed against him involved a *peine afflictive et infamante,* and in such cases the code expressly forbids bail to be taken.

Already the procedure has presented one striking feature, which stands out in strong contrast with our own. This is what Mr. Stephen, in his work on English criminal law, terms the "inquisitorial" principle which pervades the French system. From the first stage to the last, the leading idea in the French system is that the object of a criminal investigation should be to ascertain whether or no the crime has been committed. In order to carry out this idea consistently, the Code d'Instruction Criminelle has invested the Crown officials with power and discretion, which in practice have been construed in the widest sense, and certainly have invested the pursuit of crime with the worst attributes of an inquisition.

"The Procureur-General," says Mr. Stephen, "is himself a sort of Judge-Advocate, being so far a member of the Cour Imperiale that he sits on the bench during trials, and interferes ex-officio on many occasions, in the course of them. The functions of these various officers (constituting the Ministère Public), who constantly correspond with each other, and stand in the closest official relation, are almost entirely inquisitorial. They constantly interrogate the accused upon every point of the charge, and confront him from time to time with the witnesses. They have it in their power to place the accused in solitary confinement (*au secret*), and constantly exercise it; the object being to prevent him from communicating with his friends, and from forming any systematic defence. They keep him in ignorance of the depositions which may have been made for or against him, and then question him on the facts to which they refer. By comparing together these various sources of information, they gradually elaborate a theory on the subject, and it is supported not only by arguments of a most refined character, but also by considerations drawn from the manner in which the witnesses gave their evidence, the degree of frankness shown by the accused in his answers, and many other circumstances." *

The two principles, however, on which this, the main feature of the French system is based, namely, that the government should undertake the duty of pursuing crime—and that the accused should be subject to examination, are both perfectly correct. Mr. Stephen observes that "the inquisitorial theory of criminal procedure is beyond all question the true one. It is self-evident," he says, "that a trial ought to be a public inquiry into the truth of a matter deeply affecting the public interest."† We confess we cannot see any reason for agreeing with him, however, in his view that "in our own time and country it may be and possibly is the case that the best means of conducting such an inquiry is to consider the trial mainly as a litigation." It is admitted on all hands that the inefficiency of our procedure is chiefly due to its being thus conducted. And we think that "in our time and country" there is little danger to be apprehended from allowing the executive really as well as nominally to pursue and detect crime. Mr. Spedding, in his "Letters and Life of Lord Bacon," gives *in extenso* articles of examination of one Sheldon, who was suspected of having been concerned in the plot of Richard Williams against Elizabeth. From this curious and interesting document, which is all in Bacon's own handwriting, it appears that the system of examination was almost precisely the same as that now pursued in France.

* Stephen's Criminal Law of England, p. 162. † P. 167.

It is thus described by the learned editor: "Information is received which throws suspicion upon A. of having been party to some treasonable correspondence. A. is apprehended and questioned upon the particular matters in which he is suspected of having a hand. He must say something, and if he cannot give the true account of what he has done he must give a false one. The questions and answers are carefully set down, generally signed by himself, always signed by the Commissioners before whom the examination is taken. He is then remanded. Upon a careful scrutiny of his statement it appears that if true it will be confirmed; if false, confuted by the evidence of B. and C., whom it implicates. B. and C. are then sent for, and severally questioned. Not knowing what A. has said they can hardly invent statements which shall agree in all particulars with his, and with each other, unless all be true. Their answers are taken down in like manner, and are found upon a like scrutiny to involve new particulars. This supplies matter for a fresh examination of A. The same process is repeated as long as it promises to bring out anything new, until at last by successive shiftings the several witnesses (each being carefully kept in the dark as to the other's tale), find themselves involved in irreconcileable contradictions."* We think Mr. Spedding's position incontrovertible, when he says that such a course is in principle at least, rational, and the likeliest that could be adopted for the discovery of truth, supposing that to be the object.

He says that he has carefully perused a large number of state papers relating to similar proceedings in this reign, and that he had discovered no trace of hardness or injustice in the procedure even in those arbitrary times. But he admits that in the hands of an unscrupulous government it might readily be made an engine of tyranny and oppression. The danger is one which besets this, in common with every other scheme for administering public justice. It is liable to constant abuse and corruption, however admirable it may be in theory, unless it be raised

* Vol. I., p. 317.

above the possibility of state influence, and unless it be under the constant and direct control of public opinion. It is scarcely necessary to observe that these, the only conditions under which a pure and incorruptible system of public justice can exist, are not at the present time to be found in France. State influence is exerted and felt everywhere, and acts silently but irresistibly in every direction. On the other hand, public opinion—though it necessarily must exist in an empire where there is such wide-spread intelligence as in France—scarcely produces any impression on the course of administration. It makes itself known only by sullen and significant suspiciousness such as that shown during the trial of Greco and his fellow conspirators. There are, indeed, the gravest objections to the manner in which these principles are applied in the French system. It is "inquisitorial" in the worst sense of the word. Its great object is to compel the accused by every artifice to criminate himself. It puts his whole life under examination; it treats him as guilty from the first, and tries to torture him into an admission of his guilt. It introduces, too, an element of secrecy which is particularly odious. All these defects in practice are, however, quite separable from the principle on which they are founded—that the accused is himself the best source of conviction or acquittal. We have shown in a previous number of this journal* how this principle might be consistently and simply carried out in our own procedure, by a public examination of the accused at the preliminary inquiry which should not be given in evidence, and by an examination at the final trial as to the facts sworn to for the prosecution.

To return to the unfortunate Armand. The result of the inquiry made by the Juge d'Instruction had been to create in the mind of that official a strong conviction, or as Mr. Stephen terms it, a "theory" of his guilt. There is no reason to doubt that it was a sincere conviction. His inquiry had been made in the centre of the district which was full of popular preju-

* Article on Criminal Procedure, No. 31, N.S.

dice against the accused. The accused himself seems, from ill health and the unexpected circumstances he was placed in, to have become unnerved, and in his private interrogation evidently lost his self-possession. With this theory the Juge d'Instruction had gone to the Procureur-General. The intimate connexion which exists between all the branches of the Ministère Public, from the lowest official to the highest, has fitly gained for it the name of a "hierarchy." The views of the commissionnaire and his subordinate officers of police are laid before the Procureur du Roi; he submits them, as the case requires, either to the tribunal of simple police, the correctional tribunals, or the Juge d'Instruction. By the time the matter has reached the Procureur-General a case has been constructed. This case is elaborately reduced by the Procureur-General into the form of an acte d'accusation. At this point the English and French practice diverges widely. With us the statement to the jury of the acts charged against an accused is rigidly confined to the offence itself, leaving the case to be opened by the counsel for the prosecution. The French law expressly directs that the acte d'accusation shall state "First, the nature of the offence which forms the basis of accusation. Second, the facts and all the circumstances which can aggravate or diminish the punishment."* This direction interpreted in our own courts would mean such a bare statement of the facts and circumstances tending to support a conviction as were to be put in evidence by the prosecution in addition to the formal statement of the offence charged. This is, indeed, the plain intention of the article. But, unfortunately, the Ministère Public have been allowed to construe it in a sense quite foreign to its real intention. They have converted it into an instrument for embodying the theory of the prosecution. "It not only recapitulates all the grounds from which the Ministère Public infers the guilt of the accused, but also frequently states and refutes by anticipation the arguments for the defence."† These grounds are not confined

* Code d'Instruction Criminelle, Art. 241.

† Stephen.

to a statement of facts which can be put in evidence, nor even to facts which bear upon the criminal issue. Being founded on an assumption of guilt, that assumption is enforced by every artifice of rhetoric, and very often, as we shall see, by strong invective. Circumstances which cannot be proved, assertions founded on a simple train of reasoning are put forward with all the confidence of witnesses deposing to actual facts within their own personal knowledge.

That the power thus exercised is in excess of that legally conceded to them is well understood in France. We find Mons. Jules Favre protesting against its flagrant use at the Aix trial, and objecting to a statement in the acte d'accusation, "which was not a statement," because it "affirmed things that were still in doubt." The objection is most significant. But the most curious feature in this part of the French system is the tone in which the acte d'accusation is drawn up. The chief object of the composer seems to be to make it melodramatic in its form and expression. The narrative is taken back as far as possible, so that the past history of the accused may be brought out effectively. Every stage in his career is separated by a moral disquisition, often on the heinous nature of some past offence, or the general turpitude of the accused. For instance, at the recent trial of Greco and his four fellow-conspirators at Paris, the acte d'accusation begins, in the most approved style of the late Mr. G. P. R. James, thus: "On the 24th December, 1863, four strangers entered France at the same time by the Swiss Frontier." The four strangers are M. M. Greco and his three friends. The instrument gives the past history of these four men in full detail, explains how they came together, introduces and gives a long account of Mazzini, whom it denounces as the "head of the plot," and describes the manner in which he concerted and directed not only this but the Tibaldi conspiracy of 1857. The acte d'accusation, however, in the case of Armand, offers a still more striking instance of the absurdity and impropriety of such statements. The popular feeling against the accused had grown so strong, that his counsel applied on that ground to the Court of Cassation for an order that the trial should take place at Aix, which is in the adjoining department of the Bouches du Rhone. After some delay, the order was made. The prisoner had succeeded in escaping from an atmosphere of prejudice, which had even begun to mount from the rabble to the better classes. But he had not escaped from the Juge d'Instruction and the Procureur-General. The theory they had constructed was this: that the accused had committed the assault under the impulse of a fit of sudden passion. This theory the Procureur-General proceeded to unfold and explain in a manner which, to those accustomed to the dignified and impartial course of English criminal inquiries, sounds incomprehensible. It is difficult to realise the scene which occurred at Aix on the morning of the 14th of March, when the acte d'accusation was read. We try to picture to ourselves a learned counsel for the prosecution opening his statement to an English jury in the following terms:—"The accused, whom you see before you, gentlemen of the jury, is rich: he is very rich. Of all that people have been able to say of him that is perhaps the only fact that is true. But if he is very rich, he is very haughty; and more than that, very brutal, very violent, and very hard-hearted to his inferiors. I do not mean to say that he may not have gained some friends. A man worth a million—and the accused must have, at least, a million [francs]—as he has no children, always has friends. But there is one thing undeniable which will be proved on the trial, namely, his harshness towards his inferiors. Indeed, there is something incredible in the violence of his temper. At the slightest word and for the most frivolous cause, Armand gets excited either against his servants or his workmen; he makes use of the grossest invectives, and many times passes from words to blows. I have to observe," continues the prosecutor, "that whenever he assaults anyone, he begins always at the head. It is at the head he always aims whenever he has a weapon in his hand. In this fashion he has wounded many persons, and he would have wounded more if some, who knew his violence and who dreaded it, did not defend themselves and threaten to kill him if he approached them." Apart from the ludicrous tone of melodramatic exaggeration, such a style of prosecution would never be tolerated for a day in this country. But let us suppose for a moment that officers for Crown prosecutions were created with full latitude as to opening statement, it is equally impossible to conceive a prosecutor opening after the fashion above quoted. How is it then that amongst our neighbours the most solemn proceedings of their highest tribunal are disfigured by this foolish and indecent exhibition? If the truth be told, we fear the French people themselves are in no slight degree accountable for it. They are fond of theories, fond of excitement, and slaves to effect. They are ready to sacrifice everything to sensation. Had the English people received a written law, like that which regulates the drawing up of the acte d'accusation, they would have never ceased to watch jealously any attempt to enlarge its scope; they would have bound it down by rules of practice, so that it should remain as it was intended to be—a simple statement of the charge and the evidence. Not so the French. The highly flavoured address of the public prosecutor—its dramatic touches—its thrilling episodes—its ingenious explanations, are delightful to the Frenchman. Here, as in so many other cases, he has sacrificed to vanity, or present gratification, privileges which go to form the happiness and glory of a free people.

From such men as MM. Jules Favre and Lachaud, who defended the accused, a protest against the tone of the acte d'accusation came as a matter of course. They waited, however, until the case for the prosecution was exposed in the following terms. "Now, suppose such a man heard that his servant wanted to leave him, saying that his house was a hovel; to any other man it would be a trifle, but to him, puffed up with conceit as he is, it would be a deep offence, and you will easily understand that he said, when speaking to his imprudent servant, 'I will pay you out for this.' But how has he paid him? Why by means of the correction which is familiar to him (and he knows no other), by striking him on the head. On the 7th of July last, between half-past eight and nine o'clock, Armand goes down to his cellar, where he knows his servant went to fetch wood"—Here Mons. Favre interposed with the objection we have already quoted. To his protest the President replied, "You do not know whether witnesses may not come to depose to what the Procureur-General has advanced." The Procureur-General then said, "I state I cannot prove." Whereupon Mons. Favre made another strong and spirited protest against an acte d'accusation in which it is stated as a fact, "that a man is rich, haughty, violent, brutal, and that he goes down to his cellar to murder his servant, when in point of fact this is the very gist of the charge." He was told by the President that he had no right to criticise the manner in which the Procureur-General made his statements. That official, therefore, went on with the acte d'accusation, which was throughout of a piece with the introduction.

At this point we are again brought into contact with another strange feature in the French procedure:—the identification of the judge with the prosecution. This grave defect has been attributed to that principle of inquiry which lies at the root of French criminal jurisprudence. It has, in fact, only sprung from the same abuse of that principle which has distorted the system in every other direction, and has made conviction, not impartial examination, the chief end every official has in view. The efficiency, and, consequently, the promotion of a judge is in this way tested by the proportion of convictions to acquittals which have been obtained before him.

The injustice and scandal thus caused appear prominently in the trial of Armand. The presiding judge adopted the theory of the prosecution, and urged the guilt of the accused upon the jury with such indecency and violence as absolutely to recall to our minds Lord Macaulay's description of Jeffreys, "the most consummate bully ever known in his profession," from whose mind "all tenderness for the feelings of others, all self-respect, all sense of the becoming were obliterated." When any fact favourable to the accused was elicited he did his best to destroy the effect of it on the jury. He abused the counsel for the defence at every turn. In his examination of the prisoner in the presence of the jury, he insisted upon his confessing that he had committed the assault without intending to kill the accuser, merely "to administer one of those corrections which he was in the habit of administering to his servants, but that having miscalculated his blow, having gone further than he meant, intoxicated with terror, and stupified, he threw himself on his victim to finish him!" The only reply he obtained from the accused was a solemn assertion of his innocence. No browbeating or bullying could however, intimidate the prisoner's counsel, or prevent them from doing their duty. They submitted to the court the most convincing evidence of his innocence. They established beyond all moral doubt the conviction that the accusation had been falsely preferred by Roux in order to extort money in his claim for damages as *partie civile*, and that the injuries had been inflicted by himself. This defence was supported in the strongest manner by the behaviour of Roux himself in the witness-box, by the demeanour of the accused throughout his trying examination, by the evidence as to the worthless character of Roux, by the highest testimony in favour of Armand, and lastly by the most skilled medical evidence, which showed conclusively that the apparent torpor and insensibility of the accuser were feigned, and that he could easily have tied himself up in the position in which he was found.

When Mons. Lachaud concluded an eloquent speech for the defence the audience greeted him with loud cries of "Bravo!" That public spirit is not dead in France is proved by the fact that the jury refused to be dictated to by the court, and acquitted the prisoner. The shameless partisanship of the President was so undisguised that it defeated its own object, and even the populace cheered outside when they learnt that Armand had escaped from the hands of this unjust judge.

Mr. Stephen, in the comparison which he institutes between our own and the French system, speaks of the French jury as "an anomalous excrescence," and expresses it as his opinion that it is of no use, because the inquisition already carefully made by the Ministère Public has settled the question of guilt or innocence beforehand. He seems to think that they are only convened for effect, and that in fact they simply return a verdict in accordance with the direction of the prosecution. The case of Armand signally disproves this position. Here the whole weight of the Ministère Public and of the Court was against the unfortunate accused. The Juge d'Instruction who had made the first inquiry, who had taken the depositions of the witnesses, was examined and gave his evidence—particularly as to what took place in his private interrogation of the accused, in the tone of an advocate for the prosecution. The judge was shamelessly partial to the accuser, and throughout the proceedings took for granted the guilt of the accused. No greater pressure could have been brought to bear by the prosecution; yet the jury with scarcely any hesitation brought in a verdict of not guilty. It is plain that this institution is in France, as it has proved in England, a most important means for maintaining, and it may be, gradually extending their existing privileges. For though it may be true that nearly nineteen-twentieths of the criminal offences are tried before the Correctional Tribunals which have no juries, all the trials of real gravity or importance are included in the remaining twentieth; and these are tried at the Court of Assize before a jury.

We have gone briefly through the leading incidents in a prosecution which was singularly disfigured by all that is harsh and repulsive in French criminal process. We have dwelt upon all those features in it which are open to the strongest objection: the secret examination of the prisoner, the assumption throughout the written statement for the prosecution, not merely of his guilt, but of every allegation in his disfavour, whether to be produced in evidence or not: the appeals by the prosecution and the bench to the passion or the prejudice of the jury; the production against the prisoner on his final trial of the statement made by him in a previous informal inquiry: the examination for the prosecution of the very magistrate who had conducted this preliminary inquiry: the attempts made from the bench to surprise, to frighten, to cajole the accused into a confession of his guilt. But with the exception of the preventive imprisonment of the accused for many weary months we do not think that any of these evils are fairly traceable to the principles or, indeed, to the express rules laid down in the French criminal code. The system there constructed taken as a whole is rational and simple. It proposes nothing more than to obtain by inquiry the exact truth as to every offence committed throughout the empire. For this purpose it appoints a Crown prosecutor in every town. It erects tribunals of simple police for the trial of all minor offences, in every centre of population, and provides them with judges, who are not merely honorary but paid and responsible magistrates. It provides accessible local tribunals (correctional tribunals), at which all offences not of the first magnitude may be tried. It charges one of the judges of this tribunal (the Juge d'Instruction) specially with the preliminary examination of all important criminal matters. It creates two intermediate courts—the Chambre de Conseil, and the Chambre des Mises en Accusation—whose duties are to sift again all the facts before sending the case for trial. In the Procureur-General it provides an official of high standing, whose express duty it is impartially to superintend on behalf of the public every grave criminal charge, from the time of its remission to its final hearing before a jury in the Cour d'Assize. It gives an appeal from each of the minor tribunals to the higher. And, in the last resort, it allows an accused as a matter of right to carry any decision, except on a mere question of fact, to a special court of criminal appeal which has been described by an eminent authority as "one of the most important institutions of modern France, giving to the whole jurisprudence of the country, criminal as well as civil, coherence and uniformity without endangering the necessary independence of the inferior tribunals."* It even gives the Crown prosecutor discretion to summon, at the expense of the prosecution, witnesses for the defence, where he shall think that their testimony will serve to discover the truth. The only objectionable features in the code itself are —the absence in the correctional tribunals of a jury, which should always be interposed between the executive and the accused in the final trial of all but the most trifling offences; the rule which allows the majority of a jury to convict;† and the absence of any discretion to grant bail, in cases where the charge involves an infamous and afflictive punishment.‡

For the abuses which reflect such discredit upon the procedure, and which were so prominent in the case of Armand, the system constructed in the Code Napoleon is clearly not responsible. They are due partly to the social and political conditions in which France has existed since that code was promulgated, partly to the fact that when that system was first established it was supplemented by no rational or precise rules of evidence, and partly to the character of the French people. The system itself is in many respects far more philosophical and consistent than our own. If it were transplanted with some modifications into this country, there can be no doubt that it would prove more efficient, more exact, and even more humane than ours. We should of course apply to its machinery all the rules of evidence which we have so carefully devised, and so jealously preserve, in our criminal procedure. But it must be remembered that most of these rules, essential as they are to a just and impartial administration, have only been

* Macqueen Reports House of Lords, Vol. II. Account of Court of Cassation.
† Code d'Instruction Criminelle, Art. 317. ‡ Art. 113.

established even in this country by the decisions of our judges within the last century. They were wrought with infinite patience and determination out of rules of practice equally harsh and irrational with those that now obtain in France, by a Bar who here only reflected the temper and feelings of the English people. There is, indeed, but one lesson to be learnt from a study of the French procedure: that, however perfect theoretically a system of criminal jurisprudence may be, its administration can never be pure, upright, and incorruptible, unless it be open to the freest inspection and criticism, and carried on under a sense of responsibility to the people.

There remains still the civil phase of this curious trial, which is more extraordinary than all. The accuser claimed 50,000 francs compensation for the injuries which he had alleged to have been inflicted. But as a *partie civile*, or indeed as a simple informer (*denonciateur*), the accuser is liable to be condemned in damages himself if he fail to establish the charge. The Code d'Instruction Criminelle provides that "when the accused has been declared not guilty the President shall announce that he is acquitted of the charge, and shall order him to be set at liberty, if he is not detained for any other cause."* It then directs by the same article that "the court shall decide as to the damages (*dommages intérêts*) respectively claimed." And by another article (the 366th) it declares that "in the case of absolution, as in that of acquittal or condemnation, the court shall decide as to the damages claimed by the partie civile or the accused." The accused is "absolved" when he has been found guilty, (*coupable*) of an act which is not forbidden by a penal law (Article 364). Such an act though not constituting a penal offence may constitute a civil injury; and in such a case it would be quite consistent that the court should give damages for the civil injury, though the accused were absolved as to the penal charge, if it appeared that the act done had been injurious to the partie civile. It appears, however, that the question of damages is so entirely left to the discretion of the

* Code d'Instruction Criminelle, Art. 358.

Court of Assize that it may not only refuse to give them to, but may award them against, an accused who has been absolutely acquitted. "The declaration of the jury that not only was the accused not guilty, but that he had not shown imprudence on his part, does not bind the Court of Assize so that it cannot in deciding the civil question pronounce that there has been fault (*faute*) on the part of the accused, and in consequence award damages against him."* Acting, doubtless, upon this construction of the article the court on the following day adjudged that Mons. Armand should pay 20,000 francs to the man Roux, as compensation for the injury he had sustained; the jury having the day before declared virtually that the claim was an infamous fabrication. Of course an appeal was at once lodged against this monstrous sentence, and doubtless the Court of Cassation will deal with it in a way to justify its high reputation. There is, however, nothing objectionable even in the wide discretion which has been given as to damages, though we quite concur in the view which we understand is strongly urged in France, that this discretion should be given not to the court but to the jury.

ART IX.—AUSTIN'S JURISPRUDENCE.

Lectures on Jurisprudence, being the sequel to "The Province of Jurisprudence Determined." To which are added Notes and Fragments—now first published from the original manuscripts. By the late JOHN AUSTIN, Esq., of the Inner Temple, Barrister-at-Law. Vols. II. and III., 8vo. London: John Murray, Albemarle Street.

THE students of the science of law at home and abroad, the members of that distinguished profession to which the late Mr. Austin belonged, and of which he was so bright an ornament, and not a few philosophers and statesmen, will rejoice at the rescue of these scattered fragments of excellency from that oblivion to which it was feared the MSS. of Mr. Austin

* Note 62 to Art. 358 of Code d'Instruction Criminelle. Paillict, Vol. II.

were consigned. It is pleasant to acknowledge a boon, and to point with grateful recognition to the source from whence it is derived. We are often placed under obligations to ladies in the department of general literature. Occasionally, also, in the department of language and the classics some fair one steps forth —like Fulvia Olympia Morata, whose neat little mural tablet we see in the porch of the old St. Peter's University Church in Heidelberg—and weaves for herself a garland of imperishable fame. Rarely is it that the legist has to bow with grateful genuflexion to acknowledge a costly gift in his department of study from the hand of a woman. Such, however, is our duty now: a duty we most willingly perform. We sincerely thank Mrs. Sarah Austin for these valuable volumes. We honour the earnestness which she has exhibited in the collating and the editing of these memorials of her highly gifted husband. We thank Mr. Murray, the publisher, and those *innonimate* members of the profession who have encouraged and aided in the production and completion of Mr. Austin's Jurisprudence.

There are, at intervals of longer or shorter duration, certain works given to the world that stamp the epoch in which they are produced. Such works challenge the attention of mankind, and exert an influence far beyond the limits of the age and the country in which they first appear. The collection of the "Corpus Juris Civilis," in the sixth century, the "Divina Commedia di Dante Alighieri," in the fourteenth; the dramas of Shakspeare, the "De Jure Belli et Pacis" of that learned man, who has not been inaptly termed the legislator of nations, were works of this character. In our own day some few works containing the exhibition and development to a greater or less extent of principles destined to exert the greatest possible influence have appeared. Among such books we may mention the economical writings of Adam Smith and David Ricardo, and in the department of general jurisprudence those of Bentham, and Mackintosh, and Austin.

In the year 1828 there appeared a small thin volume, containing only 89 pages, entitled "A Discourse on the Study of the Law of Nature and the Law of Nations," by Sir James

Mackintosh, M.P. After the publication of these brief lectures by Mackintosh nothing attracted attention in this country on the subject of general jurisprudence till Mr. Austin published his able treatise in the year 1832.

The first edition of Austin's Jurisprudence was soon exhausted, and for many years it was only accessible to the student at our public libraries. So rare did the book become that it was necessary for those who wished to have the principal points of the work at hand for reference to make lengthy written excerpts from the copy possessed by some private or public owner. The writer of this article has now before him an epitome of this work, which occupied the spare time of several weeks to compose. Twenty-nine years after the publication of the first edition, and when the writer had passed away, the long looked for treasure was reproduced under the auspices of the author's esteemed widow. The volume had been out of print for many years, and Mr. Austin had received earnest and flattering entreaties from various quarters to publish a second edition. Mrs. Austin tells us in her own touching words the reason of the non-production of the work by her husband. She says :—" The hope, the animation, the ardour, with which he had entered upon his career as a teacher of jurisprudence, had been blighted by indifference and neglect; and, in a temper so little sanguine as his, they could have no second spring."

It is to be regretted that a man of Mr. Austin's power and wisdom did not perceive that devotion to the study of the abstruse propositions of general jurisprudence is not generally the condition of success in that profession which he had chosen. If a man wishes to be honoured as a Deity in the Temple of Law, it is more than possible that he will find himself destined to repose in awful briefless grandeur in the solitude of his chamber. If the choice is made, it is useless to repine at the dreary neglect to which one is likely to be reduced. It is quite natural that the admirable woman who has given us these three noble volumes should feel as she does, but it is to be regretted—much to be regretted—that Mr. Austin should, by his refusal to reproduce his valuable volume, have shown anything like disappointment at a result which might almost infallibly have been predicted.

It is then in these three volumes that we have the result of the labours of a thoughtful and painstaking man on one of the most momentous topics to which it is possible to direct our attention. The first impression made upon the minds of those who are acquainted with the subject, or who have perhaps pursued a similar course of investigation, will be that of profound regret, that a work so elaborately planned—that a temple, for the construction of which such choice and rare materials had been collected, should be left unfinished and unadorned. A fine ruin is beautiful in its decay, for when Time places upon it his mouldering hand, he at the same instant, and as it were to hide its desolation, reaches forth another hand to clothe with moss and varied verdure its decaying arches and falling columns. But it is not so with an unfinished work. It is not so with Mr. Austin's projected edifice. Some portion of his goodly temple is indeed reared—we can scarcely say adorned, for whilst he paid great attention to the exactness of his expression, he had little time, and perhaps little inclination, to attend to style. To pursue the illustration, the scaffolding is unremoved, materials of great value, which have cost time and enormous labour to procure, lie in heaps and masses all around. In some instances, we see the skill of the workman upon some block intended to be reared to its place in the building. It is squared or cut to the pattern required for some important point; but it has never been uplifted and placed upon the spot for which it had been designed and wrought. The mallet has been cast aside, and the chisel flung from the hand of the workman, from a sense that his labour was unappreciated and his toil unrequited. Many may be disposed to blame Mr. Austin for this, and perhaps he was not altogether without blame; but it requires a large amount of moral and mental sinew for a man to continue at a task the object of which his superiors are too busily engaged to notice, and too remiss to reward. It is perhaps worth calling attention to the different treatment such a man as Mr. Austin would have experienced in a continental State. In Germany, for instance, Mr. Austin would probably have started as a "Privatdocent" or tutor in one of the universities. His talents and industry would very soon have brought him under the special notice of his seniors in the university. Some "Professor ordinarius" would have referred to the rising man in his lectures, or in his works. As the universities are in close connexion with the Government, the Dean of the faculty in which he taught would have made such representations in the proper quarter as would have procured for him the position of a "Professor extraordinarius." His star would have arisen; the rank and emolument of "Professor ordinarius" would have been, in his case, soon reached. Then the Government would have decorated him. He would have been made first a "Hofrath"—a Court-councillor, and then a "Geheimrath"—a Privy-councillor. Then would have come the struggle between rival universities to obtain the aid and distinction of the enrollment of such a man among their staff of professors. This would assuredly have secured for Mr. Austin wealth, if not riches. It is a sad reproach to us as a nation that it should come to pass that Mrs. Austin should have to utter her mild and gentle reproaches at the neglect and poverty to which a great and wealthy nation exposed so learned a man. We boast that we are a practical people, and it must be admitted that in many things we are. But if we are great, as the Germans express it, in the "practical life," we are, to use another of their expressions, anything but great in the "scientific life;" and in the present instance we have the mortification of beholding an unfinished work with scaffolding unremoved, and heaps of unemployed materials lying in confusion all around, instead of a structure at once noble and complete. A philosopher has passed away before he has taught us all the lessons he was willing and able to impart. The stately column is broken—the beacon fire is extinct.

In the republication of the volume Mr. Austin himself gave us, now so many years ago, Mrs. Austin was kind enough to present some particulars of her husband's life and struggles. When first perused they must have produced in many minds the deepest regret. A brief review of this sketch will refresh the memories of those who read the narrative at the time, and prepare us for the perusal of the recent volumes.

Mrs. Austin tells us that: "At a very early age our author entered the army, in which he served for five years." This imprinted permanent traces in his character and sentiments. "Though he quitted it for a profession for which his talents appeared more peculiarly to fit him, he retained to the end of his life a strong sympathy with, and respect for, the military character, as he conceived it. The high and punctilious sense of honour, the chivalrous tenderness for the weak, the generous ardour mixed with reverence for authority and discipline, the frankness and loyalty which were, he thought, the distinguishing characteristics of a true soldier, were also his own; perhaps even more pre-eminently than the intellectual gifts for which he was so remarkable."

Mr. Austin was called to the Bar by the honourable Society of the Inner Temple in 1818. He was himself never sanguine; but "the eminent lawyers in whose several chambers he had studied, spoke of his talents and his application as unequalled, and confidently predicted for him the highest honours of his profession." Four years before his marriage, he concluded a letter addressed to the lady who was to be his future wife in the following desponding tone:—"and may God, above all, strengthen us to bear up under those privations and disappointments with which it is but too probable we are destined to contend."

Mrs. Austin informs us that it was not long before one who watched him with the keenest anxiety, detected that he would not succeed at the Bar. "His health was delicate: he was subject to feverish attacks which left him in a state of extreme debility and prostration; and as these attacks were brought on by either physical or moral causes, nothing could be worse for him than the hurry of practice, or the close air and continuous excitement of a court of law." And then Mrs. Austin adds: — "He was more disqualified by the constitution of his mind. Nervous and sensitive in the highest degree, he was totally deficient in readiness, in audacity, in self-complacency, and in reliance on the superiority of which he was conscious, but which oppressed rather than animated him. He felt that the weapons with which he was armed, though of the highest possible temper, were inapplicable to the warfare in which he was engaged, and he gradually grew more and more self-exacting and self-distrusting." These habits of mind were fatal to his success in business. Before he was called to the Bar, in a letter addressed to his future wife, dated 1817, when he was in the chambers of an equity draftsman, he himself detected the peculiar characteristics of his mind, and wrote to his future wife as follows:—"I almost apprehend that the habit of drawing will in no short time give me so exclusive and intolerant a taste (as far, I mean, as relates to my own productions) for perspicuity and precision, that I shall hardly venture on sending a letter of much purpose even to you, unless it be laboured with the accuracy and circumspection which are requisite in a deed of conveyance." Such was the habit and disposition of Mr. Austin's mind, and we are not surprised to find that his conflict for forensic honours was of short duration. In one short sentence his widow tells us of the advent of the anticipated result. "After a vain struggle, in which his health and spirits suffered severely, he gave up practice in the year 1825. He entered now upon a new epoch of his life. The building in Gower Street, now known as University College, had been reared, and in 1826 the University of London was established within its walls. The title was subsequently ceded to that *universitas juris* composed of a number of affiliated institutions, of which the original institution, to use the phase of the German civilians, is a "*civis.*"

A Professorship of Jurisprudence was founded, and Mr. Austin was chosen to fill the chair. He resolved to go to Germany to study under the great jurists of the Fatherland. He at once set about learning the language. No mean task this, as all know who have attempted it late in life. "In the autumn of 1827, after visiting Heidelberg, he established himself with his wife and child at Bonn, which was then the residence of Niebuhr, Brandis, Schlegel, Arndt, Welcker, Mackeldey, Heffter, and other eminent men, from whose society he received equal pleasure and instruction." Mr. Austin secured the assistance of a tutor or *Privatdocent*, and combined the study of the German language and of law in one process. His stay in Germany was but short, for Mrs. Austin tells us that "He left Bonn in the spring of 1828, master of the German language, and of a number of the greatest works which it contains." There can be no doubt of Mr. Austin having made the most of the time he spent in the interesting Rhenish town over against the "Liebengebirge," but that he could have mastered the language and the jurisprudence of the country in so short a period was not to be expected. Fidelity compels one to say that his knowledge of the Roman law, though considerable for the period he spent in Bonn, is neither sharply defined nor exact. It is impossible that it could be otherwise. There is a certain confusion and want of clearness at times pervading this part of his writings which a longer study of the Roman law would have dissipated and removed. It is exceedingly difficult to master the elements of a language and any great branch of its literature at the same time. He returned to London the subject of those peculiar feelings which many have experienced upon first entering upon a professorship. He left Germany with that regret which those who have gone there to drink of its fountains of learning, upon leaving its land and its professors, have perhaps always experienced. "Spite of the hopes," says Mrs. Austin, "the profits, and the acquirements with which he entered upon his new functions, it was not without much regret and some forebodings, that he quitted a life so full of interest and so free from care, for the restraints and privations which London imposes on poor people, and for the anxieties of a laborious and untried career." His health, always feeble, had been but partially restored by the comparative tranquillity of mind which followed his appointment, and by his solitary and agreeable residence on the Rhine. "His lectures opened with a class which exceeded his expectations. It included several men who are now most eminent in law, politics, or philosophy. He was much impressed and excited by the spectacle of this noble band of young men, and he felt with a sort of awe the responsibility attaching to his office. He had the highest possible conception of the importance of clear notions on the foundations of law and morals to the welfare of the human race; the thought of being the medium through which these were to be conveyed into so many of the minds destined to exercise a powerful influence in England, filled him with ardour and enthusiasm. As might be expected from his susceptible nature and delicate conscience, these were not unmixed with anxiety too intense for his bodily health." The position for which he was richly endowed had been reached. He was eminently qualified to discharge the duties of a teacher; but his chair was unendowed, and the first flush of success was followed by that disappointment which might certainly have been anticipated. "In spite," says the illustrious writer of a notice of Mr. Austin's death in the LAW MAGAZINE, "of the brilliant commencement of his career, as a Professor, it soon became evident that this country would not afford such a succession of students of Jurisprudence as would suffice to maintain a chair, and as there was no other provision for the teachers than the student's fees, it followed of necessity that no man could continue to hold that office unless he had a private fortune, or combined some gainful occupation with his professorship. Mr. Austin, who had no fortune, and who regarded the study and exposition of his science as more than sufficient to occupy his whole life, and who knew that it would never be in demand amongst that immense majority of law students who regard their profession only as a means of making money, found himself under the necessity of resigning his chair."

"Such," says Mrs. Austin, "was the end of his exertions in a cause to which he had devoted himself with an ardour and singleness of purpose of which few men are capable. This was the real and irremediable calamity of his life—the blow from which he never recovered."

It was in the month of June, 1832, that he gave his last lecture. In the same year he was enabled by the assistance of the late Mr. Murray to publish that which now constitutes the first volume of his lectures. The book attracted but little attention at the time. Neither of the Reviews which profess to guide public opinion on serious subjects took the slightest notice of it. The volume, however, won its way to fame by its sterling merit. In the year, 1833, Mr. Austin was appointed by Lord Brougham, then Lord Chancellor, a member of the Criminal Law Commission. According to Mr. Austin's views the proceedings of the Commission were of so unsatisfactory a nature that he even felt repugnance at receiving the public money for work from which he thought the public would derive little or no advantage. His next brief employment was in consequence of the determination of the honourable Society of the Inner Temple to make some attempt to teach the principles and history of jurisprudence. Mr. Bickersteth, afterwards Lord Langdale, was one of the most earnest promoters of this scheme. In the year 1834, Mr. Austin was engaged to deliver a course of Lectures on Jurisprudence at the Inner Temple. Law students have a morbid objection to lectures. Forms and office-*cram* are deemed of more importance by them than the science of law. The latter may make a jurist, but the former pays best. Even at the present time when what may be denominated a legal university exists in connexion with the Inns of Court, now that learned and labourious men have been appointed to occupy the chairs appointed for the readers—gentlemen who prepare themselves most thoroughly for their work; this vile prejudice against legal lectures still exists among our students for the Bar. It is fostered by causes and circumstances which it is here unnecessary to enumerate. This prejudice, however, should be discouraged by the advocates of the study of scientific law in this country. Is it of no advantage for the young man fresh from school or college, or for the middle aged man who is looking forward to the county magistracy or to the chairmanship of sessions, or for the Member of Parliament who looks to the Bar as a stepping-stone to office and promotion, to gain a clear systematic knowledge of the fundamental principles of that law which is our best inheritance; and to have a careful analysis presented to him of some of those leading cases which stand like marks in the great unexplored forest to guide the footsteps of the traveller? When we have before us the example of a philosopher constantly depressed in spirits and broken in heart from want of success as a teacher through causes entirely beyond his control—may not another question be put? Is it right to make the success of a great experiment at legal education depend upon the prejudice or the caprice of unfledged and inexperienced law students? A learned lecturer on a great subject like law, perhaps a Q.C., should certainly have no anxiety or fear lest, perchance, through the forgetfulness of some students to enter their names upon entrance the number in attendance upon his class should appear small to the "Legal Council of Education," and the whole scheme of legal education with its learned readers be deemed and adjudged a failure. If we are aiming at anything like an accurate knowledge of the science of law in this country assuredly this should not be. Apparent success is easily obtained. The Professor's Chair may be "rigged for a rise," like the Stock Market. It may be done as follows:—Let the Reader in his private class give a *minimum* of instruction and consume a *minimum* of time; let him in his public class think but little of his subject and everything of style; let him strive to make his public lecture as pointed, pithy, and antithetical as an article in a popular review; let him entirely banish from his mind those anxious thoughts which made Mr. Austin feel that the teacher of a great subject like jurisprudence must be in earnest; let him "polish his pebbles" so brightly that the fashionable languid student may be even induced to close the novel he has taken into the hall to read during the lecture, and he will be sure to succeed. It was just because Mr. Austin was too conscientious and great a man to do this that he failed. It was because his successor at the Middle Temple, Mr. George Long, was too honest and able a scholar to do this that he has been long since extinguished and has become an editor of the classics and a teacher of boys. It is because Sir James Mackintosh would not do this that a small volume in the shape of a book of devotions is the principle fruitage on this subject of his noble mind.

But let us return to our brief review of Mr. Austin's life. "Depressed by failure, unsustained by sympathy in his lofty and benevolent aspirations, or by the recognition of his value as a teacher; agitated by conflicting duties, and harassed by anxiety about the means of subsistence . . . he resolved to abandon a conflict in which he had met with nothing but defeat, and to seek an obscure but tranquil retreat on the continent where he might live upon the very small means at his disposal."

He quitted England and settled at Boulogne, his heart smarting under a sense of neglect and failure. It was indeed a truth that he expressed to one with whom he ever talked freely, when he said: "I was born out of time and place. I ought to have been a schoolman of the twelfth century—or a German professor." About a year and a half after his retirement from England a proposal was made to him by the Colonial Office, through his much esteemed and faithful friend Sir James Stephen, to proceed to the Island of Malta as Royal Commissioner, to inquire into the nature and extent of the grievances of which the natives of that island complained.

Two great men—Sir George Cornewall Lewis and Mr. Austin—both now no more, rendered to the Island of Malta services of the utmost moment, still remembered with lively and affectionate gratitude. Mr. Austin returned to England, and was preparing to enter upon his more peculiar province of legal and judicial reforms, when he was called to endure a new disappointment. Lord Glenelg had ceased to be in office, and Mr. Austin was abruptly dismissed. No reason was assigned for this, nor was his dismissal accompanied with a single word of recognition for his past services.

He returned from Malta in 1838 so feeble in health that in 1840 his medical friends exhorted him to try the waters of Carlsbad. From these waters he received so much benefit that he determined to return to them, and the summers of 1841, 1842, and 1843 were spent there. The winters he spent at Dresden and Berlin. At Dresden he wrote for the "Edinburgh Review," his answer to Dr. List's violent attack on the doctrine of Free Trade. In 1844 he removed to Paris. In that year an earnest appeal was made to him to publish a second edition on "The Province of Jurisprudence." Letters from friends—Mrs. Austin says—and even from strangers, arrived, lamenting the impossibility of getting a copy, and setting forth the constantly increasing reputation of the book." At this period he seems partly to have resolved to re-cast and re-publish his great work, under the title of "The Principles and Relations of Jurisprudence and Ethics." This intention was announced to Sir William Erle, the present Chief-Justice of the Common Pleas, the companion of his early studies, the beloved and faithful friend of every period of his life. In the fragment of a letter still preserved by the Chief-Justice, Mr. Austin says: "I intend to show the relations of positive morality and law (*mos* and *jus*), and of both to their common standard or test; to show that there are principles and distinctions common to all systems of law (or that law is the subject of an abstract science); to show the possibility and conditions of codification; to exhibit a short system of a body of law arranged in a natural order; and to show that the English Law, in spite of its great peculiarities, might be made to conform to that order much more closely than is imagined." He had finally established himself in Paris when the Revolution of 1848 once more uprooted him. After this event he remained only a few months in Paris, watching the course of events when, submitting to a severe pecuniary loss, he returned to England and took a cottage at Weybridge in Surrey, near enough to London for convenience, and for occasional visits from his only child, and far enough to enable him to enjoy the retirement he coveted. Here he spent the last twelve years of his life in *otium cum dignitate*—his health improved, surrounded by the charms of a rustic home, with the guardian angel of his life for his solace and support. Of Mr. Austin M. Guizot said, "L'etait un des hommes les plus distingues, un des esprits les plus rares, et un des cœurs les plus noble que j'ai connus. Quel dommage, qu'il n'ait pas su employer tout ce qu'il avait, et montrer tout ce qu'il valait!" "*Quel dommage*" indeed, in this land of wealth and office and power! But regrets are now too late. The wisdom that would have instructed us is dumb, and the hand that could have penned pages of priceless value to us and to future generations lies palsied in the tomb. Mrs. Austin properly informs us that it was not through the wilful negligence of her husband that we have lost this rich inheritance. She says: "In giving this short account of his troubled life and baffled designs, my object has only been to show what were the circumstances by which he was forced out of the tract on which he had entered, and which his whole mind and soul were engaged, and why it was that he seeméd to abandon the science to which he had devoted his singular powers with so much ardour and intensity."

When in 1861 Mrs. Austin reproduced the lectures of her late husband, she made the following statement. "The volume now re-published includes, as the author's preface states, the first ten of the lectures read at the London University; which, though divided into that number for delivery, were," in obedience to the affinity of the topics, "reduced by him to six."

"There remained unprinted, all the rest of the lectures given at the London University. These I propose to print exactly as he left them. I shall alter nothing. There is also the short course delivered at the Inner Temple. But as this necessarily went in a great measure over ground which had been traversed in the earlier courses, it does not appear to the friends I have consulted that it will afford matter for a separate volume. It is thought that it will be expedient to collate these with the earlier and far more numerous lectures, and to insert, as notes or appendix, any matter which is not found in these. The state of the manuscript seems to show that the author meant to incorporate them with the former; or rather, to employ both in the combination of the great work he meditated.

"Lastly, I find a considerable mass of papers on Codification; an Essay on Interpretation; the 'Excursus on Analogy, referred to at the beginning of Lecture V. in the present volume; and the commencement of a project of a Criminal Code." Thus wrote Mrs. Austin in 1861. Since that time she has been constantly occupied in preparing these materials for the press. The collating of the course of lectures delivered at the Inner Temple was rendered unnecessary by the fact that on a nearer examination it was found that the author had marked with his own hand the parts of the Inner Temple course which were to be added to, or substituted for, passages in the earlier lectures. The lectures as now printed in the second and third volumes are the two courses consolidated by the author himself. It appears that there were some passages through which Mr. Austin had drawn a faint pencil line. These passages are mostly retained, and are distinguished by brackets. We have also the notes on Criminal Law and those on Codification in their original though rough and imperfect state, so much so, that Mrs. Austin says, "I should not have ventured to publish them had I not been assured that they would, as models of arrangement, be of the utmost value to future inquirers." Of the two volumes just published, forming the second and third of Mr. Austin's Jurisprudence, the first contains his lectures—from Lecture XII. to Lecture XLVII. Lecture XL., however, is wanting. In the end of this volume are found a few fragments on Method. The third volume concludes the lectures. We have Lectures XLVIII. to LVII., whilst in addition to these lectures, and, constituting three-fourths of the volume, we have, "Notes on Contracts and Quasi-Contracts." Then follow tables and notes, extending from page 143 to page 226. Here we have a mine of wealth, but, unfortunately, in an imperfect state. These are followed by an Essay on Interpretation, an Excursus on Analogy, Notes on Codification, Notes on Criminal Law, an Essay on the Study of Jurisprudence, and an Essay on "Codification and Law Reform." The third volume closes with an index to the two volumes recently published. When new editions shall be called for, it will be convenient for reference to consolidate the indices into one, and to enlarge the index for convenient reference. We would also suggest the propriety of republishing the reviews referred to, so that a complete edition of Mr. Austin's works may be presented to the public and the profession.

In the lectures contained in the first volume of the work now before us, Mr. Austin treats of law in the strict sense of the term. "Every *law* or *rule* is a command which obliges a person or persons." Being liable to evil from you if I comply not with a wish which you signify, I am bound or obliged by your command, or I lie under a *duty* to obey it. The evil which will probably be incurred in case a command be disobeyed, or (to use an equivalent expression) in case a duty be broken, is frequently called a *sanction*, or an enforcement of obedience. Differing, and rightly so, from Bentham, he affirms that rewards are not sanctions. This word sanction stands in close connexion with the idea or notion of the nature of offence. An offence may be considered as committed either against the Superior Being, or against the State or the Crown regarded as the embodiment of the nation, or against the Clan. In the different periods of the world, and in different nations, crime has been viewed in all these aspects. Now it was at a period when a crime was considered as an offence against the god that the term *sanction* originated and was applied to the punishment contemplated and inflicted by the law. That alone was criminal which was deemed to be offensive to the presiding deity of the family or the nation. The idea prevailed that it was only by surrendering the offender as a victim on the bleeding altar of the god, that his fury could be propitiated, and his favour continued to the *gens.* The victim thus deemed as sacred was offered up, and in the Roman law the formal words of condemnation to sacrifice, pronounced by the judge and priest, were preserved in the utterance—*sacer esto.* The punishment awarded to the guilty was the *sanctio* —it was something sacred and holy, and wiped out the stain of crime. Mr. Austin is thus historically and legally correct in confining sanctions to punishments. In his first and second lectures our author having discussed the notion of law, in his third he presents for consideration the principles or doctrines of utility. As this is the very key-stone of his method, it may be well almost in his own words to state his views. Mr. Austin first states the objections which may be urged, namely, that if utility be the proximate test of positive law and morality, it is impossible that the rules of conduct *actually obtaining amongst mankind* should accord completely and correctly with the laws established *by the deity.* The index to his will is imperfect and uncertain. His laws are signified obscurely to those upon whom they are binding, and are subject to inevitable and involuntary misconstruction. For, first, positive law and morality, fashioned on the principle of utility, are gotten by observation and induction from the tendencies of human actions. Consequently, till these actions shall be marked and classed with perfect completeness, positive law and morality, fashioned on the principle of utility, must be more or less defective, and more or less erroneous. And these actions being infinitely diversified, the work of classing them completely, and of collecting their effects completely, transcends the limited faculties of created and finite beings. And, *secondly*, if utility be the proximate test of positive law and morality, the defects and errors of *popular* or *vulgar* ethics will scarcely admit of a remedy. For, if ethical truth be matter of science, and not of immediate consciousness, most of the ethical maxims, which govern the sentiments of the multitude, must be taken, without examination, from human authority.

To these objections he replies:—*First*, that the diffusion of ethical science amongst the great bulk of mankind will gradually remove the obstacles which prevent or retard its *advancement*. *Secondly*, though the many must trust to authority for a number of subordinate truths, they are competent to examine the elements which are the groundwork of the science of ethics, and to infer the more momentous of the derivative practical consequences. And, *thirdly*, as the science of ethics advances, and is cleared of obscurities and uncertainties, they, who are debarred from opportunities of examining the science extensively, will find an authority, whereon they may rationally rely, in the unanimous or general agreement of searching and impartial inquirers. And, as a further answer to the objection, Mr. Austin maintains that—admitting the imperfection of utility as the index to the Divine pleasure—it is impossible to argue from this its admitted imperfection, that utility is *not* the index.

In his fifth lecture he proceeds still further in his examination of laws proper or properly so called, and laws improper or improperly so called. Lecture VI., which concludes the volume, treats of the distinguishing marks of sovereignty and independent political society. This is introduced with the strictest regard to philosophical method—"I shall analyse," says our author, "the expression *sovereignty*, the correlative expression *subjection*, and the inseparably connected expression *independent political society*." These notions are examined to distinguish completely the appropriate province of jurisprudence from the regions which lie upon its confines, and by which it is encircled. "Every positive law, or every law simply and strictly so called, is set by a sovereign person, or a sovereign body of persons, to a member or members of the independent political society, wherein that person or body is sovereign or supreme." In the language of Hobbes—"The legislator is he, not by whose authority the law was first made, but by whose authority it continues to be a law."

It will be obvious to most readers of this article that Mr. Austin, in basing all law upon command, agrees in the main with Puffendorf, and differs from Hugo Grotius. Puffendorf affirms that in themselves actions have no moral quality whatever—that if a superior being commands or forbids certain actions, they then become right or wrong by virtue of such command or prohibition. On the other hand the principles of Grotius differ from this in the following respects,—Grotius holds that "Morality and law being independent of command, the customs and moral principles which *proprio vigore* have won the assent of separate communities, and the great system of international law which has bound these communities together are all law, and would be law, though no judge had ever recognised them, and no king ever decreed their observance." This accords with the great Roman Jurist who says, "Sed et omnes gentes et omni tempore una lex et semipiterna et immutabilis continebit, unusque erit communis quasi magister et imperator omnium Deus, ille hujus legis inventor, disceptator, lator." Cie de Republic III. 17. Lord Bacon seems to have had the same idea in his mind when, in his own poetic style he says: "For there are in nature certain fountains of justice whence all civil laws are derived, but as streams; and like as waters do take tinctures and tastes from the soils through which they run, so do civil laws vary according to the regions and governments where they are planted, though they proceed from the same fountains." Bacon's Dig. and Advt. of Learning Works, vol. 1, p. 101. It is in the same spirit that Sir James Mackintosh defines law in his "Law of Nature," as "a supreme, invariable rule of conduct to all men, of which the violation is avenged by natural punishments which necessarily flow from the constitution of things, and are as fixed and inevitable as the order of nature." P. 11, Law Nature and Nations.

Before closing this part of our subject it may be observed that Mr. Austin has perhaps scarcely presented with sufficient clearness the grand distinction that exists between the principles of legislation and those of private morality. This distinction is admirably pointed out by a modern writer. "Moreover," says Mr. Morrell, "there is a fundamental distinction between the principles of legislation and those of private morality, which should never be lost sight of. The former principles *suppose* the existence of the latter, and must proceed in strict accordance with them, whether it appears a matter of policy to do so or not. The object of the jurist is, simply to take men with their moral feelings as they are; already fixed and determined, and so to direct their actions, as to bring about the greatest welfare of the community. Morality says, "Fiat justitia ruat celum," jurisprudence points out *in what way* justice is to be done, so as to tend to the happiness of the whole nation. The one gives the absolute rule of action, the other only directs the details for social purposes. Moral law is immediately from God; political law, though springing from moral principles, is an adaptation of man—the one is a code written upon the human heart; the other, a code written in the statute book of the empire, conformable, indeed, to moral law, but compiled for social utility. To morality, as a science, the utilitarian ground is entirely destructive, altering its universal and necessary aspect; in politics, utility, directed by moral precept, must be a chief element in every enactment." Morrell, History of Philosophy of 19th Century; vol. 1, p. 447.

The lectures contained in the second and third volumes of Mr. Austin's Jurisprudence, are conformed in their topics and treatment much more to the questions and principles discussed in the Roman law. To a student of the civilians and a man of Mr. Austin's mind and studies, this might have been anticipated. The consistency, the elegance, and the exhaustive method of the Roman law are so satisfactory and complete, that they forbid the disjointed and fragmentary mode of most modern writers on Jurisprudence. The subjects treated of in these volumes are the following:—Rights and Obligations, Persons and Things, Motive and Will, in connexion with which we have a discussion and examination of what the civilians call the doctrine of *culpa* in the most extensive signification of the term. This leads to the consideration of Crime, Tort, Error, Infamy, and Insanity. Jus scriptum and jus non scriptum, and matters correlate thereto, are then brought under review. This is followed by the consideration of Customary Law, and the *jus prudentibus compositum*. The "jus naturale," the "*jus civile*," and the "*jus gentium*," are treated in connexion with the Edicts of the Prætors. Then follows the subject of Equity, and an inquiry into the nature of the Edict, the Power of the Prætor, and Civil Process. Statute and Judiciary Law and Codification; Status and the Capitis Deminutio; Primary Rights and Primary Duties, conclude the second volume. This range of topics the student of the Roman law, will at once perceive includes almost the whole of what the Germans call the "*Rechtsinstitute*" of classical Jurisprudence."

The lectures in the third volume continue and complete what remained. The Consideration of Property—that is to say of Dominium, and the various kinds of Servitudes. In these concluding lectures the principal maxims of Servitudes are discussed, namely, "res servit," "nulli res sua servit," and "servitus in non faciendo consistit." This is followed by the Law of Pignus and Hypotheca, whilst the whole concludes with some further investigations as to rights *in rem*, and rights *in personam ;* the consideration of Titles, or of Investitive and Divestitive facts. Such are the contents of the noble volumes before us. We have felt a strong temptation to present the views of Mr. Austin on some of the more prominent points of this book, and for this purpose had selected as topics, Rights, Obligations, and Interpretation. But the limits of a review preclude the consideration of these themes. To compare Mr. Austin's views and treatment with those of the classical jurists would be interesting and instructive. This must, however, be reserved for another place, and another opportunity. It is due to Mr. Austin to observe, that in these lectures there is a freshness of style and treatment which, notwithstanding the technical nature of the topics on which he writes, renders the book deeply interesting. Although an unfinished production there is a freedom even in the style and composition that contrasts favourably with the earlier lectures. Notwithstanding the rigid scientific exactness of the language employed in the first lectures, it has been felt that there was a certain hardness about the phrase that was in many instances apt to repel. We have observed years since in the first edition certain amusing notes in the margin of a copy belonging to a public library reflecting upon our author for this very defect. As a somewhat frequent reader of the copy alluded to we felt it our duty to explain to the librarian that we had not the honour of the authorship of these annotations. As this "*cacoethes scribendi*" is always infectious, it is possible that these interesting comments on Mr. Austin's style have obtained since the period referred to considerable additions. This, however, is a small matter. Mr. Austin's work will remain an imperishable monument of his industry, his rare intellect, and his devotion to the Science of Law. These volumes are assuredly the productions of a genius and a profound thinker. They treat upon the highest topic save one that can engage the human intellect. They ought to find a place in the library of every jurist, philosopher, and statesman in the empire. What was said by Quintilian of Cicero may be appropriately applied to Mr. Austin:—"Ille se profecisse sciat, cui Augustino valde placebit."

Art. X.—EQUALITY BEFORE THE LAW IN THE COURTS OF THE UNITED STATES.

LETTER of the Hon. John Appleton, Chief-Justice of Maine, to the Hon. Charles Sumner. Appended to a Report of "the Committee on Slavery and the Treatment of Freedmen," printed for the use of the Senate of the United States.

Bangor, *January* 24, 1864.

My dear Sir,—During the second session of the thirty-seventh Congress, when the Bill "in Relation to the Competency of Witnesses" was before the Senate, I perceive that an amendment you proposed, "that there shall be no exclusion of any witness on account of colour," was rejected after debate. In the present session, a Bill to effect the same object has been offered by the Hon. Mr. Lovejoy, of Illinois. As this question may again come up for discussion, and as it appertains to the domain of jurisprudence rather than of politics, I propose to call your attention to the present condition of the law on the subject, and to show the imperative need of a radical change therein, so far as relates to the administration of the law in the courts of the United States.

The due enforcement of the law in no slight degree depends upon its rules in reference to the admission or rejection of testimony. The law to be enforced—the substantive part—that which commands or prohibits, may be the perfection of legislative wisdom; yet, if by reason of exclusionary rules, the proof necessary for the establishment of existing facts is not forthcoming, the law however wise, becomes powerless, and to the extent thus rendered powerless might as well not be.

By the Act of July 16, 1862, chap. 189, "it is provided that the laws of the State in which the court shall be held, shall be the rule of decision as to the competency of witnesses in the courts of the United States in trials at common law, in equity, and in admiralty." That Congress can, constitutionally, fix and determine the rules of evidence by which the courts of the United States shall be governed in all cases within their jurisdiction, was assumed in the Judiciary Act of 1789, and is assumed in and by the passage of the Act just referred to.

But the laws of the several States are at variance as to the admissibility of witnesses. In some there are exclusions enormous in extent and disastrous in result. I refer to the exclusion of negroes and those of mixed descent, whether bond or free, and to Indians—by the former of which, in some of the States, the majority of the whole population are disabled from testifying for or against the dominant class; by the latter of which, the original occupants of the soil are denied by the higher civilisation, which has wrested from them their lands, even the capacity to be heard as witnesses in the courts of those who now occupy and enjoy them.

I shall enter into no discussions as to the morality of slavery. Its rightfulness; its patriarchal antiquity; its Christian graces, and its moral beauties may be admitted; it may be conceded to be what many learned divines claim it is—an institution alike beneficial to master and to slave, sanctioned and approved by the laws of God and of man—the grandest and purest realisation on earth of the golden rule, "that whatsoever ye would that men should do to you, do ye even so to them;" or it may be what the illustrious founder of methodism so pithily and tersely described it—the sum of all villanies. In either view, for the institution is one in regard to the character of which theologians differ where moralists agree, the need of the testimony excluded is none the less apparent, and its reception none the less important.

In relation to all matters over which Congress has jurisdiction, or which are within the cognizance of the courts of the United States, we must be regarded as one nation. The acts of Congress extend over the whole people. They should be everywhere the same; they should be uniform in their operation. The idea of opposing and conflicting legislation for the several States no one would entertain for a moment. If, instead of a general law embracing all the States, there were several and distinct statutes on the same subject-matter—as one tariff for South Carolina, and another and distinct tariff for Massachusetts, to say nothing of its unconstitutionality—such legislation would never be submitted to. We should cease to be one people.

But if the rules of evidence, by and through which alone the facts to which the law is to be applied are ascertained, are diverse and conflicting in different States, it is manifest that in fact the laws to be enforced will be thus diverse and conflicting in their operation, because by reason of such admissions of witnesses in one State and the exclusions of the same in another, different judicial results must necessarily ensue. The statute may be the same in each State, but it is only so in name. A murder is committed on the high seas by a white man. The only witnesses to its commission are black men. The murderer, if tried in South Carolina, is acquitted—black men not being permitted there to testify. If tried in Massachusetts, with the same proof which existed and was attainable in South Carolina, but the reception of which was prohibited by its laws, he would be convicted. Practically, the law of the United States, as thus administered in accordance with the local law of evidence, prohibits and punishes murder only when committed in the presence of white men in certain States of the Union, and in the rest when committed in the presence of any man or men without respect to their colour. Crime is punished or not according to the statute law of the State in which the trial is had, and the legislation of Congress ceases to be uniform over the whole nation.

Uniformity in the administration of the law is unattainable if the rules of evidence, by and through which it is administered, are conflicting and contradictory. It would be deemed absurd enough if a State were to establish different rules as to the admission or rejection of witnesses in its several towns and counties. If a bill were before Congress by which interested witnesses were to be admitted to testify in Maine, and were excluded in Massachusetts; by which the colour of the witness should suffice for rejection in Virginia, but should not in Maryland; by which all copper-coloured men were declared to be so untrustworthy in Mississippi that they should not even be heard, while in Alabama no objection to their admission was allowed, and so on, with varying rules in the different States, propably few members would be found to give it support. But if these different rules exist in the several States, and receive the sanction of congressional adoption, wherein consists the difference? There can be no uniform administration of justice. If the rules of evidence vary; if the witnesses by whom the facts can be proved are received in one State and rejected in another, it is obvious, that with the same facts existing, provable by the same witnesses, before the same judge, under the same law, the results will vary as the needed and indispensable proof is admitted or excluded. Thus, while the statutes of the United States extend in terms over its whole territory, their successful enforcement will depend upon the latitude and longitude of the place where the attempt is made.

Were Congress to pass a general law defining the acts which shall be deemed offences and prescribing the punishment consequent upon their commission, and should further enact that when committed in the presence of black men or Indians they should not be punishable in one half of the States, and that in the other half, when so committed, they should be punished, the advocates of such legislation would not, it is to be hoped, be very numerous. But passing general statutes creating offences, and then enacting another general law adopting the rules of evidence of the several States by which blacks and Indians are excluded, and at the same time those of other States, where they are admitted, is doing this and no more.

The consequence of all this is, that while by one and the same statute a general law is established over the whole Union, by another and equally general law adopting the discordant and conflicting rules of evidence of the different States, the first is in part repealed, and its uniformity of action and effect is prevented. The same law is to be administered, but with contrariant and opposite rules of evidence, and of necessity with different and opposite judgments. Now, it matters little whether there be different statutes for the different States prescribing different laws, or whether there be one and the same statute for all, with another statute commanding the judges in administering the law to adopt different and conflicting rules in the ascertainment of facts in the different localities in which it may be their duty to administer it. Uniformity in legislation is an axiomatic principle. But here disconformity is required and established by statute.

Of the various and conflicting rules of evidence thus adopted by Congress, some are good and some are bad, some are wise and some are unwise. Thus, in some States, interested witnesses are excluded, in others not. In some, men are prohibited from testifying because their bodies are black or copper-coloured. In others, these formidable proofs of testimonial untrustworthiness are disregarded, and black and copper-coloured men are examined as witnesses. Of rules thus opposed, both cannot be right, both cannot be equally wise and equally conducive to the ends of justice.

In this conflict as to the rules of evidence in the several States, it is not the duty of statesmen to adopt all, good or bad, and with an impartial indifference to their goodness or badness, but to select the good, those which are conducive to the great end of justice, correct decision, and to reject those which, in their tendency lead to misdecision.

Unless this be done, unless uniform rules of evidence are established throughout the whole Union in the courts of the United States, the uniform action of any statute passed by Congress is delusive and unreal.

The expediency and necessity of uniformity in legislation being seen, the inquiry naturally arises, Which of two conflicting and opposite rules of evidence is to be preferred, regard being had to their conduciveness to correct decision. In other words, is the admission of negroes and Indians as witnesses favourable or adverse to the judicial ascertainment of the truth? They have the form of our common humanity; they have all the organs of sense; they can perceive, and perceiving, can make known their perceptions to others; that is, they have all the essential requisites of witnesses. Why not hear them?

The sources of evidence are everywhere the same. Shall those sources be rendered available for the purposes of justice? The gravity and importance of the question will be more fully appreciated when it is remembered that the inquiry relates not to the exclusion of a solitary witness—as the exceptional atheist or the occasional convict—but that it involves that of millions; the rejection of distinct races of men; the aborginal inhabitants of two continents, and their descendants, as destitute of testimonial veracity. As though there were any races—as though the Almighty had so failed and bungled in the great work of creation that there was any race of men of whom falsehood was the rule, and truth the exception.

That judicial action requires, or should require, for its basis, proof; that this should be sought for from all available sources; that existing, no matter where, it should be rendered forthcoming for the purposes of justice, would seem to be propositions so self-evident as to require neither argument nor illustration. That the sources from which evidence would be sought should vary in relative trustworthiness was to be expected, for witnesses in a cause cannot be selected in advance. When the burglar will enter the dwelling; when the assassin will stab; when the knave will defraud; when the dishonest will evade the obligations of his contract, can neither be foreseen nor foreknown; for if foreseen or foreknown, the entry of the burglar, the stab of the assassin, the frauds of the knave, would have been guarded against and prevented; the violated contract would not have been made. Proof, therefore, must necessarily be had from sources corresponding to the act or contract to be proved; from the parties to the act or contract; from their accomplices and associates; their friends and relatives; from any and all who may have had knowledge of the transactions to be investigated.

No rule can be established in advance by which the degree of credit to which a witness should be entitled can be predetermined. The same law of nature by which the size, the strength, the complexion, is seen to vary, will equally exist in reference to clearness of perception, strength of recollection, and integrity of narration. Whether the perception of a witness is acute, his memory good, his integrity unimpeachable, can only be known after and consequent upon examination. Common-sense requires a hearing in each particular case before deciding upon the greater or less degree of credence to be given to the witness. Of individuals, or of classes, there are none of whom falsehood can certainly be predicated in any particular instance. Exclusion, because of anticipated falsehood, is decision without and before hearing; decision adverse to the integrity of the witness. The law in one phase of its action, when the criminal is on trial, presumes his innocence; when a witness is to be called in all its exclusions, the presumption is of guilt—anticipated perjury—to prevent which the witness is excluded; crime on the part of the witness, on its own part incompetency utter and irremediable, else there would be neither fear nor danger in receiving proof, against the truth of which the court excluding seems to be so fully and entirely warned.

However difficult it may be, after the full benefit of examination, and cross-examination, after a careful comparison of one witness with another, to award to each the precise degree of credence which his testimony may merit, it is still more difficult to decide this without and before such hearing and comparison. Caution necessary in all cases may be more particularly required, therefore, when there is danger of undue credence. But caution and exclusion are entirely different. Caution places the judge on his guard against sinister bias, gives him all possible material for correct decision, but demands discretion and judgment in the use of the means furnished. Exclusion withholds and denies, in whole or in part, the materials indispensable for just decision. If the evidence excluded be true, no conceivable reason can exist for its rejection. Whether it will be true or false cannot be foreknown. Neither legislative nor judicial assumption can claim infallibility, yet excluding, such is the assumption. Misdecision, the excluded evidence being material, true, and unattainable from any other source, is seen to be inevitable. If the evidence be not true, that misdecision would ensue from its reception, is by no means certain. If false, its very falsity, made manifest from other sources, would be an article of circumstantial evidence of no ordinary probative force in inducing correct decision. Presumed imbecility on the part of the judge of fact; presumed guilt, or rather guilt presumed on the part of the witness, if an opportunity to testify should occur: such the logic of exclusion. How can legislators foreknow that future judges, whose capacity and whose person are alike unknown, will be deceived by unknown witnesses of whose integrity and existence they are equally ignorant. But exclusion presupposes a judgment of which such exclusion is the consequence—a judgment without knowledge, or the possibility of knowledge of the veracity or want of veracity of those excluded, which determines the future perjury of the excluded class as preponderantly probable, and the future inability of all judges to justly decide on their testimony as reasonably certain.

The exclusion of testimony from whatsoever source

is presumably wrong. Exclude evidence material and unattainable from any other source for whatsoever reason, plausible or otherwise; exclude evidence, and to the extent of and in proportion to the importance of the evidence excluded, the judge of fact is deprived of the means of forming a correct judgment upon the facts. Exclude for any reason all evidence, and it remains only to determine the rights of litigants by lot.

He who would exclude material evidence, attainable from any source, is bound to give satisfactory reasons for such exclusion.

The reason assigned for excluding negroes and Indians as witnesses is "the degrated state in which they are placed by the laws of the State." They will steal and lie. Finding their own labour appropriated for the benefit of others, and looking at the subject from a somewhat different stand-point from that of their masters, that slaves, whenever they have, or deem they have, a safe opportunity, should, without fully appreciating the heinousness of their offence, or the benefits conferred by mastership over them, make reprisals of their own earnings, may well be deemed a natural result of "the degraded state in which they are placed by the laws of the State." So it would be strange if they had a chivalric regard for truth or were models of veracity. The plantation is hardly a better school for morals than for manners. The slave will probably be more addicted to falsehood than the freeman. It is the result of his condition. Falsehood is perhaps the weapon, whether of offence or defence, most readily available, and the use of which is attended with the least danger.

But whether there will be truth or falsehood in any case, and from any individual, will depend upon the motives acting upon him, when and where he may be testifying, and upon their strength. The black as the white man, the bond equally with the free, are influenced by motives, and their testimony will be the resultant of those motives and their strength. There are no motives impelling one race to truth or to falsehood, which do not operate upon the other. The same motives at different times and under different circumstances may vary in their strength and intensity with different individuals or with the same individual. So, too, the tendency of the same motive may at one time be in the direction of falsehood, at another in that of veracity. Neither the motives nor their strength nor their direction depend upon the colour of the skin or the woolliness of the hair. So far as the motives to the action of which an individual stands exposed tend in the direction of truth, the testimony delivered under their influence may be expected to be true. Wherever their tendency is adverse to the truth, falsehood may be anticipated. Motion is never in a direction contrary to that of the force impelling. The laws of matter are no more constant and unvarying than those of the mind. In no instance will the testimony, whether of the black, the copper-coloured, or the white man, be adverse to the balance of motives affecting his mind and determining his conduct.

All men, the most vicious, the most false, the most indifferent to the obligations of integrity, utter the truth rather than falsehood. Truth is the language of nature; falsehood the rare and occasional exception. The greatest liar, no matter how depraved he may be, usually speaks the truth. The reason is obvious. Invention is the work of labour. To narrate facts in the order of their occurrence, to tell what one has seen or heard, is in accordance with the very laws of our being. To avoid doing this is a work of difficulty. Falsely to add to what has happened, carefully to insert a dexterous lie, requires ingenuity greater or less, according to the greater or less skill with which the lie is dovetailed amid the surrounding truths. No matter how cunning the artifice, the web cannot be so woven that the stained and coloured thread shall not be perceived. Love of ease, fear of labour, the physical sanction, are ever co-operating in favour of truth. Any motive, however slight and infinitesimal it is, may be sufficient to induce action in a right direction, unless overborne by other and superior motives in a sinister direction. By a sort of impulse, by the very course of nature, the usual tendency of speech is in the line of truth. There lives not, there never lived, there never will live the man of whose statements truth may not be predicted as the rule, and falsehood the exception. Society could not subsist were it otherwise. Even in plantation life, the same rule must apply. In the intercourse of slaves with each other, with their masters, with all, truth must be the rule, falsehood exceptional. As in the ordinary intercourse of life, so it would be with judicially delivered statements. Indeed, his testimony, when uttered under the sanctions of an oath, and under the penalties of the law, would be more likely to be true, however rude and uncultivated the witness, unless those sanctions and penalties are to be regarded as in their tendency adverse to the truth.

In the great mass of cases truth might be expected. Intentional falsehood could never be anticipated unless when the witness is exposed to the influence of some motive acting with overwhelming force in a sinister direction. But no motive tending to falsehood, and every motive tending to truth, or the balance of motives having such tendency, truth would necessarily be the result, for men, however black, copper-coloured or white, never act without motive, nor against motives, nor the balance of motives. There is no greater probability of any or all motives acting in a sinister direction upon one race than another, for are we not all children of our common father? There may be errors, but they will be those of deficient perception, defective memory, or inadequate expression—sources of error arising not from the colour of the skin or the crisp of the hair.

The truth being the general rule, if the testimony is received, is material, and true, and being true is believed, justice is done; when, without its reception, injustice must have inevitably occurred.

But with the black, copper-coloured, bond or free, as with the white man, the motives operating upon the witness may tend in a sinister direction and the testimony may be false. This, however, is no more peculiar to one race than to another. May not the same be said of the white man? But what does the judge in case of the white witness? He is exposed to the same danger. He cannot foreknow his truth. He may therefore be deceived. Does he then decline to hear him? Not he. Hearing, he weighs, compares, and decides. Falsehood by its very nature is ever a source of danger to the person uttering it. Inconsistent with every true fact, inconsistent with every true witness, it is by its very nature exposed to detection and liable to refutation from any and every quarter. Of the statements of any witness part may be true and part false. The truth ever endangers the lie.

In the case of white witnesses, the judge relies upon the efficacy of cross-examination. Is that any the less efficacious with the slave than with his master? Is the intellect of the black man so acute, that he can baffle the sagacity of counsel? Are his perceptions so quick, that he can elude vigilant watchfulness of the experienced judge?

But suppose falsehood the exceptional case by the very constitution of our nature, still the danger of deception is not as the danger of falsehood. If the testimony, being false, is not believed, injustice is not done. But too implicit credence is not a danger to be feared on the part of those who would exclude. Is the intellect of the judge darkened by hearing black witnesses? Is the judge, distrustful and diffident, competent to weigh white testimony and to accord to it the just measure of its trustworthiness, and does his capacity fail him when the colour of the witness changes?

Where the witnesses are of either of the excluded races, and their testimony, being true, material, and necessary, is not received, injustice is inevitable.

The exclusion cannot be on account of the falsehood of the excluded witness, for in no particular instance can it be known in advance, by the legislation which excludes what the witness would say.

The judge will hardly rest the exclusion of this testimony upon his incapacity to give it its due weight, he being capable to weigh that of the dominant race.

Neither is the exclusion on the ground of the servile condition of the excluded testimony, for when the black man or Indian is on trial, whether bond or free, the black witness or the Indian, whether bond or free, is permitted to give testimony for or against those of his own race. Such is the general rule.

Now it may be fairly assumed that the dominant and law-making race, when enacting laws for and imposing penalties upon the servile class or upon a degraded caste, do not desire that innocence should be punished, or that guilt should escape. When a black man is tried and black witnesses are examined, the judge of fact, by whatsoever name called, hears the evidence, and decides in whole or in part upon it. Is it deceptive? If so, why receive it? Is he incompetent to determine its just force and effect? If so, why make the attempt? Or does this species of evidence afford a satisfactory basis for a decision? If it affords no true basis for decision—if it is productive of misdecision—if such is the teaching of experience, why not repeal the law? Why receive testimony intrinsically untrustworthy against anybody? Is the law-giver or the judge indifferent to injustice? is it immaterial to him whether it be done to the black man or not? To him justice is none the less desirable than if his complexion were lighter. Nor is his condition so desirable that he can any better dispense with justice than those of the dominant class.

Assuredly the master, purporting to administer justice, will not admit that he is indifferent whether it be administered or not; still less will he deny that he administers it. Judicially determining controversies between black men in criminal prosecutions against slaves, he had admitted witnesses of the same race, and of the servile class. He had found their reception, on the whole, favourable, or adverse to the ends of justice. If adverse, and such testimony continues to be received, then does the dominant and law-giving race stand self-convicted of the deliberate and wanton infliction of the deep wrong of injustice upon the servient race. If tending to misdecision, and that fact is known, as it must be known, no language of indignant reprobation and scorn can be undeserved.

If, on the other hand, the testimony is conducive to correct decision, when blacks are parties, and its continued admission is proof of the fact, what reason can be given why the same testimony should not be received between free men of the different races, and in prosecutions against slaves? The experiment of black witnesses has been tried. The evidence trustworthy as between blacks, would it at once become deceptive if admitted in suits where the parties were of the black and white races?

The importance, the necessity of the testimony of black men and Indians, bond or free, in controversies between those of their respective races, is recognised. None the less important and necessary is the admission of the same evidence in suits between those of the master class and those of a degraded caste. Is it any the less desirable that the white man should do justice to the negro or the Indian, than that the negro or the Indian should do justice to the white, or than that the black and copper-coloured men should do justice to each other? If the black man or the Indian is to have his rights as against the white man, is he not entitled to the same witnesses against the white man which the latter has against the former?

Is justice to be administered according to colour? At Athens, in ages past, justice was symbolled as blind, with bandaged eyes, that she might not know the parties. No such symbolic impartiality can be ascribed to American justice. The bandage is removed that she may discern the colour of litigants and witnesses, for she metes out her judgments, not upon inflexible principles of right, but according to the varying complexions of her suitors. Between black litigants she receives all men as witnesses. When the parties are black and white, or copper-coloured and white, she receives only white witnesses, and excludes the black or copper-coloured.

The law-making class receive testimony in suits between parties of the black race, which they reject when they are of that and the white race: the colour the cause of the difference. Was the testimony rightfully received in the one case? Why not in the other? There may have been no other attainable proof in the former: equally so in the latter. *Penuria testium* a civil law excuse for admitting testimony, the reception of which needs no apology, applies alike in each case, provided correct decision be the object sought to be obtained.

In controversies of this character it can hardly happen that there shall not be percipient witnesses of the facts in dispute belonging to each race. Those of one are received, while those of the other are rejected. The deliberate exclusion of testimony is the deliberate self-deprivation of the means of correct decision. With but half of a cause, with but fragments of the truth, what hope can there be that justice will be done?

But here, too, it may be urged, the testimony may be false—a reason applicable to all testimony; valid for disbelief after hearing, never for rejection before hearing; for whether true or false, could never be foreknown of any witness before hearing. Excluding is judging without hearing. Of what conceivable witness, of what race, can it be predicated with absolute certainty that the testimony will be true or will be false? The contingent possibility of falsehood is no reason for the exclusion of probable truth.

But the testimony being false, the judge may be deceived. What likelihood of deception and consequent misdecision on his part, adverse to the law-making and testimony-excluding class? His sympathies are adverse—so adverse to the admission of the testimony that he would not even hear. Hearing, will he be unduly credulous of witnesses, of the untrustworthiness of whom he was beforehand so fully satisfied that he insisted upon their peremptory exclusion? If hearing, he should believe, what stronger, what more assured proof of its truthfulness than that, forgetting the prejudices of colour and of caste, he has given reluctant credence to testimony he would not willingly have heard? By so doing, justice is done to the black. Is not that what the judge wishes to do—insists he is doing—seeks all available means of doing; but which the law denies him the opportunity of doing, whenever the requisite proof is withheld?

If disbelieved, still the wisdom of the admission is none the less apparent. It is not merely desirable that justice be done, but that it seem to be done. When all the material needed for correct decision is before the court, it may, nevertheless, err; but possible error with the means of correct decision, affords no reason for withholding the means essential to that end. If the certainty of correct decision is not greater with than without proof, better resort to chance, to the lot, and abide the issue.

Whether justice is to be administered to the rich man or the poor, to the native-born or the foreigner, to the slave or the freeman, to the white, the copper-coloured, or the black man, the rules of evidence best fitted to elicit truth from every source, from lips willing and unwilling, should be adopted. The object, in all cases, the same—the ascertainment of the truth. The rules for the black man cannot vary from those for the white—for the bond from those for the free. The same end being alike sought, the means for its attainment cannot be variant.

It was decided in Com. *vs.* Oldham, 1 Dana, 466; and in William *vs.* Blincoe, 1 Lit., 171, that a free man of colour might, by his oath, require a white man to keep the peace. "A free man of colour," remarks Robertson, C.J., "may sue and be sued. When he is plaintiff he may swear for the continuance of the cause. He may make an affidavit requiring bail. They are incident to his freedom, and without them he would be virtually disfranchised. And when he swears to facts against a white man to compel to keep the peace, he is not a 'witness,'* but a party swearing to what any

* A free person of colour is not a witness in the courts of South Carolina, even when the parties are of his class.—Groning *vs.* Devana, 2 Bailey, 192.

other party may." The black man is allowed to swear the peace against his white neighbour and compel him to give bonds to keep the peace. But is he not a witness then? Does he not testify? Is not an oath administered; and, being administered, does not the magistrate base official action upon his testimony? Does he not so far believe the witness as to require the white man to give security to keep the peace? A witness thus far, because, if not to this extent, "he would be virtually disfranchised." Suppose the white man breaks the peace; is the black then received to testify? Not at all. Is he not then virtually disfranchised, if, on a trial for a breach of the peace for an assault committed, his testimony is rejected? If allowed to testify for the purpose of preventing a wrong, why should he be prohibited from testifying when the wrong is done? What is the security good for if, when the bond is broken, he cannot be a witness in a suit for its enforcement?

Indeed, as the law now is in all the slave, and in many of the free States, a white man may commit any and all conceivable outrages upon the persons and property of the negro and Indian, in the presence of any number of either of those races, bond or free—he may perpetuate any fraud upon, or violate any contract with them—and all this with entire impunity, unless they can establish the facts required for redress by the testimony of white witnesses. Unlimited license to commit any crime upon, or to do any wrong to, the black and copper-coloured races, is thus awarded to the white man, unless those of his own complexion are present. Shall Congress sanction the enormities resulting from such laws, by establishing them as those by and under which its own statutes are to be enforced? Well might Montesquieu say, "it is impossible for us to suppose these creatures to be men; because by allowing them to be men, a suspicion would follow that we ourselves are not Christians."

In cases, civil and criminal, in which the dominant race are the litigants, the necessity of this testimony is none the less than in those where the parties are of different races, yet the exclusion is made peremptory "when the parties are free white Christians."*

It seems to have been settled with great deliberation that a master may shoot his slave, male or female, by way of correction, and that he is not liable therefore to indictment.† This general right of shooting is recognised as one of the necessary incidents of ownership, and its exercise is limited to the owner. If a white man, therefore, having no right of property, should shoot a slave, he would be held liable to the owner for the injury done his property.‡ Suppose the slave only wounded and the only witness, or, if killed, black men only witness his murder; is property not to receive protection? Is not the owner entitled to his actual damage? Without this evidence anybody may shoot slaves for amusement or revenge, with great detriment to the rights of property, provided it be done out of sight of white men.

So, too, in criminal cases, the black man may be the only

* In Rusk *v.* Sawerwine, 3 How. and Johns., 97, Nicholson, C.J., held Minta was an incompetent witness; the plaintiff and defendant being free white Christian persons. The plaintiff appealed, and the case was argued before Chase, C.J., Buchanan, Gant, and Earl, justices, when the judgment was affirmed.

† In State *vs.* Mann, 2 Dev., 263, the defendant was indicted for an assault and battery upon Lydia, the slave of one Elizabeth Jones. On the trial, it appeared that the defendant had hired the slave for a year; that during the term the slave had committed some small offence, for which the defendant undertook to chastise her; that while in the act of so doing, the slave ran off; whereupon the defendant called upon her to stop, which being refused, he shot at and wounded her. The judge in the court below charged the jury, that if they believed the punishment inflicted by the defendent was cruel and unwarrantable, and disproportionate to the offence committed by the slave, that in law the defendant was guilty, as he had only a special property in the slave. A verdict was returned for the State, and the defendant appealed. The judgment below was reversed; and judgment was entered for the defendant.

‡ Trespass for killing the plaintiff's slave. It appeared the slave was stealing potatoes from a bank near defendant's house. The defendant fired upon him with a gun loaded with buck and killed him. The jury found a verdict for plaintiff for one dollar.

Nott, J., held there must be a new trial; that if the jury were of opinion the slave was of a bad character, some deduction from the usual price must be made; but the plaintiff was certainly entitled to his actual damage for killing his slave.—(Richardson *vs.* Duke, 4 McCord, 156; Wallis *vs.* Frazier, 2 N. and McCord, 516.)

witness by whom the innocence of the accused can be established. Innocent, and the witness black, if the testimony is rejected, the innocent white man must suffer the penalty of guilt. The accused guilty, the testimony of black men the only existing proof, its rejection necessitates an acquittal, and guilt escapes punishment.

The need of this testimony becomes still more apparent if it be the design of government to enforce its own laws. If half the population of a State capable of being witnesses were to be excluded on account of size or sex, how manifest it is that with such exclusions the attempt to do justice would be almost hopeless. Colour affords no more logical reason for exclusion than size or sex.

In controversies between those of the white race, it is not a matter of privilege to the black man, who has no interest in the controversy, that he be permitted to testify, any more than it would be to the white man under like circumstances. If being a material and needed witness, either is excluded, it is the cause of justice that is endangered. Justice is equally denied when suitors are refused access to her temple, as, when having access, they are prohibited the use of the testimony by which alone right can be established.

But why not hear this testimony in suits between, or in prosecutions against, white persons? It is none the less needed because the parties are white. Is the judge of fact, howsoever called—chancellor, judge, or juryman—any the less able to weigh the evidence of black persons because the colour of the parties litigant differs from that of the excluded race? Self-satisfied with his ability to judge of the trustworthiness of black witnesses, when the parties are of the same colour, does his judicial ability vanish upon a change of colour on the part of the suitor? Receiving this testimony with parties of the black or Indian races, and weighing or assuming to weigh it, cannot he do the same thing when white men are litigating before him? The judge competent for his position, is he so afraid of the seductive influence of black witnesses that he will not trust himself to hear them? Is the black man more untrustworthy when parties are white than when black? Is he more deceptious? Does the ability of the judge vary with the varying races and conditions of those to whom he is meting out justice? If not, then he can weigh this testimony as well when one race is litigating as another, and it has been seen he has no scruple to use it where the parties and the witnesses are of the same colour The real danger is not of undue credence, but that, hearing, the judge will not give it the weight to which it is justly entitled. But that objection is not open to the advocate of exclusion, who protests that it is so utterly unreliable that he is unwilling even to hear it.

Exclusion, let it be remembered, depends not on the *status* of the witness, for free blacks and slaves are alike admissible for or against those of their own race, whether bond or free. Where the rights of the dominant race are involved, the black, though free, is excluded. The admissibility of witnesses is made to depend not upon their condition, but upon their colour alone.

No other instance can be found in the legislation of any nation, civilised, semi-civilised, or barbarous, in which free men have been rejected as witnesses because of their colour. By the civil law slaves were not admitted to testify. Such, too, is the Mahometan law on this subject. But the exclusion is limited to the slave. When free, he is at once a competent witness, irrespective of his colour or his descent.*

The negro and the Indian are excluded on account of colour. After successive intermixtures of their races with the white, varying in the different States, their descendants are received. The white race being regarded as the type of truth, the more it is intermingled with the degraded castes, the more trust-

* By our treaty with Mexico, by which we obtained California, we guaranteed that citizens of the ceding republic should have equal rights with those of the republic to which the cession was made. Yet the moment California became ours, the negro and the Indian, though citizens of the ceding republic, and by their law s witnesses, were at once deprived of testimonial capacity.

worthy the witness—the mulatto than the negro, the quadroon than the mulatto—till, at length, after sufficiently numerous acts of illicit intercourse, continued through successive generations, testimonial trustworthiness is restored.

The exclusion of evidence is the unmistakable proof of deficient civilisation. The barbarian refuses to have witnesses, and resorts to ordeals by fire and by water. Unwilling to trust his own judgment, he is willing to trust to chance. He prefers exclusion to investigation. Rather than weigh testimony he would reject it. He excludes the Mahometan, and is in return excluded by him, and for the self-same reason that the belief of the judge excluding differs from that of the witness excluded. Of all exclusions, the one most libellous upon humanity, most blashemous to Deity, is that by which whole races of men are prohibited from testifying on account of their colour, as if mendacity were the result of their having a greater amount of pigment cells, and a greater number of cutaneous glands; as if the Almighty had so failed as to have created whole races of men so untrustworthy that it would be unsafe even to hear their testimony. But barbarous methods for the investigation of truth recede before the advance of civilisation. The ordeal has passed away. The judicial lot has ceased. Interested witnesses are received. The Christian hears the Mahometan, and whether the Mahometan reciprocates depends upon the distance he has receded from barbarism. Testimony is judged by weight, not by count—after, and not before and without hearing. I trust the time will soon come when it will cease to be a reproach to this age and nation that whole races of men are prohibited from testimony, not from any fault of theirs, but because God in his wisdom has seen fit to impress upon their form a browner or a blacker skin than upon the bodies of the race by whose legislation they are excluded. I am, very truly, yours, &c., JOHN APPLETON.

Hon. Charles Sumner,

Senate of the United States.

Art. XI.—RESTRAINT OF CORRUPTION AT ELECTIONS.*

THIS paper has a practical object and one idea. Can a moral enthusiasm be roused, and moral influences brought to bear widely and effectively, by combined efforts of individuals, against bribery and extravagant expenditure at elections which legislation is powerless to destroy? Can this Association organize or initiate such an action?

I couple extravagant expenditure with bribery, and need hardly explain that the greater part of the expenses of expensively contested elections are virtual corruption. The expensiveness of elections, independently of bribery, may be regarded as a social question deserving the attention of social reformers, inasmuch as it restricts the area of choice of representatives, helps wealth against intellect, thwarts political earnestness, and degrades constituencies. Mr. John Mill, in denouncing the expenses of elections as "one of the most conspicuous vices of the existing electoral system," forcibly points out the importance of the ruling idea under which elections are conducted and votes sought and given, and suggests the effect on an elector's mind, auxiliary to corruption, of the simple fact of a patent large expenditure by candidates to gain a seat in Parliament. "In a good representative system," says Mr. Mill, "there would be no election expenses to be borne by the candidate. Their effect is wholly pernicious. Politically, they constitute a property qualification of the worst kind. Morally, it is still worse; not only by the profligate and demoralising character of much of the expenditure, but by the corrupting effect of the notion inculcated on the voter, that the person he votes for should pay a large sum of money for permission to serve the public. They must be poor politicians who do not know the

* A Paper by Mr. W. D. Christie (late Minister at Brazil), read at a Meeting of the Jurisprudence Department of the National Association for the Promotion of Social Science, held on Monday, 22nd February, 1864.

efficacy of such indirect moral influences. The incidental circumstances which surround a public act, and betoken the expectation entertained by society in regard to it, irrevocably determine the moral sentiment which adheres to the act in the mind of an average individual. So long as the candidate himself, and the customs of the world, seem to regard the function of a Member of Parliament less as a duty to be discharged than as a personal favour to be solicited, no effort will avail to implant in an ordinary voter the feeling that the election of a Member of Parliament is a matter of duty, and that he is not at liberty to bestow the vote on any other consideration than that of personal fitness. The necessary expenses of an election, those which concern all the candidates equally, should, it has often been urged, be defrayed either by the municipal body or by the State. With regard to the sources of expense which are personal to the individual candidate, committees, canvassing, even printing and public meetings, it is in every way better that these things should not be done at all, unless done by the gratuitous zeal, or paid for by the contributions, of his supporters. Even now there are several Members of Parliament whose elections cost them nothing, the whole expense being defrayed by their constituents: of these members we may be completely assured that they are elected from public motives; that they are the men whom the voters really wish to see elected, in preference to all others, either on account of the principles they represent, or the services they are thought qualified to render." *

Perfection is unattainable in this world, and a perfect representative system is an impossibility. Human nature has everywhere engendered bribery and rioting in popular elections for places of honour, and corruption in parliamentary government. But, though perfection is unattainable, improvement is best effected by keeping a perfect system in view as a goal, which may be neared, though it cannot be

* "Thoughts on Parliamentary Reform," by John Stuart Mill. 1859.

reached; and moral influences have already done much to purify English government. In the seventeenth century there was not only general corruption of constituencies and notorious bribery of members of Parliament, but there were also venal ministers of State. It is long since there was even a suspicion that an English Minister of State could be bribed. The corruption of members of Parliament by government bribes was rampant in the last century, and there are men living who may remember traces of it; but we may say that bribery of members of Parliament has been for many years extinct. The corruption of constituencies remains to be cured. Words used by Andrew Marvel in 1678, to describe the evil which had then suddenly assumed large proportions, are still applicable to a large number of English constituencies. "It is not to be expressed, the debauchery and lewdness which upon occasion of elections to Parliament are now grown habitual through the nation. So that the vice and the expense are risen to such a prodigious height that few sober men can endure to stand to be chosen on such conditions." *

Bishop Burnet, in the general review of the moral and social condition of England, with which he winds up the History of his own time, covering four reigns and half a century, wrote thus in 1708 on bribery at elections:—"All laws that can be made will prove ineffectual to cure so great an evil till there comes to be a change and reformation of morals in the nation. We see former laws are evaded, and so will all the laws that can be made, till the candidates and electors both become men of another temper and other principles than appear now among them." †

Since the Reform Act, and more especially since the general election of 1841, Parliament has passed a number of acts against bribery at elections; and an able historian of our

* Marvel's "Growth of Popery and Arbitrary Government in England." Works, vol. 1, p. 540.

† Burnet's "History of His Own Time," VI. 208, ed. Oxford, 1823.

own time, having passed in review this series of acts, each rapidly proved inefficacious, makes some remarks which, after the lapse of a century and a half, are an unconscious reproduction of Bishop Burnet's observation. "To repress so grave an evil," says Mr. Erskine May, in his "Constitutional History," published in 1861, "more effectual measures will doubtless be devised, but they may still be expected to fail, until bribery shall be unmistakably condemned by public opinion.' The law had treated duelling as murder, yet the penalty of death was unable to repress it; but when society discountenanced that time-honoured custom, it was suddenly abandoned. Voters may always be found to receive bribes if offered; but candidates belong to a class whom the influence of society may restrain from committing an offence condemned alike by the law and by public opinion."*

I wish to suggest whether at this moment, when a general election cannot be far distant, but while there is yet time to act on public opinion, and while, before parties are engaged in passionate contention, the voice of reason may yet be heard, an Association might not be called into existence to rouse, concentrate, and guide the moral feeling of the nation, and to arrange and superintend an extensive system of concerted practical effort, for an object which all respectable men desire, and which laws will not accomplish.

The sudden turn of feeling, which within our memories suppressed the long-cherished and strongly rooted fashion of duelling, gives encouragement to hope for good effects of a well-aimed impulse to public feeling on corruption at elections, which is not favoured, as duelling was, by opinion, but which is connived at from habit, and sheltered by charitable indulgence, and practised with compunction of conscience under the influence of circumstances, passion, rivalry, and temptation. I believe that the formation of the Anti-duelling Association in 1844 had some share in bringing about the sudden great change of public opinion on duelling which

* May's "Constitutional History of England," I., p. 390.

occurred shortly after, and I feel sure that the formation of an Association against corruption at elections, comprising the leading men of all parties, and perhaps combining for a social reform dignitaries of the Church and of the Law with the most eminent in political life, would be itself a great stride towards success.

Such an Association might of course act on opinion by large public meetings and circulation of suitable pamphlets; but I look chiefly to the following mode of action, aided by the enthusiasm which the existence of the Association would engender:

Endeavours should be made to include as many Members of Parliament and candidates for seats, and leading members of constituencies, as possible, of all parties. Every one in becoming a member of the Association would thereby pledge himself to abstain from corrupt expenditure by himself or friends, and to do everything in his power to discourage and prevent it.

Local committees composed of leading men of all parties should be organised through the constituencies. Endeavours should be made everywhere to procure agreements between opposing candidates, and opposing leaders of parties in constituencies, to abstain from bribery and to limit expenditure. Such agreements could probably be made without much difficulty in most cases some time before an election. All candidates have a strong common interest in abstaining from bribery, and election expenditure is for the most part a matter of forced habit and involuntary rivalry. There can be no doubt that it is generally the wish of the respectable leading men in all constituencies to put down bribery and profligate expenditure at elections. They know and regret the bad effects on the classes which furnish the bribed, and must care something for the reputation of their own communities. But in this as in other matters, what is everybody's business is nobody's; no one initiates a reform; political opponents do not naturally come together to talk of joint action; there are those interested in keeping up the system; the election comes on, candidates spend largely because they cannot help themselves, following the habits of the place, and one doing what the other does, and bribery is practised at the last to win, or to meet bribery. In many boroughs compulsion is put upon candidates by inferior persons, having influence among the poorer electors which they use for their own profit, and encouraging large expenditure for the same object; where one such middle-man of corruption exists on one side, his fellow is generally to be found on the other; these men might generally be overcome by previous concert between candidates and leading electors.

It is to be expected that these agreements deliberately made between gentleman and gentleman, and comprising the leading supporters on each side, would in general be honourably and completely fulfilled.

Public meetings might, if necessary, be held in constituencies to promote the desired end: in some cases, perhaps, a body of electors of different politics might act together to require from the candidates and leaders on both sides abstinence from corrupt expenditure. I should look for much aid from the clergy both of the Church and of the dissenting bodies for this movement in constituencies.

In many cases, parties will remain in the same relative position in constituencies after such an agreement. Candidates will save their money, the cause of public morality will gain, and the result of the election be the same. In other cases where a candidate could only gain his end by bribery, he and his party will make up their minds to lose by the agreement only what could not be securely won (for there always remains the danger of an election petition and its consequences;) and what one political party loses in this way in one constituency, the other will probably lose in another. The balance of parties will probably be little affected on the whole. In some of the many boroughs, where parties are nearly balanced, and a small corrupt phalanx turns the scale (and some of these are among the worst cases of corruption), there will probably be compromises, by which each party will obtain an uncontested seat. Here again the cause of public morality will gain, and the peace of the borough will be secured; and in these cases of nearly balanced parties a large minority, which a few accidents or more care in succeeding registrations might convert into a majority, has a fair claim to a share of the representation. Such compromises occurring in several constituencies would probably not disturb in the end the balance of parties. This may be considered a low mode of treating the subject, but it is well to endeavour to conciliate political partisanship.

All the money comes from candidates and wealthy supporters. If these can be got by agreement to abstain from spending money there will be no corruption.

A witness before the Committee of the House of Commons of 1860, on the Corrupt Practices Prevention Act, a gentleman of large experience in elections, Mr. Philip Rose, used a phrase in recommending suspension of writs for corrupt boroughs, which I would appropriate. Mr. Rose said, "I should treat a venal constituency as I would a drunken man, I would take away the stimulant in the hope that it would recover, and if Wakefield or Gloucester, for instance, were kept without their members for five or ten years, a new class of voters would arise in those boroughs, and corruption would be very much lessened." Now this is my plan, to take away "the stimulant." I propose to invite and incite candidates through the country to co-operate and combine to keep "the stimulant" in their own pockets. The suggested agreements and compromises will take away "the stimulant." Habits of corruption may then die away by disuse, and the appetite for bribes decay for want of the food which it has fed on.

Let us ascend from the leaders of constituencies to the leaders of parties. It is generally known that there is an organization for promotion of elections at head quarters in each party, and that, on the occasion of a general election, there have been always large subscriptions on the side of the

Government and on the side of the Opposition. The Association might begin by addressing itself to the head of the Government and the leader of the Opposition, in order to obtain their co-operation in this movement, and assurances that they will urge those, with whom respectively a word from either would be a command, and who influence many others, to abstain from everything which can excite or facilitate corrupt expenditure, and to give every aid in promoting agreements and compromises, whose object is to prevent corruption.

Patronage provides other modes of influencing votes at elections, less gross and palpable than bribery, and "lends corruption lighter wings to fly." This brings us to the subjects of our administrative system and party-government, admitted, I believe, to be within the limits of social science, but whose bounds are divided by thin partitions from the questions of passionate politics, which here must be avoided. There are thoughtful men who regard the rivalries of party and the possession of large patronage by the Government for distribution among political supporters, as necessary to good parliamentary government. I cannot think this. I regard these things as defects and blots. One of the chief advantages, I conceive, of the system of examinations for appointments which has of late years made progress among us, is its tendency to purify representative government. The full advantage can only be derived from free competitive examinations. The small places given away in all the boroughs and counties by the great public departments, the Treasury and General Post Office for instance, through political supporters, might be given as prizes of local examinations; a suggestion of this sort was made in 1844, some years before the first introduction of examinations into our administrative system, by the present Lord Grey (then Lord Howick) in the House of Commons, on the occasion of a motion by Mr. William Ewart, on public education. Lord Grey urged the institution by Government of periodical examinations in districts, for the benefit of schools of the lower orders, and added:—" Government might bring candidates to their examinations by holding out more substantial rewards to a few of the children. This could be done at no expense whatever. They all knew how earnestly situations in the lower ranks of the public service were looked for among the classes likely to send their children to these schools, and if a few such situations as those of tide-waiters for example were made prizes for perseverance, attention, and ability, the hope of winning them would attract great numbers of persons to the examinations. By a small sacrifice of patronage this important object might be attained."* I remember that I myself recalled attention to this suggestion in the House of Commons, on the occasion of another motion of Mr. Ewart's in 1846, and then read an excellent passage in recommendation of it from a letter of Mr. Dawes, the present Dean of Hereford, then a clergyman in Hampshire, zealously promoting public education in his parish, which is printed in the Minutes of the Committee of Council on Education for 1845.† I believe this to have been one of the earliest, as it is one of the most practical, suggestions of a plan which combines the advantages of extension of education, improvement of local administration, and lessening of electoral corruption. This plan of giving local appointments to local examinations has never been adopted. The plans which have been generally adopted, of appointment subject to an examination, and of nominations for limited competition, fall short of producing all the desired good. The patronage system remains. Patronage is even increased by the system of nominations for limited competition, each nomination being a favour. Members must still go to the Treasury to ask favours for their constituents, like the Roman clients thronging the patron's doorstep for the well-filled basket.

> "Nunc sportula primo
> Limine parva sedet, turbæ rapienda togatæ."

Constituencies can only be made thoroughly pure by removing all sources of corruption. So long as nominations

* Hansard, July 19, 1844. † Hansard, July 21, 1846.

can only be got by application to the Government, how can voters and Members help, or how can they be blamed for, making applications? How can the Government be expected, while the system remains, to favour their opponents?

When, eighty years ago, Mr. Pitt had defied a large adverse parliamentary majority, and successfully appealed to a general election, and stood by the result on a supereminent pinnacle of personal ascendency, one of his most attached and most celebrated friends, Mr. Wilberforce, thought (as it is recorded in his Life) that "he was then able, if he had duly estimated his position, to cast off the corrupt machinery of influence." * "Party on one side," said Mr. Wilberforce, "begets party on the other." The ungoverned fury of contending parties begets and perpetuates corruption.

The leader of a great party is in this matter in the same position and difficulty as a great many candidates for seats in Parliament, that he does not know all that is done by others. But this can hardly ever be altogether an innocent ignorance. Friends and supporters will not in the end do what the chief is really determined shall not be done. As it is, leaders and candidates are not told what goes on, and they do not inquire, contented, like Wordsworth's poet—

> "Contented if they may enjoy
> The things which others understand."

They resign themselves not without reluctance and misgiving to this contentment; and the action of public opinion is needed to save them from it and its consequences.

To return to the subject of agreements to abstain from corruption; where any candidate or his committee should refuse on being formally applied to for the purpose, to join in such an agreement, he will be an object of suspicion. Amid the hubbub of a general election, the suggested Association may be a central eye to watch everywhere, and a central head and hand to aid in exposure and punishment through existing laws.

* "Life of William Wilberforce," vol. I., p. 64.

I have not mentioned coercion and intimidation, but these also may be regarded as forms of corruption, and the proposed agreements should include all illegitimate influences, such as of customer over tradesman, landlord over tenant, &c.

In a paper read by Mr. Chadwick before the Law Amendment Society, in February, 1859, the collection of information on a large scale by a Commission as to existing constituencies in order to lay a basis for a measure of parliamentary reform was powerfully recommended. I have only to do here with so much of Mr. Chadwick's proposal as concerns corrupt proceedings. Men of all opinions on parliamentary reform will concur in an observation of Mr. Chadwick's that the Legislature cannot be in the best position for extending or lowering franchise until it has obtained full knowledge of the kinds of corruption prevailing in constituencies, and while so much corruption exists, and is even in some places increasing. A similar opinion was intimated before the Corrupt Practices Prevention Committee by a gentleman, whose profession, experience, and well-known political opinions, give peculiar value to his statement. I refer to Mr. Joseph Parkes, who said, "A certain class of boroughs are much influenced by attorneys on both sides, and also by the licensed victuallers and beerhouse keepers, which latter I consider the most growing evil of the day, *particularly if the franchise is to be lowered.*" The suggested Association may do the work of Mr. Chadwick's proposed Commission, as regards corrupt practices, by collecting information about bribery and corrupt expenditure. By printing and widely circulating facts as to corruption in constituencies, it will do further good;—strengthen the feeling against the existing evils. The misdeeds of corrupt constituencies may thus be widely made known for shame, and in the same way the conduct of pure boroughs returning members in the public-spirited manner mentioned by Mr. Mill, may be held up in tracts widely circulated for general admiration and example.

In constituencies like the large metropolitan boroughs,

where there is no purchasing of votes with coarse money bribes, it would well become leading men to combine to regulate and limit expenditure, the greater part of which leads to virtual corruption, and which has often notoriously become so large in amount as to deter candidates. In the evidence already referred to, taken by the Committee of the House of Commons of 1860 on the Corrupt Practices Prevention Act, there are many interesting and instructive particulars as to the corruption involved in general expenditure, showing what perhaps does not need to be shown, how voters who let carriages are secured by hiring their conveyances, printers by lavish printing, publicans by refreshments to supporters and hire of committee-rooms, and how an unnecessary number of voters and their relations are engaged as paid canvassers, messengers, &c., &c. These expenses which the fury of election rivalry carries beyond bounds might, by agreement between the leading men of a large borough solicitous for its political reputation, some of them be got rid of, and others reduced to the limits of necessity.

Mr. James Vaughan, who was the chief Commissioner for the inquiry in 1859 at Gloucester, strongly recommended the prohibition of paid canvassers, and limitation of messengers. A great deal of this might be effected by agreement. It would be, in the long run, the same for both parties. "In the evidence we received," Mr. Vaughan said, "we found 112 messengers employed on the one side, and 150 on the other, and it was stated that ten or twenty could do the work."

Mr. Vaughan also conducted an inquiry at Tynemouth, in 1852, and says, "There were 882 on the register, and 669 polled; the publicans who voted were 108, and in that case we found scarcely a single instance where there were not either refreshment orders, or dinners, or suppers provided by the publicans, and the publicans were wavering backwards and forwards as they received a good order from one party or the other."

Mr. Vaughan says of paying expenses of voters from a distance, "We found at Gloucester there were a great number of voters brought up upon either side, and the result was that the expenses to the candidate were largely augmented, with no practical result as regards the success of the candidate; there would be ten men brought up on the one side and ten on the other."

I should think that in large boroughs where public spirit prevails, there might often be no difficulty about the appointment of a Committee, having the confidence of the whole constituency, to regulate the mode of conducting elections, with a view to limitation of expenses and suppression of corruption; and he would be a rash candidate who would not thankfully abide by the rules.

The limitation of the number of attorneys employed to one for each candidate was strongly recommended by Mr. Pigott, the present Judge. Of the employment of attorneys, he said, "I am sure that it leads to undue influence. If you employ attorneys, they have influence over a great number of voters; in a borough particularly. Some are debtors, some have mortgages, some expect a lawyer's letter; in one way or another there are numerous modes in which an attorney has influence over voters." Mr. Vaughan said on the same subject: "We found that there were a large number of solicitors employed at Gloucester. Solicitors know a great deal about people in a town, and they are no doubt employed in consequence of the influence which they can bring to bear. I recollect that one voter mentioned he felt he must vote on a particular side, because the solicitor on that side had a mortgage on his cottage." Mr. Joseph Parkes, a distinguished member of the profession, and most experienced manager of elections, strongly protested against payment of attorneys as agents, and made the following statement. "I think that it is an evil to the public and an evil to themselves [to pay solicitors as agents;] nearly all the professional men in towns and counties act gratuitously. I myself, after 1826, never took a fee in my life, and I never would. I know all the valuable agents in Warwick, in Coventry, and at Birmingham, and I know that at the town and county elections most of them, whether upon the Conservative side, or upon the Liberal side, are volunteers; they are the men who do the work, and it is the class of the young solicitors, and the class of generally inferior men, who do a great deal of mischief, and incur useless cost. I should wish to state only one reason why I should object to the employment of solicitors. It is notorious that every agent causes more people to vote in consequence of the fee given to him, and I think it is a gross anomaly, that, because he is a lawyer, he is to be receiving the candidate's money; you might just as well give a fee of fifty guineas or five guineas a day to a medical man, who would be equally influential. A general practitioner, from his influence among families, would bring up more people to vote than even the lawyer could. How absurd it would be that you should retain a surgeon! Why should the legal profession alone be a paid class? I take it to be a custom fraught with evil."

There is no class of men whose co-operation would be so important as that of solicitors in a general movement for the diminution of election expenditure and the destruction of corruption. Other eminent solicitors versed in elections gave evidence before the Committee, Mr. Rose, Mr. Clabon, Mr. Drake, and others. The members of the profession throughout the constituencies, animated by the spirit and example of these witnesses, would be invaluable aids for the proposed Association.

I will only mention the notorious fact of a great increase of corruption in many boroughs by corrupt practices at the annual municipal elections. Mr. Philip Rose speaks of the municipal contests as the "nursery of the evil." He says, "These oft-recurring contests have led to the establishment of what I might almost term an organised system of corruption in the municipal boroughs throughout the kingdom, which provides a machinery ready made to hand, available when the parliamentary contest arrives. I am sure that if Members of Parliament on both sides of the House will inform the Committee accurately, it will be admitted that the great strain upon them by their constituents is not so much for the support of charities or public institutions, as it is for the support of the municipal contests in November, the argument invariably being, on the part of the local agents, that £10 spent at a municipal contest is better and more advantageous than £100 spent at the parliamentary contest." Other witnesses called attention to this subject. Boroughs rapidly get worse and worse under an annual administration of "the stimulant" at municipal elections; and a strong impulse from without for local organization against corruption becomes more and more necessary.

Mr. Erskine May's condensed account of the general results of the inquiries which have been prosecuted by Commissions since 1852 is a painfully striking statement:

"At Canterbury, 155 electors had been bribed at one election, and 79 at another; at Maldon, 76 electors had received bribes; at Barnstaple, 255; at Cambridge, 111; and at Kingston-upon-Hull, no less than 847. At the latter place, £26,606 had been spent in three elections. In 1858, a Commission reported that 183 freemen of Galway had received bribes. In 1860, there were strange disclosures affecting the ancient city of Gloucester. This place had been long familiar with corruption. In 1816, a single candidate had spent £27,500 at an election; in 1818, another candidate had spent £16,000; and now it appeared that at the last election in 1859 250 electors had been bribed, and 81 persons had been guilty of corrupting them. Up to this time, the places which had been distinguished by such malpractices had returned members to Parliament prior to 1832; but in 1860, the perplexing discovery was made, that bribery had also extensively prevailed in the populous and thriving borough of Wakefield, the creation of the Reform Act; 86 electors had been bribed, and such was the zeal of the canvassers, that no less than 98 persons had been concerned in bribing them."*

And how many more boroughs may there be equally steeped in corruption which have escaped inquiry? Let the leaders in all such boroughs, if they care for the reputation of their towns, bethink themselves that detection may another time fall on them. The above statement, in a work which will live, casts discredit on English civilization. Should not every effort be made to diminish such an evil? Every Act of Parliament proves inoperative. May not the evil increase?

The Association might also make it one of its objects to consider, prepare, and urge measures for restraining bribery and expenditure, which require the interposition of the legislature; and among such measures which have been from time to time suggested, are a comprehensive declaration for members on taking their seats, so framed as to prevent evasion by a man of honour, and the plan of taking votes by voting-papers collected from the voters' houses, which has been often strongly pressed by Mr. Chadwick, and was recommended by Mr. Philip Rose in his evidence before the Corrupt Practices Prevention Committee, which was the subject of a bill proposed by Lord Shaftesbury in 1853, and was introduced into the Reform Bill proposed in 1859, by Lord Derby's Government.

But the great object is to rouse an enthusiasm against electoral corruption, and to cover the country with it, and to carry it into every constituency. We have this advantage to begin with, that the moral sense of the nation already unmistakably condemns bribery. There is no need to create a feeling; we have to intensify it, and to make it conquer. It is only among inferior people who profit by corruption, and whom temptation and habit have degraded, that there is any insensibility or want of conscience on this subject. The classes from which candidates for seats in Parliament come, are entirely opposed to bribery. Suggestions have latterly

* May's "Constitutional History of England," I., p. 364.

often been made for the application of degrading punishment to candidates convicted of bribery, which could never have been put forward, if bribery were not condemned by opinion. Such punishments were recommended by several witnesses before the Corrupt Practices Prevention Committee, among others by the present Baron Pigott. This distinguished witness recommended that the punishment should be incapacity from holding any office of trust or public employment. Even stronger measures had been previously suggested by one whose name occupies the highest place of authority, and whose opinions must ever be most valued here. There is in print a letter written in 1856 by Lord Brougham to Mr. Hastings on the occasion of an anniversary meeting of the Law Amendment Society, from which I will make an extract. "With our distinguished colleague, Sir John Pakington," said Lord Brougham, "I have long been in co-operation upon this important subject, and I retain, as I believe he does, confidence in the beneficial tendency of a stringent declaration exacted from members on taking their seats. But I conceive that we should also go to the root of the evil as regards the agents of corruption. Why may we not deal with this as five and forty years ago I dealt with the execrable slave trade? For the gains of that infernal traffic we found that men would run the risk of heavy pecuniary penalties, but they shrunk from the risk of being transported as felons, and the traffic ceased. So the prize of a seat in Parliament will tempt some men to run the risk of being unseated on petition, and even of being exposed as having furnished the means of corruption to their agents; and the guilty profits will induce those agents to accept the employment with the comparatively trifling hazards that now attend it. But neither the candidate nor his supporters will encounter the danger of the treadmill or transportation; and we may see bribery, as we have seen slave-trading, cease to bring disgrace on the country." *

* "Law Amendment Journal," vol. 3, p. 115.

Let us hope that such strong measures may not be necessary. Let us make one great endeavour to attain the desired end by a large plan of co-operation for prevention by persuasion and agreement. I have thought that such an effort might well be made, at this moment, under the auspices of an Association, whose object is to utilize social science and promote all social reform, which numbers among its members leading men of all the parties that divide the State, and the name of whose President is already conspicuously associated with this question.

Notices of New Books.

[*** It should be understood that the Notices of New Works forwarded to us for Review, and which appear in this part of the Magazine, do not preclude our recurring to them at greater length, and in a more elaborate form, in a subsequent Number, when their character and importance require it.]

Wrongs and their Remedies: being a Treatise on the Law of Torts. Second Edition. By C. G. Addison, Esq., of the Inner Temple, Barrister-at-law. London: V. and R. Stevens, Sons, & Haynes. 1864.

THIS second edition of Mr. Addison's very complete and very compact book on the "Law of Torts" must be welcome to all branches of the profession as a work of ready and real practical utility. We must confess that we much incline to the plan that is now-a-days adopted, not only by Mr. Addison, but by many other legal writers—viz., that of composing a book anew from beginning to end on a law subject, instead of editing and bringing down to the present time some quondam popular treatise on the same theme. In new editions of old works, however standard and able, the original author, despite of the modernising notes and supplements, remains in the atmosphere of his own time, and his production savours of it; he has all the narrow notions and restricted views of a period unsuited to the actual enlarged and enlightened state of reformed jurisprudence. Again, much that he puts forth has become entirely obsolete, and his editor is driven into the dilemma of either preserving a great deal that is worse than useless, or of garbling the text and making a medley of the whole. As to garbling or curtailing, another inconvenience may arise, which this very work of Mr. Addison's avoids, and which is this: the original author may have cited a case in one particular view, which view an act of Parliament may have put an end to. The editor thereupon omits the case altogether, yet it may be still, in some other respect, of general utility. Thus the well-known case of *Scott* v. *Shepherd*—the Squib case—was usually cited in support of a now obsolete question of pleading; consequently the last edition of "Selwyn's Nisi Prius," having the pleading only in sight, leaves the case out; but Mr. Addison acts otherwise. He, at the very beginning of his treatise, retains the famous precedent, as lucidly showing what is damage without wrong, and introduces it thus:—

"A man may, however, sustain grievous damage at the hands of another: and yet, if it be the result of inevitable accident or a lawful act, done in a lawful manner, without any carelessness or negligence, there is no legal injury, and no tort giving rise to an action for damages. An act of force, for example, done in necessary self-defence, causing injury to an innocent bystander, is *damnum sine injuriâ*, for no man does wrong or contracts guilt in defending himself against an aggressor." Lord Ellenborough, *Leame* v. *Bray*, 3 East, 595. Thus, if a lighted firework is thrown into a coach full of company, and is thrown out again in necessary self-defence, and falls against and burns a bystander, or explodes in his face and blinds him, the person throwing out the firework is not answerable for the damage, as his act was inevitable, and he has done no wrong. The wrong-doer is the party who originally threw the burning material into the coach; and as against him there is that conjunction of damage and wrong which constitutes a tort, and will support an action. *Scott* v. *Shepherd*, 2 W. B., 892.

In contradistinction to editors of bygone books, a thorough new writer, like Mr. Addison, while he can act more freely and independently, for the public benefit, has greater responsibility thrown upon him, since everything depends on his own personal search and elaborate care. He writes, too, for to-day, and in the spirit of to-day, casting aside all that has fallen into inutility beneath the scythe of acts of Parliament. The student or practitioner should of course be familiar with past digests of note and importance, while in Mr. Addison's book he finds apt and at hand, the law that he is every day to make us of. This is, no doubt, one great reason of the popularity of Mr. Addison's former volume, "The Law of Contracts," and of the probable equal success of the production now before us. Mr. Addison has another striking merit: he condenses and contrasts cases well. We give the following example of this from his very first chapter:—

"If a landowner whose land is exposed to the inroads of the sea, or to inundation from the overflowing of an adjoining creek or river, erect sea-walls, groins, or dams, for the protection of his lands, and by so doing causes the tide, the current, or the waves to flow against the land of his neighbour and wash it away, or cover it with water, the landowner so causing an injury to his neighbour is not responsible in damages to the latter, as he has done no wrong, having acted in self-defence, and having a right to protect his land and crops from inundation; *Rex* v. *Pagham*, 8 B. & C. 360. But if he runs out a wharf for embankment into the stream for the mere purpose of acquiring additional land, and improving the value of his property, and encroaches upon the waterway of a navigable river, and thereby gives a new direction to the current, and causes his neighbour's land to be washed away, he commits a tort or wrong, and is responsible for all its injurious consequences; for if an individual, for his own benefit, makes an improvement on his own land, and thereby unwittingly injures his neighbour, he is answerable. Gibbs C. J., 6 T. 44.

"If a man sells a house commanding a fine sea view or a lovely prospect, and then builds on his own adjoining land, so as to shut out the sea view or the prospect, and thereby greatly diminishes the marketable value of the house he has just sold, a great damage is done to the purchaser thereof; but there is no tort or wrong, as the vendor has done nothing which restrains him from interfering with his neighbour's prospect. *Aldred's Case*, 9 Co., 58 *b*."

We quote this latter passage, because, though law, it is very unfair law, and really requires some statutable remedy. Nothing can be, often, more injurious than to take away from a man that very prospect and wide range of air which have formed probably the chief motive for his choosing his house in that particular locality. Nay more, we have heard that it has become a practice with some builders, when they have let a whole row of houses with a fine prospect, to then, and not till then, begin to raise up another row in front of the former. Therefore, we may remark *en passant* that this law should be looked to.

Mr. Addison's chapter on the subject of distress, or rather wrongful distress, is a remarkahly clear and comprehensive summary of the entire law on the subject. Locomotive engines, it seems, may, like cattle, be damage feasant:—

"*Distress by Railway Companies of Locomotive Engines Damage Feasant.*—All Railway Companies have a common law right to distrain engines and carriages encumbering their railway and obstructing the right of passage along the line; and the provisions of the Railway Clauses' Consolidation Act, with respect to the introduction of engines upon the railway and the removal of improperly constructed engines, do not control or qualify this right, but give a cumulative remedy. *Ambergate Rail. Co.* v. *Mid. Rail. Co.* 2 Ell. & Bl., 793."

On the whole, we do not hesitate to recommend Mr. Addison's book as one of the most learned and available treatises of the present day.

International Commercial Law: being the Principles of Mercantile Law of the following and other countries, viz., England, Scotland Ireland, British India, British Colonies, Austria, Belgium, Brazil, Buenos Ayres, Denmark, France, Germany, Greece, Hans Towns, Italy, Netherlands, Norway, Portugal, Prussia, Russia, Spain, Sweden, Switzerland, United States, Wurtemberg. By Leone Levi, Esq., F.S.A., F.S.S., of Lincoln's Inn, Barrister-at-Law; Professor of the Principle and Practice of Commerce in King's College, London, Doctor of Political Economy, Fubingen, &c. &c. Second Edition. London: V. & R. Stevens, Sons, & Haynes, 1863.

IN these days of lengthy statutes and well reported judgments, legal authorship has become a cheap and profitable pastime.

Given access to a law library, leisure, and a moderate amount of method, a text-book may easily be compiled, after the fashion now current, in a few weeks upon any subject in any department of law. There was a time when men were content to spend years in reading, noting, digesting, and comparing, for the purpose of leaving behind them some lasting memorial of their laborious thought. Authorship had not then become a trade, nor had neglected young men learnt to regard the making of a book as a professional advertisement. Money was also dearer, and the facilities for printing less, so that the publishing of a law book was something more than a bagatelle to an enterprising tradesman. *Tempora mutantur.* Every third man we meet in the Temple is an author, and our libraries groan with bulky text-books. It is also remarkable that our legal authors are young men ; for while the learned judges, our great jurists, and counsel of ripe experience within and without the Bar, favour us seldom with their valuable works, those who have just attained the dignity of "utter barrister," pour down upon us a torrent of paraphrastical editions of the Statutes at large, with interpolations of elaborate judgments. The truth is, it does not pay to write a good law book. Years of arduous research and thought, would be ill requited by the scant reward offered by the publishers, while ephemeral treatises, involving little more than a certain amount of physical toil, are sold rapidly, and with very good profits. Hence our legal literature is monopolised by a few third or fourth rate lawyers and some dozen publishers, who together, constitute a kind of joint-stock company for the supply of cheap law. Nay, we are not quite accurate perhaps in saying cheap law ; for considering, with what little talent and labour such cases may be prepared for the market, the present scale of prices might fairly be reduced, at least, to one-half. In justice to the publishers, it should also be remembered that the habits of the profession are very much altered. The race of black letter lawyers is of course completely extinct. It is out of fashion to ponder over the old authorities, or to pursue an original and independent course of reading in a purely scientific spirit. Many are satisfied if they know where to get at the law ; so books of reference, with judicious indexes, and well selected cases are in the highest demand, and fetch the highest prices. The urgency of this demand is an unanswerable proof of their utility. Considering the habits and wants of the profession perhaps we could not now do without them, and provided they be finished in a workmanlike manner why should we complain ?

The author of the work entitled "International Commercial Law," is not altogether unknown in our legal literature. Dr. Leone Levi, is a professor, a pamphleteer, a lecturer, as well as an author ; and appears to possess the plodding genius of the German philologist, not less than the concomitant dulness which imparts weight and gravity to that type of intellect. "The Annals of Legislation" (which by the by is published too late to be of much use), also exhibits Professor Levi's fondness as well as capacity for collecting scattered materials, and with the least possible waste of labour, moulding them into shape and unity. Upon the whole, we feel bound to consider the author as a good representative of the popular text-book writers of the day, and a useful member of the aforesaid joint-stock company for the promulgation of cheap law. As to the work now before us on "International Commercial Law," it is not inaptly described in a passage from Lord Bacon's preface on "The Elements of Common Law in England,"—"You have here a work without any glory of affected novelty, dedicated only to use, and submitted only to the censure of the learned, and chiefly to time." "It is the object of the present work," observes the author, "to bring the fundamental principles of the law merchants and the rules which have been superadded to them in different countries into contact with each other, so that we may profit by each other's experience, and at the same time gather materials for the attainment of solid and permanent progress in mercantile legislation. . . . The laws of foreign countries are put side by side with our own, because commerce is essentially international, and we are deeply affected by the laws and procedure of other States. Hence the distinctive title of 'International Commercial Law.'" The idea of collecting and contrasting the mercantile laws of Europe, of America, of India, and of the British Colonies, was really a good one, and Professor Levi is entitled to considerable praise for the manner in which it has been worked out in these two volumes. We should also state that the plan was submitted to the late Prince Consort, and His Royal Highness, writing to the author, in anticipation of the work, thus expressed his views on the subject, "Nothing would tend more to give public opinion a proper direction than such a publication as yours, where the legislative enactments of different countries upon the same subject would be found in juxtaposition, and where the ready means thus afforded for comparing their relative merits would infallibly lead to a certain degree of assimilation, the advantage and convenience of which would be made obvious. Or should it not lead to this result, the publication would at all events afford to the mercantile world, the means of knowing the points of difference in the various commercial codes, on which it is most important for them to be correctly informed." The task which the author had set for himself was fraught with difficulties, and required the nicest judgment. First of all, it became necessary to consider how far our own mercantile law should be incorporated in a work which was also to contain the leading principles of the laws of three continents, that is to say, of some twenty States. Nor was it an easy matter to determine the relative importance for the purposes of transcription and comparison, of the different foreign codes. Finally, there was the remaining difficulty (not so formidable as it may at first appear), of collecting the characteristic principles of foreign laws. We have much pleasure in stating that Professor Levi has mastered these difficulties in some, nay in many, of the chapters composing these two volumes. For example, the long and elaborate chapter on Bills of Exchange, on Shipping, on Marine Insurance, and the chapter on General Average, are carefully and judiciously written. Even here, however, we observe the prevalent fault of the whole work, namely, that of assigning too much space to the explanation of the English law, while the laws of Foreign States and of the Colonies, upon which we more especially seek information are passed over with a single page, sometimes with a single paragraph. Read for example, the chapter on Bankruptcy, to which nearly one-half of the second volume is devoted, and eliminate those paragraphs explanatory of the laws of foreign countries, and they will be found to make up only a few pages. We have also marked chapters and chapters which are really nothing more nor less than a paraphrase of Acts of Parliament. This is too bad. We are willing to give honour to whom honour is due, and to the extent that it is due. There is much valuable information in these volumes, which many engaged in the profession could not collect for themselves without infinite trouble and at an immense loss of time and money. For this the profession is under great obligation to Professor Levi. But having the Statutes at large, Smith's Mercantile Law, Chitty and Boyles on Bills of Exchange, Addison on Contracts, &c., and we should willingly have consented to dispense with paraphrases and transcripts of those works, for information which they do not contain, and which Professor Levi is we doubt not, well qualified to give.

Notanda in Law, Equity, Bankruptcy, Admiralty, Divorce, and Probate Cases. By Tenison Edwards, Esq., of the Inner Temple, Barrister-at-Law. London: T. F. A. Day, Carey Street, Lincoln's Inn.

We must take some blame to ourselves for having allowed so long a time to elapse before welcoming this most useful publication. We find that the first number was published so far back as the 25th April of last year, and that it now contains, including the number for March last, no less than 2,010 notes of decisions of all the Law Courts of England and Ireland, commencing with the reports published since the 1st of January, 1863.

The notes are printed on one side of the paper, when intended for insertion in the text books or statutes, and are now we understand made adhesive; but they are printed on both sides when intended to be used as a digest.

In the notice to Notanda, No. 8, 1863, we find the following remark, in which we fully agree:—"When the notes are cut up and placed in the text-book the practitioner finds the new law by looking to the old; so that, in fact, the index of the text-book becomes the index to 'Notanda.' On the other hand, when the 'Notanda' is kept whole, the index to it forms a partial index to all the text-books referred to in the 'Notanda.' By these means we have both an analytical and synthetical process of arriving at all the law upon any given subject."

We cannot conceive anything more useful to the really working barrister or lawyer, than this little work, for by its means, and a little manual labour of the clerk, text-books can always be kept up to the latest law upon every subject, thereby rendering the constant purchase of new editions unnecessary.

This at first sight might incline law publishers to look with disfavour upon the work; but in reality this should not be so; for they must well know that the very knowledge that an edition of any work becomes comparatively valueless after a few years, prevents thousands of persons purchasing that work. The notes are not intended to be gummed on the margins, but merely to the back margin and to each other, by which means an entire double page can be formed back to back, rendering the space, as the editor observes in one of his notices, practically inexhaustible.

The notes being consecutively numbered renders the work available also as an exceedingly handy digest when kept entire, and a short index of the subjects, referring to the number of the notes, enables one at once to discover what is sought for. The index to the decisions on the statute law is particularly convenient, being simply a tabular arrangement of all the statutes and sections which have been the subject of judicial decision, with a reference to the numbers of the notes. We find by a "Notice to Notanda, No. 2, 1864," the following announcement:—"It is in contemplation to bring out with every fourth number a consolidated index to, or analysis of, all the previous notes, so that the previous index may be thrown aside. . . . . By this means it will be unnecessary to refer to more than one digest for the next 15 or 20 years, or perhaps longer."

This latter idea is truly novel and most excellent, we only wonder how it has happened, that where the labour annoyance and loss of time must have been so great in looking into a number of annual and other digests, the above plan has not been adopted long since.

We were nearly omitting to notice another merit of this useful compilation, which is the concise and accurate manner in which the notes are framed by Mr. Edwards, giving, as they do, so clearly and tersely the pith of every decision; indeed, we think they may be taken as model of head notes. No one can fail to observe how much of labour and skill have been brought to bear upon the work by its talented Editor; and we recommend it heartily to the notice of both branches of the profession, feeling assured that its general adoption would save them both time and labour, and that as its practical utility becomes known, the profession will not be slow to reward the ingenuity and industry of the Editor.

Private Conveyancing Reformed; or, Dealings with Land rendered Secure, Simple, and Easy, by Registration of Title. A Lecture delivered at Belfast, the 18th March, 1864, on the invitation of the Belfast Chamber of Commerce. By Henry Dix Hutton, Esq., Barrister-at-Law. Belfast and Dublin.

We can at present do no more than notice the publication of Mr.

Hutton's pamphlet, which has only just appeared. Referring to the lecture delivered by Mr. Robert Torrens last year in the same place, Mr. Hutton states that his object is to examine this important question from a professional point of view, pointing out the essential principles on which conveyancing by the registration of title rests, and indicating the historical growth of the idea. While doing ample justice to the merits of Mr. Torrens' particular system, the author, in a spirit of impartial justice and conciliation, shows that the general idea of registering title has been gradually elaborated by many independent thinkers in England and Ireland, whose points of resemblance are mainly traceable to the fact that they naturally have all gone back to the one great type of simple conveyancing—that furnished by dealings with personal property. Their differences are also traceable, in a great measure, to those which subsist between the several modes of dealing applied respectively to stock shares and shipping. Mr. Hutton has, we observe, prefixed to his lecture a preface, intended, more especially, for professional men ; calculated to reconcile them to the change, and at the same time to enlist their sympathies with a measure so eminently required for the public good.

An Essay on Waste, Nuisance, and Trespass ; chiefly with reference to remedies in Equity. Treating of the Law of Timber, Mines, Lights, Water, Supports, the Construction of Public Works, &c. By George N. Yool, M.A., of Lincoln's Inn, Barrister at Law, late Fellow of Trinity College, Cambridge. London : W. Maxwell.

The author of this work has introduced it by no preface. He justly thinks that the title page will itself indicate the importance and use of the treatise, and he leaves the reader to judge by the results of the labour bestowed. We think that the labour and skill employed must have been considerable. The book seems clear and intelligible. The text sets out law at length, so far as is requisite, to enable the reader to grasp the principles ; and no one can read the work (which is pleasant reading), without feeling that in a short space he has gained that preparatory knowledge of the whole subject, which it is the office of a text-book to communicate, and that by the aid of the numerous references in the notes he can apply the law safely. The writer must have been sorely tempted to diverge occasionally from the narrow path he had laid down for himself. Thus, when treating of "nuisances to dwelling-houses," it seems almost a waste of labour to give the law relating to the reservation or grant of lights on the separation of ownership of adjoining tenements, and to the obstruction of lights, and not to complete the subject by adding the little that would be required about the implied grant or reservation, and the obstruction of continuous and apparent casements generally. We trust that in this and other directions the author will enlarge his treatise when he issues another edition.

A Manual of Common Law, comprising the Fundamental Principles and the Points most usually occurring in Daily Life and Practice for the Practitioner, Student, and General Reader. By Josiah W. Smith, B.C.L., Q.C., &c. Second Edition. London: Stevens, Sons, & Haynes. 1864.

This is another of the manuals necessitated by the system of "cramming," to which the institution of examinations seems always destined to lead. Lord Coke says, "Reason is the life of the law; the common law is nothing else but reason . . . it has by long experience grown to perfection . . . the perfection of reason;" but we don't think that anyone "getting up" the common law from this manual alone, would appreciate the justice of his remarks. It was perhaps inevitable in such a manual, that the law should be diversed from its reasons; but the student must nevertheless on that account find the subject "hard," as the author seems to fear he may; and, having mastered by a pure effort of memory the contents of the volume, would find it avail him little for any points but those expressly mentioned. We very much regret to see (what the multiplication of these manuals forces us to see and to remark) that institutions intended to promote a sounder legal education, should so rapidly degenerate into a system for the encouragement of mere memories and the production of legal indices. We hope that some day the authorities will select some few leading branches of the law, and insist upon their being thoroughly and scientifically studied; and will cease to require the student to traverse in a cursory manner the whole range of legal topics. However, here the system is, and Mr. Smith is entitled to the gratitude of the student for the great labour and pains, he tells us he has bestowed in the compilation of this work. It seems prepared with the care and accuracy generally exhibited by the author. We think the student may use this book, (as the author suggests) with great advantage, as a means of directing his studies and enabling him to investigate the subjects it treats of in detail. And, if he should thus possess himself of the reasons and foundations of the rules of law, he may afterwards recall them to his memory at once, by the mere perusal of the manual upon which his investigations were based. The "Table of Particular Contents," in which is contained a detailed summary of the contents of the chapters struck us as likely to be exceedingly useful as a means of testing the knowledge which the reader may have acquired upon their subject-matter, in fact as a substitute for "a body of examination questions."

We are afraid, however, that the lawyer would find that the limits of a manual had shut out many particulars that it would be necessary for him to know. Thus, for instance, we have looked in vain for something relative to the operation of a power of attorney in rendering a chose in action practically transferable at law, or in fact for any reference to powers of attorney at all, though the subject of the transfer of choses in action is more than once treated of. The author, too, seems to have followed the books he has consulted in distinguishing between an open account, a stated account, and a settled account, and has given definitions of the first two, but not of the last species of account.

Mr. Smith is, however, entitled to credit for the great amount of matter he has compressed into so small a space, and omissions such as those referred to, are probably only unavoidable evils attaching to manuals and the system which requires them.

A Manual of Equity Jurisprudence, Founded on the Works of Story, Spence, and other Writers, and on the Subsequent Cases: comprising the Fundamental Principles and the Points of Equity usually occurring in General Practice. By Josiah W. Smith, B.C.L., Q.C., Editor of Fearne's "Contingent Remainders," and Mitford's "Chancery Pleadings;" Author of "A Compendium of the Law of Real and Personal Property," "A Manual of Common Law and Bankruptcy," &c., and one of the Consolidators of the Chancery Orders. Seventh Edition. London: Stevens, Sons, and Haynes. 1864.

It is difficult to treat properly so vast a subject as Equity Jurisprudence in so small a volume as this manual. A text writer can certainly give a summary of some of the main principles, and show to a small extent their application; but it is almost impossible accurately to define them except by tracing out their operation in detail. Take for instance the initial question of what are the true nature, sphere, and limits of Equity Jurisprudence; Mr. Smith has attempted to give them in a page, but we very much doubt whether any mind but one already well versed in the subject could appreciate the correctness and meaning of the definition. And so in regard to the exposition of the various branches of the Jurisprudence—the doctrines of the Court have *grown*—they have been developed and modified according as novel cases have demanded, &c., and any cut and dried definitions unsupported by an ample statement of the reasoning and circumstances which led to the decisions by which the doctrines were established will frequently (even if comprehensible) fail in conveying a notion of the true bearing of such doctrines, but will still more likely remain to a student as mere forms of words of which he does not understand the value and application. To avoid this, of course, the applications of principles may be set out, but not fully and with particularity in a manual. We apprehend that the works of Story and Spence are so deservedly esteemed because they do take the form of argumentative treatises and trace the growth of doctrines. Under the present system of legal education, however, it is absolutely necessary that a student should gain some general notion of the doctrines of equity as so many *facts*, and this manual is well adapted, as its success has shown, to convey the knowledge required, and at the same time, perhaps, as accurate and full ideas on the subject as could be given by a work of the size. The law, gathered from various sources, is conveniently and correctly epitomised and arranged; and, by the original matter deduced from the latest cases, the reader will be sure that he is learning the present law, and will have nothing to unlearn. The hope which the author expresses that this edition will be found useful to the practitioner, we are glad to think will be realised. To such a one it will be a great advantage for ordinary use, that the law, scattered in several bulky text books, should be here presented in so small a compass, and that the portions of Story's work which relate to the American decisions only, should be excluded. Having previously become familiar with the subject in detail, the lawyer may hereby readily refresh his memory, and will then be in a position, with the help of the four hundred new cases which the author has added, to follow the further development of the Principles of Equity Jurisprudence.

The Law Lexicon or Dictionary of Jurisprudence: explaining the Technical Words and Phrases employed in the Several Departments of English Law; including the Various Legal Terms used in Commercial Business; together with an Explanatory as well as Literal Translation of the Latin Maxims contained in the Writings of the Ancient and Modern Commentators. By J. J. S. Wharton, Esq., M.A., Barrister-at-Law, Author of "The Articled Clerk's Manual," &c. Third Edition. London: V. R. Stevens, Sons, and Haynes. 1864.

We have much pleasure in recording the fact of this really useful book of Mr. Wharton's having reached its third edition, and we willingly admit that it is in every respect a very great improvement upon the previous editions; inasmuch as several important additions have been made, the text entirely revised, and the alterations in the law since the publication of the former works, have been here very carefully noted. The references have been brought down as nearly as possible to the date of publication, Hilary Term, 1864; and the most recent law books published have been quoted in elucidation of the subject matter of the work. Regarded as a mere compilation, quite apart from its undoubted literary merit, this Law Lexicon evinces much painstaking research, and we can unhesitatingly recommend it, more especially to the professional student, as a reference-book which will afford him incalculable assistance in his studies. While containing far more valuable information than any other book of the kind, the author has wisely omitted the insertion of much obsolete and consequently unprofitable matter, which, in the old Law Dictionaries, only perplexes the law student, however interesting it may be to the antiquarian. In the preface to the first edition Mr. Wharton says: "the aims attempted throughout its arrangement have been compression, avoiding obscurity and yielding information easily and effectually;" and we certainly think that if this difficult undertaking were not quite accomplished in the first and second editions, it has been successfully attained in this. The author is entitled to much praise for having supplied a professional want, and we have no doubt that his learned industry will be duly appreciated by the legal profession generally.

Handy-Book on the Law of the Drama and Music: being an Exposition of the Law of Dramatic Copyright, Copyright in Musical Compositions, Dramatic Copyright in Music, and International Copyright in the Drama and Music; the Law for Regulating Theatres, the Law affecting Theatres, and the Law relating to Music, Dancing, and Professional Engagements; with the Statutes, Forms, &c., referring thereto. London: T. H. Lacy, 89, Strand.

THIS little work by an anonymous writer, forms a complete *resumé* of the law on the various subjects to which it relates. The book does not appear to us to have been written exclusively either for the legal practitioner, or for those whose interest it has in view. By the former much will be found collected together in a small compass that may be useful, and to the latter the contents of the volume will be complete and interesting.

Handy-Book on Life Assurance Law, for the Use of Policy Holders and Agents, with a preliminary statement of some amendments that are desirable. By Arthur Scratchley, Esq., M.A. London: Stevens, Sons, & Haynes.

THE title of this little two-and-sixpenny book points out its use, and the name of Mr. Scratchley is sufficient to guarantee its value.

The Bankruptcy Act, 1861. Classified Synopsis of Bankruptcy Proceedings in the County Courts; with the Sections of the Acts, the Rules, the Official Constructions, and the forms arranged in consecutive order as required in practice. Forming a Simple Guide to the Law and Practice of Bankruptcy in the County Courts. By Benjamin Page, Grimsby, Deputy Registrar of the County Court of Suffolk at Ipswich. London: Stevens, Sons, and Haynes.

THIS little compilation is exactly what it professes to be, namely, a simple practical guide to the Law and Practice of Bankruptcy in the County Courts. The Acts, the Rules, the Official Instructions, and the Forms having been methodised, placed in consecutive order as required in practice, and so arranged that the eye has within its survey at once each Enactment, the Rule thereupon, and the Form applicable. It is printed in tabular form, and in size and type uniform with the General Orders last issued. To the regular practitioner this synopsis will be invaluable.

Transactions of the National Association for the Promotion of Social Science, Edinburgh Meeting. Edited by G. W. Hastings, Esq. London : Longman & Co.

THIS volume, the seventh issued by the Association, has just reached us. The Department of Jurisprudence is unusually full and interesting, as was to be expected at Edinburgh, though many of the subjects belong to Scotch law.

Events of the Quarter.

Electoral Corruption.—The movement originated by Mr. W. D. Christie, a member of the Bar, and late Ambassador to the Brazils, for checking bribery and corruption at elections, will, if adequately carried out, be one of the most remarkable of the day. It is simply the overt expression of an opinion which has long been gaining ground with all who reflect on the practical working of our constitution. The effect of the Reform Act has been, it is now seen, to substitute the power of unscrupulous expenditure for that of aristocratic influence; and the evils which Burke so forcibly described as resulting from the introduction of the "nabob" element into elections have come with tenfold force upon us. Whether the organisation which Mr. Christie desires to bring into existence would really suppress the nuisance must be matter of doubt: but it may be worth trying. The following observations were made by Mr. John Stuart Mill, and Mr. Chadwick, at a meeting of the Jurisprudence Department of the Social Science Association, when Mr. Christie's paper (which we have printed elsewhere) was considered:—

Mr. John Stuart Mill said—It is unnecessary here, though it might be necessary in some other places, to insist upon the magnitude of the evil to which this report relates. What is at stake is nothing less than the vitality of representative government. If the majority or a preponderant portion of the House of Commons represented only their own pockets, we should, indeed, have what Mr. Disraeli called a Venetian Constitution, and that in a very bad form. It would be a great mistake to suppose that we have seen the worst of this evil. I am persuaded that we are only in the beginning of it. When we consider the rapid growth of manufacture and commerce, and the number of persons that are constantly becoming wealthy, whose sole ambition is to obtain what wealth alone has not yet given them, namely, position, we see what a rapidly increasing number of persons there is to whom it is worth any money to acquire the only thing purchaseable by money, which will give them the grand object of their desire. I have been told by one who has filled a distinguished position in Australia that there were within his knowledge five or six persons, Australians, who were only waiting for a general election to offer themselves to English constituencies, with the object I have mentioned. I mean nothing uncomplimentary to Australians. I believe them to be a very intelligent community. But the instance suggests the class of persons who make this evil an increasing one—the vulgar rich, to whom it is worth while to spend any amount of money for the sake of station in society. Persons of established position are often wishing to spend money corruptly, but there is a limit to the amount they will spend. They can gain comparatively little in importance by lavish expenditure. Their position is made, and they may even impair instead of advancing it if they spend too lavishly. But to a person of the other kind a seat in Parliament may be worth half his fortune. Now I think the society must feel that, saving exceptions (admirable exceptions there are sure to be), this class of persons, whether they act the part of flunkies, crouching at the feet of the aristocracy, or of envious demagogues anxious to bring them down, or, as will often be the case, are ready to turn from either of these parts to the other, according to convenience, are about the most undesirable and the most dangerous class of persons who can obtain admission to Parliament. It may be thought that the only evils to be apprehended from them are those of what may be called plutocracy ; but, in reality, we should have those of democracy too, for if the costliness of elections limited the choice to such men, the electors finding no one to vote for whom they could trust to act according to his own judgment and conscience, if they themselves have any regard to their own particular opinions, will bind them strictly by pledges to abide by subjects which the electors care about. The House of Commons would be an assembly of delegates, while on other subjects the member would vote according to his own interests or caprice, or according to the question in which he desired to carry favour. Now, as to the remedying of this, I am not one of those who think that legal means would necessarily be insufficient. I think there are legal measures which could be made effectual, but only if backed by a moral demonstration of a sufficient number of honest men, who would league themselves together against the political crime, expressly or virtually pledging themselves both to abstain from it personally, and to use all their influence to prevent it. They would probably be able to obtain from the Legislature any such enactments as may be desirable, while they would supply the only powers which could enable those enactments to be enforced. Great credit is due to Mr. Christie for having, as it seems to me, "hit the right nail on the head." As to the persons who should take this in hand, I think there is none so fit as this society. No individual, and no self-elected committee could address themselves to the leaders of parties, and to influential politicians throughout the country, nor would they be listened to if they did. But this association, not to mention the larger society of which it now forms a part, could address itself to anyone. The learned gentleman concluded by moving that the report be received, adopted, and consented to.

Mr. Chadwick said—I have received a letter from our noble president, Lord Brougham, who, after reading the report now submitted to the meeting, declares that, in his opinion, this association is especially bound to exert itself in this matter, and that, although his opinion remains the same, that a penal enactment would be the effectual remedy, yet he is of opinion that a declaration is advisable, and that he is willing to sign it and promote it in every way. Lord Shaftesbury writes to me that he considers the suggestion of the committee deserving of trial. Sir Fitzroy Kelly regrets his unavoidable absence, and expresses his concurrence in the object in the object in view ; and Mr. Philip Rose writes that he would be glad to see any measure adopted which would have the effect of checking the evils of bribery, and that he knows of none which will be so effectual, with proper safeguards, as the system of voting by voting-papers. * * * The exercise of public opinion obtained by the Anti-Duelling Association placed this country in advance of all Continental nations, as respects the practice of duelling. But the dormant public opinion here allows practices to prevail in our electoral and legislative organisation which are subjects of astonishment to thinking men in all Europe. At the International Statistical Congresses which I have attended, I have taken occasion to make inquiries from the delegates as to the electoral procedure in their respective States. There were, they said, occasional complaints, more or less well founded, of the exercise of irregular influences, though not very considerable, by parties in getting up voters ; but neither in France, nor in Belgium, nor in Holland, nor in the chief cantons of Switzerland, in respect to which I made inquiries, was there any such bribery, nor indeed any practice of individual bribery, nor any such extravagant electoral expenses as are known to be so common, as almost to be general in England. I say there was no individual bribery, for there were occasionally instances of what was considered collective bribery by candidates promising, if they were elected, to get a railway carried in their direction, or to do something for their peculiar local advantage. In those countries the gross debauchery and rioting at our elections, as well as the excessive expenditure, any getting in of " third men " for the sake of the electoral expenditure in contests—such scenes as those at the last election for Brighton —are subjects of surprise and disparaging comment. In respect to electoral expenditure, I am told that in France four or five hundred francs would be the usual amount of a candidate's expenses ; and that expenditures of double that amount, or thirty or forty pounds, are open to being challenged as irregular. My information related to elections before the last. Let us, however, contrast these with the electoral expenditures unchallenged, and indeed allowed, as regular in England, in counties as well as in boroughs. A very respectable metropolitan member, who had spent some two thousand pounds, but who had been beaten in a third election by another who had spent four, declared to me that his opponent, without reference to his political, moral, or intellectual merits, would be beaten by any other who spent six. A highly respectable man, Mr. Wilkinson, who spent between two and three thousand pounds, was beaten by Mr. Roupell, notwithstanding notoriously bad antecedents, who spent more than five thousand pounds, set forth in the Parliamentary returns as legal. The instruments used by Mr. Roupell were upwards of fifty committee-rooms and committees, and eight or nine hundred of paid canvassers and hired messengers. In one small country town, which had only one or two hotels, almost every public-house and beer-shop was hired as a committee-room, with its paid committee-men and canvassers, and the place was drenched with drink. Is it not possible to evoke a public opinion against the use of such machinery, which is as open and flagrant a misuse of money-power as putting money in the voter's hand in the open streets? At Southampton a gentleman, whose labours had been of material advantage to the town, was moved to consider of presenting himself to the town as a candidate, but on inquiry he was told that he must retain all the Liberal lawyers there—some dozen of them—and, unless he did so, he would have no chance, and that he must spend £2,000 at the least. He therefore left that field to Mr. Edwin James, who, however, subsequently selected Marylebone, and left Southampton to another member of the profession. The Parliamentary returns show that in the contest for Aberdeen Colonel Sykes had to retain eleven lawyers. In the evidence before the Parliamentary committee on corrupt practices, Mr. Joseph Parkes, an eminent member of the profession and an experienced agent in Parliamentary elections, gives good reasons why no attorney whatsoever should be retained. Against such gross expenditures, into which one candidate may be driven, as also of others set forth in the evidence—expenditures for the sake of which third men are sought and contests are invited by those who profit by them—will it not be practicable to evoke some check from public opinion? In the Continental examples to which I have referred for the absence of any practice of bribery, it is due to state that in each instance the ballot was in use. It is due also to state on testimony of persons like myself, who had filled public executive offices, and were in neutral positions, as well as of persons of the classes which were highly Conservative, the ballot was deemed to work on the whole most satisfactorily. We need not here, however, enter into this or any question which is the subject of party contest. I refer to it for this fact:—In Continental experience I learned that the practice of the ballot is beset with serious political difficulties in getting the electors to leave their daily money-getting occupations to give their votes. If the ballot checks bribery, it checks expenditure for getting parties up to the poll to give their votes. Its tendency was to make the working of the electoral system regular, and to give power to minorities, except on occasions of extraordinary excitement. In Holland, on ordinary occasions, the elections, I am told, often fall into the hands of one-fifth of the electors, except on occasions of great political excitement. To avoid the sacrifice of profitable time, and conflict of public duty with private interest in that respect, Continental States have been driven to take elections on the Sunday. In Switzerland it was found to be impossible to get farmer electors from their fields to attend the polling booths; and in the Canton of Zurich and other Cantons they take the elections in the Church, and after the Sunday service they turn out the women and children, and lock in the electors, until they had given their votes. In America, too, this difficulty of getting up electors is experienced, and is productive of large public consequences. Great events turn upon what is termed good or bad election weather, bad election weather being the inclement weather when people will not expose themselves to add merely an unit, as they conceive, to some thousands of a large aggregate. Here, it is testified by Mr. Sidney Smith, bribery begins with the elector, and almost always begins with the question, But who is to pay me for my lost time? I think I have shown in poor law administration, that this large source of bribery is to be met, and that it is effectually met by the house to house collection of votes, by means of voting-papers. I am glad that we have had an instance of the voluntary collection of opinion by this method, by means of returns, obtained through the post, of declarations from electors, for whom they intended to vote, and of such declarations having been made the means of reducing canvassing and avoiding contests. It would be for the organisation proposed to consider whether the voluntary use of that method may not be much extended, for the avoidance of contests altogether.

THE CONVICT QUESTION.—We have repeatedly advocated in this MAGAZINE the introduction into Great Britain of the Convict System which has been so successfully and beneficially carried out in Ireland by Sir Walter Crofton. The Government have strangely lagged behind the intelligent convictions of the country on this question, and Sir George Grey has seemed determined to resist every suggested improvement. The House of Commons, however, is more wise. On going into Committee on the Penal Servitude Bill, Mr. Hunt, the learned Member of Northampton, moved a clause establishing police supervision throughout the country over discharged convicts. This wholesome provision was carried, in the teeth of the Home Office, by a majority of twenty-eight.

COPYRIGHT AMENDMENT AND LEGISLATION.—The Sub-Committee on the Law of Copyright appointed by the Law Amendment Society, embodied the opinions arrived at by them in the following resolutions :—

I. That the British municipal laws of Copyright in works of literature, the drama, music, and the fine arts, are in a most unsatisfactory state in consequence of the legislation upon the subject being voluminous, complicated, and inefficient.

II. That such defective legislation is unjust in its operation upon authors, and other proprietors of British Copyrights; and also very injurious to the commercial interests of the British public.

III. That such defective municipal laws of Copyright are likewise very unjust and oppressive towards the subjects of those States with which Her Majesty the Queen has entered into International Copyright Conventions, because all those Conventions profess to be based upon the principle of *reciprocity*, whereas, in fact, such reciprocity does not exist in the British dominions, inasmuch as in France and other of the States in question their municipal laws of Copyright are simple and efficient, while ours are quite the reverse.

IV. That, as British Copyright is, and always has been, based upon the principle of that *property* to which an author is justly entitled in the re-production of his works *after their publication*, he ought, in all cases, to have a summary remedy for the violation of his Copyright.

V. That, in order thoroughly to reform the British municipal laws of Copyright in works of literature, the drama, music, and the fine arts, it is essential that all the existing legislation on the subject (so far as circumstances will permit) should be repealed, and the laws consolidated and amended.

VI. That, considering the existing state of the British municipal laws of Copyright, and also the conflicting legislation of other States upon that subject, especially those States with which Her Majesty the Queen has entered into International Copyright Conventions, it has become of the utmost importance, as far as possible, to promote *uniform* municipal legislation as to Copyrights upon the following points :—

1st. The works which shall be entitled to Copyright.
2nd. The period for which such copyright shall continue.
3rd. The conditions to be performed in the State where the work is first published, in order to acquire such Copyright.
4th. The prohibition of piracy of works first published in any foreign State.
5th. The remedies to which the proprietor of a Copyright shall be entitled for the protection of his property therein.
6th. That no conditions should be required to be performed for the acquisition of Copyright, except those essential according to the municipal laws of the State where the work was first published.

VII. That, considering the vast and rapidly increasing demand for works of literature, the drama, music, and the fine arts, the extensive capital now embarked in undertakings for the re-production of such works; together with the great number of persons who are directly and indirectly employed in such undertakings, it has, in the interests of *commerce*, as well as upon grounds of justice to the proprietors of Copyrights, become of the utmost importance that our legislation upon Copyright should be efficiently consolidated and amended.

VIII. That, the present defective system of Registration at Stationers' Hall should be discontinued, and that the whole system and machinery of registration in all cases of Copyright should be transferred to the Registration of Designs Office, Whitehall.

These resolutions were brought up by Mr. Serjeant Burke, Chairman of the Committee, at a meeting of the Law Amendment Society, and were adopted.

Mr. Black, the enlightened M.P. for Edinburgh, has now before Parliament a bill to consolidate and amend the whole Copyright law. It has passed the second reading, and has been referred to a Select Committee. There is, therefore, every prospect that something will soon be done to effectively put an end to the present confusing and conflicting state of our copyright jurisprudence.

APPOINTMENTS.

Mr. George Francis has been appointed Recorder of Faversham, vacant by the resignation of Mr. E. P. Alderson.

Mr. Tindal Atkinson, and Mr. John Simon, of the Northern Circuit, and Mr. Alexander Pulling, of the South Wales Circuit, and author of the "Treatise on the Laws, Customs, and Regulations of the City and Port of London," and of the "Law of Attorneys and Solicitors," have been admitted to the degree of Serjeants-at-Law.

Mr. William Field, of the Midland Circuit, Mr. D. D. Keane, of the Norfolk Circuit, and Mr. J. J. Johnson, of the Home Circuit, have been appointed Queen's Counsel.

Mr. T. E. Chitty, Barrister-at-Law, has been appointed Clerk of Assize for the Western Circuit, in the place of the late Mr. Sidney Gurney.

Mr. E. B. Church, Solicitor, has been appointed Chief Clerk in the Chambers of the Master of the Rolls, in the room of Mr. Whiting, deceased.

Mr. Jamas Attar, Solicitor of Stamford, has been appointed Clerk of the Peace for the Parts of Holland, Lincolnshire.

Ireland.—Mr. C. H. Hemphill has been appointed to the Chairmanship of Louth; Mr. Leahy to Limerick; Mr. D. R. Pigot to West Cork; Mr. Barron to Kerry: Mr. West to Wexford; Mr. Coffey to Leitrim; and Mr. John O'Hagan to Westmeath.

Mr. R. Thos. Todd, Solicitor, has been appointed Clerk of the Crown for the County of Down, in the room of the late Mr. Thomas Courtney.

Scotland. — Mr. George Moir has been elected Professor of Scot's Law in the University of Edinburgh, in the room of the late Professor Ross.

Mr. Æneas Macbean, Writer to the Signet, has been appointed one of the Clerks of the Court of Justiciary.

Gold Coast.—Mr. M. R. Barry, of the Equity Bar, has been appointed Queen's Advocate.

India.—Mr. F. B. Simpson has been appointed Civil and Sessions Judge of Jessore; Mr. G. W. Edema, Registrar of Lands for the Western Province and for the Colombo District; Mr. W. Morgan, for the Southern Province and Galle District; Mr. W. H. P. De Saram, for the Eastern Province and Trimcomalee District; Mr. A. Mainwaring, for North Western Province and for Kornegee District; Mr. J. F. Lozens, for the Cultura District; Mr. D. J. Pereira, for the Negombo District; Mr. W. L. W. Ludekens, for the Matura District; Mr. O. C. Lassossay, for the Tangalle District; Mr. J. P. Meerwald, for the Batticaloa District: Mr. W. Stock, for the Central Provinces and Kandy District; Mr. S. Waytilingham, for the Northern Provinces and Jaffna District; and Mr. J. Masselamany for the Ratnapoora District.

EXAMINATIONS AT THE INCORPORATED LAW SOCIETY.

Hilary Term, 1864.

At the final examination of candidates for admission on the roll of attorneys and solicitors of the superior courts, the examiners recommended the following gentlemen, under the age of 26, as being entitled to honorary distinction :—

C. M. Warmington, aged 21 ; T. Waterhouse, B.A., aged 25 ; J. W. Chandler, aged 25; and A. Bright, M.A., aged 23 ; J. W. Gabb, B.A., aged 25 ; J. A. Hewitt, aged 21 ; and R. B. Smith, aged 22, equal.

The Council of the Incorporated Law Society have accordingly awarded the following prizes of books :—

To Mr. Warmington, the prize of the Hon. Society of Clifford's Inn ; to Mr. Waterhouse, the prize of the Hon. Society of Clement's Inn ; to Mr. Chandler, Mr. Bright, Mr. Gabb, Mr. Hewit, and to Mr. Smith, each one of the prizes of the Incorporated Society.

The examiners have also certified that the following candidates whose names are placed in alphabetical order, passed examinations which entitle them to commendation :—

Nicholas Albert Earle, aged 23 ; John Smythies Greene, aged 21 ; Richard Hewlett, aged 22 ; Claude Ashley Anson Penley, aged 22 ; Joseph Soames, aged 23 ; and Sharon Grote Turner, aged 21.

The Council have accordingly awarded them certificates of merit.

The examiners have further announced to the following candidates, whose names are placed in alphabetical order, that their answers to the questions at the examinations were highly satisfactory, and would have entitled them to certificates of merit if they had been under the age of 26 :—

Samuel Harris, aged 39 ; Thomas Martin, aged 34 ; and Barnard Thomas, B.A., aged 27.

The number of candidates examined in this term was 122 ; of these 107 passed, and 15 were postponed.

The examiners reported that the following gentlemen, whose names are arranged in alphabetical order, have passed the intermediate examination with distinction :—

William Charles Lovelace Bowling, aged 22 ; Charles Frederick Hird, aged 20 ; Thomas M'Millin, aged 25 ; and George Francis Riddiford, aged 22.

The number of candidates examined in this term was 78 ; of these 68 were passed, and 10 postponed.

We regret to announce the death of a well-known author, Leonard Shelford, Esq., of the Middle Temple, Barrister-at-Law. He was the second son of the late Rev. Leonard Shelford, B.D., rector of North Tuddenham, in the county of Norfolk, by Ellen, daughter of William Grigson, Esq., of West Wretham, in the same county. He was one of twelve children, of whom few survive. His eldest brother was the Rev. Thomas Shelford, B.D., many years Fellow and Tutor of Corpus Christi College, Cambridge—afterwards rector of Lambourne, Essex. (Died 1846.) His next brother (third son), William Heard Shelford, M.A., Fellow of Emmanuel College, Cambridge, and afterwards rector of Preston, Suffolk. (Died 1854.)

The deceased was born July 26, 1795. He was brought up as a solicitor, and served his articles with Mr. William Repton, of Aylsham, Norfolk, from whence he subsequently removed to London, and was engaged in the office of Messrs. Boodle & Co. He afterwards studied for, and was called to the Bar, by the Benchers of the Middle Temple, in 1827.

For upwards of forty years he occupied chambers in the Temple, living the life of a student, and, with short intervals, almost of a recluse. During that period he wrote no less than fifteen works on different legal subjects, most of which have passed through several editions, and some of which have been republished in America, as is told us in a list of his numerous works, "without the author's consent."

Mr. Shelford never obtained a lucrative practice at the Bar, and although his works were most of them eminently successful, and of the greatest use to the profession, we believe that he never procured any appointment as a fitting reward of his great merits as an author, nor did his works, in a pecuniary point of view, prove as profitable to him as they must have done to others. In his private character he was held in high esteem for his high and honourable principles and his keen sense of what was just and right between man and man. This was his salient point. He seemed to be incapable of anything that was unfair or in the slightest degree dishonourable.

Though possessed of some eccentricity of manner, he had a kind heart and a disposition naturally generous, though perhaps a little soured by the reverses of the world.

He died March 17, 1864, from a disease of the liver of long standing. He was never married. Though he had been breaking up for a long time his death was sudden at the last, and his relatives were not aware even of his illness till a few hours before his death.

Necrology.

January.

17th. Rigge, Thomas, Esq., Solicitor, aged 50.

19th. Harris, Henry, Esq., Solicitor.

23rd. Parkinson, F. Dennis, Esq., Solicitor.

26th. Blood, Thomas, Esq., Barrister, aged 66.

27th. Trafford, Richard Leigh, Esq., late County Court Judge.

February.

4th. Tombe, George, Esq., Q.C., aged 80,

4th. Marshall, Henry, Esq., Solicitor, aged 45.

7th. Stirling, Thomas Henry, Esq., Barrister, aged 75.

11th. Jessop, Alfred, Esq., Solicitor.

14th. Niblett, Isaac Goodluck, Esq., Solicitor, aged 45.

19th. Tribe, John, Esq., Solicitor, aged 60.

24th. Lafontaine, Sir J. H., Bart., Chief Justice of the Court of Queen's Bench, Lower Canada.

24th. Iles, Edward, Esq., Solicitor, aged 59.

25th. Eastlake, George S., Esq., formerly Admiralty Solicitor and Judge Advocate.

28th. Carter, John Richard, Esq., Solicitor, aged 73.

28th. Clarke, John, Esq., Barrister, aged 52.

28th. Potter, Thomas, Esq., Solicitor, aged 62.

28th. Martin, Richard Thomas, Esq., Barrister.

March.

5th. Green, William Francis, Esq., Solicitor.

6th. Rothery, William, Esq., formerly Legal Adviser to the Treasury on the Slave Trade, aged 89.

9th. Gurney, Sidney, Esq., Clerk of Assize, Western Circuit, aged 56.

12th. Smith, H. W. S., Esq., Barrister.

14th. Smith, Joseph, Esq., Solicitor, aged 55.

17th. Shelford Leonard, Esq., Barrister, aged 68.

21st. HILDITCH, JOHN FREDERICK, Esq., Solicitor.
22nd. HINGESTON, Samuel, Esq., Barrister, aged 59.
26th. ROSCOE, JAMES, Esq., Solicitor, aged 73.
28th. LAWFORD, EDWARD, Esq.. Solicitor, aged 76.
30th. TUCKER, EDWARD M., Esq., Solicitor, aged 46.

April.

3rd. TURNER, ALFRED, Esq., Solicitor, aged 67.
4th. MAPLES, THOMAS FREDERICK, Esq., Solicitor, aged 82.
5th. JOSEPH, NATHANIEL, Esq., Barrister.
16th. JAMIESON, ANDREW, Esq., Solicitor.

List of New Publications.

Addison—Wrongs and their Remedies, being a Treatise on the Law of Torts. By C. G. Addison, Esq., Barrister. Second Edition. Royal 8vo. 34*s*. cloth.

Archbold—Parish Officer and Parish Law. Fourth Edition. By J. Paterson, Esq., Barrister. 12mo. 10*s*. cloth.

Archbold—The Law of Landlord and Tenant, with all the requisite Forms, including the Pleadings in the several Actions by and against Landlord and Tenant, and the Evidence necessary to support them. By J. F. Archbold, Esq., Barrister. Third Edition. 12mo. 14*s*. cloth.

Bigg—Collection of Public General Acts for Regulation of Railways, 1830 to 1863, with Index. By J. Bigg. Tenth Edition. 12mo. 8*s*. cloth.

Broom—A Selection of Legal Maxims, Classified and Illustrated. By Herbert Broom, Esq., Barrister. Fourth Edition. 8vo. 31*s*. 6*d*. cloth.

Davies—A Handy Book of the Land, Assessed, and Income Tax Acts. By R. R. Davies. 8vo. 12*s*. 6*d*. cloth.

Davis and Owston—The Overseers' Manual, showing their Duties, Liabilities and Responsibilities, to which are added an Index of Cases, &c. By H. J. Davis and H. A. Owston. Post 8vo. 3*s*. 6*d*. cloth.

Dickson—A Treatise on the Law of Evidence in Scotland. Second Edition. By J. Skelton, Esq., Advocate. 2 Vols. royal 8vo. £2 5*s*. cloth.

Glen—General Consolidated and other Orders of the Poor Law Commissioners and the Poor Law Board. By W. C. Glen, Esq., Barrister. Fifth Edition. 12mo. 12*s*. cloth.

Nicol—The Bankruptcy Acts, 1849, 1854, and 1861; with Forms and Precedents. By H. Nicol, Esq., Barrister. Second Edition. Post 8vo. 14*s*. cloth.

Oke—Friendly Societies' Accounts: A Practical Exemplification of the Instructions in Book-keeping for Friendly Societies issued by the Registrar: with directions for checking, &c. By G. C. Oke. Post 8vo. 2*s*. 6*d*. cloth.

Phillimore—Private Law among the Romans, from the Pandects. By J. G. Phillimore, Esq., Q.C. 8vo. 16*s*. cloth.

Pollock and Nicol—Practice of the County Courts. By C. E. Pollock and H. Nicol, Esqrs., Barristers. Fifth Edition. 8vo. 30*s*. cloth.

Robertson—A Hand Book of Bankers' Law. (Scotland). By H. Robertson. Second Edition. 12mo. 4*s*. 6*d*. cloth.

Taylor—A Treatise on the Law of Evidence, as Administered in England and Ireland, with Illustrations from the American and other Foreign Laws. By J. Pitt Taylor, Esq., Barrister. Fourth Edition. 2 Vols. royal 8vo. £3 10*s*. cloth.

Waddilove—The Law of Marriage and Divorce, arranged in the form of a Code. By A. Waddilove, D.C.L. 8vo. 3*s*. 6*d*. cloth.

Wharton—The Law Lexicon, or Dictionary of Jurisprudence. By J. J. S. Wharton, Esq., Barrister. Third Edition. Imp. 8vo. 40*s*. cloth.

Williams—Principles of the Law of Personal Property, intended for the use of Students in Conveyancing. By J. Williams, Esq., Barrister. Fifth Edition. 8vo. 18*s*. cloth.

THE

Law Magazine and Law Review:

OR,

QUARTERLY JOURNAL OF JURISPRUDENCE.

No. XXXIV.

Art. I.—AUDIENCE, PREAUDIENCE, AND PRECEDENCE AT THE BAR.

THE rules that govern audience, preaudience, and precedence at the Bar, have necessarily a peculiar interest for our professional readers. Questions now rarely arise on this subject. The complication that exists is for the most part attributable to innovations of modern growth.

The Bar of a judicial tribunal has associations second only to the Bench. As the latter denotes the judgment seat and all that pertains to the office of the judge, the Bar or barrier which serves to fence the Bench, calls to mind the presence of all those who are immediately interested in the business before it—the culprit, the suitor, and the advocate or pleader. When the culprit is arraigned, or placed upon his trial, he is brought to this barrier, and is styled the prisoner at the Bar: and the proclamation calls upon all informers "to come forward and they shall be heard; for the prisoner stands at the Bar upon his deliverance." When the issue in a civil cause is tried in either of the superior courts sitting *in banco*, it is properly designated a trial at Bar.* So the advocate admitted to

* *See Paddock* v. *Forrester*, 1 M. & G., 583.

plead is called to, or received at, the Bar. When a barrister obtains preaudience or precedence it has been a recognised practice to distinguish him in court by calling him *within the Bar;* and in the happily very rare case when it has been necessary to degrade an unworthy barrister, he is said to be put *from the Bar.**

The law of England confers upon the presiding judges of every court the power of regulating in what manner audience at the Bar shall be granted. This power is restricted in many cases by positive regulations or by ancient usage: but when these do not prevail, it seems to be in the discretion of the Bench to determine the restrictions under which audience is to be granted, and whether any persons, and who, shall be allowed to be heard at the Bar:† and it is well established that all the powers enjoyed by the Benchers of the Inns of Court, of calling to the Bar, have been delegated to them by the judges.‡

The positive regulations which govern the right of audience at the Bar in Westminster Hall are of very ancient date. It would seem that up to the time of Magna Charta the only *conteurs* or pleaders were the serjeants, called to that degree by writ from the Crown. The *Mirror of Justices,* which gives the form of the serjeant's oath, as it is taken at this day, describes the countors or pleaders as "serjeants skilful in the laws of the realm, who serve the common people, to declare and defend actions in judgment for those who have

* *See* 1 Roll Rep. 55, l. 40. "Ne soit oye en la Court le Roy a counter pur nulluy." Stat. West. 1, c. 29, Co. 2, Inst. 214. For some slight neglect of an old counsellor, in 1602, Chief-Justice Wray is reported to have said to him, "Get you from the barr, or I will put you from the barr for your foolish pride."—"Templar's Diary," quoted in *Pearce's Inns of Court,* 424.

† *See* per Lord Tenterden in *Collier* v. *Hicks,* 2 Barn. & Ad. 668.

‡ *See* per Lord Mansfield in *Rex* v. *Gray's Inn,* 1 Dougl. 354. In Ireland, the practice still prevails of calling to the Bar in open Court. *See* Report of Mr. Heyward's case, 107.

From the Star Chamber Book it appears that a barrister was once appointed by letters patent, who had never graduated at either of the Inns of Court, and the validity of the patent was called in question. *See Harl. MSS.,* No. 980.

need of them, for their fees: *" and it is certain that in the chief court of ordinary jurisdiction between subject and subject (the Court of Common Pleas), from the earliest time of which we have any record, up to a very recent date, serjeants-at-law were the exclusive advocates and pleaders.

The Inns of Court and the subordinate Inns of Chancery, which seem to have been established about the time of the passing of Magna Charta, gradually supplied a sufficient number of apprentices-at-law, or students to serve in aid of the serjeants, or in lieu of them, in those courts where the serjeants could not attend, *e.g.*, the local courts, and those held at different places, under commission of assize, nisi prius, oyer and terminer, and gaol delivery,† and an ordinance of 1292 directed that a certain number of attorneys and apprentices should be chosen to follow the courts on their several circuits.‡

The Inns of Court and Chancery,§ instituted for the express purpose of promoting the study of the law, and the education of the future advocates or pleaders, established in imitation of the actual proceedings at Westminster Hall a system of exercises in forensic argument denominated in the uncouth language of old time *mootings* and *boltings*: and a certain probation in these exercises was required before the student could obtain a forensic degree. From the course of learning and legal exercises, which was assiduously kept up in these seminaries, the term apprentice ‖ came to be applied to every member. The bencher or great apprentice-at-law came next after the serjeant, and then the other appren-

* *Mirror of Justices*, c. 2., s. 5.; 2 Just. 214.

† The presence of the serjeants was generally required in the execution of their commissions in the capacity of judges. *See* 14 Ed. III., c. 16, and 4 Just., 160.

‡ *See* Rot. Parl. 20 Edw. I., 84, Dugdale's Orig. 55; Spelman's Gloss. *voce* Apprentice.

§ The Inns of Chancery were the subordinate establishments in which the junior students and clerks in Chancery were lodged. They had, however, their readers and their mootings as the higher Inns of Court had, and the attendance on those moots counted in qualifying the apprentice to obtain his degree.

‖ From *apprendre*, to learn.

tices who practised the law, and then apprentices of less estate.* The honoured ancient designation of *apprentice del ley* was retained to a modern period, and Plowden and Sir Henry Finch did not disdain so to describe themselves.

The name most frequently given, however, to both serjeants and apprentices-at-law, up to quite a recent date, was counsellor-at-law; a term used as descriptive of the whole class in a number of statutes.† The shorter word counsel in time came to denote all the learned persons who were chosen to be "of counsel" to any one,‡ hence the title queen's counsel, enjoyed by so many distinguished members of the Bar, in the patents appointing the gentleman selected as "one of our counsel learned in the law."

The halls of the Inns of Court and Chancery, in imitation of the courts at Westminster Hall, seem to have been partitioned off by a bar fencing the Bench, and denominated the upper bar,§ and an inner bar within which the students were placed. The latter were called mootmen, or inner barristers, whilst those who had passed the students' bar were called utter barristers;‖ but the utter barristers of the Inns of Court were not *de facto* entitled to practise as pleaders at the Bar in Westminster

* This was the order observed in an assessment made in 1379. See Rot. Parl. 58. The Recorder of London, it is said in one of the city books, ought to be "one of the most skilful and virtuous apprentices of the law in all the whole kingdom." Liber albus. ch. xv., Riley's edition, p. 38.

† The 5 Eliz., c. 14, speaks of attorneys, lawyers or counsellors. The 3 Jac. I., c. 5, s. 8, prohibits any recusant convict practising the law as a counsellor, clerk, attorney, or solicitor. The 13 Will. III., c. 6, prescribes the oath for serjeants-at-law, counsellors-at-law, barristers, advocates, attorneys and solicitors, and this is repeated in subsequent acts. *See* also 1 Edw. I., c. 13.

‡ "What says my counsel learned in the law?"—*Pope.*

§ *See*, as to this, Dugdale's Orig. 344, ed. 2.

‖ The utter barristers were so called, because when they argued at moots they sat uttermost on the forms which constituted the Bar. The other members or inner barristers were the youngest members who for lack of learning or continuance were not able to argue and reason in the *motes*, see return temp. Hen. VIII. quoted in Manning's *Serviens ad legem*, 262: "Every fellow of those two Inns of Chancery (Furnival's Inn and Thavies Inn) who had been allowed an utter barrister there, and that had mooted there two vacations at the utter bar should pay for their admissions into the fellowship of this house (Lincoln's Inn) only 13*s*. 4*d*., but any lesser utter barrister of any other Inn of Chancery 20*s*." *See* Dugdale's Orig. 342.

Hall. A long probation was first required, and it was only by gradual innovation on the ancient rules that a call to the Bar at one of the Inns of Court conferred the privileges now possessed by barristers.

The right of practising at the Bar in Westminster Hall seems up to a modern date* to have been confined to serjeants, benchers of one of the Inns of Court, readers of one of the Inns of Chancery, or utter barristers† of one of the Inns of Court, of a certain number of years standing. The period of probation varying at different times from three years to twelve.‡

Such being the general qualifications required in order to practise at the Bar, various regulations prevailed with respect to exclusive audience. In the Court of Common Pleas, the serjeants retained their exclusive right of pleading and audience at the Bar, up to the year 1846, when such privilege was taken away by an express Act of Parliament§—a previous order‖ in Council having been deemed insufficient to effect the object aimed at.¶ By more recent regula-

* *See* Dugdale, 312: and General Orders made in 1630, cited *ib.*

† The term utter barrister has been sometimes erroneously treated as describing the Junior Bar, as distinguished from those who are within the Bar at Westminster Hall. *See* Cowel's *Interpreter*, *voce* Utter Barrister, and all the law dictionaries which have borrowed from that work. Prynn and other eminent Members of the Bar gloried in the title of utter barrister.

‡ In 1558, it was prohibited to utter barristers to plead at any Bar until they were of twelve years standing, and then with the license of the benchers, provided that they might be of counsel with their clients, and come with them to the Bar upon their business already begun. Dugdale, Orig. Jus.

By the same rules, made in 1574, it was provided that none be admitted to plead at any of the Courts at Westminster, or to subscribe any action, bill, or plea, unless he be a reader or bencher in Court, or five years utter barrister, and continuing that time in exercise of learning, or a reader in Chancery two years at the least, and upon admonition as aforesaid, shall be at common prayers as before is limited. None to be allowed to plead before the justices of assizes, except he be allowed for a pleader in the Courts at Westminster, or shall be allowed by the justices of assize to plead before them.

Dugdale, 312. By the general order made in 1630, the period of probation of an utter barrister was reduced to three years, and by the 21 Jac. I c. 23, an "utter barrister of three years standing at the Bar of one of the four Inns of Courts was qualified to act as assessor of courts of record in boroughs," &c.

§ 9 & 10 Vict., c. 54.

‖ *See* the warrant, 24th April, 1834, set out in 10 Bingh, 571.

¶ *See* the proceedings at length, in Scott Rep., and Manning's *Serviens ad Legem*.

tions for transferring the jurisdiction in probate and divorce cases from Doctors Commons to newly constituted courts at Westminster Hall, the exclusive privileges of the doctors of law, as advocates, have been taken away, and the right of audience in the new courts extended to all barristers.*

The principles of free trade, upon which these changes seem to have been based, have been also brought to bear on the general privileges of the Bar. The same year in which the privilege of audience in the Common Pleas was conferred generally on barristers, the right of advocacy in the county courts, with a most extensive jurisdiction, transferred from Westminster Hall, was legally conferred on attorneys as well as barristers:† but the principles of free trade, with reference to the Bar, have not at present progressed any further.

In all the Courts at Westminster Hall, and on circuit, the exclusive right of audience is still enjoyed by the serjeants and barristers; and at the various courts of quarter session, the Bar of Westminster Hall enjoy a practical monopoly, orders of justices having been held valid, which provided that on the attendance of a sufficient number of barristers being secured, they alone should be heard as advocates.‡

The rules that govern audience and exclusive audience at the English Bar are, however, not only prescribed by the positive provisions of the law; some also and those of no small importance are derived from the established etiquette of the profession. On these are based the old established regulations affecting the circuits, the more modern rules with reference to quarter sessions, and the still more modern

* 20 & 21 Vict., c. 79, s. 46; 20 & 21 Vict., c. 85, s. 15.

† 9 & 10 Vict., c. 95, s. 91; *see* now 15 & 16 Vict., c. 54, s. 10. Attorneys and solicitors were previously empowered to act as advocates in the Bankruptcy Court (*see* 1 & 2 Will. IV., c. 36, s. 10, re-enacted in 12 & 13 Vict., c. 106, s. 247), and also before magistrates in cases arising out of their summary jurisdictions. *See* 6 & 7 Will. IV., c. 114, s. 2, and 11 & 12 Vict., c. 43, s. 12.

‡ *See Rex* v. *Justices of Denbighshire*, 9 Q. B. Rep. 279; 15 Law Journal, N.S., Q.B. 335.

usages which have separated the Common Law Bar from the Chancery Bar, and called into existence what is sometimes denominated the Parliamentary Bar.

From a remote period—perhaps from the time of the ordnance of Edward I. already referred to *—the circuits of the judges seem to have been attended by a regular Bar, and by the existing rules of etiquette each barrister, after deliberately choosing his circuit, is precluded from practising on any other unless he has formally changed his circuit† or he be specially retained for the occasion. Similar regulations, adopted also by the profession, secure to the chief courts of quarter sessions throughout the country a regular attendance of barristers, and the etiquette that enforces these regulations is deservedly respected, having for its object the convenience of the Bar and most undoubtedly conducing to the interest of the public.‡ The attempts of unworthy practitioners of either branch of the law to frustrate such rules have generally caused only their own discomfiture.

The rules of etiquette, however, which serve to keep up such distinctions as that of the Common Law Bar from the Equity Bar, &c., are not so easily ascertained. Though the more eminent members of the Bar succeed in confining their ordinary practice to one class of business and sometimes to one court, no such self-imposed restrictions are usually adopted, many barristers of unquestionable reputation attending the civil and criminal courts on circuit, and the Chancery Courts in London, and the so called Parliamentary Bar being now protected by no prohibitive rules of etiquette.

Such being the right of audience and the rules that affect

* *See* ante, p. 205.

† Which can only be done by those of junior standing.

‡ The inducements to the Bar for keeping up the present usages of circuit and sessions are certainly not so great as they formerly were. With a large increase in the number of barristers on every circuit, not only are the cases for trial much fewer than in old times, but the fees as a general rule are small in amount; the fees for a barrister at Sessions who has to travel 150 miles or even more to reach his destination, are generally less than those usually adopted by attorneys where they act as advocates.

exclusive audience, we have now to deal with the questions of preaudience and precedence. For the proper discipline of the Bar and the benefit of the public, certain rules of precedence and preaudience must be observed. To whom should the power be left of laying down those rules? To confer the power on every occasion on the client of deciding which barrister shall be leader and which junior, would be merely to add, without any public benefit, to the already large influence possessed by the attorneys. To rest all precedence and preaudience on concessions from the Crown would be a substitute equally objectionable.

There have been great innovations upon the ancient rules with respect to precedence and preaudience. These have been of recent growth. They have crept in without any apparent object or perceptible public gain. Lord Coke describes the gradations of the Bar in his time as follows:—

"Now for the degrees of the law, as there be in the Universities of Cambridge and Oxford divers degrees, as sophisters, bachelors, masters, doctors, of whom be chosen men for eminent and judicial places, both in the Church and Ecclesiastical courts; so in the profession of the law there are mootmen (which are those that argue readers' cases, in the houses of Chancery, both in terms and grand vacations.) Of mootmen, after eight years' study or thereabouts, are chosen utter barristers; of these are chosen readers in Inns of Chancery. Of utter barristers after they have been of that degree twelve years at least, are chosen benchers, or ancients; of which one, that is of the puisne sort, reads yearly in summer vacation, and is called a single reader; and one of the ancients that had formerly read, reads in Lent vacation and is called a double reader, and commonly it is between his first and second reading, about nine or ten years. And out of these the King makes choice of his attorney, and solicitor-general, his attorney of the court of wards and liveries, and attorney of the duchy; and of these readers, are serjeants elected by the King, and are, by the King's writ, called *ad statum* *et gradum servientis ad legem;* and out of these the King electeth one, two, or three as please him, to be his serjeants, which are called the king's serjeants: of serjeants are by the King also constituted the honourable and reverend judges and sages of the law." * Other books of authority also mention as the degrees of rank at the Bar those of serjeants-at-law, benchers, and utter barrister,† and the gradations at the Bar from counsellor-at-law to serjeant are continually referred to in the regulations for the government of the Inns of Court.‡

Since Lord Coke wrote, a great innovation has taken place in the practice of promotion at the Bar. The degrees which Coke enumerates are, to a great extent, eclipsed by appointments made direct by the Crown. Instead of the one, two, or three king's serjeants in former times selected to aid the attorney and solicitor-general, it has gradually become the practice for the office of queen's counsel to be conferred on a very large number of barristers. In 1799, the number of Crown counsel had increased to fifteen. At this day we find in the law list the names of more than one hundred and thirty barristers holding these appointments.

The practice having obtained for barristers other than those actually required for the service of the Crown, to obtain patents as queen's counsel, the appointment came to be in demand§ merely as a professional degree. The creation of king's and queen's counsel extraordinary, as they were, until recently, denominated,‖ has been so much on the increase that they now far outnumber the whole body of serjeants and

* *See* 3 Co. Rep. proœm XIX.

† *Wynne's Eunomus*, p. 283, and *see* 1 Eliz., c. 1, s. 5, and 7 Jac. I., c. 6, ss. 14 and 15, as to oaths.

‡ When any serjeant or counsellor-at-law shall at any time come before the Board to move their Lordships concerning any matter, and shall not wear their gowns according to their places, upon such neglect by any of them, if it be a serjeant he to deposit 20*s*., and if it be a counsellor 10*s*." Judges Orders made at Whitehall, 19 March, 1636, Dugdale, Orig. 321.

§ The appointment of king's counsel was, in former times, always offered unsolicited. *See* Twiss' "Life of Lord Eldon," Vol. i., p. 4.

‖ *See* the formal list of promotions at the Bar, in preface to 1 Wilson's Reports.

benchers not having such appointments. The number of serjeants remain as they did thirty years ago, but the benchers' tables of the Inns of Court are so crowded with queen's counsel, that the old rank of bencher bids fair to be lost sight of. At first there seems to have been a resistance to this state of things. To use the language of the late Mr. Justice Talfourd, "The particular description of rank which was given by the Crown as matter of special favour, and has since become so frequently bestowed, was scarcely known at all in old times. Serjeant was known, and bencher was known; reader was known, and utter barrister was known; but king's counsel, except being really of the King's Council by holding office under the Crown was not known."*

The benchers of the Middle Temple demurred, after North had been made king's counsel, to call him to the Bench table,† and at a much more recent date the claim of the queen's counsel to be *de facto* elected benchers of their Inn has been successfully resisted.‡ The practice before introduced has been so far discontinued that there are now several instances of queen's counsel of long standing who have never been elected to the Bench table.§

Looking to the great increase in the number of queen's counsel, compared with that of serjeants-at-law, and the frequent applications still made for the appointment, it can be little doubted that the caprice of our time has brought about a preference among the majority of aspirants for forensic distinction for the more modern office over the more ancient rank. It cannot be denied that many of the most distinguished members of the Bar have given the preference to the modern office of queen's counsel over the degree of serjeant, but neither can it be deemed invidious to observe

* Argument in Mr. Hayward's case, p. 77.

† *See* note to Siderfin, 365, and North's "Life of Lord Keeper Guildford."

‡ *See* report of Mr. Hayward's dispute with the Inner Temple, 1846.

§ Mr. Edwin James, who obtained the office of Q.C., in 1850, and was disbarred, after practising as a leading advocate ten years subsequently, had never been called to the rank of bencher.

that others who have attained equal eminence have in their own persons well upheld the ancient dignity of the coif; and that Serjeant's Inn in our time has been enabled to bring to the public service at least as large a proportion of excellence as the modern order of queen's counsel.* There is moreover some inconvenience in the existing practice of appointing so many permanent counsel for the Crown. The practice has a tendency to fetter the independent action of the Bar, directly restricting the right possessed by the public freely to seek from the Bar the services of any of its members. When so large a proportion of the most eminent of the Bar are enlisted in the service of the Crown, and cannot be relieved from their obligation without a licence, the public are sometimes made to feel that they are unjustly restricted in their selection of counsel.†

Serjeants-at-law are still called by writ from the Crown: but, unlike queen's counsel, they are in no way in the service of the Crown, and therefore under no similar restrictions in respect to advocacy; and they certainly are never promoted from political influence of any kind. The course is now, as it has existed for many ages, for the promotion to the rank of serjeant to take place on the direct recommendation of the judges; the Chief-Justice of the Common Pleas by the advice and counsel of the other judges, when the number of serjeants is deemed insufficient,

* Of the judges now on the Bench at Westminster Hall, three have filled the office of attorney or solicitor-general, four successfully practised as serjeants, four as queen's counsel, and four were never called within the Bar.

† In cases in which the Crown is concerned, it is a constant practical hardship that in order to obtain the services of a queen's counsel for the other side, a special licence from the Crown is required. The injustice of this was pointed out many years ago, when there were not one-tenth of the present number of queen's counsel; *see* Professor Christian's note to 3 Bl. Com., 27. The practice, however, and the exactions it imposes on defendants in criminal proceedings continue. In ordinary criminal trials, the effect generally is only to impose on the prisoner the additional cost of the licence from the Crown. In prosecutions for political offences it is always in the power of the Crown to withhold the licence.

presenting to the Lord Chancellor the names of those who are fit for the degree.*

The serjeants were in former times generally selected from those who had filled the office of reader in the Inn of Court to which they belonged; and upon receipt by an utter barrister of a writ to be made a serjeant-at-law, he was at once elected reader of his own inn, and not only raised over the rest of the utter barristers, but placed at the upper end of the bench table of his inn, above all other readers, as being a serjeant elect.† At Westminster Hall too, serjeants as soon as called seem always to have been admitted within the Bar of the Court of Common Pleas, and to have had precedency and preaudience in all the courts over all barristers not having a special warrant for their preaudience or precedence. What constitutes such a special warrant it is not so easy to say.

Thus, no position at the English Bar is now more free from question than that of Her Majesty's attorney-general; and yet his precedence and preaudience in ordinary cases at West-

* *See* on this, Fortescue *de laudibus legum Angliæ*, ch. 5. That the appointment of King's and Queen's Counsel have been often made from political motives, and the applications for such appointments rejected for want of the right political influence is a matter too well established to be controverted. The refusal for political reasons of Lord Eldon to give a silk gown to Brougham when in the zenith of his glory at the Bar, is referred to with exultation in one of the published letters of the Tory Chancellor. *See* Twiss' Life of Lord Eldon, Vol. ii, p. 537. In some recent proceedings consequent on a charge of professional misconduct against a barrister having a seat in Parliament who had conferred on him after a brief Parliamentary campaign the appointment of one of Her Majesty's Counsel, it was openly stated without any contradiction, that a previous solicitation by the honourable Member in the regular way for the rank of serjeant-at-law had met with a refusal.

† "If any person receive a serjeant's writ, either in Hilary Term returnable in Easter Term, or Trinity Term returnable in Michaelmas Term, so as there be a reading time between the receipt and the return of the writ, the party to whom such writ is sent is to read in that next vacation, whether he hath before read or not. . . . . Likewise if any Member of this House receives a serjeant's writ he is then forthwith placed at the upper end of the Bench table above all other readers, as being a serjeant elect though not complete, and notwithstanding such his writ he continues still a Bencher, and in commons until the day of solemnity and receiving of the coif, at which time he takes his leave of the House."—Dugdale, Orig. Jur. 210.

The precedence of serjeants-at-law rests on legal warrant.

minster Hall, have been only gradually conceded to him. Lord Coke is reported to have denied this right when Sir Francis Bacon, as attorney-general, claimed it over a serjeant-at-law, in cases where the attorney-general did not appear on behalf of the Crown,* and the king's serjeant took precedence of the attorney-general, until, in consequence of Serjeant Shepherd being appointed to fill the subordinate office of solicitor-general in 1814, the order of precedence was altered by royal warrant.†

The precedence and preaudience of the attorney-general have now been settled by this warrant. Next in order comes the queen's advocate, and after him the solicitor-general, and then the queen's serjeants; and after the serjeants and queen's counsel, the recorder and common serjeant of London, if not already of the degree of the coif, or having an appointment as queen's counsel. Benchers not having the latter distinction do not at this day seem to assert any precedence over ordinary barristers but their seniority, to be counted from the date of their call to the Bar.

The precedence and preaudience of queen's counsel, other than the attorney and solicitor-general, over serjeants-at-law do not rest on a very certain warrant. When the practice of appointing counsel for the Crown, not of the ancient degree of serjeant-at-law, was first introduced, much difficulty arose in settling their status in court. North received his appointment in Easter Term, 20 Car. 2, but the benchers of his inn,

* Sir Francis Bacon, attorney-general, being to move, a serjeant-at-law having a short motion, offered to move before him; at which he was much moved, saying that he marvelled he would offer this to him. Upon this Coke, Chief-Justice, said, no serjeant ought to move before the king's attorney, when he moves for the King; but for other motions any serjeant-at-law is to move before him, and when I was the king's attorney I never offered to move before a serjeant unless it was for the King."—3 Bulstrode, 32. The attorney-general at this day gives place in the Court of Exchequer, when not appearing for the Crown, to the tubman and postman.

In the Court of Common Pleas, whilst the exclusive privileges of the serjeants remained, the attorney-general could not be heard at all except on the business of the Crown.—*See Paddock* v. *Forrester*, 1 M. & G., 588.

† *See* the warrant, 14 December, 1814, 2 M. & G. 253; 6 Taunton, 424.

the Middle Temple, demurred to his precedence, and considerable discussion arose before it was accorded to him.* However, he seems to have been at once admitted within the Bar of the Court of Queen's Bench,† and the practice has prevailed ever since of calling within the Bar those who have received similar appointments,‡ but the same distinction has always been conferred on those barristers who have obtained precedence or preaudience at the Bar in other ways, *e.g.*, by an express patent of precedence from the Crown,§ and there is reason to believe that previous to the great influx into the front row of so many counsel for the Crown, all serjeants coming from the Common Pleas into any other court, and those who were called to the Bench of their Inn, by seniority or merit, and had filled the office of reader, had the same distinction conferred on them by the judges.‖ The privilege of sitting within the Bar is one which seems clearly to be derived from the judges, and to have no dependence on any patent from the Crown,¶ and the judges at Westminster Hall would be deemed probably to possess the same power which they have at various times been called on to exercise, to settle for the public convenience questions affecting preaudience. Lord Bacon is reported to have claimed for the presiding judge, a

* *See* Roger North's "Life of Lord Keeper Guildford."

† *See* 1 Siderfin, 365.

‡ When Mr. Scarlett (Lord Abinger) was made a king's counsel, in 1816, Lord Ellenborough formally, or rather informally, called him within the Bar at nisi prius. *See* per Chief-Baron Pollock, in Report of Mr. Hayward's case, p. 82.

§ The custom of granting patents of precedence is spoken of by Blackstone as only then recently introduced. 3 Bl. Com. 27.

‖ "The names of such as have read double or shall read double, shall be given to the judges who have promised to give them pre-eminence of hearing after serjeants and her Majesty's counsel." Orders for regulation of the Inns of Court, 16 Eliz.; Dugdale Orig. Jur. p. 212. "Benchers also do come within the Bar at the Chapel of the Rolls, and sit their promiscuously among the serjeants-at-law and the king's and queen's counsel learned." Dugdale, 210.

¶ In the County Palatine Courts, a limited number of gentlemen at the Bar under the rank of serjeant are from time to time called within the Bar by the judges and have preaudience and precedence, next after serjeants. Gentlemen so promoted are in the *Law List* erroneously designated as queen's counsel of the County Palatine.

degree of absolute power in this respect.* Lord Mansfield consulting more the real convenience of the public contented himself with proposing a less arbitrary innovation on the old order of preaudience.† The present Lord Chief-Justice concurring with the Lord Chief-Baron, and, indeed, all the judges, has very recently made a useful regulation with respect to seats within the Bar—restoring with a very good grace to the serjeants-at-law in the Queen's Bench and Exchequer, their proper place.

The great influx of queen's counsel of late years had gone far to give them the monopoly of the seats within the Bar; and the usage of formally calling other barristers within the Bar, has been going out. The Benchers of the Inns of Court,

* "And since I am upon the point whom I will hear, your Lordships will give me leave to tell you a fancy. It falleth out that there be three of us the king's servants in great places that are lawyers by descent; Mr. Attorney, son of a judge; Mr. Solicitor, likewise son of a judge; and myself a Chancellor's son. Now, because the law roots so well in my time, I will water it at the roots thus far, as besides these great ones, I will hear any judge's son before a serjeant, and any serjeant's son before a reader, if there be not many of them." Bacon's speech on taking his oath as Lord Keeper.

† The new Lord Chief-Justice at his first setting out, instituted a different method of going through the motions at the Bar, from that which had been usually, and, indeed, most universally, practised theretofore; which new method was not only advantageous to the younger part of the barristers, but also exceedingly convenient to the suitors, as it took away that delay to business which arose from the unreasonable preference hitherto given to gentlemen within the Bar. For the repeated preaudience hitherto allowed them, had thrown almost the whole business into their hands; which as they were entitled to move only once a day, could not be sufficiently despatched. The course had been, ever since I remember, and was in Lord Chief-Justice Holt's time (as the late Mr. Justice Page has often told me), "to begin every day, with the senior counsel within the Bar, and then to call to the next senior in order, and so on, as long as it was convenient to the court to sit; and to proceed again in the same manner upon the next and every subsequent day; although the Bar had not been half or perhaps a quarter gone through upon any one of the former days; so that the juniors were very often obliged to attend in vain, without being able to bring on their motions, for many successive days." This was the settled and general rule; though, perhaps, the judges out of mere compassion to the juniors, would two or three times in a Term give them leave to move upon the next day such motions as were real remanets of the former day. Whereas Lord Mansfield professed and most punctually practised the going quite through the Bar, even to the youngest counsel, before he would begin again with the seniors; even though it should happen to take two, or three, or more days before all the motions which were ready at the Bar could be heard." Burrow's Rep. p. 57.

not holding the appointment of queen's counsel, have for many years been in a small minority,* and the serjeants who formerly attached themselves exclusively to the Court of Common Pleas, did not seek the distinction of sitting within the Bar of the other courts;† but since all the courts of Westminster Hall have been indifferently opened to all the Bar according to their rank and seniority, a different state of things has arisen. The royal warrant of 1834 expressly conferred on all the then existing serjeants precedence and preaudience in all the courts over all subsequently made king's counsel. The 9 & 10 Vict., c. 54, which affected the other objects aimed at by this warrant, left the question of precedence and preaudience of the serjeants as it was made. By the regulation already referred to in the Courts of Queen's Bench and Exchequer, the privilege has been with a very good grace conceded to all serjeants of sitting within the Bar, and they now enjoy this distinction in all courts as they always did in the Court of Common Pleas.

This very just concession to the serjeants leaves altogether open all questions of precedence and preaudience. The precedence of the serjeants for some purposes is warranted by positive law.‡ The precedence and preaudience of gentlemen holding the appointment of queen's counsel are the result of usage and practice, and a special precedence and preaudience have been conferred on certain serjeants and barristers by special patent of precedence. The result is that some confusion and complication are occasioned in settling the exact precedence and preaudience of any of the order.

* Up to 1827 the Inner Temple Benchers counted only six king's counsel among them, out of a Bench table of twenty-nine. At this day they have thirty-seven queen's counsel, and only two of the benchers are practising at the Bar without an appointment from the Crown. Well might it be remarked by the benchers that they were "deluged with silk." *See* per Sir F. Thesiger in Mr. Hayward's case, Report p. 135.

† The serjeants were on being called to that degree always admonished to keep the Common Pleas Bar. *See* the Exhortation, Dugdale, Orig. Jur.

‡ *See* as to this, 1 Edw. VI., c. 7, s. 3, and the authorities cited in the Serjeant's case, 8 Scott's Rep. 265 Appendix, and *see* the table of precedence prefixed to "Burke's Peerage."

A barrister called to the degree of serjeant has *de facto* precedence and preaudience over all other barristers not having a patent expressly conferring seniority on them; and the serjeants among themselves derive their seniority from the date of their call to that rank. A barrister appointed a queen's counsel practically at this day enjoys preaudience both over serjeants and other barristers not having such a special patent—the queen's counsel among themselves derive their seniority from the date of their appointment—but it has been the usage for many years for serjeants and barristers to obtain special patents of precedence varying their former position as regards all other serjeants and barristers; and the position at the Bar of the latter may thus be continually shifted.* This confusion and complication might be very easily put an end to with great advantage to all concerned.

Let the rules of seniority of call which prevail among ordinary barristers apply also within the Bar. Let there be in future no provision for one gentleman in the front row jumping by virtue of a patent from the Crown over the heads of all the others. Let there be no more patents of precedence, but let those who have legitimately obtained a place within the Bar by virtue of their promotion in either of the three modes already referred to keep such place notwithstanding any fresh concession from the Crown to a new comer.

By such an order of seniority being settled, all complications as to precedence and preaudience both at Westminster Hall and on circuit would be put an end to, without causing injustice to anyone.

* Erskine and Pigott (afterwards Chief-Baron) were made king's counsel one day before Scott (Lord Eldon) who was the senior of both at the Bar. After a great deal of manœuvring very special patents were made out to Scott and another senior who was promoted at the same time, giving them the precedence over Erskine and Pigott.—Mr. Twiss' "Life of Lord Eldon," Vol. i., p. 143.

Art. II.—CAPITAL PUNISHMENT.—THE ROYAL COMMISSION.

THE beneficial mitigation of the severity of our Penal Code, begun by the late Sir Samuel Romilly, and partly, though to a very small extent, effected during his life, was sure ultimately to occasion a public inquiry, as to the necessity for retaining the punishment of death for any offence. That inquiry has not arrived too speedily;* a demand for it having been accelerated by a flexible exercise, for several years, of the prerogative of pardon, whereby the law has been rendered in its operation very uncertain, and far more frequently non-capital than capital.

In the debate on capital punishment in the House of Commons, on the 3rd of May last, on Mr. Ewart's motion, which resulted in the issuing of the above Commission, it is remarkable that arguments in favour of continuing the capital penalty founded on theology or natural justice, were almost entirely abandoned, one speaker only having alluded to what he considered to be the expressed will of the Almighty. It may therefore, it is believed, now be regarded as generally admitted (at least, by all persons familiar with those facts necessary to be known in order to arrive at a true solution of the question), that necessity can alone justify the State in visiting a citizen with death; consequently, that death inflicted for sentimental reasons only—for example, for the sake of vengeance, or from a sense of justice—is a proceeding utterly indefensible, and as irrational as is beheading the corpse of a traitor, or as an attempt to wash out blood by blood. It is believed, therefore, that it would be agreeable, if not to the whole nation, at least to a large and increasing number of the most respectable and best informed portion of it, if our laws could, consistently with the public welfare, be

* The expediency of a Royal Commission to inquire into the operation of capital punishment was suggested in 1860. *See* Law Amendment Society's papers, 17th Dec., 1860.

rendered entirely non-capital. That innocent persons have occasionally been condemned and executed is a fact, alas! indisputable, and very recently some remarkable examples of the miscarriage of juries, in cases not capital, have reminded the public, that the possibility of the like fatal and irremediable error must exist, so long as the capital penalty is retained.

One of the first, and perhaps the first, of the inquiries brought under the consideration of the Commissioners, will therefore be—whether there is from any and what cause a reluctance in juries to convict on trials for capital offences; and whether any distinction is made by juries when the victim of murder is an infant; and if, contrary to our anticipations,* it should be found that there is no such reluctance, and that human life is equally protected at all ages from malicious attempts to destroy it,—advocates for the abolition of capital punishment will no longer be able to avail themselves of the reluctance of juries to convict, as one of their favourite arguments; but on the other hand, should such reluctance be found to exist, and should it appear that human life is not equally protected from murder at all ages, and that from these causes guilt is likely to escape, and occasionally escapes, conviction, it appears difficult to continue for any beneficial purpose the capital penalty. Whether it should be continued depends, however, upon many other considerations besides those last referred to. At present as regards malicious homicides the law is, and has been for several years, theoretically capital, but in the great majority of convictions practically non-capital, and hence it may be predicated that the Commissioners will recommend either the abandonment of the death penalty, or surround the sentence of death with such new circumstances, as will, if possible, render the infliction of it satisfactory to the public.

* From 1858 to 1862 convictions for murder were 322 out of 1,000; for all other offences 755 out of 1,000.—Communicated by H. T. Humphreys, Secretary to the Anti-Capital Punishment Association.

The causes that produced the Commission may be stated to be, first, the increased regard for human life arising from many years of domestic tranquillity and the consequent progress of the nation in humanity and civilisation; secondly, the belief that the death punishment is either not a deterrent, or if a deterrent, is attended with circumstances that render its infliction productive of more evil than good, or that it is, as a deterrent, not greater than, or so great as, hopeless penal imprisonment or hopeless penal servitude for life would be; thirdly, the co-existence with the two former causes of an irresponsible power in the Crown to stay the executioner's hand, after the convict has been sentenced to die. The word "irresponsible" is used because the power has been exercised on allegations brought *ex parte* to the notice of the Crown, without any public investigation, and in the absence of any agent to protect the public welfare. The first of the foregoing causes, operating on the last, has now for some years occasioned frequent and extraordinary public manifestations for mercy where the slightest doubt of guilt has appeared to exist, and in cases even where the Court has been satisfied with the verdict. It has also caused the law to be administered, not on an uniform principle, but on a principle vibrating in its movements according as it is operated upon by the public, or a portion of the public. Hence, one murderer has been executed, whilst another, for an offence precisely equal in degree, has escaped. In some cases an inquiry after verdict and sentence of death is made, in others not, although justice requires that if further inquiry be allowed in any case, it should be made in all, since all verdicts are fallible. Now a penal law ought not to be varied in its operation, for to the extent to which it is relaxable, it ceases to be penal; and yet having regard to public opinion, the death penalty can at present be carried out in a comparatively few cases only. Thus the deterrent effect of the law, if such deterrent effect exist, is so uncertain as to be reduced to a *minimum*. The second of the three before mentioned causes that occasioned the Commission, has greatly augmented the power of the first; and has also raised a question entirely independent of considerations arising from religion or humanity—in short a question of police; for the abolitionists of capital punishment, without availing themselves of the arguments in their favour founded on Christian theology or civilisation, allege that, having regard to the causes of murders, the death penalty is not only not deterrent, but that from its demoralising operation it tends to foment those vicious passions that give birth to the crime.

For the purpose of ascertaining whether the capital penalty is or is not at all, or to any, and if any to what extent, deterrent, the psychology of murderers will, it is presumed, be investigated, so that the report may be satisfactory to men of science who have made psychological facts their special study. Upon this branch of inquiry it is believed that much information, with which the public is only partially acquainted, may be adduced by the examination of physicians of experience and learning, and others. There seems, indeed, to be little doubt that the psychological causes of murder may be ascertained with exactitude, and that those murders that have been brought to the notice of the public are types of all undiscovered murders; and if by referring to trials for murder for a series of years, the motives which occasion the crime seem to be such as to defy repression by the death penalty, the Commissioners will hardly fail to point out its inutility from that cause alone. Under this head of inquiry it may possibly be ascertained, that when any passions are sufficiently excited, no self-control from reasoning about consequences exists, and that the murderous intent or passion is that on which the death penalty has, if any, the most feeble operation. Moreover, on examining the origin of murders, the Commissioners will probably discover that one and all arise from cupidity, and that cupidity has its varieties capable of classification, and is a more powerful emotion than the fear of death. The following statement shows how easily murders and the causes of them may be classed.

The Varieties of Cupidity which occasion Murders.	Cases that have actually occurred, proving each variety, with their Dates.
	21st December, 1846.
1. Despair	1st—Hannah Reid found drowned in Waterloo-dock, London, with the body of her recently born infant bound to her waist, her arms clasping the child to her bosom.
	2nd—All suicides.
2. Superstition...	Suttees and the voluntary prostration of human beings for death, before the crushing wheels of the Juggernaut.
	16th May, 1854.
3. Lust	Lewellin Garratt Talmage Harvey, aged 30, murdered Mary Richards, aged 21, having dragged her into a coppice and violated her person, and stunned her with blows of which she died.
	24th December, 1828.
4. Gain	1st—Burke and Hare, who at Glasgow had suffocated several persons to sell their bodies for anatomical purposes.
	19th July, 1849.
	2nd—Rebecca Smith, a pious and devout Sabbatarian, the mother of eleven children, ten of whom she poisoned, and was executed for poisoning the last, a month old. The reason she alleged was to save her children from want.

The Varieties of Cupidity which occasion Murders.	Cases that have actually occurred, proving each variety, with their Dates.
	1st January, 1845.
5. Love of a false but good reputation.	1st—Tawell, a married man, in apparent affluence and very charitable, murdered at Salt Hill a woman, Sarah Hart, with whom he cohabited. 2nd—All murders of newly born bastards, now so common.
	18th August, 1847.
6. Anger	The murder, early in the morning, of the Duchess de Praslin at Paris, by her husband, who afterwards committed suicide. Violent altercations had long existed between them.
	16th February, 1846.
7. Hatred	The murder of James Bostock, in Drury Lane, by his apprentice Wicks, who had received a debt due to his master of 15*s*., and could account for 4*s*. only. He told his master he had lost 11*s*. of it, and proposed paying it back at 2*s*. 6*d*. a week, but his master insisted on deducting the 15*s*. from his week's wages; for which he shot him dead a day or two afterwards.
	1st October, 1861.
8. Revenge	Murder of Mr. Mark Frater, a tax-collector, at Newcastle-on-Tyne, by a carpenter named Clark, for distraining his work tools. The distress was made in the pre-

The Variety of Cupidity which occasion Murders.	Cases that have actually occurred, proving each variety, with their Dates.
	vious July. Immediately after the murder Clark exclaimed, "It's all right, he has robbed me and I have paid him."
	20th September, 1860.
9. Jealousy	A bailiff named Harrison was in the occupation of a cottage in which the prisoner Lockey's wife lived with three children by a former marriage. Harrison slept below, Mrs. Lockey above. Lockey became jealous of Harrison, and on his way home from work was heard to use violent language, and soon after he arrived at home, he attempted to murder both his wife and Harrison, and killed Harrison.
10. Envy	The first historical murder.

Can it be for a moment credited, that fear can have had any operation in restraining any one of the foregoing homicidal passions, especially if they be excited by inebriation? and yet it is believed, that there is no cause of murder that may not be attributed to one or more of them. They are adduced here as examples. The fear of death is, in truth, a very feeble opponent to the other emotions of human nature. When contending with cupidity it invariably gives way, whether the object of the cupidity be good, for example, to save life from drowning or to win a battle in a just war—or bad, as to commit a murder from revenge, or to fight as a mercenary.

Although human nature is, as regards its elementary properties, the same throughout the world, the social institutions of one nation are not necessarily applicable to every other; and therefore no sound argument can indisputably be raised in favour of the abolition of capital punishment in this country because its abolition has worked well in others; but if the abolition of the death penalty has not increased crime, amongst a people unquestionably less civilised than we are, it is a legitimate argument to allege that it would not be followed by any increase of crime with us.

Sir James Mackintosh, who presided for seven years as Judge of the Supreme Court of Bombay, in his last address to the grand jury is represented to have said:

> "In the seven years ending 1763, there had been 141 capital convictions, out of which there were 47 executions, averaging nearly seven a year. A gradual reduction of punishments took place, and in the seven years ending 1804, under the presidency of Sir William Syer, the convictions for murder were 18, and the executions 12 (not quite two a year). During the seven years of my presidency, dating from 1804, there were but six murder convictions *and no executions.* Yet there was during that entire period no diminution in the security of the lives or property of men."

If then the fact of the abolition of capital punishment amongst a people comparatively barbarous having led to no increase of crime, affords sound ground for its abolition, how greatly is the weight of that argument increased when applied to countries as civilised as our own, in which executions have, without any public disadvantage, been abolished? How then can it be contended if the suspension or abolition of the law of death operates satisfactorily in Louisiana, Rhode Island, Michigan, and Wisconsin; in Laenwarden, Utrecht, Brunswick, Denmark, Belgium, Berne, and Tuscany, (in which last State the punishment of death has for the third time been by law abolished,) that it will not operate in like manner with us?

This will be an important and interesting subject for the inquiry and consideration of the Commissioners.

Respect for life—whether of animals or of man—is a sentiment created by civilisation. What boy ever refrained from robbing birds of their nests from any natural feeling of pity? What barbarian ever hesitated to take away life from a feeling of compassion or a sense of religion? Now surely wilful homicides must correspond in number with the degree of value placed on human life; for amongst a people by whom it is held very sacred there must be few—by whom it is lightly regarded there must be many. The object of our institutions should therefore be to consecrate human life.

Another of the objects of inquiry therefore probably will be, whether the death penalty—independently of the manner of executing it—has or has not any and what operation, either in encouraging humane feelings, or checking their development; while one of the inquiries specially mentioned in the Commission is the operation of the manner in which the death sentence is executed. Should the report advise the abolition of the death penalty that inquiry will become unnecessary except for the purpose of illustration; but it is very important that there should be very satisfactory evidence adduced as to the operation on the public morals of public executions—because, notwithstanding the report, the legislature may retain the capital penalty. Upon this head of inquiry numerous witnesses should be examined, that the tendency of public opinion may be ascertained. It is believed that much more extensive and valuable evidence may be obtained on this head, than that adduced before the Select Committee of the House of Lords on executions in jails in 1856. In Tasmania, executions are not, we are informed, conducted in public—and we are also informed that no evil has arisen therefrom—and in other countries, it may be (Prussia is one) that death sentences are carried into effect before a limited number of witnesses. The Commissioners will doubtless be able to obtain valuable evidence as to the effect of such executions—and to ascertain whether there is any reason to suppose they create suspicion of foul play, or tend to encourage assassination.

That a great change of opinion as to the expediency of retaining the death penalty has occurred, is certain, from the course taken by the House of Commons on Mr. Ewart's motion. The Commissioners will doubtless ascertain the causes of this change, with reference to which the Home Office will be able to furnish important evidence, by supplying the Commissioners with the particulars of the applications to the Home Secretary for a commutation of the death sentence during a period of years, the number of such applications, and the reasons for refusing or acceding to them. Doubtless these reasons are recorded; if not, they ought to have been. They will, if afforded, probably prove to be the most interesting and important matter adduced before the Commissioners, especially if the expediency of retaining the prerogative of mercy should, directly or indirectly, be brought under their consideration.

From what has preceded, it will be observed that the Commissioners will exhaust the subject of their commission by proceeding under four heads of inquiry, viz.

1st. The operation of the death penalty on juries.

2nd. Whether it operates at all, or to any and what extent as a deterrent; an inquiry which suggests two topics for consideration, viz.

(1st.) The emotions which end in murder, and what are the counteracting emotions, and whether the fear of death is one of them.

(2nd.) The operation of the abolition of the death penalty in those countries in which it has been abolished.

3rd. The operation of the death penalty on the morals of the people, irrespective of the manner of executing it.

4th. Its operation when publicly executed.

With reference to the first head of inquiry, it may be observed as remarkable, that after the capital penalty became a dead-letter law as regards the following offences, viz., sodomy, burglary with violence, robbery with wounds, and arson of inhabited houses, there was on the whole both a decrease of crime and an increase in the proportion of convictions.* Those who advocate its entire abolition have therefore a *primâ facie* argument in their favour. It may, indeed, be legitimately contended that the *onus probandi* is thrown on those who uphold the continuation of the death penalty, and that the moment the question presents itself, it is fairly open to grave doubts, whether a lawful penalty analogous in its results to

* The following table, communicated by H. T. Humphreys, Secretary to the Anti-Capital Punishment Association, establishes this statement.

Crimes.	Five years from 1852 to 1856.		Five years from 1857 to 1861.		Decrease of convictions per cent.	Decrease of committals per cent.
	Committed.	Sentenced to death.	Committed.	Sentenced to death.	—	—
Sodomy	228	69	183	65	5·8	19·7
Burglary with violence	55	38	39	35	8·	29·
Robbery with wounds	55	33	31	16	51·5	43·6
Arson of inhabited houses	22	12	13	5	58·5	40·9
	360	152	266	121	...	...

PROPORTION OF CONVICTIONS TO COMMITTALS.

	From 1852 to 1856.	From 1857 to 1861.
Sodomy	30 per cent.	35·5 per cent.
Burglary with violence	69 ,,	89·7 ,,
Robbery with wounds	60 ,,	51·6 ,,
Arson of inhabited houses	54·5 ,,	38·3 ,,

that of the crime it punishes, can have any operation in discouraging the crime.

The just indignation which a murder excites in the survivors of the crime, cannot be regarded as existing for any other object than to urge the survivors to prevent a repetition of the offence, for which a jail is as serviceable as the executioner, except so far as the example of death may operate. If then executions are unjustifiable simply as measures of justice, and unnecessary to prevent a second offence by the same individual, they can be maintained only for financial reasons or because they are terrific; but surely the possibility of a wrong verdict justifies the State in providing a criminal convicted capitally with food and clothing, for if he be innocent and executed he is removed beyond the power of human compensation. Is then capital punishment in murder cases deterrent? With reference to which it may be observed, that although, for example, rebellions may be suppressed, and war, and anarchy terminated, by a wholesale resort to it—(especially if the death be frightful and public, as, for example, blowing men from guns, crucifixions, and the like)—that however the law of terror may operate upon large masses of mankind, concerting and bound together for a common object, yet as regards crimes by individuals—by persons who isolate themselves from their fellow men, for the purpose of secretly committing crime—it is open to serious doubt whether the punishment of death does operate as a preventative. It has not been necessary to re-enact the death penalty for arson, cattle-stealing, forgery or burglary, or indeed for any crime great or small; and there are examples showing that, as regards murder, the death penalty has had no operation even in the vicinity of the gallows. In three successive years there were three murders in Derbyshire in two of which the murderers were brought to the scaffold at Derby, and the third was that by Townley.

In conclusion it may be observed that the Report cannot satisfactorily steer a middle course, and therefore the Commissioners must find it expedient or not expedient to retain the death penalty. If it be retained, its operation must be rendered certain and impartial, either by abolishing the prerogative of mercy, or affixing some condition to the exercise of it which will insure responsibility. It is not probable that the Crown will be advised to abandon, or even to qualify its power of mercy, and yet as long as it exists it will rest with the Crown whether the life of a convicted criminal shall be spared or not, and hence public agitation for reprieves will again and again occur, and none of the existing evils arising from the importunity of the public to save human life can be terminated. This appears to be one of the strongest arguments to prove the inexpediency of the death penalty being retained. If executions were allowed only in cases in which the jury found a verdict of guilty, and life were to be spared only when, with the verdict, circumstances extenuating the crime were found, that would be qualifying the prerogative of pardon; and there has been more than one instance in which it has been found expedient to commute the death sentence, notwithstanding an unqualified verdict of guilty, satisfactory both to the jury and the judge; and such cases will, of course, occur again. Nor would this objection be entirely removed were a second trial allowed by way of appeal, and a second verdict of guilty were found. The possibility of error would still exist, though the probability of error would be greatly diminished. At present there is no criminal appeal, nor is the subject of criminal appeals referred to the Commissioners, who must therefore proceed as if there could be no second trial for murder. Neither are they at liberty to enter into the question whether it is or not expedient to qualify in any way the prerogative of mercy. If, on the other hand, the Commissioners should report that it is inexpedient to retain the capital penalty all these difficulties would be removed. Connected with the abolition of capital punishment is that of a secondary punishment, as to which great difficulties have hitherto existed. None, however, have been found when a criminal has been reprieved, and therefore these difficulties are clearly not insuperable. Irremissible but not unpardonable life punishment would answer for the purpose of deterring others, better than death; and that punishment should be penal in a greater degree than for any other crime, but should not be accompanied by any species of torture. There would be no difficulty in defining the servitude to which murderers should be subjected, so as to mark the enormity of the offence; but one unalterable condition should be that no ticket-of-leave system should apply to them.

Much power of good and evil is vested in the Commissioners. The future social welfare of the community is largely concerned in the conclusion they may come to. The death penalty if retained, however seldom it may be inflicted, will be a fact operating on the morals and manners of the people, far and wide, on other matters of conduct affecting domestic society, besides attempts on human life the abolition of it will have an influence equally extensive. Whether of the twain is the better adapted for the security of human life, and for the progress of civilisation, the Commissioners have to decide.*

* Since the above was written Her Majesty has been pleased to direct letters patent to be passed under the Great Seal, appointing the Most Noble Duke of Richmond, the Right Hon. Lord Stanley, M.P., the Right Hon. Stephen Lushington, D.C.L., Judge of Her Majesty's High Court of Admiralty; the Right Hon. Sir John Taylor Coleridge, Knight; the Right Hon. Thomas O'Hagan, Attorney-General for Ireland; James Moncrieff, Esq., M.P., Advocate for Scotland; Horatio Waddington, Esq., John Bright, Esq., M.P., William Ewart, Esq., M.P., Gathorne Hardy, Esq., M.P., George Warde Hunt, Esq., M.P., and Charles Neate, Esq., M.P., to be Her Majesty's Commissioners to inquire into the provisions and operation of the laws now in force in the United Kingdom under and by virtue of which the punishment of death may be inflicted upon persons convicted of certain crimes, and also into the manner in which capital sentences are carried into execution.

ART. III.—CONTRIBUTORY NEGLIGENCE.

A LAW LAY.

Tuff v. *Warman.* 5 C. B., N.S. 573.

INGENUOUS Student, who, with curious eye,
Would trace the tangled threads of thought that lie
Involved in oracles of *Tuff and Warman*,
Hear, on that well-thumb'd text, a homely sermon.

The text, though cumbered much with clause on clause,
Reads fairly plain, till near an end it draws;
But at the end, through devious ways, we come
To rule that gravels pleaders, all and some.
Here Wightman, Justice, tells us, in effect,
Plaintiff stands none the worse of's own neglect,
If but Defendant, when default is made,
Its consequences could with care evade.
The canon at first blush reads all too wide,
Unless a triple caution be supplied;
Which to supply, and point you out the way,
To find where wanted, here, in loyal lay,
Contributory Negligence I sing,
The rule of Law, and reason of the thing.

Both are in fault: else, 'tis a simple story,
The negligence were not contributory.
Then, either both have been in fault together,
Or else the one's in fault before the other.
If both together, neither bears the blame;
The wrongs concurrent, and the rights the same:
If fault of one the other's fault precede,
He pays the penalty: unless, indeed,
The other, by some little common sense,
Could shun that first misconduct's consequence.

Say, I lie drunk, a trespasser besides,
On *Marcus'* avenue; and *Marcus* rides,
Or stumbles o'er me: still, first question is,
(Be it, the broken bones are mine or his,)
Could *Marcus*, by an ordinary care,
Have shunned the danger, and so gone elsewhere?
If *yea*, he pays me for my hurt; altho'
I was in act the first to blame: if *no*,
Since but for me he ne'er had been o'erthrown,
I pay him for his hurt and bear my own.

What then, whene'er by night I walk or ride,
Must I a link-boy or a scout provide,
Lest *Davies'* donkey in my path should roll,*
Or *Forrester* have left his building pole†
To trip me up? nay, Law was never heard,
To sanction charge of caution so absurd.
I must not, if I'd not be brought to book,
Run blind-man's muck, and leap before I look;
(Though some that leap'd and never looked, have found
A verdict 'twixt the foot-board and the ground;)‡
But if with eye-sight such as bless'd withal,
I keep my head from contact with the wall
By ordinary care, the law demands
No weightier charge of caution at my hands.
But say I'm blind; or one of tender years,
Insensible to age's prudent fears?
Your case thereby nor better is nor worse,
Your leader answers for you, or your nurse.§

Of these collateral moot-points enough,
Return we now to *Warman* versus *Tuff*.

* *Davies* v. *Mann*, 10 M. & W. 546.
† *Butterfield* v. *Forrester*, 11 East, 60.
‡ *Scott* v. *Dublin* and *Wicklow Ry. Co.*, 11 W. C. L. R. 377.
§ *Lynch* v. *Nurdin*, 4 P. & D. 672. *Waite* v. *Nth. Ln. Ry. Coy.*, 1 Ell. Bl. & Ell. 719.

The judgment's truly neither less nor more
Than, done in doggrel, is set down before;—
One's first in fault; then, could the other one
That fault's effects by common caution shun?
But there you stop: else, caught in Pleaders' Pound,
Each cries *Tu quoque!* in an endless round.
As, say that when, a log, in *Marcus*' way
By want of ordinary care I lay,
Marcus athwart me falling breaks his head,
And brings his suit: if, in defence 'tis said
"You might have shunned me, had you used your eyes;"
And *Marcus* then with Wightman, J., replies
"And *you* shunned *me!*" the altercation tends
To circular dispute that never ends. (*c*)
Or, say two runners, each a careless spark,
Have clashed their heads together in the dark;
It lies not in the mouth of one to say
"Sir, you by caution could have kept away,
And so I had not dashed, and lost, my tooth
'Gainst your *Os frontis:*" for the other youth,
With equal justice may in turn reply,
"Nor had *I* dashed 'gainst *yours,* and lost, my eye."
For here the active fault of both concurr'd
And left to neither, in the law, a word. (*a*)
Or say two barges insecurely moor'd
Drift in a stream, with neither crew on board:
Borne in an eddy of the wind or tide,
The barques approach, and with a crash collide:
My planks stove in afford as little room
For just complaint, as does *your* broken boom.
For here, the passive fault of both together
Has shut the mouth of each against the other. (*b*)

But two, each so in fault, will yield no more
Predicaments of blame, but only four:*

And Wightman's canon, as above we see,
Holds not, of these, in categories three:
Wherefore his " Plaintiff's non-disabling fault,"
Must needs be taken with three grains of salt,
And limited to that one category
Where Plaintiff's fault's the first contributory.
As if, say last, when *Marcus* o'er me rode,
Broad day-light had the present danger show'd,
And I, as Plaintiff, my crushed ribs had mourn'd,
Whereto " *Tu quoque* " *Marcus* had return'd,
Then, in that case, but in that only one,
May I reply as Wightman, J., has done,
" True, 'twas my first default that brought me there,
But you, good *Marcus,* could with common care,
Have shunned me where I lay, and in that state
Of things, 'tis lawful to recriminate." (*d*)

By Wightman's judgment, then, 'twas never meant
That Plaintiff's negligence should not prevent
Plaintiff's success, in any of the three
Firstly above-put cases:—Wherefore ye
Who scan that clause so oft misunderstood,
Read " If Defendant by due caution could
(*When Plaintiff has been first to blame in fact*)
Have shunned the consequence of Plaintiff's act,
The Plaintiff shall not thereby be undone,"—
So shall the Law and Judgment be at one.

S. F.

* Viz.,—

- Negligence in both
  - Concurrent
    - Both active. (*a*)
    - Both passive. (*b*)
  - Non-concurrent
    - Plaintiff active; Defendant passive. (*c*)
    - Plaintiff passive; Defendant active. (*d*)

Art. IV.—THE PEERS, BARONETS, KNIGHTS, AND LANDED GENTRY, AND THE BOOKS ABOUT THEM.

The Historic Peerage of England, being a new Edition of the "Synopsis of the Peerage of England," by the late Sir Harris Nicolas, G.C.M.G. By William Courthope, Esq., Somerset Herald. 1857. Murray: Albemarle Street.

The Noblemen and Gentlemen of England. Attempted by Evelyn Philip Shirley, Esq., M.A., F.S.A., one of the Knights of the Shire for the Co. of Warwick. Westminster: J. B. Nichols and Sons.

The Peerage, Baronetage, and Knightage of Great Britain and Ireland for 1864, *including all the Titled Classes for* 1864: *twenty-fourth year.* By Robert P. Dod, Esq. Whittaker and Co.

A Dictionary of the Peerage and Baronetage of the British Empire. By Sir Bernard Burke, Ulster King-of-Arms. 26th Edition. 1864. Harrison: 59, Pall Mall.

A Dictionary of the Landed Gentry of Great Britain and Ireland. By Sir Bernard Burke. 4th Edition. 1863. Harrison: 59, Pall Mall.

THE Peers, Baronets, Knights, and Landed Gentlemen of the United Kingdom form a subject of peculiar interest to lawyers, for upon these upper classes and their vast territorial possessions and manifold affairs the major portion of the legal operations of the country turn. They and their connections are the *dramatis personæ* of most of not only the parliamentary but the forensic events of the time. Equity and the civil side of the common law would have but confined action without these prominent personages, and, to their honour may it be said, there is only the criminal law with which they come little in contact. It is indeed an undoubted truth that from age to age down to the present time, the nobles and upper classes have, compared with the rest of society, been singularly free from criminal prosecutions other than those of a political nature. Look back for the last two hundred years. The charge of murder against a peer, if we except Lord Ferrers' crime—the act of a madman—and some cases of duelling, is utterly unknown. This is so; but the brighter side of jurisprudence is ever bringing the nobleman or gentleman forward. Their conveyances and their wills, their contracts and their dealings bring substantial wealth to the barrister and the solicitor, and sharpen and keep sharpened the intellect of both. The affairs of Parliament are in close alliance with the affairs of Westminster Hall. The law is, too, ever busy with the daily transactions of nobles and gentry in every county in the realm. These superior classes so link one with another that, in conveyancing particularly, reference to their *status*, alliances, and descents, becomes frequently indispensable. A knowledge therefore, of the peerage, baronetage, knightage, and gentry of the United Kingdom cannot but prove of very great advantage to all practising lawyers.

In another sense, British rank and dignity must ever be of interest to the British bar: for it is the goal to which all successful members of that bar have a right to aspire. Every French soldier, it is said, carries a Marshal's *bâton* in his knapsack; the observation may be also ventured that every barrister bears in his forensic bag the patent of a peerage. At any rate, if any barrister thinks that too strong an assertion, and will not indulge in such proud pleasures of hope, he has at least the pleasures of memory. Let him but look over the past roll of nobility of the United Kingdom, and how illumined will he find it with the talent and the virtue that the bar has brought it. The peerage is big with the history of the bar. The peerage, however, includes Wellington and Nelson, and therefore we cannot say of it that *cedant arma togæ*, yet, in the acquisition of titled rank, the bar has done much to acquire a parity of fame. Histories, rolls, and records of the *noblesse* titled or untitled should therefore, for many reasons, be perused and studied by the lawyer. We now, with the reader's permission, propose to take a cursory glance of some of the best modern books on the subject of family dignities. Of old works thereon we would refer to Collins' "Peerage of England," edited by Sir Egerton Brydges, Bart., whom the House of Lords would not make Baron Chandos; to Archdall's "Peerage of Ireland;" to Douglas's "Peerage of Scotland," edited by Wood; to Cruise upon Dignities; to Playfair's productions; and to the county histories and published visitations; all admirable bygone authorities.

Modern peerage books are not so diffuse, and generally, it is to be regretted, do not cite their references; but as they adopt the alphabetical form, and are far more clear and concise, the knowledge they contain is imparted more readily and pleasantly.

The "Historic Peerage" or "Synopsis of the Peerage," by that most able, most learned, and most industrious but ill-rewarded lawyer and genealogist, the late Sir Harris Nicolas, is a volume of infinite research and utility. Its plan is to bring, in a kind of tabular and explicit form, each peerage before the reader, as it has been borne from age to age, either by inheritance, revival, or new creation. The title of "Bath" we here give as a specimen of the whole:

Earls.		Bath.
"I.	1485.	Philibert de Shaunde, called "consanguineum nostrum" by Hen. VII., created Earl of Bath, 6th Jan., 1485, but nothing further is known of him.
II.	1536.	1. John Bourchier, X., 12th Baron Fitz-Warine; created Earl of Bath 9th July, 1536, ob. 1539.
III.	1539.	2. John Bourchier, s. and h. who became sole heir general of the Barony of Daubeney, on the death of Henry Daubeney, Earl of Bridgewater, 1548, ob. 1560.

IV. 1560. 3. William Bourchier, grandson and h., being s. and h. of John Bourchier (ob. v. p.), eldest son of the last Earl; ob. 1623.

V. 1623. 4. Edward Bourchier, s. and h.; ob. 1636, S. P. M.

VI. 1636. 5. Henry Bourchier, cousin and h., being s. and h. of Sir George Bourchier, 2nd son of John III., 2nd Earl; ob. 1654, S. P., when the title became extinct.

VII. 1661. 1. John Granville, created Baron Granville of Kilkhampton and Biddeford, Viscount Granville of Lansdown, and Earl of Bath, 20th April, 1661, and by Royal licence 26th of same month was permitted to use the titles of Earl of Corboile, Thorigny and Granville; ob. August, 1701.

VIII. 1701. 2. Charles Granville, s. and h. summ. to Parl. by Writ, v. p., 16th July, 1689, and placed in his father's Barony of Granville; ob. twelve days after his father, 1701.

IX. 1701. 3. William Henry Granville, s. and h.; unm. ob. 1711, when all his honours became extinct.

X. 1742. 1. William Pulteney, created Baron of Hedon, co. York, Viscount Pulteney of Wrington, co. Somerset, and Earl of Bath, 14th July, 1742; ob. 1764, S. P. S., when these dignities became extinct.

MARQUESS.

I. 1789. 1. Thomas Thynne, 3rd Viscount Weymouth, created Marquess of Bath, 29th August, 1789, K.G.; ob. 1796.

II. 1796. 2. Thomas Thynne, s. and h., K.G.; ob. 27th March, 1837.

III. 1837. 3. Henry Frederick, s. and h.; ob. 24th June, 1837.

IV. 1837. 4. John Alexander, s. and h., present Marquess of Bath, Viscount Weymouth, Baron Thynne, and a Bart.

Baroness.	Countess.	
I. 1792.	1803.	Henrietta Laura Pulteney, dau. of William Pulteney, Esq. (formerly Johnstone), by Frances, dau. and h. of Daniel Pulteney, s. and h. of John Pulteney, next bro. of William Pulteney, father of William Pulteney, X., 1st Earl of Bath; created Baroness of Bath with limitation of the dignity of Baron Bath, co. Somerset, to her issue male, 26th July, 1792, and Countess of Bath, co. Somerset, with the same limitation of the Earldom of Bath, 26th Oct. 1803; m. Sir James Murray, Bart., who assumed the name of Pulteney; ob. 14th August, 1808, S. P., when these titles became extinct."

Sir Harris Nicolas called this work "The Synopsis of the Peerage;" but its present editor, Mr. Courthorpe, the Somerset Herald, has changed the name to that of the "Historic Peerage." Mr. Courthorpe's editorship is carefully and diligently carried out, and does him much credit.

"The Noblemen and Gentlemen of England," attempted by Shirley, is a quaint and fantastic production, very capricious and uncertain in its details, but by no means uninteresting or unprofitable to read. The families mentioned in it are certainly of old and honourable position, but the author omits many other families equally so. It is, therefore, good as far as it goes, but is imperfect.

Mr. Dod's well-known annual "Peerage, Baronetage, and Knightage of Great Britain and Ireland," is a book of great and ready practical utility. Its plan is original, and supplies a great deal that may not be found elsewhere. Beyond the marriage, parentage, and eldest son, of each bearer of a title, Mr. Dod gives little or no genealogical details, but the articles all contain biographical particulars of the parties mentioned which are most valuable for reference. It should be added that Mr. Dod's is the only present work of credit (beyond the excellent summary in Thom's famous Almanac) that furnishes full information as to knights and privy counsellors.

We now come to an author who may be well termed the giant of modern genealogical literature, Sir Bernard Burke, Ulster King-of-Arms. No author, byegone or existing, has written so largely or so effectively on those "institutions which have been adopted for giving body to opinion and permanence to fugitive esteem." The ennobling principle which he has felt in his own heart, he has spent his life in endeavouring to impart to others; and it is not too much to say that his labours have had a beneficial effect on the society of this country. A taste for genealogy and heraldry is, we maintain, a wholesome and a refining taste; for they are sciences which resuscitate and retain each particular action of the good and great; and keep in perpetual and gorgeous array before us all the pomp, pride, and circumstance, of a glorious past. The love of rank and title necessarily includes the love of order, and it has been well said that "it is one sign of a liberal and benevolent mind to incline to them with some sort of partial propensity." "Thank God, we have a House of Lords!" exclaimed Cobbett; and we may render further thanks to Providence that we have not only that chamber of peers, but a whole country full of nobles, baronets, knights, and gentry, serving as a broadstone of honour on which the foot of coward or traitor cannot stand, and as a front of resistance which the leveller or revolutionist can never overcome. It is, however, on the refining influence of heraldry and genealogy that we would particularly insist, for we have remarked that wherever those sciences prevail or flourish, there also may be found a degree of courtesy and elegance which soften while they elevate the daily intercourse and amenities of life. The extensive circulation and popularity of Sir Bernard's works afford a strong proof of how much the public adopt and appreciate his views; how much they accord in the notion that due and proper homage to and respect for rank and title tend to burnish and embellish social civilisation. Sir Bernard Burke's heraldic and genealogical works are too numerous for us to be able to recall even the names, much less the contents, of all of them. We shall here confine ourselves to his most prominent and constant publications, "The Peerage and Baronetage" and "The Landed Gentry." These books are as near perfection in their way, as the mass of compilation, correction, and constant change will permit, and they are the tomes that ought to be found in every lawyer's office or chambers.

Sir Bernard's "Peerage and Baronetage" teems with interesting genealogical and biographical particulars of successful practitioners of the law, past and present. At the very outset of the volume we find elaborately given the descent of our present Lord Chief Justice, Sir Alexander Cockburn, from a Sir Alexander Cockburn of Langtoun, who was Keeper of the Great Seal of Scotland in 1389. A subsequent page tells us that our newest judge, Sir William Shee, is allied to the premier Baronet of Nova Scotia. We also learn from an earlier article that a Baronet now also a peer, Sir John Yarde Buller, Lord Churston, springs from a great jurist, of whom the following neat biographical sketch is given:—

"Francis Buller, Esq., b. 27th March, 1745-6, a very eminent lawyer, was educated in a private school in the West of England, on leaving which he was admitted of the Inner Temple, in February 1763, and became a pupil of Sir William Ashurst, at that time a great special pleader, whom he afterwards excelled. His own practice, on becoming a special pleader, was very quickly established, and it increased to a vast amount. After spending some years in that branch of legal business, Buller was called to the bar by the Hon. Society of the Middle Temple, in Easter term, 1772, and his earnings as a counsel soon equalled those of almost all his brethren of that day. His complete devotion to his profession prevented his ever going into Parliament. He was made a king's counsel, 24th Nov., 1777, and three days afterwards second judge of the Chester circuit. His friend, Lord Mansfield, however, who had the highest opinion of his talents, would not be satisfied till he sat by his side, and Buller was appointed, 1st May, 1778, a judge of the Court of King's Bench. The indisposition of Lord Mansfield, not long after, compelling his absence, gave Buller the prominent part in the proceedings in the court, and he conducted the business there with consummate ability. He was a strict and stern judge, but ever acted on the most enlightened views, and on legal principles correct to a nicety. When Mansfield resigned, everyone looked to Buller as his successor, but from some political reason of the moment, Sir Lloyd Kenyon was preferred, and became the new Chief Justice. Buller, disappointed, and his health declining, exchanged the King's Bench for the Common Pleas, and succeeded Mr. Justice Gould as a judge of the latter court, 1794, but his health still continued to decay, and he was about to resign altogether, when he died suddenly, at his house in Bedford Square, 4th June, 1800, leaving behind him a name of lasting note in the annals of English jurisprudence. His talents have survived the display and success of his lifetime, for his judgments and his writings are still continually looked upon as among the most valuable and unerring of expositions of our common law. His work relative to trials at nisi prius is to this day a standard book. Mr. Justice Buller was created a baronet, 13 Jan., 1790. He m. when only 17 years of age, Susannah, only dau. and heir of Francis Yarde, Esq., of Churston Ferrers, and Ottery St. Mary, co. Devon, and dying 4th June, 1800, was s. by his son.

"II. Sir Francis, b. 28th Sept., 1767, who, in pursuance of the will of his maternal uncle, assumed the surname of Yarde, but afterwards, by sign manual, added to it his patronymic of Buller."

The second Sir Francis's son, the article goes on to show, is the present Lord Churston.

We might multiply citations of this kind, for Sir Bernard never lets the opportunity of a great lawyer pass without note and comment, whether it be a Bacon, Lyttelton, or Coke, of past ages, or a Lyndhurst, Campbell, or Brougham, of modern times. It is this mixture of family and public history which gives a charm to the work.

The "Landed Gentry," follows, out the exact plan of "The Peerage and Baronetage," but the details are more curious, as they relate to people not quite so generally known. In it much light is given throughout on byegone and actual members of the bar. For instance, here is a puzzle cleared up as to who were the two Goulds, of whom as judges frequent mention occurs in the law books.

"John Gould, Esq., of Dorchester, co. Dorset, purchased Frome Bellet of the Long family, 1610. He m. Joan, dau. of — Hellier, and widow of John Roy, of Dorchester; his will, preserved among the family documents, is dated 11th June, 1630; he d. 13th June, 1630, and was buried in St. Peter's Church, Dorchester, leaving issue."

His second son's seventh son,

"Henry Gould, studied the law, and, as king's serjeant, conducted the evidence for the Crown in the House of Commons, on the Bill of Attainder against Sir John Fenwick, in 1696. He was made judge of the King's Bench, 30th Jan., 1698, and knighted. He m. Miss Davidge, of Dorchester, and left (with one dau., m. to Lieutenant-General Edmund Fielding, kinsman to the Earl of Denbigh, and father by her of Henry Fielding, the celebrated novelist), one son, Sir Henry Gould's younger brother.

"Davidge Gould, Esq., barrister-at-law, Middle Temple, m. Honora Hockmore, of Buckland, Baron co., Devon, and had issue:

I. William, D.D., Rector of Stapleford Abbots, co. Essex, d. unm.

II. Thomas, barrister d. unm.

III. Richard, of Wells, m. Susan, dau. of — Maundrell, Esq., and had issue:

1. Henry, Canon of Wells, d. unm.
2. William, m. Elizabeth, dau. of Henry Strangways, Esq., of Shapwick; d. s. p.
3. Davidge (Sir), Admiral, K.C.B., who commanded a vessel

at the battle of the Nile, and d. in 1848, s. p.; he m. Elizabeth, eldest dau. of Archdeacon Willes, and grand-daughter of Bishop Willes.

IV. Henry (Sir), Knt.,* a Judge of the Court of Common Pleas, m. Elizabeth, dau. of the Ven. — Walker, Archdeacon of Wells, and d. 5th March, 1794, leaving two surviving daus. co-heiresses."

The following article, relating to a deservedly popular judge, we are glad to come across, and cite it as a bit of information interesting to most in the legal world:

"ERLE, the Right Honble. Sir William, of Bramshott Grange, co. Hants., Lord Chief Justice of the Court of Common Pleas; b. 1st Oct., 1793, m. 30th Sept., 1834, Amelia, eldest dau. of the late Rev. David Williams, D.C.L., Warden of New College, Oxford, by Amelia, his wife, dau. of the Rev. William Goddard, of Stargroves, East Wordhay, co. Hants., and Castle Eaton, co. Wilts. This able and distinguished lawyer, who was called to the bar in 1819, and practised for many years with pre-eminent success, sat in Parliament for the city of Oxford from 1837 to 1841; and became one of the judges of the Court of Common Pleas in 1845. In 1846 he was transferred to the Queen's Bench, and in 1859, succeeded Sir Alexander Cockburn as Lord Chief Justice of the Common Pleas.

"LINEAGE.—The Erles are a very old family, originally temp.

* This Sir Henry Gould, nephew of the first judge of the same name, entered the Middle Temple, 16th May, 1728, was called to the bar, 13th June, 1734; made king's counsel, 3rd May, 1754, and was raised to the Bench, 1761 as Puisne Baron of the Exchequer, but was removed to the Court of Common Pleas, 24th Jan., 1763, where he continued till his death, in 1794, having seen the Bench three times cleared by the vicissitudes of time. He retained his faculties to the last, and died at his house, in Lincoln's Inn Fields, at the advanced age of eighty-four. He was distinguished for his extreme urbanity and merciful disposition, as well as for his eminent abilities. In him the English law lost one of its steadiest luminaries. His remains were interred at Stapleford Abbots, Essex, of which parish his brother William was the Rector. The following characteristic anecdote is recorded in the *Gentleman's Magazine*—"During the riots of 1780, after the attack on Lord Mansfield's house, the King sent to offer each of the twelve judges the protection of a military guard, which offer Mr. Justice Gould, with equal courage and equanimity, declined, saying, 'that he was persuaded, however some persons might be misled, the people in general loved and respected the laws, and he would rather die, than live under any other protection.'"

Hen. II., of Beckington, co. Somerset, and subsequently of Ashburton, co. Devon, and Charborough, co. Dorset. In the great Civil War, Sir Walter Erle, of Charborough, was a distinguished Parliamentarian. The late Rev. Christopher Erle, a descendant of the Erles of Dorsetshire, m. Margaret, dau. of Thomas Bowles, Esq., of Shaftesbury, and had issue:

I. Christopher, in holy orders.

II. Walter, in holy orders.

III. William, the present Lord Chief Justice Erle.

IV. Peter, Q.C., m. Mary F. Fearon, and has issue, four children.

I. Jane, deceased, m. to William Fenwick, Esq.

II. Margaret S., m. to John Lucius Dampier, Esq., and d. leaving three children.

Arms.—Gu. three escallop shells, or.

Seat.—Bramshott Grange, Lapbrook, Hants."

Many other legal names, with family particulars, appear in the "Landed Gentry," such, for instance, as Bere, Bain, Cresswell, Evans, Fortescue, Grattan, Hill, Lefroy, Murray, O'Connell, Pennefather, Pigott, Plowden, Roupell, Smith, Spinks, Treby, and Woolrych.

There are many smaller publications on the titled and upper classes, but we may pass them unnoticed, as they are mostly either abridgements or colourable piracies of the works we have already mentioned; or mere catchpenny compilations got up by unlearned and inexperienced authors. One book of some pretension is entitled "The Peerage and Baronetage of the British Empire," and is said on the title to be by "Edmund Lodge, Esq.," but as that able genealogist and Norroy King-of-Arms is now dead some fourteen or fifteen years, and as he could never have had much to do with the book in question, we may look on it as more of an heraldic delusion than a reality.

In conclusion, we may quote the words of Cicero: *Omnes boni semper nobilitati favemus;* and repose in satisfaction on the agreeable idea that we lawyers have full claim to be put among the good men thus favouring our country's nobility, whether inherited by descent or got by worth—whether ancestorial, or the acquirement of ability carried out with energy, industry, and honour.

ART. V.—BRIBERY AT ELECTIONS.

A Letter to the Editor of the Law Magazine and Law Review.

A PAPER on Bribery at Elections, read by Mr. W. D. Christie before the Social Science Association, appeared in our last number. We need hardly say that when papers of this nature are printed in this MAGAZINE, by virtue of a long-standing arrangement, we do not consider ourselves responsible for the facts or opinions expressed therein. We think that the plan originated by Mr. Christie deserves examination, and are happy to afford any facility in our power for its public discussion. We thought it right to forward to Mr. Christie a proof of the following letter, and the reply of that gentlemen is subjoined thereto.—ED. L. M. & L. R.]

SIR,—Your last number contained a paper by Mr. Christie, on Corrupt Practices at Elections, which its learned author characterises as having "a practical object and one idea." The "object" is the very laudable one of repressing electoral corruption; the "idea" is to obtain an answer to the inquiry "whether moral enthusiasm can be raised, and moral influences brought to bear by the combined efforts of individuals against bribery and extravagant expenditure at elections, which legislation is powerless to destroy?" Mr. Christie is disposed to answer this question in the affirmative. He thinks that "the moral sense of the nation already unmistakably condemns bribery;" and that we have only "to intensify this feeling and make it conquer;" and he would accomplish this end by getting everybody, from the Earl of Derby and Lord Palmerston, down to the local politicians of their respective parties, to join in a society for this purpose. To the same end, he would abolish, or at least greatly diminish, patronage; would suspend the writs of delinquent boroughs, and, finally, would subject to the pains of imprisonment, and the discipline of the treadmill, every one who surrenders his own political virtue, or tempts his fellow-citizens to do the like. He cites Lord Brougham to show that though men were willing to carry on the slave trade at the risk of incurring heavy pecuniary penalties, they gave it up at once when it involved a chance of transportation; and he argues from the success of penal laws and the Anti-Duelling Association in abolishing mortal combat as a mode of settling differences, to a like success when the Legislature has passed stringent statutes against bribery, treating, and intimidation, and the Anti-Corrupt-Practices-at-Elections-Society has had time to imbue the nation with a wholesome abhorrence of all unfair agencies in political warfare.

I doubt whether any one of practical experience or extended observation in election matters, will assent to Mr. Christie's premises, admit his conclusion, or adopt his analogy. It is true that in the abstract, public feeling is adverse to bribery, but facts only too conclusively show that this feeling is a mere sentiment, very different in character from that hearty hatred which promises an abatement of the evil. It is, I think, generally true, that what public opinion unequivocally condemns, imperial legislation can effectually suppress; while on the other hand, evils at which society winks, or which it condemns, as it were, *pro formâ*, will continue to flourish in spite of accumulated Acts of Parliament. Hence, laws against robbery and violence will, in general, be obeyed, while other laws, levelled at social evils of a different class, will be evaded or neglected altogether.

Mr. Christie will not find much evidence in support of his

estimate of public feeling in the history of legislative efforts towards the suppression of the evil. We have now between fifty and sixty Acts on the Statute Book for regulating parliamentary elections, and of these nearly one-fourth have been added during the present reign, for the express purpose of preventing corruption in one form or other. Besides these, there have been statutes for regulating and for shortening the duration of polls; for diminishing the expenses of elections, and for amending election procedure in various ways. Within the same time, we have disfranchised Sudbury and St. Albans, have visited Nottingham, Wakefield, Gloucester, and other boroughs with pains and penalties; have sent commissions of inquiry to Reading, Berwick, Stafford, and other places. All this action, legislative and judicial, has been taken in the interest of electoral purity, and for the purpose of cleansing the Augean stable of electoral corruption. And how do our legislators speak of their own work? To go back no farther than last year's debates, we find Mr. Bentinck characterising the annual discussion "as an annual farce, which led to no good result, because neither in nor out of the house was there any feeling that acts of bribery involved any moral culpability." On the same occasion, Mr. Berkeley spoke of election law as "the laughing stock of every attorney's clerk," for a candidate's seat was perfectly safe so long as he did not bribe personally, or by an agent previously named, while any unnamed agent might do what he liked and the candidate would not be responsible; for "by good management he might indulge in illegal expenditure at discretion without running any risk," so that "under cover of the Act, whenever the next election should come, the richest man would win."

It may be said that these are but opinions. Then let us look to facts. Even before the misapplication of trust funds was made a criminal offence, an unprincipled trustee whose delinquencies were known to the world, would have been very coolly received in decent society, and since the passing of sundry recent Acts, no one would receive him with open arms, simply because he had escaped punishment through the skill of a clever counsel, and an opportune spiriting away of the prosecutor's witnesses. But we find no such trace of society's aversion to members or candidates against whom similar things can be said in connexion with offences against our statutes for securing purity of election. No one cut Mr. Bell, because his bribery had caused the disfranchisement of an ancient borough, and Messrs. Charlesworth and Leatham were regarded rather as martyrs than as delinquents, for the part they took in corrupting a modern one. The gallant General who sits for Chatham did not lose caste when he was unseated some years ago for his own, or his agent's use of Government appointments, and all the ugly things said about the Dover contract have not affected the status of the worthy Admiral who represents that enlightened constituency. Sending "a good and safe man" to Derby, cost "W. B." his place, but it did not affect his social status, and no one thought a bit the worse of the gentlemen who have at different times represented Rochdale and Berwick, because the witnesses upon whom the petitioners against their return relied, were, by some strange coincidence, not to be found when their presence in the Committee Room was most desired. Nay, in the case of George Hudson, there were not a few who reproached the electors of Sunderland with ingratitude, because, some years after his fall, they rejected the man who had benefited them on a grand scale by dock improvements and railway facilities.

It would be easy to protract this catalogue indefinitely; to call up the memories of elections at Bewdley and Cheltenham; at Stafford and Shrewsbury; at Harwich and Horsham; at Carlisle and Preston; at Nottingham and Northampton; at Beverley and Northallerton; at Kinsale and Lisburn; at Hull and Bristol; at Norwich and Maldon; and scores of other places, where bribery has been actually proved or rendered morally certain, and yet no one ever heard of any of the bribers incurring social penalties as a consequence of their delinquencies. Coming from the procurers to the instruments of corruption, do we find any class of them, from the solicitors at head quarters, down to the "men in the moon" who pour auriferous streams into the hands of easy-conscienced voters in darkened chambers, losing one jot of the estimation of their fellows, simply because of their share in these practices? Let any one who has watched these things answer, and I am sure the reply will be in the negative. The truth is that so far from public opinion being strongly adverse to bribery, there is a large class who view it with favour because of the gain it brings, and another class, less numerous, but more powerful, who look upon the power to bribe and intimidate, as part of the legitimate influence of property. It is true that there are few boroughs where such people form anything like the majority, but the experience of every election shows that they exert considerable influence, even upon those who in their hearts disapprove of any but legitimate means. The fact is, that at such times men seem to lose their moral balance. In the midst of a contested election, they forget their ordinary rules of life and conduct. Parties, it may be, are pretty nearly matched, and it is known that many voters are holding back for the best bidder. One or two of these doubtfuls go to the poll; the presumption that they have been bribed is accepted as a "confirmation strong;" the chances are ten to one that some enthusiastic friend then resolves that his side "shall not be beat for the sake of a few pounds;" and that resolution at once lets in all the machinery of corruption, even where, up to the polling day, the candidate and his immediate friends have persistently endeavoured to keep their hands clean. The would-be M.P. may know nothing about it till the fight is over, and then the plea, "it was all for the good of the cause," like charity, covers a multitude of sins. Public opinion against bribery, indeed! Did not the electors of Beverley fête the victims of a Government prosecution?

Did not Chatham, for the first time in its history, reject a Government candidate, because he had procured the unseating of a gallant officer, who, having stood when a different ministry was in office, had known how to employ Government patronage as an instrument of corruption? Was not public sympathy in favour of Messrs. Charlesworth and Leatham so strong, that the Government, after spending an enormous sum in obtaining their conviction, were content to drop the proceedings? And were there many men of either side in politics, who did not admire and sympathise with Mr. Charlesworth's partisan, who defied Baron Martin in the witness-box, and went to prison for six months rather than divulge the malpractices of his party in a court of justice?

Mr. Christie's paper contains one sentence which is almost equal to a foregone conclusion against his entire scheme. He "has no hope so long as the candidate and the world regard the functions of an M.P. less as a duty to be discharged, than as a favour to be solicited." The candidate and the world certainly hold this view now, and it is by no means clear that they are in the wrong. A seat in the legislature imposes a duty it is true, but does it not also confer advantages otherwise unattainable? Cadets of noble houses seek it as a school for the Upper Chamber, and county gentlemen as a means of gratifying a lofty and honourable ambition; aspiring lawyers must enter it, for it is the avenue that leads most surely and directly to the highest prizes of the profession; successful merchants and manufacturers feel that until they can write M.P. after their names, the edifice they have reared wants something "to cap it." From the Carlton and Reform Club Registers, and other sources, it is said that a list of 4,000 or 5,000 names may any day be obtained, of gentlemen desirous of the honour, and not unwilling to incur the expense of winning a seat in Parliament. The development of trade, and the increased facilities for obtaining a liberal education, are likely to cause an increase rather than a diminution in these numbers, and so long as the demand for seats is eight or ten times as great as the supply, candidates, and electors too, will adhere to their present estimate of their mutual relations. Till a change in this particular seems much nearer than it does at present, we need not spend much time in considering "whether the State should pay the candidates' expenses," or whether nothing should be done "save by the zeal or the contributions of the electors." Mr. Christie's quotations from Bishop Burnet and Andrew Marvell, seem to mean that he has no hope save in "a change and reformation in the manners of the nation." He might go farther, and say in human nature itself.

Mr. Christie trusts partly to moral, and partly to legal means. He would unite candidates, their supporters and agents, in a mutual bond to abstain from corrupt practices, and he would punish severely those who violate such an agreement. Offending boroughs he would temporarily or permanently deprive of their franchise; delinquent individuals he would send to the treadmill, or to penal servitude. Are not both these remedies sadly wanting in the equitable, as well as in the practical element? You may, perhaps, be able to form "the leading men of all parties, the dignitaries in Church and State, the candidates, and the leading men of the constituencies" into an Anti-Bribery Union; but no one who knows the intensity and the bitterness of political hostilities in many boroughs and counties will believe that "Local Committees of all parties" will work together. But even if they would, how can you be sure of the unauthorised acts of individuals, acting "for the good of the party," on their own responsibility? At the recent election for Barnstaple, the successful candidate gave orders that no bribery should be allowed; was assured by his leading supporters that none was practised, and was only undeceived when he had undertaken to defend his seat, and had paid his counsel's fees. Similar complaints are continually made in at least half the election inquiries that take place; and in how many instances candidates "grumble and pay" in silence, none but those who are behind the scenes have any idea. Mr. Christie's scheme for binding over election agents of a certain class to electoral purity by moral suasion, is something like using the same means to convince a *chevalier d'industrie* of the advantages of keeping honest. Both may listen to you with a sober face, and may yield an outward assent to your arguments, but for all that the one will bribe your voters, and the other will steal your pocket-handkerchief, on the first opportunity.

In common with many others, Mr. Christie falls foul of that much abused class, the attorneys. He looks upon their employment as objectionable, and approves of Baron Pigott's suggestion to limit the number that candidates may retain, though he thinks "such men as Messrs. Rose, Clabon, and Drake, would be invaluable aids for the proposed association." The Bill of last year was framed in this spirit, and contained a clause for disfranchising any attorney who acted as a paid agent, but it was observed with much force during the debate, that "the management of elections was quite as much part of an attorney's business, as drawing a conveyance;" that "attorneys were employed according to their political principles, and it was not to be expected that they would for the time give up their regular business, and employ their clerks and others about election matters without receiving remuneration;" that it was "unreasonable to expect that they should give their votes and their services into the bargain;" for "the same principle applies to every person employed; if he does work, he has a right to be paid for it." The fact is, an attorney is employed for his peculiar knowledge, and that knowledge makes him the best man for a canvass, just as a printer's types and presses make him the fittest agent for issuing the candidate's address, or publishing an election squib. If you exclude the one, you cannot consistently retain the other.

As to the proposal to send honourable members and their friends to county gaols or model prisons, we are quite sure that, even if Parliament were to pass such a law, it would remain a dead letter. It is always "a mistake to impose on an offence a punishment disproportioned to its magnitude, or to the sense of its seriousness entertained by the country at large." In the Wakefield case, where the parties had confessed their acts of corruption, convictions were obtained with difficulty, and "the feeling of the House and the country was against the proceedings, because it was felt that the persons had been trapped into an admission of guilt."

Even now, it is not easy to make out a case of bribery before a Committee of the House of Commons, and when "the cold fit" is on, honourable members are very slow to put an unfavourable construction on an equivocal act. How much this feeling would be increased by the proposed legislation, it is needless to point out. There is too much reason to fear that if ever a prosecution under such an Act took place, we should see an amount of prevarication, not to say flat perjury, by respectable witnesses, frequent repetition of which would go far to lower the moral tone of the community in other and still more important matters. The same objection applies, though in a less degree, to Baron Pigott's recommendation that the punishment should be incapacity for holding any office of trust or employment, and to Lord Brougham's comparison of bribery and the slave trade. His Lordship argues from the preventive power of degrading punishment in the one case, to similar results in the other. But not even his Lordship will maintain that the moral guilt of the two offences is equal, or so nearly equal as to render it possible to visit both with the same punishment without shocking the moral sense of the entire nation. A stringent declaration by all members on taking their seats has been proposed, but probably the only result of such an expedient would be that the agents would keep the details of the contest entirely in the dark until after the declaration was made, and then of course no one would expect the sitting member to give up his seat when he had made the statutory declaration *bonâ fide,* and without notice of any flaw in his title. By the combined operation of law and equity he might claim the right to retain what he had won, even if it afterwards appeared that his declaration had been made under a mistaken impression.

With patronage and exclusive dealing, those more subtle methods of corrupting a constituency, it is pretty generally admitted that legislation is scarcely competent to deal, but bribery, treating, and the grosser forms of intimidation may be proved in evidence, and dealt with by statute. No one defends these evils, but very few really and heartily condemn them, and even the punitive measures occasionally taken by the House in its fits of virtuous indignation, seem to show that it is not in earnest even when it strikes. Quoting Blue Books, Mr. Christie tells us that at different elections, the number of persons bribed was 155 at Canterbury, 111 at Cambridge, 183 (freemen) at Galway, 255 at Barnstaple, and 847 at Hull, while at the Gloucester election, which nearly cost the city its franchise, 250 persons were bribed by 81 agents, and at Wakefield, the bribed were 86, and the bribers 98. Mr. Christie, in such cases as these, would suspend the writ or disfranchise the place altogether. Where there is, it may be, "a small corrupt phalanx which turns the scale," he would not select the "small corrupt phalanx" for punishment, but he would "take away the stimulant" of corruption by depriving the place of its representatives for five or ten years, so that the "habits of corruption may die away by disuse." But though the Government adopted this idea in their Bill of last Session, and carried the clauses containing it through the Commons, the Lords struck out those clauses in Committee.

Indeed, it is hard to defend on any principle of justice a mode of punishment by which innocent and guilty suffer together. This argument against the ministerial proposal was ably placed before the House during the debate by Mr. J. J. Powell, Q.C., of the Oxford circuit, who had not long before been elected for Gloucester, when its franchise was restored after two years suspension. Mr. Powell is a native of the city he represents, and is therefore well able to speak to the state of parties there. He referred to the fact that "the Inquiry Commissioners had reported that at Gloucester there were a number of gentlemen who had for many years associated themselves together for the express purpose of insuring purity of election, and that, in 1852, they brought about a perfectly pure and free election. But because they had not always succeeded; and because in a large constituency, a comparatively small number were corrupt, these gentlemen, who had greatly exerted themselves to secure purity of election, would nevertheless be disfranchised by the bill. Such a clause would prove inoperative, for the reason that all would be desirous of evading the law. In a constituency of, say 2,000,—200 were proved to have been bribed, and all the 2,000 were to be disfranchised, for the sake of purifying the 200."

There is much force in these remarks, for we are sure no one would advocate an extension of this mode of administering justice, from electoral to ordinary offenders. Mr. Powell deserves the credit of having made in this debate the most valuable and practical suggestions for meeting the evil, that we have yet seen. He said, that as the object of legislation was not to disfranchise but to purify, that object could best be attained "by excising from every constituency, every elector against whom a charge of bribery can be made out, and disfranchising inexorably not only every one who took, but every one who gave a bribe."

These recommendations are much more practical than Mr. Christie's proposal for a society for putting down bribery by mutual agreement, as experience at Gloucester shows that such agreements, even if successful once in a dozen years, are broken through as soon as party contests become as fierce, or party men as excited, as usual. By disfranchising those who had taken bribes at an election, we should, in many cases, get rid at once of the great source of corruption. We should remove the "small corrupt phalanx" with whom a vote is only worth having for what it will fetch, and we should exercise a wholesome influence over any like-minded electors who might for the time escape detection. This would be directly contrary to the present working of our Parliamentary Law, which seems designed to hold out the greatest possible amount of encouragement to the venal portion of a constituency. As matters stand at present, Tom Trueman and Sam Sordid may vote at the same election, the one from conscientious motives, the other for a pecuniary consideration. If their candidate loses, Sordid has, at any rate, the money in his purse, but in the contrary event, he has, in addition, the chance of being summoned to London to give evidence on the petition. After a stay of some days, or it may be weeks, at a good hotel, he gives his evidence, and gets a very respectable sum for his attendance as a witness; the member is or is not unseated, and the process is repeated greatly to Sordid's satisfaction, till the borough gets notorious, and a committee reports its delinquencies to the House. Then comes a repetition of what we have already seen—a commission of inquiry, the discovery of an immense amount of bribery, a long and expensive investigation, and ultimately a suspension of the writ. Sordid and his class have brought all this upon their town and order, and it might be expected that they would be marked out for severe punishment. Not a bit of it. They, and they alone, have enjoyed the profits of corruption, but Trueman and his fellows are now to share their punishment. They have taunted Trueman with his folly in "letting the ready money pass him," and now they twit him with being "tarred with the same brush" as themselves. Can a more effectual mode of debasing the voters be imagined? Ought we not to be surprised, not that many yield to the temptation, but that any remain proof against it? Granting that very often "a corrupt phalanx turns the scale," are we not likely to make that phalanx more important and more influential, by allowing it to retain all the advantages of corruption, and only imposing penalties upon it, which are laid upon the more virtuous members of the constituency as well? The proceedings of an election commission are essentially judicial. The commissioners ask the help of everyone who can give them information on the subject of the inquiry; persons accused are summoned and heard, and then they in turn can subject others to the same ordeal, and the commissioners make their report on the information thus obtained, "this result being arrived at in great measure through assistance rendered to them by the honest portion of the community. The house, therefore, knows who the corrupt persons are, and it knows also substantially, that all the rest of the community are not corrupt." But the tendency of this wholesale and undiscriminating disfranchisement is "to give every honest man the same interest as a rogue in concealing corrupt practices; for how can one expect a man to expose the offences of others, when he is himself to be punished for them?" Is it not like enacting "that every person reported guilty of bribery and corruption should receive a certain number of lashes, and every honest man who will give such information as shall lead to the conviction of the offenders, shall receive precisely the same punishment?"

It has been objected to these arguments that as witnesses at an election commission give their evidence under promise of indemnity, you break faith with them if you take away their right of voting. To this it is replied, indemnity is oblivion for offences past, not licence to commit offences future. To allow a delinquent to escape punishment is one thing; to put him in a position where you are certain he will do the same again, is quite another. If you commit a breach of faith by punishing the guilty, do you make that breach of faith less by extending your punishment to the innocent? You make the inhabitants of a hundred pecuniarily liable for damage done by rioters, but you do not hold them criminally responsible. How, then, can you justify depriving seven-eighths of the electors of a given place of their right as Englishmen, because they have honestly exercised that right in spite of great temptation, while the remaining eighth have sold their birthright like a set of venal slaves?

But besides the multitudinous objections on equitable grounds, which may be urged against the suspension of writs, it can hardly be denied that the course the House has hitherto adopted is highly unconstitutional. Of its own mere motion it has taken on itself to deprive large constituencies of the right of election and of their share in the representation. Precedents for this course are not wanting, but to quote the words of Hallam on a somewhat analagous question:—"If a few precedents, and those of recent date, are to determine all questions of constitutional law, it is plain enough from the journals, that the House has assumed the power of incapacitation; but such an authority is highly dangerous, and unnecessary for any good purpose, and, according to all legal rules, so extraordinary a power cannot be supported except by a kind of prescription, which cannot be shown."

Even an infraction of the constitution might, in the public interest, be excused, where the evil is great, if the punishment be discriminative, and the remedy effectual. But this is not the case. As soon as the appointed time is over, the House becomes "as indiscriminate in its mercy as in its severity, and allows the writs to issue without restriction, though it knows the name of every person guilty of corruption."

There is little to be said in favour of a scheme of law reform which is at once unjust in principle, unworkable in practice, ineffective alike to punish evil doers, or to protect those that do well. Differing with great humility from an opinion which the LAW MAGAZINE has to some extent approved, I think that Mr. Christie has failed "to hit the right nail on the head." Not even the high authority of Lord Brougham will satisfy me that bribery and the slave-trade should be put down by the same means and visited with the same punishment. Nor can Mr. Christie's analogy between corruption and duelling be seriously supported. Stringent laws and heavy punishments did not put down the latter practice, nor did any "sudden change of public feeling" take place in consequence of the labours of the Anti-Duelling Association. So far back as 1830, the case of *R.* v. *Helsham* shows that duellists escaped, not because our laws were uncertain, or our judges unwilling to administer it, but because jurors paid less regard to their oaths, than to the prevailing feeling of society. The duel between Colonel Fawcett and Lieutenant Munro, which led to the formation of the Anti-Duelling Association in 1844, was chiefly remarkable for occurring at a time when such a mode of settling differences between gentlemen had gone out of fashion, and the Association was not a cause, but a consequence, of that dislike to duelling which has rendered it an obsolete barbarism. Yet though a coroner's jury returned verdicts of wilful murder against the parties, one or both of the seconds were acquitted, and not without some hesitation did a jury find the principal guilty. The palmy days of duelling were over; human life had been lost in the encounter, and, before the trial, the Anti-Duelling Association had had plenty of time to imbue society with a wholesome horror of its own favourite aversion; but nevertheless, the prosecutions were not much better than failures. How then could we expect convictions, when the politician in the dock would probably have ardent sympathisers among the politicians in the box, and when an adverse verdict would be *primâ facie* ground for suspecting that the jury and the prisoner were of opposite politics?

It may be mortifying to our national vanity, but there is no gainsaying the fact, that bribery prevails too extensively to be abated by such measures as those Mr. Christie proposes. His Anti-Bribery Union would be but a rope of sand, and his penal legislation, by shocking the country's sense of justice, would bring the law into disrepute, and introduce evils far greater than those it was designed to destroy. We must rely upon other means for the removal of this plague-spot in our political system. To this end, statutes for shortening proceedings and limiting expenditure may in some measure contribute, but we can never hope for any great improvement till we have a radical change in our mode of investigating charges of bribery when made, and of punishing offences against purity of election when proved. The House of Commons claims the sole right of determining all matters relative to the election of its members, but the manner in which that right is exercised makes election law uncertain and variable to the last degree. Hence we have contemporary decisions on precisely similar facts, in which diametrically opposite views are taken; a disregard of precedent which makes the award of a committee almost a matter of guess work; and which gives to committee decisions the character, not of a current, but of an ever varying succession of eddies, from whose erratic motions no one is able to deduce a clear and consistent rule. The remedy for this is to erect a tribunal for the trial of election matters, which, like every other tribunal, shall be bound by fixed rules and presided over by men of legal experience. The sittings of such a court should be, not in the committee rooms of the House, but in the borough or place to which the inquiry refers, and the witnesses should not be those whom the parties to the petition choose to keep in town at a fabulous cost, but anyone and everyone whom the Commissioners should see fit to summon before them. The expenses of such an inquiry should fall on the parties, whether bribers or bribed, whose misconduct made it necessary; and, in the last place, the power of disfranchisement, which the House now exercises capriciously and indiscriminately, should be brought to bear only upon those who have shown that they do not deserve the right of voting, by basely bartering that right for gold. If these changes were effected, the guilty would no longer trust to the expense of a petition, as their great safeguard against the exposure of their misdeeds, nor would they, after selling their votes, be able to make a further profit by "selling" the man who bought them. Finally, there would be, between the pure and the impure, between the precious and the vile, a broad and appreciable distinction. The one would remain in the exercise of their franchise, while the other would be ignominiously debarred from it; the one, having suffered a temporary injury by the rejection of their candidate through corrupt influences, would secure a permanent benefit by the excision of those by whose venality that injury had been inflicted. The cause of political honesty would immensely gain; the moral tone of the political world would be greatly raised, and a clear field and a fair prospect would be secured for the operations of Mr. Christie's Anti-Bribery Society.

I remain, Sir,
Very truly yours,
FRANCIS TURNER.
Middle Temple.

MR. CHRISTIE'S REPLY TO THE FOREGOING.

I have been permitted by the Editor to read Mr. Turner's letter as it passed through the press, and to make such remarks on it as I may desire.

Mr. Turner has greatly misunderstood the object of my paper entitled "Suggestions for an Organization for Restraint of Bribery and Corruption," has sometimes misstated my opinions, and has ascribed to me several recommendations of specific measures against bribery which I have simply mentioned as those of others.

The object of my paper was to suggest an organization or association which should strive to create a general strong feeling against bribery and corrupt practices, promote agreements between candidates and leaders of parties in boroughs to abstain from or avert bribery, as well as mixed Committees for diminution of expenditure, and give special attention to the law as to bribery and to the consideration and preparation of measures for repressing it.

I have not proposed the entire abolition of patronage. I have not recommended suspension of writs in the case of delinquent boroughs, or disfranchisements, or punishment of bribers by imprisonment and the treadmill. I have mentioned these recommendations of others incidentally: but they form no part of my plan for an organization. It is Lord Brougham who has proposed to deal with bribers as he dealt with slave-traders, and to confront candidates and their supporters with the treadmill or transportation. I have said that I hope that such strong measures may not be necessary, and am disposed to agree with Mr. Turner that such legislation would not be backed by opinion, and so would fail. I have not said that I have "no hope so long as the candidate and the world regard the functions of an M.P. less as a duty to be discharged, than as a favour to be solicited." A similar sentiment, but not in these words, occurs in a passage which I quoted from Mr. John Stuart Mill's "Thoughts on Representative Reform." I have not proposed to "unite candidates, their supporters, and agents, in a mutual bond to abstain from corrupt practices, and punish severely those who violate such an agreement." I have not said anything about "binding over election agents of a certain class to electoral purity by moral suasion," which would have been stark nonsense. I have not "fallen foul of attorneys;" I quoted the opinions of Baron Pigott, Mr. James Vaughan, and Mr. Joseph Parkes, himself an attorney, on the employment of attorneys in elections. Mr. Turner completely misquotes and misrepresents me when he says that I "would 'take away the stimulant' of corruption by depriving the place of its representatives for five or ten years, so that 'the habit of corruption may die away by disuse.'" I have not put forward "a scheme of law-reform."

I wish to have an association which shall make it its special business to do everything that can be done for the restraint of bribery and expenditure at elections, and such an association would consider, with others, the proposal, ascribed by Mr.

Turner to Mr. Powell, the member for Gloucester, for disfranchisement of every voter proved to have taken or given a bribe, and Mr. Turner's own excellent suggestions for a thorough reform of the system of trying elections. Indeed, the Committee, which has been appointed by the Council of the Association for the Promotion of Social Science, for the establishment of such an organization as I have suggested, have already announced that, "the whole law and procedure of election-petitions will merit special attention."

There is not, perhaps, really much difference of opinion between Mr. Turner and myself, as to the feeling about bribery. Mr. Turner says, "It is true that in the abstract public feeling is adverse to bribery." I say, "The great object is to rouse an enthusiasm against electoral corruption, and to cover the country with it, and to carry it into every constituency. We have this advantage to begin with, that the moral sense of the nation already unmistakeably condemns bribery. There is no need to create a feeling; we have to intensify it, and to make it conquer." Anyhow, if the feeling is to be created, it is all the more necessary to make a great effort to create it, and the weaker the feeling, the more need to labour to strengthen it.

I certainly have not expected to find any horror of corruption among the "men in the moon," or the solicitors who employ them.

Mr. Turner must exaggerate when he says that a list of five or six thousand names of gentlemen anxious to pay largely to get into Parliament can be obtained any day at the Carlton or Reform Club.

My quotations from Andrew Marvel and Bishop Burnet do not mean that I have "no hope in a change and reformation in the manners of the nation." That is what I hope for, and wish to strive to effect.

The unauthorised acts of individuals, such as those which lately compelled Mr. Lloyd to renounce his seat for Barnstaple, would cease if candidates placed in similar positions would generally act like Mr. Lloyd, or refuse to reimburse unauthorised expenditure.

The plan of repressing bribery through agreements in constituencies, which Mr. Turner decries, was advocated by the late Sir Robert Peel in a speech delivered in the House of Commons on the 6th of June, 1842:

"In every borough there are certain individuals who take a lead in all political matters, and who altogether influence the electors in their respective places. Now, I believe that if these influential persons of both parties in boroughs set their faces against bribery, and came to an understanding to discourage all unnecessary expenses, they would do a great deal more towards the suppression of the evils complained of, than all the acts of the Legislature. I do not therefore underrate the law, but I think that good example and improved habits will more effectually lead to the diminution of bribery—its extinction I scarcely hope for—than any legislative enactment whatever, and I do hope that the leading men of the country will set their faces so effectually against it, that after the next general election, come when it may, there shall be little or no cause to complain on the score of bribery."

I end, as I began, by remarking that Mr. Turner has misunderstood my proposal; and I append a short summary of the objects of the proposed organization, which has been circulated by the Committee of the Association for Promotion of Social Science.

W. D. CHRISTIE.

"The proposed organization will have for its object the reform of a great moral and social evil. Originated by the National Association for the Promotion of Social Science, which unites members of all political parties, it will be sedulously kept aloof from party politics.

"The great object of the suggested organization would be to act on public opinion and endeavour to rouse a moral enthusiasm through the country, which might enable much to be done through voluntary efforts of individuals and by voluntary agreements, and which might also effectually aid the action of legislation.

"Endeavours may be made to form local Committees composed of leading men of all parties, and to procure agreements between opposing candidates and opposing leaders of parties in constituencies to abstain from bribery and to limit expenditure.

"Public opinion may be acted on by public meetings, where they may be thought desirable, and by the circulation of suitable pamphlets. Information may be collected about boroughs where elections are stained by corruption, and as to the various kinds and forms of corruption prevailing.

"It will be an object to restrain, not only the direct purchase of votes by money, but all forms of unnecessary expenditure involving or easily turned to corruption. The employment of paid agents and canvassers, of clerks and messengers, the conveyance of voters to the poll, the bringing up of out-voters, the use of public-houses for committee rooms, might all be made subjects of agreement between opposing candidates, or of regulation by a mixed committee of leading electors, to the general advantage of all candidates as well as to the benefit of morality.

"Attention will also be directed to legislation against bribery, and to the preparation of measures which may be recommended to Parliament. The whole law and procedure of election petitions will, under this head, merit special attention.

"It will be important to obtain the cooperation of as many Members of both Houses of Parliament and candidates for seats in the House of Commons as possible; and the cooperation of solicitors and election agents through the country is particularly desired. It is hoped that the leading men of all political parties, some of the most distinguished in literature, and the most eminent in the Law and the Church, will combine for this object."

Art. VI.—COOKE ON INCLOSURES.

The Acts for facilitating the Inclosure of Commons in England and Wales, with a Treatise on the Law of Rights of Commons, in reference to these Acts, and of the Jurisdiction of the Inclosure Commissioners. By George Wingrove Cooke, of the Middle Temple, Barrister-at-Law. Fourth Edition. London: Stevens, Sons, and Haynes. 1864.

THE law of commons, speaking in a strict sense, has undergone but little alteration. When the ancient wastes and common lands become inclosures, the statute law interferes extensively and introduces a new description of ownership, together with a confirmation of title after proof before the valuer of enjoyment of the commonable privileges for a certain number of years. To use the words of Mr. Cooke:—"There is a provision in the new General Inclosure Act (Sect. 54.) that rights of common not sustainable in law may be allowed* after sixty years' user. No decision has yet occurred upon the effect of this enactment."† With the exception then of the 2 & 3 Will. IV., c. 71 (the Prescription Act), which confers a provisional right after thirty, and an absolute right after sixty, years, unless some consent to the enjoyment should appear by deed or writing, the pasturage and feedings on wastes and lammas or other such lands are governed, as of old, by the common law. For the Act of George III. (13 Geo. III., c. 81) regulates the user rather than disturbs the right. Mr. Cooke is much of this opinion. He remarks that Bracton "has a chapter on rights of common which would not be out of place in a modern treatise, and even Bracton is compelled to cite anterior writers, and expresses himself in terms frequently drawn from the

* That is by the valuer. † P. 25, 214.

Civilians."* Following this view, we are not surprised to find that the able writer of the "History of Party" should have enumerated the various rights of commons, appendancies, appurtenant rights, rights in gross, common pur cause de vicinage.† Then, common of pasture, of piscary, of turbary, and of estovers. We think that Mr. Cooke's observation concerning the confusion of appendancies, &c., with the subject matter of the right, is commendable, and deserving of attention. But he shall speak for himself—"It has been the custom of writers upon this department of our law to confuse their subject by a faulty division. Thus, Bacon, Cruise, and Woolrych, all treat of 'the several kinds of common,' first, as common appendant, appurtenant, in gross, and by vicinage, and then as common of pasture—turbary, piscary, and estovers. In truth, however, the first division applies only to rights of common, and the second only to the subject matter of that right."‡

Yet, admitting, as we do, the value of the suggestion, it is doubtful whether criticism bears out the author's comment on these works. It is, at all events, a refinement; for, upon turning to the older writers, we find that the species of commons flow naturally from their original elements or principles, and that, if there be error, it has arisen rather from redundancy than confusion.

Passing by this episode, the various descriptions of the intercommonable privileges are related according to the views of the author, and with correct succinctness. The common pur cause, &c., is well illustrated, as separate from common appendant where the rights are not co-extensive. Speaking of this partial admixture of neighbours' cattle, the author says, "Such cases are, in fact, very frequent in some parts of the country, where the commoners of A. have common over wastes A. and B., but the commoners of B. are confined

* P. 5.

† This common ought not to have the title of a right, for it is but an excuse for a trespass, and may be at once extinguished by inclosure.

‡ P. 6. n.

to waste B. The right of the commoners of A. over the waste of B. is frequently, but erroneously, spoken of as a right of common by vicinage. In truth, the commoners of A. in the case put, have a right of common, either appendant or appurtenant, over the wastes of A. and B."* This point is not inaptly tendered, because common of vicinage is an appendant common. And the quotation above is not a conceit, but is in strict accordance with the opinion of Lawrence, J., in *Hollinshed* v. *Walton*,† only amplified.

With the observations contained in subsequent pages on the "common *sans nombre*," we are not so well prepared to agree. There is said to have been such a right attached to a Lincolnshire cottage by way of common appurtenant, and in gross by grant. The Lincolnshire case was attributed to the encouragement of habitation in a fen country. This has been accepted as the ordinary reason, but Mr. Cooke will have it, that "it was probably upon some part of the wolds of Lincolnshire, and not in the fens that the prescription was found."‡ The writer remarks upon the absence of agricultural knowledge amongst the lawyers and judges of former days, and doubts whether the "power of turning out sheep to rot in a fen country would be an encouragement of habitation."§ The idea of the wolds, which are more to the north, is an ingenious, though venturesome conjecture. We are willing to prefer the history which has been handed down to us.

Many commons are tenanted by cattle in Cambridgeshire, yet that is a fen country. The same may be said of Essex, and of other places where there have been marshes, and yet beasts in abundance.

It must have occurred to the learned author that the labours of sewerage were originated at a very early date. Before the days of Henry VI., indeed far earlier, the escape of the waters which deluged the neighbouring lands

* P. 18.
† 7 East, 485.
‡ P. 21. n.
§ *Ibid.*

was promoted. There was the bane and antidote, the disease and the remedy. Drainage was to some extent made available in a natural channel long before the artificial power was applied. Lincolnshire has been a stronghold of sewerage for generations. The experienced Inclosure Commissioner could not have been ignorant, seeing that he has brought the drainage law before us, that whilst fever and ague were assailing the fen inhabitants, the encouragement for men to settle there was furthered by a liberal, perhaps not unlimited, permission by the lords of manors, or owners of land, to use the extensive wastes with sheep which could scarcely be numbered. *Sans nombre;* that is, difficult to tell the exact amount; indifferent as to the quantity; the tract of pasturage being so large. Then, the great Statute of Sewers, 23 Hen. VIII., "The Bill of Sewers" exhibits the zeal of the times for maintaining outlets for the inland streams and the prostration of annoyances calculated to retard the exit of those floods and waters. We are not confounding sewerage with drainage, but we can understand that statutory provisions like those of the Act of Henry, would, with their wide grasp and application, give assurance to people coming towards a place not densely populated, especially with the accompaniment of extensive feedings, or lands where those feedings would be deemed, at common law, incident to the grant. Common in gross *sans nombre* receives a better explanation at the hands of Mr. Cooke. He sums up by observing on the existence of such an user being possible in law: "That a right of common of pasture in gross *sans nombre* is limited to a right to turn on so many cattle as the common will maintain beyond the *levant* and *couchant* cattle of the lord and the commoners."*

We incline to the opinion that there never was such a right as an unrestricted power to turn on in the plain sense of

* P. 27. This is an expression more applicable to the commoner than the lord. The lord cannot common in his own land, but he can depasture as lord.

the word, and that the ordinary interpretation of so large a privilege was never realised. We conceive, that a man might have made a grant by deed to this effect: "You may turn on as many as you like, I shall not put any stint upon you." But if subsequently appealed to, that he would reply, "I never meant to confer the power of sending such a number of beasts to the moor as you have put on. I only intended a reasonable user, consistent with the rights of others, and, probably, a slight overflow would not have been noticed." This happens in a minor degree not unfrequently upon wastes, or upon greens. An infinitely larger portion of animals is found depasturing than the owner can justify, and he has not even a deed to help him. But indifference and the difficulty of obtaining redress are such as to leave the transgressor in full enjoyment of his surcharge. So, upon a larger scale, many use the wide spreading tracts of downs and walks without question as to numbers, and many compester without any right at all. So that common *sans nombre* is a kind of mystical term which signifies, in itself, nothing, but, if interpreted, means, either such a flock or herd as cannot be easily counted, or rather an excess, concerning which the owner, or grantor, or lord, *de minimis*, as it were, *non curat*. When the mischief or the population increases so as to produce inconvenience, the matter is taken in hand, and, unless time has passed so that it becomes too late to arrest the false claim *in toto*, for even then the *unlimited* assertion can be resisted, the user is narrowed within reasonable bounds, and the thesis of the common *sans nombre* is not verified. Indeed, the fact of the usual grant of a common in gross for so many cattle has alone a tendency to negative the wild assumption of unmeasured user.

Farther on in the work, Mr. Cooke says, "It has been doubted whether a stinted right of pasture is in reality a right of common."* This observation must be confined to common lands, cattle gates, and lands in severalty to which common

* P. 43.

appertains at certain periods. It was, no doubt, so intended by the author. For, of course, a right on the lord's waste for so many beasts is as much a right of common as an appendant or appurtenant common.

In another page* the learned writer speaks of "the old lot meadow, in which the owners draw lots for the choice. They all, however, agree in that as soon as the crops are removed, they become commonable." We have known a lot mead always pasture, and where the lord's waste nearly adjoins. This was probably severed from the waste by encroachment, but we merely quote it to show that the lot meadow might have been originally pasture as well as arable, there not being any contiguous commonable arable lands to identify it with severalties.

The account of these different rights is wound up with the shack common. "After the crop has been removed, these lands become commonable to all the parties having a severalty right, but to no others."† "The severalty holders upon shack lands are usually the holders of the fee of their several portions."‡

Lammas lands are open after a particular day when the crop is in general removed, and commonable lands, for the most part, obey the same rule, which distinguishes them from shack. Lammas lands likewise are open to others than owners in severalty. Shack lands are confined to such owners.§

There are other incidents belonging to commons; alienation; extinguishments; the respective rights of lords and commoners; all these have been dealt with in the book under our view. There is, however, one subject which has a claim upon our attention. To use the words of our text, "This (non-user) is, perhaps the most difficult of all the ordinary

* P. 48. † P. 50. ‡ P. 51.

§ "These commonable lands," says Mr. Cooke, "have hitherto been unnoticed by our law writers," p. 51 n. We think this too broad an assertion.

points that come before the valuer and assistant commissioners." The question is whether a commonable right can be lost by non-user. Mr. Cooke's illustration is this: "It must frequently happen that although two estates may be equally entitled to turn out on a waste, the tenant of one will exercise the right, and the tenant of the other will abstain from so doing. The better farmer will keep a herd of sheep that will not live upon the waste, or the more distant farmer may not find it profitable to drive his beasts there. Yet it would be manifestly unjust if upon an inclosure the waste were so divided as to be a valuable premium for bad husbandry; the chief reason for inclosing waste lands being that land in an uninclosed state is useless to the skilled farmer."*

It is not easy to say how a common can be lost by an acquiescence in abstinence. Light; way; water-course; these may be lost by certain acts which establish a positive abandonment. You may abolish the spring from whence the ancient light, the right of passage, and the stream flow, but you cannot extinguish the waste so as to raise the question of non-user. Unity of possession is quite beside the question.

We conceive, therefore, that common can scarcely be destroyed by merely forbearing from taking the profit *à prendre*. There was a case of *Manifold* v. *Pennington*, in Barnewall and Alderson. The result of that decision seems to have been, that if a man did not keep, and was never known to have kept, a particular species of cattle, he could not be said to have surrendered his right, nor to have lost any right of action, nor was he liable to be proceeded against, for he had not exercised the privilege to which he was entitled. Had he kept the stock, as sheep, for example, it might have been left to the jury to say whether there had been an abandonment. We do not, however, place too much reliance on that case as authority. It often happens that landowners having an undoubted right to the waste, keep commonable cattle, but,

* P. 59.

for various reasons, it is inconvenient for them to send their stock to the pasture. Can anything be more unreasonable than to compel the owner to use the common by way of asserting a claim which belongs to his estate, or which is his by grant? It might be a wise policy to make an occasional visit to the common-field or waste, taking care to have evidence of the user, however rare. But we recognise a plain difference between this profit and easements, the former being of a substantial character, the latter, comparatively speaking, of a fugitive or evanescent nature.

When the valuer and assistant commissioner are called upon to decide upon claims under the Inclosure Act, it seems to us that they should, as far as possible, relieve themselves from the embarrassing principle of legal non-user, and rather look with jealousy at the fact of long neglect or absence of user, not in the light of extinguishment, but of evidence that there has never been any user. So many fictitious claims are put forward at the approach of a division of the waste, that the officers whose duty it is to settle these pretensions, may justly require proof, not so much limited to a prior user, as of the existence of the very right itself.

We take our leave at this point of the first portion of Mr. Cooke's useful work. It is a valuable and compendious narrative of a subject of some complication, and the professional inquirer will find in the terse yet luminous pages of this treatise a clue to further information, if he be not already satisfied with the materials before him.

The plan adopted by many law writers of supplying or inserting all the statutes concerning the subject of which they treat is judicious, and consequently, useful. The second part of this work consists of the Law of Inclosures. The author has not only placed together all the Acts: he has also added those which have any relation to the subject.*

* Mr. Woolrych, the Police Magistrate, has upon the same principle, collected the Local Government Acts with success.

There is a useful chapter "of the evidence in claims before the valuer or assistant commissioner," and the question of encroachments has received attention. A curious point has been offered in the chapter of evidence. The extent of the right being measured by the ancient inclosures, *i.e.*, the wintering of commonable beasts: does the 5th section of the Act 8 & 9 Vict., c. 118, enable the valuer to reject a sixty years' claim which is founded upon a *surcharge?* In other words, admitting the right to a certain extent, will a constant trespass work itself into an indefeasible privilege after the lapse of that period? "No case has yet been decided by the courts upon the construction of this section of the Act; but the assistant commissioners have held that a right claimed under it must be a legal and a limited right."*

The gist of the matter is in the word "right." The words of the 2 & 3 Will. IV., c. 71, are, "where such right, profit, or benefit shall have been actually taken and enjoyed by any person claiming right thereto." There must be an enjoyment as of right, and although there may not have been an absolute determination upon the point, the authorities are strong in favour of the views assumed by the assistant commissioners. If a commoner should be found to have usurped a right in respect of a messuage and land, which element will confer the legal privilege, he cannot be molested after thirty years user; but if he should have intruded on the waste, and upon investigation his claim should be for common appendant or appurtenance, without the messuage, &c., any user he may have enjoyed ought not to weigh against the words of the statute, "nevertheless such claim may be defeated in any other way by which the same is now liable to be defeated." To maintain a legal right by usurpation by virtue of an act of the Legislature, is very different from assuming a right which has no foundation at all, and which, therefore, cannot come within the scope of the remedy. A surcharge does not negative the limited profit, but if such an excess were to be sanctioned

* P. 105, n.

after sixty years, a principle would be sustained which neither the common law, nor the prescriptive Act, nor the Inclosure Acts, could warrant.

The jurisdiction of the Inclosure Commissioners with reference to commons has not been forgotten. For instance, as to exchanges, partitions, intermixed land, drainage, rent-charge. The author rightly observes, that the drainage jurisdiction is foreign to the original purpose of the commission,* and to the scope of his work.† Yet having introduced the Acts 9 & 10 Vict., c. 101., 12 & 13 Vict., c. 100, and 13 & 14 Vict., c. 31., he might, perhaps, have adverted, however slightly, to the statute, 24 & 25 Vict., c. 133, an important code as to recent agricultural drainage and commissions of sewers, and the more so as the Inclosure Commissioners have, by it, another trust confided to them; the issuing with their sanction new commissions of sewers. It is true that the Act has but little connection with commons, but as we find in the title page "The jurisdiction of the Inclosure Commissioners (amongst other things) under the Public and Private Money's Drainage Acts and under the Companies' Acts relating thereto," we may be pardoned if we just allude to this Drainage Act of 1861. The Inclosure Commissioners are important officers under the Act, for, upon their recommendation, commissions of sewers may be granted for new areas, regard being had to the levels and other facilities of drainage, or for an area wholly or partially within the limits of an existing commission. The powers of present commissioners are saved, and the Queen's power to issue commissions is expressly saved. Nevertheless, the change is of a very striking character, and it will probably lead to consequences requiring fresh labours from Commissioners of Inclosure. For they are already provided by this Act with considerable powers in forming the new areas.‡ The subsequent division of the Act provides

* That is the Inclosure Commission.

† P. 148.

‡ *See* the early clauses of 24 & 25 Vict., c. 133.

for the appointment and arrangement of Electoral Drainage Boards, but with these we have no concern, although we will conclude our remarks with this observation of Mr. Cooke: "Like other provisions which have the effect of allowing land owners with limited estates to let their lands upon equitable terms, or to improve their cultivation, they are very beneficial in their operation, and it is well that the power should be known to exist."*

Without an appendix of forms a work is considered incomplete. We have here a copious list of forms. They are ever acceptable to the practitioner, who, if he be a practised lawyer, takes all forms, statutable or otherwise (not being imperative), as guides, not as masters.

We now take leave, for the present, of the commissioner, whose office is the reward of his knowledge and his labours. When a treatise has arrived at its fourth edition, a guarantee for its value is revealed which needs no other record than a kindly remembrance to the public of its appearance. We may not agree with every sentence of the commonable discussions, but we regard the whole as a work of considerable utility, not too short, so as to raise a suspicion of want of care, but sufficiently explicit to win the watchful reader to the belief that he has found the chief points he has been looking for, well and lucidly explained.

ART. VII.—JUSTICES' OF THE PEACE PROCEDURE BILL.†

THE object of this Bill is "to consolidate and amend the Acts regulating procedure before Justices of the Peace out of Quarter Sessions in England," and its preamble succinctly recites that "it is expedient to reduce into one Act

* P. 148.

† Brought in by Mr. Paull, Mr. Richard Hodgson, and Mr. Staniland, 8th June, 1864.

the existing enactments regulating the procedure before Justices of the Peace out of Quarter Sessions in England, to simplify and amend those enactments and the forms of such procedure, and to provide uniform Tables of Fees to be taken by Clerks to Justices and Constables." It is understood to have been prepared by Mr. Oke, of the Mansion House justice room, whose works upon this extensive branch of the law are in universal use, and to be framed in accordance with the valuable paper upon the subject read by him at the annual meeting of the National Association for the Promotion of Social Science, held at the Guildhall, London, in June, 1862, and published in the *Transactions* of the Association for that year.* In that paper we repointed out the numerous practical defects in the present procedure before justices in England, with suggestions of the fitting remedies; and after remarking that the procedure is principally regulated by Jervis's Act, 11 & 12 Vict., c. 43, passed in 1848, which, although it effected many improvements in the practice, fell very short of what it professed to be, a consolidation Act, and did not give that facility to the justices in the exercise of their increasing duties, which was expected; the author says—

"It does not create a uniformity of practice, for it exempts from its operation so many offences and matters to which some, if not all, of its provisions might advantageously have been applied, and contains in every fourth or fifth section some exception or proviso as to portions of procedure supplied by other enactments, which should have been repealed, that its utility is much impaired; it being in fact and practically of limited operation, and, in many cases, only of a cumulative character, thereby creating confusion and uncertainty in the application of its provisions, as the questions submitted to the superior courts from time to time abundantly testify. It has likewise in many cases of modern legislation been referred to as the Act containing the procedure, without due consideration of the

* Page 146. "Magisterial Procedure: Reasons for its Revision, Simplification, and Uniformity." By George C. Oke, of the Mansion House Justice Room, author of "The Magisterial Synopsis," and other legal works. Reviewed L. M. and R. August, 1862, page 367.

nature of its provisions, to many of which it was never intended to apply, and, as respects others, it provides no adequate machinery to carry out; whilst many statutes passed afterwards, to which it would have applied, have, regardless of the procedure provided by it, embodied similar clauses to those in it on procedure, and others have contained new and unnecessary enactments, applicable, in some instances only partially, to the steps taken in the same class or description of cases. As an illustration of recent date—in four of the important Criminal Law Consolidation Acts of the last session,* there were upwards of twenty clauses as to procedure which are unnecessary, or were already law and enacted in almost similar terms in the 11 & 12 Vict., c. 43, which is also specially, though unnecessarily, referred to in those statutes, and which clauses would have been more appropriate in a Consolidated Procedure Bill, and must be repealed when such a measure is brought before Parliament. In confirmation of this view, it is considered necessary in this present session, by a Bill promoted by the Government,† to amend these four Acts in regard to Ireland, by enacting that certain provisions in them as to procedure for offences punishable summarily should not extend to Ireland, which had already a better and more comprehensive code of procedure, provided eleven years since, in the 14 & 15 Vict., c. 93, which is admirably suited to the petty sessions courts in that part of the kingdom (and which the officials there do not, I understand, desire to see altered), and is three years later in point of time than our own incomplete measure, the defects in which were avoided although in England the summary jurisdiction is far more extensive and important."

The defunct Statute Law Commission, in March, 1857, gave instructions for the preparation of a Consolidation Procedure Bill, and it was partially proceeded with by Mr. Macnamara under the direction of Mr. Greaves, Q.C., but ultimately abandoned; Mr. Greaves, however, in the Introduction to his edition of the Criminal Law Acts of 1861 (pp., xxviii and xxix), expresses his regret that such a Bill had not been passed before the latter Acts were prepared, so as to simplify their procedure clauses. Ireland, as above observed, had

* 24 & 25 Vict., c. 96, 97, 99, & 100. † Now 25 & 26 Vict., c. 50.

a general Procedure Act in 1851, the Petty Sessions Act, 14 & 15 Vict., c. 93; and during the present Session of Parliament, a similar measure has been passed for Scotland.

Mr. Oke has, in the Bill before us, carefully carried out his scheme of a comprehensive code of procedure for justices, and has, we believe, cured, in a very satisfactory manner, all the defects which have been found to exist in the present General and Special Acts, as well as afforded many facilities in the administration of the onerous and vastly increasing duties of the magistracy.

The Bill is, from the large and miscellaneous character of magisterial jurisdiction, necessarily of considerable length—115 pages, containing 145 clauses with schedule,—and is divided into fourteen parts, viz.:—

Part		Clauses
	Preliminary	1—5
I.	Jurisdiction and authority of justices ...	6—17
II.	Clerks to justices, their fees and duties	18—36
III.	Preferring complaints and charges ...	37—40
IV.	Process to enforce appearance	41—43
V.	Witnesses	44
VI.	Adjourning and remanding cases	45—51
VII.	Place of hearing and proceedings thereat.	52—57
VIII.	Summary jurisdiction	51—83
IX.	Indictable offences	84—90
X.	Summary jurisdiction over certain indictable offences	91—103
XI.	Special sessions matters	104—120
XII.	Execution of warrants	121—126
XIII.	Recognizances	127—129
XIV.	Repeal of Acts and miscellaneous provisions	130—145

Schedules.—1st. Table of justices' clerks' fees.
2nd. Forms for justices and others.
3rd. Acts repealed, thirty-two in number, either wholly or partially.

The general enactments which the Bill proposes to repeal specifically are more than double the number of its clauses; the forms in the second schedule are not on the whole one-third of the length of those now in use; and the various and dissimilar procedure provisions, relating to upwards of 2,000 offences and divers matters of a civil character, including about eighty appeal clauses, each averaging a page of a printed Bill, will be entirely removed from the Statute-book if this Bill should pass into law; while future legislative measures conferring jurisdiction on justices, or creating summary offences, would be much shortened by the omission of all such provisions, and need only refer, if at all, to the General Procedure Act. It will also materially assist in the work of consolidating the statutes.

The Bill is prepared somewhat on the plan of the Irish Petty Sessions Act of 1851, which is much better drawn and arranged, and more complete than Jervis's Acts passed three years previously; but as the summary jurisdiction in England is far more extensive and complicated than in Ireland, this Bill is necessarily more comprehensive in its application, and is intended to apply to all cases coming before justices, except to some extent those relating to the revenue, which are already regulated by a special procedure.

The principal points or details, and the proposed new provisions, may be thus summarised:—

1. A repeal of Jervis's Acts, 11 & 12 Vict., cc. 42, 43; 20 & 21 Vict., c. 43; 21 & 22 Vict., c. 73 (in part); procedure clauses in Acts creating summary jurisdiction, and special sessions procedure; procedure clauses in the Metropolitan and City Police Acts; also sections as to justices', clerks', and constables' fees: (part xiv., sect. 130, and part ii., and 3rd schedule.)

2. Provisions defining jurisdiction and powers of all descriptions of justices, and when they shall be disqualified from determining cases by reason of interest, relationship to the parties, or being members of corporate bodies, &c.: (part i.)

3. Procedure provisions, in most instances similar to those in the

Irish Act, 14 & 15 Vict., c. 93, applicable to the whole of the cases within the summary jurisdiction (except revenue and a few other cases which have their own peculiar laws), and giving an uniform mode for the preferring of the complaint to the final appeal against the justices' decision: (part viii. and portions of the previous parts).

4. Allowing a more simple mode of making complaints and issuing summonses, similar to that in the practice of County Courts; limiting the period for recovering local rates (now without limitation) to twelve months from their dates; giving power to summon witnesses wherever resident, and to produce documents; to impose full amount of penalties, &c. upon each offender where several are concerned; to mitigate penalties and terms of imprisonment; to substitute imprisonment in gaol for the stocks; to permit sums, as distinguished from penalties, to be paid by instalments; to allow a deposit of money instead of sureties in certain cases; and to impose consecutive terms of imprisonment in those cases which are not provided for by 11 & 12 Vict., c. 43, s. 25: (part iii., part v., and parts v., and viii., sect. 67.)

5. Allowing proof of service of summonses and orders at a distance to be made by affidavit, obviating the necessity for constables being taken from their duties to attend the petty sessions solely to prove such service: (part iv., sect 43.)

6. Providing that justices' warrants may be executed anywhere in England without being indorsed where executed, like those of the metropolitan police magistrates may now be (2 & 3 Vict., c. 71, s. 17), and as proposed in the Scotch Summary Procedure Bill of this Session, the present practice of getting warrants backed being a great hindrance to their execution: (part xii., sect. 122, par. 3.)

7. Providing an uniform scale of imprisonment in default of payment of all penalties, sums and costs: (part viii., sect. 68.)

8. Providing an uniform mode for the application of penalties to the superannuation, county or other funds, to informers (not being constables), &c., and removing the doubts as to the appropriation of penalties in certain boroughs: (part vii., sect. 77.)

9. Providing a summary mode before justices of estreating recognisances for appearance of parties at petty sessions, &c. (without going to the Quarter Sessions or requiring the aid of the sheriff), as

allowed in the metropolitan police courts in certain cases and in Ireland: (part xiii., sect. 128.)

10. Providing a comprehensive series of short forms for the use of justices and others: (part xiv., sect. 137 and 2nd schedule.)

11. Substituting a record or register of decisions in each district of petty sessions for the present long and formal convictions and orders, which in future are not to be filed with the clerk of the peace, as this record, or a certified copy of any entry in it, is proposed to be evidence of a conviction or other decision: (part viii., sect. 66.)

12. Allowing an appeal in the cases now allowed, and in most others from any justice's decision upon the facts or law to the Quarter Sessions (as in the Irish Act, 14 & 15 Vict., c. 93, s. 24, and Metropolitan Police Courts Act, 2 & 3 Vict., c. 71, s. 50, Jervis's Act, 11 & 12 Vict., c. 43, containing no provision on that subject), and in all cases upon the law only to a Superior Court as now permitted by 20 & 21 Vict., c. 43;—with uniform provisions as to time of appealing, notice, recognisances, &c., in each mode of appeal: (part viii., sects. 73, 74, 75, 76.)

13. An improved procedure in preliminary examinations in indictable offences, now regulated by 11 & 12 Vict., c. 42, and providing for the receiving of evidence for an accused, and further facilities as to bailing, &c.: (part ix.)

14. Extending the present summary jurisdiction over certain indictable offences under the Criminal Justice and Juvenile Offenders Acts (18 & 19 Vict., c. 126, 10 & 11 Vict., c. 82, 13 & 14 Vict., c. 37) to frauds and embezzlements, &c., of a small amount, and enacting an uniform and more simple procedure than now exists by those Acts: (part x.; *vide* G. C. Oke's letter in the *Times* of 12th May, 1864, hereon.)

15. Providing an uniform mode of appointing and convening special sessions, in lieu of the present circuitous one through the high and petty constables, and general powers of adjourning and holding special sessions, &c.: (part xi.)

16. Defining the tenure of the office of clerk to justices in counties similar to that existing in boroughs, with the disqualifications from acting for parties before their justices, and conducting prosecutions emanating from them, unless with the justices' consent or direction: (part ii., sects. 18, 21.)

17. Providing an uniform table of fees to justices' clerks of counties as well as boroughs (which now are very dissimilar) adapted to all duties they are likely to be called upon to perform, and to future legislation, similar to the table recommended in the commissioners' report on "Costs of Prosecutions," 1858-9 ; giving the Home Office power to alter the items from time to time, instead of the sessions or borough council, as now ; also similar but amended regulations as to the payment of such clerks by salary instead of fees, as now allowed under 14 & 15 Vict., c. 55 : (part ii., sect. 24, and 1st schedule ; sects. 30, 31, 32.)

18. Giving the Home Office power to make an uniform table of fees and allowances for the service of summonses and execution of warrants by constables, the same now differing in each county : (part xiv., section 141.)

19. Providing for the recovery of justices' clerks' and constables' fees before a justice instead of in the County Court : (part ii., sect. 34 ; part xiv. sect. 141.)

20. Many of the general provisions of the Bill have, where it appeared necessary, been extended to revenue and other cases, advisedly excepted from many of its provisions, as was done by the 11 & 12 Vict., c. 43, s. 35, and 14 & 15 Vict., c. 93, s. 42 ; but the whole or other portions of the Bill may readily be adapted to all such cases if the revenue solicitors see fit : (part xiv., sect. 140.)

These are the main points of the measure, many of the new details of a minor character being omitted. Many other provisions might be usefully introduced, such as an amendment of the Parish Constables Acts, and the abolition of the office of high constable, whose functions have been gradually taken from him by the County Rate Act of 15 & 16 Vict., c. 81, the Juries Act, 1862 (25 & 26 Vict., c. 107), s. 3, and the remainder of them is now proposed to be done away by the Bill which dispenses with his services in reference to convening special sessions. He is now appointed by justices in special sessions under 7 & 8 Vict., c. 33, s. 8, which is the only section of that Act now in force, except sect 7, proposed for repeal in this Bill.

In the margin of the Bill reference is made to the Acts as

to the present procedure in England and Ireland containing the analogous provisions, or provisions relating to the subject of the clause; most of those in the English Acts being proposed to be repealed in the third schedule, clause 130. Where no section is mentioned in the margin of the provision, it is entirely new.

We ought to mention, as a new and useful feature in a Parliamentary Bill, that the present one has prefixed, in addition to the usual "Arrangement of Clauses," a "comparative Table of repealed Acts and new provisions," showing at a glance where the re-enactments or new provisions for those repealed are to be found in the Bill, or the reasons for their omission. This table will materially facilitate any critical examination of the proposed enactments; at the same time it shows the care and labour which have been bestowed by its framer in maturing what we think will be found on perusal to be one of the most important measures of law reform for the consideration of the next Session of Parliament (as we understand, it has been introduced in order to its being considered by the magistracy during the recess), and we doubt not that its provisions will generally receive the sanction of the legislature; for the details of which must necessarily be entrusted to those who are practically acquainted with the working of the present system.

We may add, that Mr. Oke, in a circular which he has issued to the Magistracy and their Clerks, invites suggestions upon the provisions of the Bill before the close of this year.

Art. VIII.—TWISS AND WHEATON ON INTERNATIONAL LAW.

The Law of Nations considered as Independent Political Communities—on the Rights and Duties of Nations in Time of War. By Travers Twiss, D.C.L., Regius Professor of Civil Law in the University of Oxford, and one of Her Majesty's Counsel. London: Longman, Green, & Co. 1863.

Elements of International Law. By Henry Wheaton, L.L.D. Minister of the United States at the Court of Prussia, &c. Second annotated Edition, by William Beach Lawrence, Author of Visitation and Search, &c. Boston, U.S. London: Sampson, Low, & Co. 1863.

THE treatises at the head of this article possess a special interest, not only for the statesman and the jurist, but also for the community at large; the one being the result of English, the other of American learning and research. Mr. Wheaton's work on International Law is so instructive, and is so universally known and appreciated, as to be considered the standing text-book on that intricate subject, and thus it has been adopted by our Inns of Court as the means of instruction for legal students. This results from its clear but comprehensive style. It is what it professes to be—an elementary work. The annotations of Mr. Lawrence in this edition, bearing on the unhappy conflict between the Northern and Southern States of the American Continent, give it an additional interest at the present day. Dr. Twiss's volume is of a more recondite and philosophical nature; its title denotes its character,—"The rights and duties of nations in time of war." The learned author truly describes his work in his preface, when he says that, "History, in its relation to the rights of war, may be truly said to be philosophy teaching by examples;" following out that principle, Dr. Twiss gives an historical account of the sources from which International Law has flowed; for example, he traces reprisals from the 17 Edw. III. (A.D. 1355), and founds on the right of redress the origin of letters of marque.

And in pursuing this branch of his subject farther (Chapter 10), in connexion with privateering, he says the term is of English origin, and appears to have been employed to designate a particular class of private armed vessels in the reign of Charles II., and this is followed by an elaborate but interesting inquiry, showing the countenance given to, and the restraints imposed upon, private armed vessels by the several leading States of Europe. Again, he deals in the same manner with the doctrine of "Free ship, free goods." He traces it from a rule of the "Consolato del Mare," the supposed production, as he also informs us elsewhere (p. 146), of the fourteenth century; and after showing the different fluctuations it has undergone, and submitting it to the ordeal of the armed neutrality (out of which it came unscathed as far as England was concerned), he brings it down to the Declaration of Paris (April, 1856), whereby it was agreed (Art. 2) that the neutral flag covers enemy's goods with the exception of contraband of war. These examples might be multiplied, but these are sufficient to indicate the nature of this elaborate treatise, evincing, as it does, a vast amount of research and a thorough knowledge of the subject. Dr. Twiss also compares the manner in which different States have dealt with most of the leading maxims which have tended to establish the law of nations, and enables his reader to deduce therefrom, as far as the nature of the subject will admit, a practical system of action. We must, however, point out one error into which the learned civilian has fallen whilst informing us how the different States of Europe have viewed the maxim of "Free ship, free goods." At page 158 he writes, "The convenience of the principle that the neutral flag covers the cargo, had thus been very generally recognised by the nations of Europe prior to the first French Revolution." If by this it is meant that Great Britain, with the other "nations of Europe," recognised the principle, we must take occasion to observe that it was in defiance of the armed neutrality of 1780 that Great Britain maintained that doctrine; and that, until the Crimean war rendered it incumbent upon her to change her policy in consequence of her alliance with France, she never flinched from it; and that although at the Conference of Paris of 1856, she, in conjunction with the other parties to that treaty, declared, "that the neutral flag covers enemy's goods," she is still at liberty, apart from that declaration, to seize enemy's property on board a neutral's vessel; never having recognised the counter-principle in any other way, and then only as a matter of expediency for the occasion, as we shall hereafter show.

We would now make some general observations on international law in its practical bearings: it is a subject fraught with interest at the present day, when the peculiar state of Europe, and even more that of the Continent of America, revive old controversies and raise questions of a novel and intricate nature with no authority to resort to for solution. In Mr. Lawrence's treatise before us, Wheaton's definition of international law is given thus: "international law, as understood among civilised nations, may be defined as consisting of those rules of conduct which reason deduces as consonant to justice from the nature of the society existing among independent nations, with such definitions and modifications as may be established by general consent." This is not a satisfactory definition; a law, as the word implies, ought to be inflexible, and not liable to change, even with such modifications as may result from general consent, even if that could be had. He then enumerates the sources of international law thus:—

1. Text writers of authority, showing what is the approved usage of nations, or the general opinion respecting their mutual conduct, with the definitions and modifications introduced by general consent.

2. Treaties of peace, alliance, and commerce; declaring, modifying, or defining the pre-existing international law.

3. Ordinances of particular States, prescribing rules for the conduct of their commissioned cruisers and prize tribunals.

4. The adjudication of international tribunals, such as boards of arbitration and courts of prize.

5. Another depository of international law is to be found in the written opinions of official jurists, given confidentially to their own governments. Only a small portion of the controversies which arise between States become public. Before one State requires redress from another for injuries sustained by itself or its subjects, it generally acts as an individual would do in similar situations, it consults its legal advisers, and is guided by their opinion as to the law of the case. Where that opinion has been adverse to the sovereign client, and has been acted on, and the State which submitted to be bound by it was more powerful than its opponent in the dispute, we may confidently assume that the law of nations, such as it was then supposed to be, has been correctly laid down. The archives of the department of foreign affairs of every country contain a collection of such documents, the publication of which would form a valuable addition to the existing materials of international law.

6. The history of the wars, negociations, treaties of peace, and other transactions relating to the public intercourse of nations may conclude this enumeration of the sources of international law.

We must repeat that this definition of the law of nations and the authority on which it is based, is not very satisfactory to the legal mind, and yet it is doubtful whether any better can be given. Well might a learned author * write thus; "What are these laws? Where are they written? What authority do they command? They are a body of usages, for the most part traditional, which have arisen principally from reasons of convenience, assisted by those instincts of humanity and justice which belong to man in a natural (that is, a social) state; viz., the sense of military honour, the progress of civilisation, and the extension of commerce."

And when we consider the conflicting interests of different

* Mr. Bernard, Professor of International Law, &c., at Oxford. "Oxford Essays," p. 856.

nations, their ambition—whether for conquest, fame, or possessions—and, it must be added, their jealousy of other powers, it is a marvel that there should have been so many uncontroverted maxims regulating their conduct towards each other; and the more especially so, if we bear in mind that there is no generally recognised tribunal to enforce those maxims,—that it is the fear of forfeiture of moral respect which prompts obedience, rather than the dread of punishment or resentment. To this may be added the surprise that the opportunity offered to States in adjudicating in their own courts on the legality of the capture of prizes taken at sea from other States, to strain those maxims in their favour, or disregard them altogether, has but in a few instances been abused. But notwithstanding these remarks, there remain several questions upon which nations are not agreed. Truly does Monsieur Guizot write ("History of his Own Times," vol. iv. p. 1., Mr. Cole's translation)—"For nations as well as for kings, for statesmen and warriors, foreign policy is the field in which imagination, ambition, and pride, display themselves in their unfettered rage. In domestic legislation, present and ostensible interests, recognised rights and legal powers, imperiously restrain pretensions and hopes within fixed limits. In external dealings with foreign States, and in front of prospective views of power and glory both national and personal, a great temptation presents itself to yield to passion, to appeal to force, and to rely on success." This explains the tenacity with which some nations have clung and still continue to cling to rights and powers denounced by others. International Law is in theory represented as being based on the general welfare of the world at large. Treating the several nations of the earth as one community, it prescribes for the general weal. This may be true in the main, but witness the conflict of opinion on some of the most vital points; *e.g.*, the questions—free ships, free goods; enemy's ships, enemy's goods; the right of search; the abolition of privateering; contraband of war; the right of a belligerent to deal with a captured vessel as prize without her being condemned as such—these are some of the questions in which the peculiar position of a State, or its individual interests prompt that State to disregard the policy or feelings of other States, and to assert its own will. And not only have nations contended for rights and powers in opposition to the views and maxims of other nations, but they have shifted their ground as occasion required, and even adopted, at one period, the very maxim denounced at another. Witness our own conduct on the question, "Free ship, free goods." By the Treaty of Utrecht, entered into between England and France in 1713 (Art. 17), "It was stipulated concerning goods and ships, that free ships should also give freedom to goods; that everything should be deemed to be free and exempt which should be found on board belonging to the subjects of either of the confederates (that is the parties to the treaty), although the whole loading or any part thereof should appertain to the enemies of either of their Majesties." Here we have the maxim "that free ships make free goods," clearly enunciated. It must, however, be admitted that this was but the expression of a special treaty in derogation of the common law (so to speak) of nations. To injure your enemy to the utmost of your power, to cripple or destroy his commerce, and thereby reduce him to poverty, were viewed as the most sure aids to conquest, especially by those nations who were powerful at sea, of whom England was the foremost. Treaties, however, are annulled by war between the parties to them; thus, when war broke out between England and France in 1756, England at once renounced the maxim of "Free ships, free goods," and enforced the contrary maxim that "enemy's goods were seizable whereever found at sea" with all her power and energy. This provoked the resentment of the other European powers, and the confederacy followed, known as the Armed Neutrality.*

* Mr. Lawrence, at p. 744 *et seq.*, gives a full historical account of the origin and progress of this alliance against England.

England, however, braved that formidable opposition single-handed, and triumphed in the determination to maintain her asserted right. The peace of 1783 set the question at rest for a time. But when war again broke out between England and France, in consequence of the French revolution, England again insisted on her right of searching neutral ships, and seizing them if their enemy's property were found on board. Again, the Armed Neutrality, now aided by the United States, endeavoured to crush the maritime power of England, but in vain; she still clung to the doctrine of "enemy's goods, enemy's ships," and adhered to it as being part of the common law of the sea (Twiss, p. 158). Even when peace was established between England and the United States, which had most vehemently opposed England's demands, and the treaty of Ghent was concluded (1814), no allusion was made to the subject; and moreover, when general peace was proclaimed throughout Europe, in 1815, although several treaties were entered into, still (whether from accident or design) the question whether neutral property on board an enemy's ship was to be respected or not remained untouched, and England was at liberty to act as she might think fit. It has been said she adopted the maxim—"Free ships, free goods," by joining in the Declaration of Paris (April, 1856), but she did so only on the expediency of the occasion. In that year France combined with England in declaring war against Russia. It was therefore necessary that those two powers, acting in hostile concert, should adopt the same rule as to belligerents at sea; but at the very threshold of the agreement was a barrier. France held to the doctrine that the property of a neutral power on board an enemy's ship was lawful prize. England held the contrary, viz,—that it was free from seizure; on the other hand, England held, as has been said, that enemy's property on board a neutral ship was lawful prize. When the two nations were to act as allied belligerents at sea it was absolutely necessary that they should adopt one and the same course of action, thus they each gave way, and each relinquished the doctrine they had theretofore maintained. An Order in Council of the English Government, dated March 28th, 1854, promulgated that, "To preserve the commerce of neutrals from all unnecessary obstruction, Her Majesty is willing for the present to waive a part of the belligerent rights appertaining to her by the Law of Nations. It is impossible for Her Majesty to forego the exercise of her right of seizing articles contraband of war, and of preventing neutrals from carrying enemy's despatches, and she must maintain the right of a belligerent to prevent neutrals from breaking any effective blockade which may be established with an adequate force against the enemy's forts, harbours, or coasts."

"But Her Majesty *will waive the right of seizing enemy's property laden on board a neutral vessel* unless it be contraband of war."

Thus England for the present acceded to the doctrine, "Free ship, free goods," in deference to the alliance with France. That country, in the same spirit and under the same influence, relinquished her maxim that enemy's ship made enemy's goods, which England did not recognise. Hence, from the sheer force of necessity resulting from this alliance, a great stride was made in softening the rigour of maritime warfare as regards neutrals. The Congress of Paris (April, 1856) has we trust irrevocably confirmed these mutual concessions.* Before we quit the question of free ship free goods and its opposite, we must cite the words of Wheaton as given by Mr. Lawrence (p. 73):—"Whatever may be the true original abstract principle of natural law on this subject, it is undeniable that the constant

* The terms of that Declaration are—

1. Privateering is and remains abolished.

2. The neutral flag covers enemy's goods, with the exception of contraband of war.

3. Neutral goods, except contraband of war, are not liable to capture under enemy's flag.

4. Blockades in order to be binding must be effective, that is to say, maintained by a force sufficient really to prevent access to the coast of the enemy.

usage and practice of belligerent nations from the earliest times have subjected enemy's goods in neutral vessels to capture and condemnation as prize of war. The constant and universal usage has only been interrupted by treaty stipulations forming a temporary conventional law between the parties to such stipulation." Notwithstanding this, the United States of America have struggled to support the contrary. Mr. Lawrence continues (p. 747):—"During the wars of the French Revolution, the United States, being neutral, admitted that the immunity of their flag did not cover enemy's property as a principle founded on the customary law and established usage of nations, though they sought every opportunity of substituting for it the opposite maxim of 'free ship, free goods' by conventional arrangements with such nations as were disposed to adopt that amendment of the law." Thus we arrive at the conclusion that unless there are stipulations between States, or a voluntary abandonment of the doctrine and practice, neutral's property on board an enemy's ship is liable to seizure by the general law of nations. A proposition which jars harshly with the advance of civilisation and humanity in other quarters; but from the unanimity with which the maritime powers and minor States of Europe, and even Asia and South America, have concurred in the Paris declaration,* let us hope that Europe at least will not again witness the spoliation of an unoffending neutral—whether his property be on board an enemy's ship, or an enemy's property be on board the neutral's ship. The right of search is closely connected with the subject we have been considering, that is, search in time of war. The United States

* Baden, Bavaria, Belgium, Bremen, Brazil, Duchy of Brunswick, Chili, the Argentine Confederation, the Germanic Confederation, Denmark, the two Sicilies, the Republic of the Equator, the Roman States, Greece, Guatemala, Hoyle, Hamburgh, Hanover, the two Hesses, Lubeck, Mecklenburg-Strelitz, Mecklenburg-Schwerin, Nassau, Oldenburg, Parma, Holland, Peru, Portugal, Saxony, Saxe-Altenburg, Saxe-Coburg Gotha, Saxe-Meinengen, Saxe-Weimar, Sweden, Switzerland, Tuscany, Wurtemburg, Anhalt-Dessau, Modena, New Granada, Uruguay, have joined with Great Britain, Austria, France, Prussia, Russia, Sardinia, and Turkey in acceding to the terms of this treaty (Twiss, p. 164, note).

of America have shown great indignation at England's asserted right to search their vessels in time of peace, even for the prevention of the traffic in slaves, and Mr. Wheaton not only in the volume before us (p. 258, *et seq.*) goes fully into the subjects, but he has compiled a treatise wholly devoted to it. Although belligerents under the Declaration of Paris will not seize neutral property at sea unless there has been a violation or intended violation of a blockade; still, to prohibit the transport of contraband, and to detect the violation of a blockade in order to learn whether a suspended ship is offending, or has offended, in either case she must be boarded. Mr. Lawrence supports this maxim (p. 852) by citing the well-known judgment of Lord Stowell in the "Maria" (Ch. Robinson's Rep., p. 340); one brief paragraph we will quote :—"This right is so clear in principle that no man can deny it who admits the right of maritime capture, because if you are not at liberty to ascertain by sufficient inquiry whether that is property that can legally be captured, it is impossible to capture. The matter, however, provoked a hostile feeling between England and America when the former insisted on searching the vessels of the latter for British seamen, and in a great measure tended to produce the war of 1812; but although when peace ensued there was a treaty between them known as the Treaty of Ghent (1814), no allusion was made to the subject, and it might be a question of serious embarrassment, were war again to break out between them, whether England could enforce its formerly asserted right."

The most direct and effective means of injuring your enemy in his commercial relations, is supposed to be the blockade of his coasts, whereby the ships of neutrals are to be deterred from entering or leaving his ports. This has been always considered the most effective means of reducing your enemy to submission, to isolate him from the commerce of, and communication with other nations, to prevent him from acquiring the comforts or necessaries which other nations might supply to him, and to prevent him from reaping the benefit of supplying other nations with the produce of his own specialities; in short, to destroy his trade and thus impoverish him, are the objects and purpose of blockade. After the relaxations of the Conference of Paris of 1856, whereby both an enemy's and a neutral's property were made exempt from seizure, the only way in which belligerents could weaken each other in commercial relations was by preventing the ingress to, and the egress from, their respective ports. The right, therefore, of blockade has been sedulously maintained. At the present day we find Denmark, in retaliation for the injuries inflicted on her by the Prussians in Jutland and Schleswig, notifying her blockade of the Prussian ports in the Baltic, and the ports of the States composing the German Confederation in the North Sea. To this, as sanctioned by international law, no objection can be raised; but let us for a moment consider the effect of this exercise of power. To blockade a country not completely insular is of little avail, it is only its seaboard that is affected by it, the whole of its land frontier is free. Thus, in our late Crimean war, we blockaded the Russian ports in the Baltic, but Russian produce, tallow, hemp, flax, and bristles, found their way into this country through Prussia in rather an increased quantity, but at a greater cost to us, since we had to pay for the land carriage to the Prussian port of Memel instead of receiving them direct from Riga, Revel, Abo, or other ports of Russia. Again, at the present day, the blockade of the Southern ports of America has not worked the injury anticipated from it. Charleston and Wilmington are represented as being closely blockaded; but we read that during fifteen months from Jan. 1st, 1863, to April, 1864, out of 590 attempts to run the blockade of Charleston, 498 were successful; and that between the 1st of May and 1st of June, 1864, no less than 24 vessels ran the blockade of Wilmington,* and hence a

* The *Times* newspaper, July, 1864.

question has arisen whether vessels seized for violation of the blockade have not been unjustly seized, and our Government has been accused of deserting the interests of British commerce. It is a question of some nicety to determine what amounts to an effective blockade. "There must be so many armed vessels watching the blockaded port either stationary or sufficiently near, that there is *evident* danger in entering them," says Wheaton; "That it shall be apparently dangerous," says Chancellor Kent; "I think" says Dr. Lushington, "that these definitions are, and must be, from the nature of blockades, loose and uncertain. The maintenance of a blockade must always be a question of degree—of the degree of danger attending ships going into or leaving a blockaded port." Again, a knowledge, or a fairly presumed knowledge of the fact of a port being blockaded must be established against a vessel before she can be condemned as prize for violating a blockade. Again, it is uncertain what will constitute the termination or legal suspension of a blockade. The Berlin and Milan decrees of Napoleon Bonaparte, and the Orders in Council of the English Government in 1806-7, are instructive incidents in the history of blockade.

When the kingdom of Hanover was, in 1806, taken possession of by Prussia, at the instigation of Napoleon Bonaparte, a proclamation issuing ostensibly from Prussia, but virtually the act of Bonaparte himself, was put forth declaring the ports of the North Sea, as well as the rivers flowing into it, closed against British shipping and commerce as they were at the time the French troops occupied Hanover. As a measure of retaliation, the English Government declared the mouths of the rivers Ems, Weser, and the Elbe, blockaded, and also laid an embargo on all Prussian vessels and property in the ports of Great Britain; less than a month afterwards another more comprehensive order was issued, extending the blockade to all ports between the Elbe and Brest, thus including the ports of Holland, those of Prussia on the German Ocean, and the whole seaboard of France; this was derisively styled "the paper blockade." Hence resulted the Berlin and Milan decrees of Bonaparte, and the Orders in Council of the British Government, put forth, the former in 1806, and the latter in 1807, the combined effect of which for a time paralysed the industrial energies and all but annihilated the trade of Great Britain. After being in force for nearly five years, the Orders in Council were rescinded, in consequence of their manifest disastrous results having been incontrovertibly proved by evidence taken before the House of Commons, and so clearly and forcibly demonstrated by Lord (then Mr.) Brougham in his well-known speech in Parliament. The history of these Orders in Council is thus briefly but graphically given in the *Edinburgh Review* for July, 1812. These Orders in Council took their origin in a decree promulgated by Bonaparte in Berlin, on the 21st November, 1807, by which, in the usual style of that personage, he declared the United Kingdom to be in a state of blockade; that all commodities of English origin, or belonging to Englishmen, were good prize; and that no ship from England or her colonies, or which should have touched there, should be admitted into any harbour belonging to France, or occupied by her troops. This bravado was followed on our part by an Order in Council, dated 9th January, 1807, by which we interdicted neutrals from the whole coasting trade from one part of France to another; and in November, 1807, a series of new orders was promulgated, by which we declared that we would permit no trade with France and her dependencies, except through England; all neutrals bound to these countries being required in the first instance to touch at our ports and pay a duty to our Government; and that every vessel which had not a certificate of origin on board, should be declared lawful prize. To which extraordinary edict, France finally replied by what has been called the Milan Decree, declaring in substance that any vessel, which in any way submitted to our orders of the 11th November, or which had been searched in the course of her voyage by an English cruiser, should be considered as lawful prize. This is the sum of these unprecedented state documents, and the consequence was that between their decrees and the English orders, all neutral trade was effectually annihilated. Thus the evils resulting from blockades are not always confined to the intended object of them.

Treaties are justly described as being modifications of the law of nations; in other words, they tend, as the interests, policy, or inclination of States may sway them, to soften the rigour of their conduct as sanctioned by the general law of nations in the abstract, or to adjust what is called the "balance of power;" and the frequent resort to them as emergencies arise, shows the imperfect and unsatisfactory nature of international law as a system. Hence, the innumerable treaties to be found in Monsieur Marten's collection. But even treaties are ofttimes set at nought by the very parties to them; witness, within these few years, the violation of the Treaty of Vienna by Russia, in her conduct towards Poland, the severance of Milan from Austria, and the encroachments of France on the borders of the Lake of Geneva, nay, whilst we write, mark the disregard by the leading powers of the German Confederation of the Treaty of 1852. By that document, the King of Denmark was supposed to be constituted Duke of Holstein; we purposely omit the *questio vexata* whether Schleswig is an integral part of Denmark proper, or is inseparably connected with Holstein, and therefore not subject to Danish sway. Be that as it may, Austria and Prussia, although parties to that treaty, avowedly repudiate its obligations, under the pretext that Denmark has not fulfilled her obligations, by not giving, as she was bound to do, certain privileges to Schleswig; moreover, they assert that, hostilities having arisen between them and Denmark, the treaty is at an end, and therefore they are at liberty, as they have done, to act towards Denmark as they please; that they are not bound to respect the claims of Denmark to the Dukedom of either Holstein or Schleswig, but are free to support the claim of any pretender to the sovereignty of one or both of those Duchies. Again, Prussia and Austria threaten—notwithstanding that they were parties to the declaration resulting from the Paris Conference of 1856, that "privateering is abolished"—to resort to that barbarous mode of warfare, urging as a pretext, the non-efficiency of the Danish blockade, it having been laid down by one of the canons of the Paris Conference, in accordance with the recognised rule of public law, that blockades to be binding must be effectual. It is clear that these are but the domineering acts of two strong powers against one comparatively weak, deserted in her misfortune by the other powers of Europe, and left gallantly but hopelessly to contend alone against two far superior but merciless foes.

Mr. Lawrence in his note (p. 458) draws a distinction between the view taken of a treaty by Great Britain and America. "A treaty is in its nature a contract between two nations, not a legislative act, and does not generally of itself effect the object to be accomplished, but is carried into execution by the sovereign power of the respective parties to the instrument." (This may be said to be the European custom.) "But in the United States," continues Mr. Lawrence, "the Constitution declares a treaty to be the law of the land. It is consequently to be regarded in courts of justice as equivalent to the act of the legislature, whenever it operates of itself without any legislative provision, but when the terms of the stipulation import a contract, when either of the parties engages to perform a particular act, the treaty addresses itself to the political, not the judicial department, and the legislature must execute the contract before it can become a rule of the court." He then gives an instance in which the President (Washington) was overruled by the House of Representatives, when he denied the right of that body to call for papers connected with the negotiation with Great Britain previous to the Treaty of 1794; he gives other examples, and sums up by saying, "The conclusion on all these occasions would seem to have been, that as the President and Senate are by the Constitution fully authorised to enter into treaties whenever the aid of Congress is required to carry out its provisions, if the treaty be within the constitutional limits, free from fraud, and not destructive of any of the great rights or interests of the country, then there is a moral objection to grant the aid required. When a treaty comes before the House of Representatives, they are not to proceed in the discussion and examination of it as an act of ordinary legislation. Such a construction would, in fact, repeal the constitutional provision respecting treaties, and nullify the whole power of the Government in its intercourse with foreign nations." It may here be added that our constitution has left in the hands of the sovereign alone the prerogative of making treaties, leagues, and alliances with foreign states and princes, and the only check upon the abuse or ill use of that power would be the disapproval of Parliament of the conduct of the ministers who advised or permitted it, or their formal impeachment.

Although we trust privateering, as far as Europe is concerned, is abolished, let us devote a few lines to it. Privateers are armed ships which are fitted out by private persons, and sail under a commander to whom a belligerent power has granted a commission to seize and take ships and goods of an enemy power. The term is of English origin, and appears to have been employed to designate a peculiar class of private armed vessels in the reign of King Charles II., but it is applied at the present day indiscriminately to private ships which sail under commissions of war, and to private ships sailing under letters of marque and reprisals.* Such is the history of this legalised piracy called privateering, as given by Dr. Twiss. Lord Clarendon, in his Life (vol. ii., p. 335) tells us that "In the year 1665 it was resolved that all possible encouragement should be given to privateers; that is, as many as would take commissions from the Admiralty

* Twiss, p. 374, note.

to let out vessels of war, as they call them, to take prizes from the enemy." When the Americans declared their independence and established themselves as a nation, they adopted the rules of naval warfare as recognised by other States. But it is but an act of justice to say that they have steadily endeavoured to render the property of a neutral safe from seizure, and in the same spirit they have negociated with England for the abolition of privateering. Mr. Lawrence, at page 631, (note) gives us a striking instance of this.

The subject was fully brought to the notice of the British Government during the negociation at London, in 1823-4, between the American Minister, Mr. Rush, and the British plenipotentiaries, Messrs. Huskisson and Stratford Canning. Mr. Adams, Secretary of State, in his instructions of July 28, 1823, said:—"We press no disavowal on her (England) but we think the present time eminently auspicious for urging upon her and upon others an object which has long been dear to the hearts, and ardent in the aspirations, of the benevolent and the wise; an object essentially congenial to the true spirit of Christianity, and therefore peculiarly fitting for the support of a nation, intent, in the same spirit, upon the final and total suppression of the slave trade, and of sovereigns who have given public pledges to the world of their determination to administer imperial dominion upon the genuine precepts of Christianity. The object to which I allude is private war upon the sea. It has been remarked that by the usages of modern war the private property of an enemy is protected from seizure or confiscation as such, and private war itself has been almost universally exploded upon the land. By an exception, the reason of which it is not easy to perceive, the private property of an enemy upon the sea has not so fully received the benefit of the same principle. Private war, banished by the tacit and general consent of Christian nations from their territories, has taken its last refuge upon the ocean, and there continues to disgrace and afflict them by a system of licensed robbery, bearing all the most atrocious characters of piracy. To a government intent from motives of general benevolence and humanity upon the final and total suppression of the slave trade, it cannot be unreasonable to claim its aid and co-operation to the abolition of private war upon the sea. From the time the United States took their place among the nations of the earth this has been one of their favourite objects. 'It is time,' said Dr. Franklin (in a letter of the 14th March, 1785), 'it is high time, for the sake of humanity, that a stop were put to this enormity.' The United States of America, though better situated than any European nation to make profit by privateering, are, as far as in them lies, endeavouring to abolish the practice by offering in all their treaties with other powers an article engaging solemnly that in case of future war, no privateer shall be commissioned on either side, and that unarmed merchant ships on both sides shall pursue their voyages unmolested. This will be a happy improvement of the law of nations. The humane and the just cannot but wish general success to the proposition."

"It is well known a treaty between the United States and the King of Prussia was concluded, by the 23rd article of which this principle was solemnly sanctioned in the form of a national compact. The 26th article of the treaty between the United States and Great Britain of the 19th November, 1794, carries it, in some respects, still further, though in others falling short of it. The articles of the enclosed draft combine the special stipulations of both those articles."

In rendering an account of this negociation, at its close Mr. Rush writes to the Secretary of State, August 12, 1824, "I next said to the British plenipotentiaries that the question of abolishing privateering and the capture of private property at sea, whether by national ships or by privateers, was one that I considered as standing apart from those to which their decision had been given to me. Upon this question, therefore, I desired them to understand that I was ready to treat as of one, occupying ground wholly its own."

But notwithstanding this expression of feeling on the part of the United States of America, it must be remarked that after the Orders in Council were promulgated by the British Government at the commencement of the Crimean War, one of which contained the words, "It is not Her Majesty's present intention to issue letters of marque for the commissioning of privateers;" the then President of the United States, Mr. Pierce, states in his message (a State document answering to our speech from the throne on the assembling of Parliament) that "When on the alliance of England and France, in hostility to Russia, those two countries determined to be exempt from the seizure of neutral property on the ocean, the United States and Russia entered into a convention guaranteeing the same privileges to their respective subjects, and that the Kings of Prussia, and Naples, and Sicily, expressed their readiness to adopt the same course. The former, however, qualifying her assent by the suggestion that the practice of privateering should be wholly abandoned. But to this American authorities were unwilling to assent, assigning as a reason their inability to cope with other nations whose navy was larger and more powerful than their own, unless by resorting to reprisals by means of their private mercantile marine. Should, however," the message continues, "the leading powers of Europe concur in proposing, as a rule of international law, to exempt private property upon the ocean from seizure by public armed cruisers, as well as privateers, the United States would readily meet them upon that broad ground." The Treaty of Paris (dated April, 1856) unequivocally renounces privateering.

Its first article runs thus: "Privateering is and remains abolished." Seven powers concurred in that declaration, and many others gave in their adherence (*ante*, p. 297). America and Spain are the only powers of any consideration who have not done so. Prussia, however, in her present war with Denmark, threatens to repudiate her obligation and to resort to privateering in retaliation for the blockade of her ports. America being free to act as she pleases carries on her present war between North and South with the most inveterate hostility. The North denounce the South as rebels and pirates, and thus deserving of extermination, the South retaliate in their own fashion—thus each seizes and destroys the property of the other by any and every means; private as well as public armed cruisers traverse every sea in quest of hostile vessels, and the savage edict has gone forth—burn, pillage, and destroy.

To determine what is contraband of war is a very nice and difficult question, since there are so many articles which are either directly or indirectly aids to warfare, the more especially since the introduction of war steamers and other scientific appliances; it is therefore in vain that efforts have been made to define them. Dr. Twiss devotes a whole chapter (the 7th) to its consideration; and Mr. Lawrence, with the text of Wheaton and his own annotations, extends the subject over nineteen octavo pages, but after all this elaboration of the question, what is contraband of war and what is not, is left in doubt and uncertainty, and must so remain until a general rule is laid down and assented to by all the world, specifying what articles may be carried or in what quantities. A question involving much difference of opinion and angry controversy between the Northern States of America and England, and which nearly resulted in hostilities, arose at the latter end of 1861, in consequence of the seizure of two Confederate envoys on board a neutral ship. The facts were these: The "Trent," a packet ship belonging to the British Mail Steam Company, which runs from Vera Cruz to Havannah and thence to St. Thomas's (where her passengers and mails are transferred to another steamer to be conveyed to Southampton), had touched, in the beginning of November, in the usual course of her voyage, at Havannah, to take in passengers and letters. Four gentlemen, Messrs. Slidell, Mason, Eustace, and MacFarlane, who had paid their whole passage money for the whole route from Havannah to Southampton embarked on board. Messrs. Slidell and Mason had been sent as envoys from the Confederate States to Europe, Mr. Slidell being bound for France and Mr. Mason for England. They came, however, on board, as ordinary passengers at a neutral port in a neutral ship. On the 7th November, the "Trent" sailed for St. Thomas, and when she reached the old Bahama Channel she observed a ship lying stationary. The "Trent" hoisted her flag, the British ensign, but no flag was then shown by the other vessel. As the "Trent" approached a shotted gun was fired across her course, and the United States flag was then displayed at the peak of the other vessel; she proved to be the United States war steamer "San Jacinto," commanded by Captain Wilkes. The British flag was again hoisted by the "Trent," and so remained; she continued her course, when a shell was fired, which burst across her bows; a boat put off from the "San Jacinto," followed by two other boats full of armed men with a lieutenant in the uniform of the United States, who boarded the "Trent" and demanded from Captain Moir, the commander, his list of passengers. This was refused, and Captain Moir formally protested against any right to visit his ship for such a purpose. The lieutenant of the "San Jacinto" announcing his commission, said that two gentlemen, named Slidell and Mason, were known to be on board, and that his orders were to carry them on board the "San Jacinto." Commander Williams, R.N., the British Admiralty agent, who was in charge of the mails on board the "Trent," protested vehemently against the act, and denounced it as piratical; but notwithstanding his remonstrance, as well as that of Messrs. Slidell and Mason, they were compelled by a show of force to leave the "Trent," and were taken on board the "San Jacinto" and there detained. Dr. Twiss thus briefly disposes of the question raised by this conduct of the Federal States of America. "'If any prince,' observes Grotius, 'shall *out of his own territory* contrive to surprise the ambassadors of another State, this would be a direct breach of the law of nations.' The case of the seizure of the envoys of the

Confederate States on board the British post-office packet, the "Trent," by an United States cruiser would seem to come within the prohibition laid down by Grotius. Their seizure was justly resented by Great Britain as a direct breach of the law of nations, and the envoys, at the demand of the British Government, were set at liberty by the government of the United States, and allowed to proceed to Europe in a British vessel."[3] This, however, was not done until a strong remonstrance had been made by Great Britain, and a determination had been evinced by her to resort to hostilities rather than yield in her demand; it must be added that the Emperor of the French and some of the European powers strongly expressed their disapproval of this violation of international law. America had to defend and justify her act. Mr. Lawrence gives in his appendix (p. 939) a full account of the correspondence between Earl Russell and the American Secretary of State, Mr. Seward. The former complains that two individuals had been taken from on board a British vessel whilst she was pursuing a lawful and innocent voyage. The latter replies "that the act of Captain Wilkes (the commander of the 'San Jacinto') was undertaken as a simple legal customary and belligerent proceeding to arrest and capture a neutral vessel carrying contraband of war for the use and benefit of the insurgents;" he then cites Vattel and the opinions of Lord Stowell; and concludes by saying, "I trust that I have shown that the four persons who were taken from the 'Trent' by Captain Wilkes, and their despatches, were contraband of war." Much stress was also laid upon the fact that we ourselves, in our war with France in 1812, had taken from American vessels British seamen who had deserted from our ships. What tended to complicate the question was the peculiar position of the Confederate States; they were not admitted to be belligerents, although their ports were blockaded; but they were styled rebels in hostility to their Government. As to the question whether the envoys and their despatches were contraband of war or not, that should have been by the law of nations decided by a prize court. The lawful mode of procedure would have been for the "San Jacinto" to have made prize of the "Trent" with a view to her condemnation, instead of forcibly taking the envoys out of her. The matter was however brought to an amicable conclusion by the surrender of Messrs. Slidell and Mason; but the points in dispute were not yielded by the United States.

The peculiar position in which the Northern and Southern States of America have placed themselves by their internecine war, not only as regards each other, but also in relation to other States, was recently exemplified in the case of the "Tuscaloosa;" she was originally a Federal merchant vessel, named the "Conrad;" when she was off the coast of Brazil with a cargo of wool on board, she was captured by the Confederate cruiser the "Alabama," whose captain put some guns on board of her and ten men, changed her name to the "Tuscaloosa," and employed her as a tender to the "Alabama." The two vessels were together off the Cape of Good Hope, when the "Tuscaloosa" was ordered to Simon's Bay, for the purpose of obtaining provisions and undergoing some slight repairs. Her Britannic Majesty, at the commencement of the war in America, for the purpose of acting with strict neutrality towards each of the combatants, had issued a proclamation, prohibiting the ships of both parties from bringing their prizes into the ports, harbours, or roadsteads of the United Kingdom, or of any of the British colonies or possessions. This, it was conceived, was in conformity with a recognised rule of international law. The English Admiral on the station being aware of what had taken place, and having regard to the Queen of England's proclamation, doubted whether the "Tuscaloosa," being an uncondemned prize, could be admitted within the roadstead of Simon's Bay, and sent to the Governor of the Cape for instructions how to act. He having consulted his law officer there returned for answer that the

"Tuscaloosa" having been converted into a vessel of war, and armed by her captors, and having had an officer and crew put on board, had become a vessel of war, and was, therefore, privileged to enter the Bay; she accordingly entered Simon's Bay. The American Consul whilst she was lying there demanded her detention on the part of her original owners. Here arose an important question, on which not only did the English and American authorities differ, but even some of our own statesmen and most eminent jurists in open discussion in the legislature pronounced different views and opinions. It was said on behalf of the English Government, that this was not a *bonâ fide* conversion of a merchant prize into a war tender; that it was merely a subterfuge, and that if Confederate ships of war were allowed to send in prizes with their cargo on board (it appeared that the wool remained on board the "Tuscaloosa" after the guns and men were put into her), and by putting a few guns and a Confederate officer on board to call them ships of war, Her Majesty's Proclamation would become null and void. But it was said that there were exceptional circumstances in the case. The Confederates having no ports but what were blockaded it was not possible for them to take their prizes to their own country to be adjudicated upon; they were, therefore, obliged to burn, to sink, and destroy them, or act towards them as they had done to the quondam "Conrad." The general right of an enemy to destroy the captured vessel of his enemy without her condemnation, and as a corollary thereto his right to turn a captured vessel into a vessel of war of his own authority without first taking her into one of their own ports, was warmly discussed both in the Houses of Lords and Commons, and it is to be lamented that the debate was tinged with so much party feeling. The fact that the "Tuscaloosa" was not interfered with on her first resort to Simon's Bay, but was allowed to remain and depart without inquiry, and that it was only on a second visit that any objection was raised to her character or conduct, tended to throw doubt on the sincerity of the proceeding. The conduct of Government was, however, approved by a majority in the House of Commons; in the House of Lords there was no division. The view of our Government on the whole question was summed up in the despatch of the Duke of Newcastle to the Governor of the Cape: "The mode of proceeding in such circumstances most consistent with Her Majesty's dignity, and most proper for the vindication of her territory, would have been to prohibit the exercise of any further control over the 'Tuscaloosa' by the captors, and to retain that vessel under Her Majesty's control and jurisdiction until properly reclaimed by her original owners." * This, however, does not settle the general questions involved in the case. It having occurred since the publication of either Dr. Twiss or Mr. Lawrence's work, we lose the benefit of any comments they might devote to it, as directly bearing upon it. But in the volume of the former, at the head of this article, at page 344, under the subject of re-capture, we read: "It is within the province of every country to regulate by its municipal law all questions of re-capture between its own citizens, but an exception has been maintained in our prize courts in the case in which the enemy has fitted out his prize as a man-of-war." He also states (page 340), as bearing on the power of restoration by the authorities at the Cape of the "Tuscaloosa" to her original owners:—"Every capture of a vessel is complete as between the belligerents when the surrender has taken place, and the *spes recuperandi* is gone, but as between the original owner of the vessel and a third party in respect of the *jus postliminii*, if the vessel should be re-captured, or as between the captor of the vessel and a third party, Mr. Wheaton states as a general proposition that where

* Subsequently, however, a despatch was sent to the Governor of the Cape, in these words: "Her Majesty's Government have therefore come to the opinion on the special circumstances of this particular case, that the 'Tuscaloosa' ought to be released, with a warning, however, to the captain of the 'Alabama,' that the ships of war of the belligerents are not to be allowed to bring prizes into British ports; and that it rests with Her Majesty's Government to decide to what vessels that character belongs."

the capture of enemy's property is made within the territorial limits of a neutral State, or by armed vessels fitted out within the neutral territory, in either of these cases, the judicial tribunals of the neutral State have jurisdiction to determine the validity of the captures thus made by restoring the property of its own subjects or of other States in amity with it to the original owners." It was urged on the part of the Government that the principle here evolved applied to the present case; that our neutrality had been violated by the "Tuscaloosa" being brought into one of our colonial roadsteads in defiance of Her Majesty's Proclamation. But it was justly observed by those in opposition to the Government that the capture had not taken place in neutral territory, or by an armed vessel fitted out there, nor had there been any judicial inquiry for the purpose of condemning the "Tuscaloosa" as legal prize, and therefore the authority of Wheaton was inapplicable. But we would refer those anxious to learn all that was said on the subject to the Parliamentary debate, which is full of learning and interest.* The fact is, the case was one of a very peculiar nature, which had not before arisen, and to which therefore no definite rule of international law could be applied—analogy was substituted for precedent.

We cannot but express our satisfaction and thankfulness at the advance which humanity and civilisation have made towards mitigating the evils of war, the more especially as regards neutrals; still much remains to be accomplished. It has been said that owing to the greater vigour and energy with which hostilities would be carried on in these our days, war would sooner be brought to an end, and instead of being extended over years, as heretofore, would quickly end by the defeat of the less powerful or skilful combatant. The battle of Solferino may perhaps have justified this speculation, but our own Crimean war, and the prolonged

* And to the correspondence presented to the House of Lords in pursuance of their address of Feb. 16, 1864 (North America, No. 6, 1864).

strife in America, with no probable end, and a very uncertain result, do not tend to support the prediction. But even granted that these results might follow, it is not humanity which has prompted the increased power of destruction. But humanity has had a powerful influence in mitigating the evils of war as regards neutrals; the Declaration of the Congress of Paris does honour to the age in which we live, and leads us to hope that a day is not far distant when the humane principles there enunciated will induce the freedom from capture of neutral's property at sea under all and every state of circumstances, so that nations may adopt and fulfil in some measure towards each other, the Christian and charitable precept, "Do unto others as you would have them do unto you."

Art. IX.—THE POLICY OF PATENTS.

Libre Travail, ou l'Abolition de la Proprieté Intellectuelle. Par P. Vermeire. Paris: *Guillaumin et Cie.*, 1864.

THE number of recent publications on the question of the policy of patents is but limited. Not long ago we inserted two very able articles by Mr. William Hawes, and as the subject becomes more and more seen, so will contributions towards its elucidation be multiplied. A thorough and exhaustive treatise on this branch of the larger subject of intellectual property (to use the term adopted by the *industriel* whose *brochure* heads the present notice), is a desideratum we long to have supplied. Meanwhile we welcome every worker in this field of inquiry; every vindication of the great principle of freedom of industry. Each new writer appears to impart some new views, or to set some old views in a new and strong light. We gladly acknowledge the obligation due to M. Vermeire. His pamphlet is a republication of papers from the *Economiste Belge*, together with correspondence of other economists of the Continent, where the question has been agitated more than in our own country. Our readers may remember an illustration of the boldness with which monopoly of inventions is contested abroad, in the prominent place given to denunciations of the system as an interference with manufacture and trade, in the French official reports upon the Great Exhibition of 1862. Mr. Macfie gave extracts from these in an appendix to the paper which he read at the Edinburgh Meeting of the Association for the Promotion of Social Science, which he has since published. A more striking proof of the advance of what we must characterise as sound and sensible opinions, is afforded in the circumstance mentioned by M. Vermeire, that thirty-one out of forty-seven chambers of commerce existing in Prussia, have declared in favour of abolishing patents. This declaration has been given, as we understand, in answer to queries judiciously submitted to these bodies by the ministry of commerce of that kingdom. The whole of that gentleman's little work deserves attention. The following extracts (the imperfect translation of which we beg our readers and the author to excuse) will show his style and general sentiments. He contends, it will be seen, not only against patents, but against all recognition of intellectual property of whatsoever sort.

"Property implies an idea of possession, but possession does not imply an idea of property. In other words, that which is a possession is not necessarily called property. In order that possession may constitute property, it must not be or cannot be within reach of all. Light, for instance, which is one of the elements existing everywhere in nature, is a thing which every one possesses, and which has never been called property.

"The man who first thought of making himself a bow and arrows, and who made them, possessed at the same time the idea of making these instruments, and the instruments themselves. That bow and arrows were his property because they belonged to him alone; to deprive him of them one would be committing a theft, which is punishable throughout all non-communist society. Is it the same with the idea attached to the manufacturing of the objects which we take as examples? Could not some one else come into possession of that idea without robbing it of the man who had first conceived it? Evidently, yes.

"The ideas of invention come from one knows not where, if they are not rather to be spoken of as inspirations flowing from a Supreme Being, and the same thought may be born in thousands of heads at the same time, and in millions in a certain lapse of time.

"The man who had made for himself a bow might say to himself, This bow, I hold it, it is mine, and belongs to none but me. A possession of that nature has been called property. But he could not say to himself, The idea of making a bow, I have it, and none can possess it without they come and rob me of it. Therefore legislators up to the time when the sophisms of civilisation had succeeded in obliterating the good sense of people, have taken good care not to call an idea a property, and much less did they call thief, the man who thought like another man.

"All positive religion, as well as natural religion, reproves the theft of a thing which is the tangible property of an individual, but there is none which has ever condemned the profit which society has received from inventions, by the appropriation of ideas put forth.

"Have those been called robbers who have armed themselves like the first inventor of the bow; those who have clothed themselves like the first man who had the idea of covering himself with skins as clothing; those who have fed upon flesh, taking example from him who first was not content to support life on fruit and vegetables; those who first built themselves houses after the pattern of the man who first had that thought? Is that person a thief who imbibes the virtues of others; he who in conversation collects a phrase, a word, serving as the theme to a speech, he who enriches his mind by the observations and studies for which he is indebted to another mind than his own? Is he a thief who scours through far off lands to study manners, laws, industry, trade, and who wishes to apply in his native land the result of his wanderings? No, no. The action of thought itself proclaims everywhere the community (*communisme*) of ideas as a constitutive law of the mind, in the same manner that the vibrations of ether spread everywhere the communism of light as an essential condition of the fluid which lights up all nature.

"With regard to ideas, we declare ourselves, therefore, radically communists, and we say, not only that the property of ideas is theft, but also that it is barbarism, the annihilation of progress and the deterioration of mankind.

"What are civilisation, sciences, arts, industry, if not a continuous chain of ideas, having at one end the first man of creation, and at the other the last-come thinker? Cut the chain asunder, no matter where, and you destroy all the prodigies of the human intellect.

"The propagators of the property of ideas, do they do any less? No! they do much more, for with one stroke of their pen they would snap at once all the links of man's perfectibility, by forcing back in the mind of all thinkers any intellectual spark likely to enlighten, animate, or to excite minds on the road of progress.

"In these days, when society has made so many discoveries, when industry has reached to such a high degree of perfection, people seem to think that there are no more inventions wanted, and are blinded as to the bearings of a doctrine which must bring universal trouble to industry whenever applied in the absoluteness (*absoluteisme*) towards which it tends in so very perceptible a manner; but, as we have already shown, it is sufficient to carry back one's mind to the principle at the original development of anything valuable within the sphere of social activity, in order to perceive that property of ideas is calculated as its destination to break down all incentives to labour, and to break up all the springs of production.

"In the primitive state, all combination, all action, all manners of thinking or of doing, were everyone's inventions and discoveries, because man, a new comer in creation, could produce nothing but novelties. But as soon as there has been a society, there has also been an imitation of processes, a reproduction of movements, a repetition of methods and systems. It is thus that the world has travelled on from progress to progress, heaping up traditionally all the improvements which the spirit of invention had produced.

"If, from the beginning of the growth of society, the imitation called in our days infringement (*contrefacon*) had been forbidden, where would the civilised world be, where sciences, arts, literature—where would be every sort of social advancement? Of course, in a state of infancy; for all progress made by society implies in itself the application of a new idea issued from the mind of an individual. If the inventor of the alphabet and of the formation of words by the help of signs, had had the property of his invention, and of the latter had passed to his heirs, where would be the art of writing? If the first poet who had the idea of putting together rhythmed phrases and rhyme had had the exclusive privilege, he and his heirs, to handle in this fashion his language, where would poetry be? If the discoveries of all those who have only practised calculation, mechanics, chemistry, botany, geology, medicine, surgery, &c., &c., had not been within the reach of all to practice, where would sciences be? If people had not been able to profit by all the progress made in the producing, the transformation and carriage of useful things, where would agriculture be? Where industry and trade? Evidently, all would be in a primitive state, and instead of engaging in trades and professions we should be living under a system of costs, restrictions, and privileges a thousand times more formidable and repressive than all that has ever existed of this nature.

* * * * * * * *

"The priest, the professor mounting the pulpit to preach

virtue or to instruct, render service to their audience by a work consisting in making the circumambient air vibrate with speech, which these collect and pay for either directly in countries where worship or instruction is free, or by means of contributions in countries where worship and instruction are subsidiary to or provided by the State. But if this priest be a model of wisdom; if this professor is a genius of knowledge; the services they render are not confined to their audience; their words are propagated from country to country, from generation to generation, and everything in this indirect service is gratuitous, because Providence has willed it so, and makes use of His creatures to finish His work of redemption.

"The advocate, pleading before a tribunal, renders a service to his client. This service is a property in so far as it concerns the client; but if the advocate, endowed with a profound mind, criticises with success a vicious interpretation of the law which cramps the action of a number of citizens, he renders service not only to his client, but to an entire population, because other advocates would be able to copy, or, in order not to use this word, which is applied to industrials as an injury, *make use* of the same means as their associate. The doctor who cures a patient by a new surgical operation or by the use of a new medicine renders service to this invalid. This service is a property acknowledged and paid for, and it results that economically medicine or surgery can be called trade. In what is the profession of healing a liberal profession? Once more, by the right of imitation which society enjoys and by nothing else, unless the doctor, working only for philanthropy, does not wish any remuneration for his direct services.

"The writer making a book finds himself in a position identical with that of any other worker; he is but an artisan if he is a man of mediocrity; he is a regenerator, if he is a man of genius.

"The author, who would wish to proceed like a professor, can, like him, collect an audience and read his writings to persons who will pay a pre-arranged price. This lecture would be an industrial work, a service rendered and paid for. The moralist will admit the force of these appeals. But the author, we fear, is in advance of his age. Wisely, therefore, have the advocates of a change in the patent laws kept their cause distinct from that of copyright."

We wish we could share the author's faith in the substitutes he proposes for patent-right in the following paragraphs, which form the concluding part of his treatise.

"To find a means at once efficacious and natural, to pay in a substantial form and in a sufficient measure, the type-products of intellect called manuscripts, machines, models, designs, without checking the course of progress, without casting trouble and disturbance into business occupations—that is the great social problem which has to be solved.

"We think we have proved that the monopolies of sale and enterprise called 'intellectual property' must be given up, and that for two principal motives. First of all, because those monopolies, if they are profitable in a few and rare individual cases, are in general rather ruinous to those to whom they are granted, and secondly because these anti-economical monopolies violate the liberty of labour, and, if they could be worked on an important scale, would cause to society more loss than the spirit of invention could bring it advantage. Is it necessary for that purpose to have recourse to governmental rewards or to State subsidies? We repudiate again such a system, because governmental intervention can here produce nothing truly salutary. What resources have we then left? There remains to us association, which has become at the present time a new power. Each association prosecutes some end. If it is a religious association it prosecutes the propagation of its faith and the defence of its liberties; if the association is scientific it has for its end the dissemination of science; if it is artistic, it desires the progress of arts; if it is political it has rights to defend or to conquer; if it is commercial and industrial, it has economical interests to gain.

"Now we bring forward, as a fact, that all moral, philosophical, literary, scientific, artistic, and political works—that all invention, all discovery, all novelty, come within the aim of a certain group of associations which are interested, on the one side to encourage by all possible means all men of talent in their line, and which, on the other hand, are interested that the works and inventions in the same line should become freely available for general use at the cheapest rate possible.

"Why then could not these national and international societies, so powerful because of the number of their adherents, so indefatigable by reason of the desire of proselytism,—why could not those numerous associations which have lately been constituted everywhere for the propagation of faith, of science, of art, why could not these substitute themselves, with advantage to writers worthy of encouragement, for trading publishers who absorb the rights of authors and enrich themselves at their expense? Why could not these associations treat with the writers and take charge of the publishing of books without exclusive copyright, as well as newspapers and periodical writings, of which the elements are in that manner treated as public property? Inventors might address themselves to industrial associations with better luck than that furnished by the legal guarantee, which is always, as we have said already, a source of law-suits, torment, and ruin.

"The system, therefore, which we put forward in order to provide for types of work the most advantageous position, would be to create, through association, funds that would serve to buy and to sell again, without monopoly of copy or working, manuscripts, works of art, machines, models, drawings, &c."

We fear such associations as the author contemplates would be on the whole too rare to be taken much account of. We rather incline in the case of inventions to the plan of public grants, surrounded with difficulties and objections as we know it to be, while as a substitute for copyright—or as a modification of it, we should rather say—the following may appear to our readers worthy of consideration; viz., to limit the exclusive privilege of publication to a period of one year, and thereafter to allow every publisher to issue editions on paying the author a fair percentage on the selling price of such a number of copies as might be printed. Thus, if this royalty were ten per cent., the author would receive from the publisher of 1,000 copies of a guinea volume £105; if the price were half-a-guinea, £52 10*s.*; if half-a-crown, £12 10*s.*; if a shilling, £5. A glance at these figures shows in a moment what great inducement the abolition of monopoly and the substitution of royalties in its stead would present to sell books cheap. How beneficial, therefore, would the action of such a system be to the bulk of the population, and especially to the poor, who, as things are now, seldom or never get a new book into their hands—for as a general rule, the so called "popular" editions or issues that are small in price, suitable to their means, come forth, if at all, only after the lapse of too often many long years, when freshness is gone, and the stimulus and pleasure are to a great extent evaporated. What with paper freed from duty, and competition for the first time introduced into the supply of new books, we should not despair of seeing editions of fifty-fold the magnitude that is now current, and new books at prices so comparatively small that everybody in easy circumstances may ungrudgingly buy, in place of borrowing, and, after perusal, give away or tear to pieces instead of hoarding them. In that future happy time the labouring man may, almost equally with his master, enjoy what is now the expensive luxury of fresh cotemporary literature.

We are sorry to notice some seeming inaccuracies in M. Vermeire's statements; for instance, we are not aware that the Commissioners for the Great Exhibition of 1862 had ever considered the subject of Patent Law; nor that the German Economists, who met in congress last year, at Dresden, were affected in their decided verdict against patents by any of our countrymen present; nor that the Chambers of Commerce of this country had shown leanings towards advanced opinions on the question. As to these last associations, the indications are rather of indifference or adherence to prevailing prejudice and abuses, the result this, no doubt, of a strange illusion that we meet with on all hands, that the subject of the patent system is too involved and intricate to be mastered, whereas, indeed, it is in its principle most simple. The question, we are satisfied, has yet to be studied, even by the parties whom it most directly and seriously affects. Meanwhile, the public suffers from the pretensions that are stoutly urged on behalf of inventors as men of pre-eminent merit, and even as distinguished national benefactors, in disregard of the circumstance that it is not inventors but patentees that we have to do with, very few of whom would the most ardent admirer elevate up to these pretensions. The demand is not for honour and gratitude, but for exclusive privileges; in plain English and law English, too, for monopoly—coupled with the right of exacting, where they can, for the favour of licences royalties without limit. Far be it from us to repudiate the just claims of merit, but as little are we prepared to subject producers to restrictions and burdens that are inconsistent with that equality which is the first requisite of freedom of trade. There is, we observe, in the New World the same partiality for the few, and neglect or compromise of the interests of the many, that is the vice of the Old. Let the reader who cares to inquire into this refer to the latest American Patent Office Report.

We do not indeed know if Yankee cuteness has gone so far as to enlist in its support of patent monopolies the semi-religious press. If the Americans consult the "Leisure Hour," they may learn a lesson we have no wish to see repeated in this country.

We are glad to notice in our own country a healthier tone manifesting itself in some quarters. But this is a point on which we have not space to enter. May we not attribute the disappointing delay of the Royal Commissioners' Report, so long after the reception of evidence has been closed, to difficulties in determining a course such as shall at once maintain the principle of patents, and free inventive talent and productive industry from the shackles it is seen to forge, and the wrong it is seen to inflict?

Art. X.—THE ROMAN ELEMENT IN ENGLAND.

A Neglected Fact in English History. By Henry Charles Coote, F.S.A. London: Bell and Daldy. 1864.

IN our last Number we remarked with some severity on the publication of a work, which, beyond a general design to exalt the Roman civil law at the expense of our own jurisprudence, appeared to us to have no practical object, and which was in our opinion a very uncalled for display of questionable learning. We, of course, regarded the work in question from the point of view presented by the author, and which exhibited a certain degree of contrast between some of the more salient doctrines of the Roman system and the modern development of the law of England. Mr. Phillimore, the author of the work referred to, would, if we understand him, incorporate the Pandects in our Statute-Book bodily, hoping in that way to inaugurate a system of juridical training by which, instead of "Wrights, Norths, Wedderburnes, and Eldons," we might expect to have "De Thous, Hôpitals, Molès, and Lamoignons," and, in the result, and as a consummation devoutly to be wished, at once destroy the servility of the Bar and the tyrannical privileges of the attorneys! But here is a book the object of which is to rescue "a neglected fact" in our history, and which demonstrates to us very plainly that the evils and barbarism which so grieve Mr. Phillimore's ingenuous spirit are more deeply rooted, and have come upon us more sadly, than even he had imagined; for if Mr. Coote is to be believed we are the barbarians and vulgarians Mr. Phillimore so pleasantly describes us to be, not for the want of, but in spite of, the possession and influence among us of Roman law and of Roman institutions; and that is a fact which has been neglected by historians and literati, and in particular most shamefully neglected by our uncompromising censor, Mr. Phillimore. It is a mistake, Mr. Coote tells us, by his remote and quaint research, that we were Germanic in our original existence as a nation. On the contrary, everything about us at the period of which he speaks, and that was worthy of being noted as evidence of our civilisation, was Roman—we were Roman socially, Roman municipally, Roman legally. Indeed, if our worthy and industrious author, Mr. Coote, had lived and studied in 1253, it might be doubted whether the statute of Merton would ever have been passed, and at least he might have been able to have held his own with the old barons. The position taken may be received incredulously by many, and some may not like to be told that such was the effect to any extent of the Roman occupation of our island. But if not approved by our genuine John Bulls, Lord Palmerston may possibly feel interested when he is told, as we all are, by Mr. Coote, that "the Anglo-Saxon *thegn*" (gentleman), "in the peculiarities of his position, is no other than the provincial landholder and gentleman, the possessor and the *civis Romanus*." Yes, notwithstanding the recent debate, and all our political and patriotic reclamation, John Bull is neither Saxon nor German, but a veritable *civis Romanus!* And there are many other synthetic pleasantries in the work which might be developed in a manner not more amusing than instructive. It is, of course, chiefly as bearing on the early history of our law that we are concerned with it; but the author's thoughts have worked themselves out in such a manner as to make it exceedingly difficult to separate the strictly legal from the other portions of the book. As a contribution to our libraries we are obliged to say that the book is distinguished by many defects, so much so that we fear none but the most persistent student and resolute antiquarian would care to encounter its exposition. And not to speak of the material inconveniences of being without an index, or even table of contents, it is unmarked by points or positions in its argument. In reading and considering its 180 pages, the mind from beginning to end finds no resting-place, but is fatigued by one continuous uninterrupted stream of remote tradition and pristine lore, which tradition and lore are not generally stated in a manner calculated to attract the attention of the intellect. Our author would have done his work better if its arrangement had been characterised by divisions or chapters, which would have been in themselves inductively complete, historical, and argumentative theses; the matter, too, of the work should have been summarised more clearly and logically.

Notwithstanding, however, these and other rather repellent qualities of the book, we have risen from its perusal with feelings of great respect for its author. The expression "neglected fact" may indeed suggest the idea of a hobby, but if the subject of the book be of that character, Mr. Coote's hobby is one of those which do not detract from, but add to the esteem with which he may otherwise be regarded. He is evidently a man of considerable attainments and historical learning, and if he has not the faculty of clear logical statement, his capacity for laborious and persevering industry in studious acquisition shows that he has a mind which can perceive and grasp its purpose with great tenacity. And no doubt the learned matter with which every page of the book may be said to be replete, is from its remotely antiquated, and not very accessible, character, exceedingly difficult of treatment. The following extract from the preface gives a pretty faithful idea of the author's purpose.

Of the elements which compose the English nationality the most obvious is attributable to a Germanic stock,

But however clearly this element may exhibit itself, the specific source to which it is truly to be ascribed has been unaccountably misunderstood and mis-stated. For it has been commonly agreed, both at home and abroad, to find the required ascription in a theory that Englishmen (on the Germanic side at least) are the descendants of the immigrants of the fifth and sixth centuries solely.

Of this prevalent theory it is to be observed, that it involves the extermination of the provincial Britons as a condition *sine quâ non*, and makes a *tabula rasa* of Roman Britain.

But such an assumption is attended with this great difficulty,— it is entirely irreconcilable with the leading phenomena displayed in the political, social and legal condition of England, as it is found during the period of the Anglo-Saxon *régime*.

The phenomena which Anglo-Saxons exhibit are these :—

They are divided into the two classes of the privileged and the unprivileged, distinctions which the philosophy of history has demonstrated to contain within themselves the fact, that a nationality from without has mastered another and a native nationality, which survives in a subject condition.

In the next place, this general society of masters and subjects is steeped in Roman institutions and observances.

No part of its life is free from these impressions, which dominate alike the thane and the churl.

The master holds his land and the servant occupies and tills it in unhesitating submission to rules and conditions which the law of the Empire had inculcated and enforced.

The master condescends to Roman taxation in order to maintain in their pristine state the bridges and causeways of Rome, and the warlike defences of those *municipia* which the Eternal City had founded in Britain.

In the civil, as in the territorial law, the Roman element prevails.

The Roman *civitates* continue in life and action, and the burgesses still follow and obey the *lex municipalis.*

The civilisation and art of the country are high in degree and Roman in haracter.

The Imperial coinage virtually survives.

Roman words of art and manufacture, of weight and measure, of commerce, of law, of civilised amusement, of common and general nomenclature, spring from the lips of the Anglo-Saxon in the utterances of his daily life.

Pure doctrinal Christianity, such as existed before the fall of Imperial paganism, is traceable in the land before the Roman monk has nerved himself to his task of pious ambition.

All this and more of Roman stamp and derivation are parcel of the organisation of the country.

Respecting the Anglo-Saxon, or to speak more correctly, the Anglo-Saxon immigrant, he had never belonged to Rome, but had belonged to unromanised and primitive Germany:—

"In a word, barbarism was his sole inheritance and endowment," and we are not "to attribute to him the source and origin of the Roman usages of England."

These of course are to be attributed to the Romano-Britain, and beyond him to the pure Roman. The other, that is the German, is—

An ill-considered theory, which need occasion no regret in the mind of an Englishman. The theory itself is not only untrue as a fact, but is also disparaging to the national pedigree.

It post-dates the English *origines*, and dries up the springs of our early history, the merits and interest of which are by this supposition lavished upon a race of strangers. It disentitles a large proportion of the Britons of Imperial Rome to the sympathies of the present race of Englishmen. It asserts that the arts and civilisation which the Mistress of the World imposed upon her subjects and pupils have conferred no derivative benefit upon ourselves, between whom and the Eternal City it leaves a gap without connexion or transition. Provincial Britain becomes a lost nation, and four centuries of historical associations, with their momentous consequences, are divorced from our annals.

And he further observes:—

In excuse for the superficial old theory which has been so long and so unhesitatingly received, it must be admitted that there are difficulties attending the treatment and solution of this interesting question; these difficulties having reference to the paucity and smallness of the direct evidence which now exists upon the subject: Yet there is a mass of circumstantial proof, sufficient, if carefully and conscientiously handled, to afford a satisfactory induction which will discover to us the true ascription of the English nationality. And this induction, while it will identify our modern Englishman with the Romano-Briton of the Empire, will also yield the fact that his nationality owes its origin to a branch of a great Cis-rhenan people, which in its continental seat strained the nerve of the great dictator before it submitted to the genius of the Empire. Of this people, as the true continental branches have been long since lost or merged, England is now the sole representative.

And such is the neglected fact. Or, as Mr. Coote otherwise puts it:—

This induction, while it shows that the English are only Angles as the French are Franks, and the Northern Italians are Lombards, is a fact in English history which has been undeservedly neglected, and as it will assist to explain the peculiarities of Englishmen, it may go far to justify their pride in them.

The manner in which all this is worked up in the body of the essay (as the book may better than anything else be called) is very learned, but far from being satisfactory or even ordinarily attractive by the form and method of its literary statement. One would have imagined, that in order to make good his position, the author would have begun at the beginning, and traced the national phenomena up to the Anglo-Saxon conquest and supercession of the Roman Britain, pointing out, as he went on, his various Roman evidences. But instead of such a natural and progressive induction, Mr. Coote opens up with a view of society as organised by the Anglo-Saxons, who, he tells us, were divided into *gesithas* and *ceorlas*, the first of these being in fact the gentry of the period; the other being a subject population, although not servile. They were in fact distinct castes. "But," says Mr. Coote, "distinct castes in the same nation are in other words distinct nationalities on the same soil,"—and these *gesithas* and *ceorlas* were "two nationalities or peoples co-existing in Anglo-Saxon England." These Anglo-Saxon *gesithas*, or gentlemen, owed their rank and privileges to the merely military and barbarous right of conquest—with deference to the Austrians and Prussians of our day be it said—but which in the primitive times to which we are referring, conferred a high moral title; and—

The name of *gesith*, in other respects endeared to the German mind, became ennobled in the estimation of the Anglo-Saxon, and was transmitted by him to his descendents to be borne in perpetual remembrance, as well of the stupendous triumph of his race as also of the conditions upon which these properties and privileges had been obtained.

The privileges of the *gesithas* consisted of rights proprietary, political, and judicial. The *gesith* became a landholder:—

Land became his badge as well as his privilege. He was never to be disconnected from the land nor the land from him. A *gesith* and a landholder became convertible terms, and the land, from being the possession of a paramount class, became the distinctive symbol of the class itself.

As for his political privileges—

It was his exclusive right to attend the public councils of his kingdom, whether they were those general political assemblies of the nation which decided on war or peace, or the judicial meetings of his own hundred or shire.

But the *gesithas* were not only the political masters, they were also the judges of the land. This fact, however, is stated by Mr. Coote in a way less interesting and true as regards the remote ideal of the judicial office in England than as throwing light on the origin of our jury. The assembled *gesithas*, in fact, appear to have been neither more nor less than our jury, and the functions of the two bodies appear to have been not dissimilar. Mr. Coote says:—

The *scyrgemot* was composed of all the *gesithas* of the county, and their attendance upon that Court was compulsory; and though the Court was presided over by the *caldorman* of the shire, it was not that officer, but the *gesithas*, who determined the questions of life and property submitted to the adjudication of the Court.

From a subsequent passage we learn that the number of *gesithas* was twelve, but strange to say they appear to have been legally and technically known, not so much with reference to themselves personally, but as representing the quantity of land which they unitedly possessed,—thus, speaking of the *hide*, as a measure of land, we are told, "Metaphor, in this measure of land, became precise and technical phraseology of Anglo-Saxon law; and an union of twelve *thegns* (or *gesithas*) to testify the innocence of the accused was known to the tribunal as an oath of sixty hides." Of course by such land hidage was to be understood, what in fact Mr. Coote states, that to be duly qualified, the *gesitha* or *thegn* must have been the possessor of at least five hides of land.

The jurisdiction, however, of these *gesithas* appears to have been something more definite and precise than the province of our juries. Mr. Coote describes it as a right of judicature, and says it was called *thegnscipe*.

These details, although they show a want of good arrangement in Mr. Coote's statement of his case, are interesting in themselves. But we pass on to the *ceorlas* or inferior class, whose position and history are more to the point. It is in truth to these *ceorlas* that the neglected fact alone applies. Although relatively subject and inferior to the Anglo-Saxon *gesithas*, it was they who claimed the Romans for their ancestors, and their civilisation was Roman and nothing else. In this respect, indeed, they were in the anomalous position of being greatly superior to their Anglo-Saxon lords, who—

"Claimed and exulted," as our author tells us, "in a descent from Jutes, Angles, and Saxons, and from those Jutes, Angles, and Saxons who conquered or occupied Britain in the fifth or sixth centuries."

Mr. Coote proceeds to observe :—

But of the origin and descent of the lower class, their masters have not left us a word of record or information.

This, therefore, is the only question left open for inquiry and decision, and its solution is the subject of this essay.

At starting, it may be observed, that this class, whatever be its origin, must either have been imported into Roman Britain by the Anglo-Saxons, or must have been a population there found and retained by them.

The first of these suppositions Mr. Coote dismisses as unfounded, labouring to demonstrate that the latter was the truth. The conclusion, therefore, is that the Anglo-Saxons found in the country a British people who had proceeded from a Roman origin, but whose laws, especially as they related to land, the successful invaders appear to have appreciated and retained. Mr. Coote here, we regret to say, does not explain himself clearly, although we think we have caught his meaning. He speaks of the laws of Anglo-Saxon England upon the subject of real estate, but his argument shows that these laws were not the laws of the Anglo-Saxons themselves, but the laws which they found prevailing in the country; in fact, the laws of the inferior and subject *ceorlas.* He, notwithstanding, describes one of these laws as "the early and true Anglo-Saxon," although in a few sentences afterwards, he demonstrates it to have been Roman, and a law which affected landed possessions in the provinces of the empire, *i.e.*, the Roman empire. There is, indeed, a most annoying confusion throughout, in Mr. Coote's application of national names, and the confusion is all the more annoying from his matter being really most valuable and interesting. The national name of a race or community should indicate with more or less precision some distinct historical epoch, but really without the closest attention to his context, it is very difficult to understand what our author means by "Anglo-Saxon" this and that.

Among the laws referred to, there was a certain imperfect

and conditional estate in land, or modified species of ownership, which could neither be alienated nor devised without the consent of the king. This estate Mr. Coote traces to have originated in the Roman *possessio*, which was a device of the governing families of Rome, and was in this wise:—the State, instead of alienating, retained the dominion of lands captured from the enemy, granting *possession* of them to tenants who, while they should pay an annual tithe of the products, should be bound to surrender their holding whenever the State should call upon them to do so. It appears to have been for financial reasons that this kind of holding was extended to the territorial conquests made by the Roman republic beyond the limits of Italy. And Mr. Coote informs us that, with few exceptions, no other estate in land was known in the provinces except this *possessio*. On this point the following extract is too interesting to be omitted:—

Provincial land accordingly was granted both by the Republic and the Emperors as possession only, the dominion remaining in the Emperors or the Roman people, liable under that title to be resumed at will, and thus made a patient producer of revenue, tamely susceptible of any obligation whose imposition the necessity of the state might demand. But, for impositions of every kind, there existed in the Empire necessities of the sternest and most exactive form. The large standing armies ramified through the provinces the immense military staff and civil establishment therein, the formation and repair of the fortifications, the bridges, the aqueducts and the roads of the provinces, the general expenses of the Empire, and the private expenses of the Emperors, unfailingly created those necessities.

We have seen that in return for the usufruct of his land, the provincial possessor paid *tributum* or land tax. This impost would go far to provide for one set of expenses. But for the other expenses an equivalent provision would also have to be made, and, accordingly, the *tributum* was not the only condition upon which the estate was conceded. The other charges to which *possessiones* were liable by law were further conditions of the holding.

In general terms these charges were denominated *onera* (or *munera*) *patrimonialia;* specifically they were *pontium refectio, arcium munitio* (or *refectio*), *viarum munitio* (or *refectio*), and *tironum productio.* Under the obligations, *the possessor* within the territory of any given *civitas* was bound to contribute, according to the extent of the acreage which he had under cultivation, to the repair of the bridges along the leading lines of road, and of those same lines of road within the territory, and also of the walls and bastions of the *civitas* itself. He was further bound to find recruits for the imperial armies, and to subsist and receive the Emperor and his attendants when they made a progress through the province.

Such was the state and condition of landed property in Britain during the imperial occupation; and the state of Anglo-Saxon land shows that it remained unaltered after the Anglo-Saxon conquest.

And the author adduces many other interesting evidences of the strong mark the Roman occupation had left on the land. Mr. Cobden, and those who agree with him, will be interested to learn that in Anglo-Saxon England real property was as a general rule legally divisible among all the children of an intestate, although in some districts the youngest son succeeded, and both the general law itself and its exception were Roman:—

By that law, an intestate's children (being *sui* or unemancipated) shared his real property upon his decease, to the exclusion of the emancipated children. At the period, therefore, when the independence of Britain was restored, all the intestate's children, or only his youngest, might take according to the circumstances of a family, as the one or others of the children were unemancipated.

Afterwards, when Roman legal rigour had relaxed itself in this country, some places may have established for themselves, as a custom, that all the children should be *sui.* This was the general Anglo-Saxon law.

Other places may have applied the principle, that all should be considered emancipated, save the youngest son. This became Borough English.

And the following, also, is too interesting for omission in this article :—

We have evidence that there was a law of distribution of intestate's personal estates in Anglo-Saxon times. Cnut expressly declares, that an intestate's inheritance shall be divided legally between wife and children, or amongst the nearest of kin, according to their degree of relationship.

This, of course, is Roman.

By the Roman law, the same persons who succeeded to the realty, succeeded to the moveable property also.

This principle prevailed also in Anglo-Saxon England, as we find by Cnut's law, and the absence of any authority to the contrary.

Besides this identity in general principle, there have been, and still are, some striking peculiarities in the English law of personal succession which, as no innovation can be shown, must also be ranked as Anglo-Saxon law, but which, at the same time, are Roman antejustinianean law.

By a peculiarity of English law, unparticipated in by the rest of Europe, the English father succeeds to the whole of his son's personalty, to the exclusion even of his other parent, for where there is a father, the mother is not next of kin to her son. There is nothing to negative this principle of law being Anglo-Saxon, and we will therefore rank it as such. But it is, in reality, the *patria potestas* of the Roman law.

There was another principle of Roman law—one of the highest equity. A testator could not wholly disinherit his wife and family, for he had the right of testation only as regarded a proportion of his property, the rest of it going under a compulsory intestacy to his wife and his issue. This was law in Anglo-Saxon England, and the testable portion was long afterwards known here as the dead man's part.

Mr. Coote might have here added, if he is aware of the circumstance, and if he is not aware we beg to inform him, that such is also the law of Scotland at the present day. We may here observe that the Scotch law also recognised another principle of the Roman law of as high equity, to say the least, and which is known in Roman and Scotch law books as the *conditio si sine liberis discesserit,* according to which if a man makes a gift or a bequest of all or the greater part of his estate when he had no children, and comes afterwards to have children, the gift becomes void, upon the presumption that if the donor or testator had anticipated having children of his own, he would not have made it.

There were two modes of sale and transfer of land recognised by the Anglo-Saxon law, which Mr. Coote shows to have been derived from a Roman source. The Roman and Anglo-Saxon forms equally required to be perfected by tradition or seisin as a legal preliminary to the registration of the title. This registration was considered by the Roman law as a judicial act, and an incident of the voluntary jurisdiction belonging to the provincial and municipal magistrates. And Mr. Coote points out that the Anglo-Saxon *gewitnesse,* which was the verbal announcement of the contract, has the sense of adjudication.

The Anglo-Saxon law regarding wills is traced in the same way to a similar source.

On this subject our author says:

The Anglo-Saxons made their wills, and we have most interesting specimens of them left. But wills were totally unknown to the Germans, and must therefore have been adopted from Rome.

There is a peculiarity about the Anglo-Saxon testaments which shows that their origin is Roman, for there is no executor, though that functionary was a canonical creation of an early age.

As the Anglo-Saxon will is Roman, so are its contents. It manumits a slave agreeably to a peculiar privilege of the Roman testament.

From things legal, Mr. Coote passes on to other aspects and conditions of the country in Anglo-Saxon times, showing a Roman hue in everything. The "shire," the "hundred," the "borough," municipal or self-government by citizens, the coinage, the adoption of the planetary week, and the religion, which was Christian, and, although Roman, not papal;

concluding with a summary of the many points and evidences of his demonstration. In the result, the Saxon having cast off the alliance of the Pict, he entered the military service of the Briton, and in conjunction with him repulsed and destroyed the other invaders of this island. Mr. Coote concludes in the following eloquent terms:—

> The result is well known. When the Pict and Scot had fled for ever from the scene of their ravages, and the Kymric Briton had suffered a retribution which has left its material traces at this day, the victorious Anglo-Saxon leaders were permitted by a gracious providence to initiate the glorious monarchy of England.

We have spoken of the book with perfect candour, indicating some of its faults, but admitting its claims to favour at the hands of the historical student, by reason of the curious matter in relation to law, politics, and social science, with which it is replete. But with the exception of possibly affording some pleasing meditations to the sentimental bookworm or nebulous politician, Mr. Coote himself probably does not expect his essay to be regarded as of much practical value, even if he made out his case more triumphantly than he does, although, as we have indicated, we consider he is fairly entitled to the concurrence and sympathy of reasonable, not to say of sanguine, thinkers.

There is one reflection which the attentive perusal of the book may suggest, namely, that mere political and social refinement, or in other words, superiority in civilisation, can never successfully contend against the material inroads of the invader's sword. Compared with the *ceorlas*, or subject portion of the population, the *gesithas*, *thegns*, or gentlemen, were, in regard to all that related to political and legal government and social organisation, neither more nor less than barbarians. But the latter got the upper hand, and became not less the social than the territorial aristocrats. And may we not tremble to think what might have been our lot if Mr. Bright and his peace party had then lived, and directed Anglo-Saxon politics? Might we not all have been Romans still, and instead of being a distinctive nation, have formed but a portion of the great Latin race? If so, there would have been no need of the Phillimores of our day. Yet had they existed, they would not of course have been without their own appropriate intellectual *mirage.*

Art. XI.—LAW REPORTING.

THE Report of the Committee of the Bar on Law Reporting is now before the profession, and the scheme which was agreed to by the majority has to be considered before the adjourned meeting of the Bar in November. The scheme proposed is simply for an amalgamation of the existing reports, and their publication in future under the control of a council, having the management of the financial department, and the selecting of a competent staff of editors and reporters.

Should this proposition bring a sufficient subscription list, one great step would be made towards an improvement on the present costly and unsatisfactory mode of preparing our law reports. The Committee, however, have not at present recommended any alteration of our *system of law reporting;* which leaves the rules of law laid down in Westminster Hall to be collected only from notes, not only unauthentic, but confined to those matters which appeared to the reporter at the moment of taking them adopted for publication, affording no guarantee against the omission altogether of decisions of the greatest importance, but which the carelessness or want of judgment of the reporter may have kept out of his notebook.

The serious evils so often described as resulting from these defects of our law reporting system, may, for anything in the proposed scheme, remain unabated; and it is certainly remarkable that the Committee, with ample materials before them, did not deal with such an important part of the subject referred to them.

The Committee, we are told, before entering upon the consideration of any scheme of amendment to be suggested by any of its members, resolved to issue a circular to the profession inviting observations and suggestions; such circular was as follows:—

The Committee are anxious, in order the better to discharge the duty entrusted to them, to collect the opinion of the profession upon the subject of LAW REPORTING; and for that purpose the Committee are desirous of receiving any observations which you, either alone or in conjunction with others, may be so obliging as to make upon what, in your opinion, are the advantages or disadvantages of the present system, and also any suggestions, either as to the principle or details of any amendment of the existing system which you may think desirable.

This circular was sent to the judges, and extensively distributed among both branches of the profession. In reply, the Committee received numerous and valuable observations and suggestions. Although these exhibited differences of opinion as to the proper mode of amending the existing system of law reporting, they exhibited, at the same time, a very general desire for amendment; and the Committee have been greatly assisted in the discharge of their duties by the observations and suggestions thus received.

The Committee, also, before entering upon the consideration of any plan of their own, appointed a Sub-Committee (consisting of the Hon. George Denman, Q.C., Mr. Serjeant Pulling, Mr. Henry Matthews, Mr. Quain, and Mr. Westlake) to inquire into the mode of recording and reporting judicial decisions in the various European States, and in the United States of America.

The Sub-Committee undertook these duties, and reported as follows:—

The Sub-Committee thus appointed have received valuable communications from a number of competent foreign jurists, and other gentlemen professionally or officially connected with the chief tribunals of the countries embraced in the inquiry, and thus conversant with the subject-matter of the reference.

The Sub-Committee have by this means obtained information which they recommend to the Committee as worthy of their attention.

To begin with the system adopted in France. Every judicial decision is required to be in writing, and to be *motivé*, *i.e.*, to disclose on the face of it the grounds and reasons on which it is founded; and when the signature of the President of the Tribunal has been affixed to these solemn judgments, it is the business of the *Greffier* to see them entered on the register of the courts, and only one version of them can therefore ever legally appear.

The records of the tribunals thus containing an authentic version of every decision, the legal profession and the public have at all times access to the register to ascertain what has from time to time been decided, and it is competent for anyone to make from the register a selection of such decisions for publication. The collections of decisions by Sirey and Dalloz, and Ledru Rollin, have been thus prepared. Though these works are deservedly held in great esteem, they are not official publications, any more than any series of English law reports.

In Norway and Sweden the judgments of the ordinary tribunals are always given in writing, and in every case entered on the protocols of the courts; and in the supreme courts of appeal, when the votes of the judges are given separately, it is the business of the registrar of the court to enter on the records of the court, not only the final judgment or conclusion, but the grounds and reasons of the decision of each judge. Here, as in France, therefore, the records of the courts supply ample materials for the preparation of books of reports or collections of decisions, and such publications are left wholly to free trade.

In Denmark, though it is competent for any one to take down, print and publish reports of cases and decisions of which he has himself taken notes, the only authentic version of judicial proceedings is the entry in the *dombistocol*, under the hand of the judge; containing not only the conclusion itself to which the court has arrived, but the facts and reasons and grounds of the decision; and from these, selections of cases which may serve for precedents are made by the direction of the courts, though it would seem that other selections made by competent private publishers would be received with equal attention.

In Italy all judicial decisions, whether civil or criminal, must be read aloud in open court, with the grounds in fact or law set out at length; and authentic minutes of the judicial opinions so pronounced are duly entered in the register of the court; and compilations of the principal decisions of the four superior courts of cassation at Milan, Florence, Naples, and Palermo are published by voluntary editors, whose province it is to make a proper selection of cases for publication, to give an analysis of them in the head and marginal notes, and to explain or illustrate them in other annotations. These compilations only so far receive the protection of the State that a certain number of copies are subscribed for out of the public treasury. The compilation entitled "La Legge Romana" is a journal of judicial and administrative proceedings for the Kingdom of Italy, published at short intervals (the judicial three times a week), and containing in an abridged form notes taken from the minutes in the registers of all the important cases disposed of.

In the United States of America there is no law requiring either written decisions or a record or register of the grounds and reasons of the decisions; but the judgments are generally in writing, and in most of the States, and in the Supreme Court of the United States, there are now official reporters, remunerated by salary as well as by a portion of the profits of the publications. These reporters are generally appointed by the State, and are always removable at the discretion of the appointing power, but enjoy in the performance of their duties the same freedom as the authors of our own law reports. In the superior court of the City of New York, the judges publish the reports of their own decisions, choosing an editor from among themselves. As a rule, the official reports omit the arguments of counsel, and give only a narrative of the facts and the copy of the written judgments. The official publication rarely appears for many months after the judgment is pronounced, and until that time publications called the *Law Reporter* and *Law Journal* are referred to, but do not profess to give more than the most important cases. No suggestion is made that the official reporters are less efficient or more dilatory than their predecessors under the voluntary system, nor is it found that they are subject to any improper influence in the discharge of their duties; and in the State of New York the official reports are required by law to be sold at a much smaller price.

The Committee, with the information they now had before them, proceeded to consider proposals for amendment.

The first proposal discussed by the Committee was a joint proposal by Mr. Serjeant Pulling, Mr. Joshua Williams, and Mr. Westlake, and was as follows:—

The present system has arisen from the default of proper records of their own proceedings being kept by the courts. The privilege which the Bar has of reporting comes to this, that any barrister may inform the court of that which the court might much better know from its own records. No remedy appears to us sufficient which does not strike at the root of the evil. It would be desirable that all judgments should be written; but this may be thought impracticable. We therefore propose as follows:—

It should be the duty of the registrar, in all cases in which judicial opinions are pronounced, to record the names of the parties, and of their counsel and attorneys, or solicitors, the authorities cited, the judicial opinion or opinions delivered, and the formal judgment, order or decree; also the substance of the pleadings and the case, and the points relied upon by counsel, wherever a mere transcript of the judicial opinions actually delivered did not render any other summary of the case, pleading and points unnecessary.

Each registrar should be assisted by one or more short-hand writers, whose duty it should be to take down all remarks of the judges, especially their judgments, and any remarks by counsel which may be necessary to render them intelligible.

The short-hand writers should be allowed to furnish notes to applicants for their own profit.

The short-hand writers' notes should be written out as soon as possible, and furnished to the registrar.

It should be the duty of the registrar, from these notes and his own, with the assistance of the judges, the other officers of the court, and the counsel and attorneys or solicitors employed, to prepare such record of the case as aforesaid.

This record should be printed as soon as possible by the Queen's printers, on paper of a given shape, each cause being on separate paper, and the transactions of each day being printed within a week at furthest.

The records so printed should be published and sold at a low price, with liberty to any person to reprint them.

The record so made should be amended by the court on sufficient evidence of its inaccuracy, and should be evidence in the same manner as the records of the courts now are.

All printed pleadings and evidence should be on paper of the same size and shape with that of the records, so that the printed documents relating to each cause might be bound up, as those relating to Privy Council causes now are in Lincoln's Inn Library; and copies of all such printed documents should be furnished to the libraries of the Inns of Court and the Incorporated Law Society.

If a ministry of justice should be established, which we think very desirable, it might be charged with the preparation of an annual or semiannual digest, and with supplying marginal notes to the records of cases, but so that such records might also be bought without such notes by those who might think it important to get them sooner.

Mr. Joshua Williams has, since the presentation of the Report of the Committee, given his own views on the subject as follows:—

I think it is due to the Bar that I should state my reasons for not concurring in the Report of the Committee on Law Reporting, of which I was nominated a member. The joint proposal of Mr. Serjeant Pulling, Mr. Westlake, and myself, mentioned in the Report, does not in every particular represent my views. I agreed to some alterations for the purpose of securing the co-operation of these gentlemen.

It appears to me that the essence of all that is practicable by way of amendment of the present system of law reporting is comprised in the three following propositions:—

1. That all judgments of the superior courts should, as far as practicable, be written.

2. That all judgments of the superior courts, not committed to writing before delivery, should be committed to writing under the authority of the court as soon as possible after delivery.
3. That access to all the judgments of the superior courts should be afforded to every member of the profession as speedily and cheaply as possible.

I moved resolutions to this effect before the Committee, but the first being negatived, I withdrew the others.

The judgments of the courts make the law. This alone is a sufficient reason why their preservation should not be left, as at present, to the care of any reporter who may chance to be present.

Accuracy is evidently the first requisite. To secure this the best means should be adopted. Writing evidently secures accuracy better than speaking. But if a judgment must needs be spoken, a a report of it, made by a practised short-hand writer and perused and signed by the judge, appears to me to be the next best means of securing accuracy.

Speedy and cheap access to the judgments when once they are accurately recorded is evidently best obtained by their being printed as soon as possible, and published at the lowest price that will cover the expense of their publication.

Reporting as now used is a complex operation. It comprises an accurate statement of the judgment so far as the reporter's means and opportunities may allow ; but it includes also selecting, digesting, and abstracting, so as to present in a readable form the decisions of such cases as the reporter thinks worthy of publication.

The great mass of materials is an evil that can never be overcome. No one can prevent two persons from going to law about any matter whatever ; and, if they do, a decision more or less valuable must be the result.

I think that the present reporters exercise functions which ought to be separated. So far as they aim merely at an accurate report of the judgment, their functions appear to me to be such as would be more properly discharged by an official person. So far as they select, digest, and abstract, so far, I think, should their duties be open to competition. The records which form the sources of history are all officially preserved ; but history itself is written by individuals, whose success is proportioned to the ability they display in selecting and digesting.

The scheme recommended by the Committee proposes to unite functions which, I think, should be kept separate. The proposed incorporation of a new body by Letters Patent or Act of Parliament appears to me to involve a constitutional change far too important for the evils complained of. But my main objection is, that it does not strike at the root of the evil, which lies in the want of an accurate official record of every judgment pronounced by the courts.

It only remains to add that were the question now entertained of securing an official record of every judgment pronounced by the courts, many of the difficulties suggested to the proposition will be found to be more fanciful than real. 1. The annual surplus of the fees paid by suitors, after defraying all other charges, would suffice to cover, and be legitimately applicable to the cost of competent recorders or registrars of decisions, and indeed in the common law courts the constant presence of such an officer would serve in lieu of the attendance of the masters, so as to reserve the latter for their more urgent business out of court. 2. The services of short-hand writers could be secured at a very inconsiderable cost, if they were allowed also to supply copies or extracts from their notes for their own profit as at present. 3. If the books of the court contained such an accurate record of every judgment the business of subsequent publication could safely be left to free trade, which would soon supply the best selections at the minimum cost. The record of the decisions would be authentic and accessible to all. The profitable work of publishing selections of cases with head and marginal notes and comments showing the principles which any decided case establishes, would not fail to find competent editors and ready publishers.

The subject is so important that we shall probably recur to it in our next Number.

Art. XII.—INDIAN AND AMERICAN CODES.

MORE than twenty years since the anomalous state of our Indian Empire as respects its laws, was pointed out by the Indian Law Commissioners, a learned body of men, who executed the task of inquiry assigned to them with indefatigable zeal and perseverance. They remarked that India was the only country in the world enjoying the advantage of a civilised Government, which did not possess any substantive law. Up to this date, indeed, India has no *lex loci.* It is true that within certain limits round the three presidency towns of Calcutta, Madras, and Bombay, the law has for a long time been fixed; but even there, there is no one body of law applicable to all persons, and deciding all actions. The Hindoo and Mahometan inhabitants, who form, of course, the great bulk of the population, are entitled by treaty to their own laws on all matters of inheritance and succession, and of contract; while on all other persons and in other matters (the criminal law, for instance) the law of England is exclusively binding. Not exactly the law of England as it is known to us, but the law of England as it existed in the 13th year of George I., when the Recorder's Court of Calcutta was established by royal charter: with the addition of any Acts of Parliament since passed expressly relating to India, of the laws and regulations enacted by the Legislative Council of India, and of the decisions of the Indian Supreme Courts. Outside the narrow areas of these presidency districts no fixed law of any kind seems to be administered by the tribunals. The Mofussil (or provincial) courts are not courts of law, but of equity and conscience, the judges being directed to decide each case as it arises on its own merits, and as far as possible according to justice and reason. But conceiving themselves bound by the maxim that "equity follows the law," the judges have generally thought it necessary to ascertain the particular law which their equity should follow for each litigant; and a custom has accordingly grown up of administering to the multifarious races and tribes of our Indian empire their real or supposed laws or customs. The codes of the Hindoos and Mahometans are indisputable, and admitted as a matter of course, but the floating usages of the Parsees, Armenians, and other "nationalities" are of a very different character, and must have afforded no small trouble to the judges before whom they were pleaded. In fact, under this singular state of things, which we believe to have been unprecedented except during the "dark ages" of Europe, when Goths, Vandals, Visigoths, and every other rabble of barbarians had their own laws or usages to which they appealed,—not only are the judges perplexed and justice is rendered uncertain by a complication of laws, but the courts, as Sir Lawrence Peel long since observed, are occasionally driven to the necessity of a preliminary inquiry into the pedigree of a litigant, before they can know what rules are to be applied to his case!

The India Law Commissioners therefore recommended as the one indispensable step towards the efficient administration of justice in India, the preparation and enactment of a substantive code of law, which should be, if possible, applicable in all respects to all the inhabitants of our Indian territories; and if this were not possible, then to all save the Hindoos and Mahometans in matters of succession and contract. It was in consequence of this recommendation that Mr. (afterwards Lord) Macaulay devoted himself, with the assistance of other able men, to the preparation of a Penal Code; and this was followed at a considerable interval by a code of civil procedure, for which we were indebted to a Commission, of which the Master of the Rolls was the head. This last-named Commission supported the India Law Commissioners in their recommendation of a civil code; and some three years since a new Commission was issued, with Sir John Romilly again at the head, and having the advantage of the presence of the Chief Justice of the Common Pleas among its members. This Commission has just presented its first report to Her Majesty, and they give therein the first instalment of the great work in which they are engaged, a substantive code of civil law applicable to the whole of India. We say "applicable," though the Commissioners do not recommend that it should be so applied; it being proposed by them that this portion of the code, which deals with succession and inheritance, should not extend to Hindoos and Mahometans. They, however, express a hope that in the process of time it may be adopted by those two great classes of the population of India, and in the meantime we believe that its promulgation would be hailed as an inestimable boon by the other subjects of the Crown in that immense dependency. The law of England has been taken as the basis of the code, but such modifications are introduced as are rendered necessary or desirable by the peculiar circumstances of India. For these we must refer our readers to the Report itself, but we may mention that no distinction is made as to moveable and immoveable property, the devolution of each being governed by the same rules. Again, a husband will not acquire by law any interest in his wife's property during her life, and a married woman will retain her powers as a *feme sole.* The age for making a will, too, has been fixed at eighteen.

But we are particularly desirous of calling attention to the observations made on the illustrations which have been introduced into the code, after the example first set by Lord Macaulay. We must confess ourselves much struck with them, and it is a fair question for consideration, whether most of the objections that are often, and reasonably enough, made to codification, would not be met by a judicious use of this expedient. The Commissioners say:—

Following the example set by the framers of the Indian Penal Code, we have made copious use of illustrations. All the Commissioners think that illustrations carefully framed are calculated to assist in the administration of the law, although we do not all take the same high view of the importance of illustrations which was expressed by the framers of the Penal Code. The advantages contemplated by those Commissioners from the use of illustrations were set forth and dilated on by them in their letter to the Governor-General in Council, dated the 14th of October, 1837, with which they submitted their draft of the Penal Code. The observations contained in that letter appear to be so pertinent to this matter that we think it desirable to quote a portion of that part of it which relates to this subject.

"One peculiarity in the manner in which this code is framed will immediately strike your Lordship in Council. We mean the copious use of illustrations. These illustrations will, we trust, greatly facilitate the understanding of the law, and will at the same time often serve as a defence of the law. In our definitions we have repeatedly found ourselves under the necessity of sacrificing neatness and perspicuity to precision, and of using harsh expressions because we could find no other expressions which would convey our whole meaning, and no more than our whole meaning. Such definitions standing by themselves might repel and perplex the reader, and would perhaps be fully comprehended only by a few students after long application. Yet such definitions are found, and must be found, in every system of law which aims at accuracy. A legislator may, if he thinks fit, avoid such definitions, and by avoiding them he will give a smoother and more attractive appearance to his workmanship; but in that case he flinches from a duty which he ought to perform, and which somebody must perform. If this necessary but most disagreeable work be not performed by the lawgiver once for all, it must be constantly performed in a rude and imperfect manner by every judge in the Empire. . . . . . We have, therefore, thought it right not to shrink from the task of framing these unpleasing but indispensable parts of a code. And we hope that when each of these definitions is followed by a collection of cases falling under it, and of cases which, though at first sight they appear to fall under it, do not really fall under it, the definition and the reasons which led to the adoption of it will be readily understood. . . . . The definitions and enacting clauses contain the whole law. The illustrations make nothing law which would not be law without them. They only exhibit the law in full action, and show what its effects will be on the events of common life.

"Thus the code will be at once a statute book and a collection of decided cases. The decided cases in the code will differ from the decided cases in the English law books in two most important points. In the first place, our illustrations are never intended to supply any omission in the written law, nor do they ever, in our opinion, put a strain on the written law. They are merely instances of the practical application of the written law to the affairs of mankind. Secondly, they are cases decided not by the judges but by the legislature, by those who make the law, and who must know more certainly than any judge can know what the law is which they mean to make."

We also wish it to be fully understood that the correctness of the decision contained in any illustration is not to be questioned in the administration of the law. The illustrations are not merely examples of the law in operation, but are the law itself showing by examples what it is. The statements that "the definitions and enacting clauses contain the whole law," and that "the illustrations make nothing law which would not be law without them," are correct if understood as merely importing that in the view of the legislature the illustrations determine nothing otherwise than what without them would have been determined by a right application of the rules to which they are annexed. As, however, much law has been made by judicial decisions, which determine questions respecting the application of written rules of law, so law may without impropriety be said to be made by the illustrations in the numerous cases in which they determine points about which, without their guidance. there would be room for difference of opinion even among learned and able judges. It is chiefly in this way that the illustrations, while they make the definitions and rules more easy to be understood, also serve to render them more precise. The operation of judicial decisions in making law precise is a natural process, and that process is adopted and improved in the use of illustrations. The laws of England, as they exist, are to be found partly in rules and principles, some of which are contained in statutes and some in books not stamped with any legislative or even judicial authority, and partly in the reports of decisions by judicial tribunals. Law framed in the way in which we have endeavoured to frame it, also consists of rules and principles combined with decided cases, but with this difference, that the decisions are not made by judges in trying causes, but by the legislature itself in enacting the law, and though they are an important part of the law, settling points which without them would have been left to be determined by the judges yet they are strictly confined to the function of guiding the judges in their future decisions, and of explaining in what manner the definitions and rules to which they are annexed are to be interpreted and applied.

Another matter of great importance is closely connected with this subject, viz., how best to prevent the law from being overlaid with an accumulating mass of comments and decisions: an evil which no mode of framing the law itself can completely exclude. On this subject also we think it useful to quote and adopt a portion of the observations contained in the letter of the authors of the Penal Code, already referred to.

"The publication of this collection of cases decided by legislative authority will, we hope, greatly limit the power which the courts of justice possess of putting their own sense on the laws. But we are sensible that neither this collection nor any other can be sufficiently extensive to settle every question which may be raised as to the construction of the code. Such questions will certainly arise, and, unless proper precautions be taken, the decisions on such questions will accumulate till they form a body of law of far greater bulk than that which has been adopted by the legislature. Nor is this the worst. While the judicial system of British India continues to be what it now is, these decisions will render the law not only bulky but uncertain and contradictory. . . . But whether the present judicial organisation be retained or not, it is most desirable that measures should be taken to prevent the written law from being overlaid by an immense weight of comments and decisions. We conceive that it is proper for us, at the time at which we lay before your Lordship in Council the first part of the Indian Code, to offer such suggestions as have occurred to us on this important subject. . . . In civil suits which are actually pending we think it on the whole desirable to leave to the courts the office of deciding doubtful questions of law which have actually arisen in the course of litigation. But every case in which the construction put by a judge on any part of the code is set aside by any of those tribunals from which at present there is no appeal in India, and every case in which there is a difference of opinion in a court composed of several judges as to the construction of any part of the code, ought to be forthwith reported to the legislature. Every judge of every rank whose duty it is to administer the law as contained in the code should be enjoined to report to his official superiors every doubt which he may entertain as to any question of construction which may have arisen in his court. Of these doubts all which are not obviously unreasonable ought to be periodically reported by the highest judicial authorities to the legislature. All the questions thus reported to the Government might with advantage be referred for examination to the Law Commission, if that commission should be a permanent body. In some cases it will be found that the law is already sufficiently clear, and that any misconstruction which may have taken place is to be attributed to weakness, carelessness, wrongheadedness, or corruption on the part of an individual, and is not likely to occur again. In such cases it will be unnecessary to make any change in the code. Sometimes it will be found that a case has arisen respecting which the code is silent. In such a case it will be proper to supply the omission. Sometimes it may be found that the code is inconsistent with itself. If so the inconsistency ought to be removed. Sometimes it will be found that the words of the law are not sufficiently precise. In such a case it will be proper to substitute others. Sometimes it will be found that the language of the law, though it is as precise as the subject admits, is not so clear that a person of ordinary intelligence can see its whole meaning. In these cases it will generally be expedient to add illustrations such as may distinctly show in what sense the legislature intends the law to be understood, and may render it impossible that the same question, or any similar question, should ever again occasion difference of opinion. In this manner every successive edition of the code will solve all the important questions as to the construction of the code which have arisen since the appearance of the edition immediately preceding. Important questions, particularly questions about which courts of the highest rank have pronounced opposite decisions, ought to be settled without delay; and no point of law ought to continue to be a doubtful point more than a few years after it has been mooted in a Court of Justice. An addition of a very few pages to the code will stand in the place of several volumes of reports, and will be of far more value than such reports, inasmuch as the additions to the code will proceed from the legislature, and will be of unquestionable authority, whereas the reports would only give the opinions of the judge, which other judges might venture to set aside.

"It appears to us also highly desirable that, if the code shall be adopted, all those penal laws which the Indian Legislature may from time to time find it necessary to pass should be framed in such a manner as to fit into the code. Their language ought to be that of the code. No word ought to be used in any other sense than that in which it is used in the code. The very part of the code in which the new law is to be inserted ought to be indicated. If the new law rescinds or modifies any provision of the code that provision ought to be indicated. In fact the new law ought, from the day on which it is passed, to be part of the code, and to affect all the other provisions of the code, and to be affected by them as if it were actually a clause of the original code. In the next edition of the code the new law ought to appear in its proper place."

Although the illustrations, we believe, will obviate many questions of construction, and will do much to fix the sense of the law, yet undoubtedly many cases will occur in which there will be difference of opinion among judges as to what the law is. Room will still be left for doubts as to the meaning of rules, and also as to the right application of illustrations; and cases will no doubt arise where the enacted law is silent; in all such cases the judges will be compelled to use their law-supplying power. It will consequently inevitably follow, if no measures are taken to prevent it, that the enacted law will ere long be incumbered with a mass of comments and decisions; and although the number of chief courts has been reduced since the letter we have quoted was written, yet such is still the judicial system of India that probably many of those decisions will be opposed to others of equal authority.

We agree with the framers of the penal code in thinking that, for the prevention of this great evil, the enacted law ought, at intervals of only a few years, to be revised and so amended as to make it contain, as completely as possible, in the form of definitions, of rules, or of illustrations, everything which may from time to time be deemed fit to be made a part of it, leaving nothing to rest as law on the authority of previous judicial decisions. Each successive edition after such a revision should be enacted as law, and would contain, sanctioned by the legislature, all judge-made law of the preceding interval deemed worthy of being retained. On these occasions, too, the opportunity should be taken to amend the body of law under revision in every practicable way, and especially to provide such new rules of law as might be required by the rise of new interests and new circumstances in the progress of society.

We have much pleasure in stating that the New York Commissioners (Mr. David Dudley Field, Mr. William Curtis Noyes, and Mr. Alexander W. Bradford) appointed in 1857, to prepare a code for that State, have issued the draft of a penal code, for examination by the judges and others, prior to revision by the Commissioners. Through the courtesy of Mr. Noyes we have received a copy of the draft, and we trust in our next number to be able to offer some observations thereupon. We cannot, however, let this opportunity pass without expressing our sense of the importance of the work in which the Commission is engaged, not only to the State of New York, but to all communities speaking the English tongue, and inheriting the laws and usages of the English race. It is singular enough that the appearance of two Reports, each devoted to the object of codifying English law, should have been nearly coincident, though prepared on different sides of the Atlantic, and intended to apply, the one to the ancient civilization of the East, the other to the young energy and boundless future of the Western Continent. It will be more singular still if England should come to be the only State ruled by the English race which does not possess a code of law.

Notices of New Books.

[*⁎* It should be understood that the Notices of New Works forwarded to us for Review, and which appear in this part of the Magazine, do not preclude our recurring to them at greater length, and in a more elaborate form, in a subsequent Number, when their character and importance require it.]

The Ocean, the River, and the Shore. Part I. Navigation. By J. W. Willcock, Q.C., and A. Willcock, M.A., Barrister-at-Law. London: Routledge, Warne, and Routledge. 1864.

THE Preface to this book tells us that it is "intended rather for the merchant, the mariner, the 'riparian' proprietor, the fisherman, the jurist, and the general reader, than for the lawyer." It is written by lawyers, avowedly, and it supplies both history and law. The "historical sketch of navigation" fills 130 pages out of 465, and would, in our opinion, have been better omitted; for we do not find in it that evidence of command of the subject and of the compendious method of treating it with advantage which, in the rest of the work, invites the confidence of the classes of readers to whom it is avowedly addressed. It is true that from none less than from "seamen" is criticism of the "history" of navigation to be looked for. Perhaps no class, as a class, has displayed less interest in the past progress of the art by which it has its being; though this, be it observed—a lack of historical interest in the bygones of the daily occupation—is by no means distinctive of seamen. We all, more or less willingly, "take for granted" in the past, what troubles us quite enough in the present. And this work, as one of practical utility, in which character it claims a high place, would, we think, have been well confined to that of which its writers have evidently a competent command, and in which its intended readers may be expected to have a direct and somewhat lively interest.

The remainder of the work is well done. A vast mass of law, complicated, in no ordinary degree, by its being derived, in many instances, from several independent sources—the products of which can be reconciled only by reference to those general principles to which, for lack of a better title, we give the collective name of international law—is brought into a space moderate enough to satisfy any reader who has intelligence enough to see that there are limits to the useful compression of such matter. It is arranged in numbered paragraphs, and under heads so distinguished as to lead the various classes of readers addressed each to its own peculiar section of the book. That so much is not done without some expression of opinion as to the reason, or rather unreason, of some of the rules laid down, is to be expected. Confusion and contradiction so inevitably beget controversy, and all three do so abound where—as in matters arising on the high seas, and involving different national interests—the conflict of laws is incessant, that it is not possible to obtain, for some problems, more than a choice of solutions, with an indication of which is most palatable to the writer who offers them. When the guidance thus offered does not run to needless refinement, is done with manifest impartiality, and with adequate knowledge, and leaves the character of the work, as a compendium, intact, it constitutes no mean addition to its value—for the occasional consultation of such books, by far the most frequent method of use, more frequently has reference to cases disputed (with or without reason) than to such as lie within, and are readily decided by, ordinary and well-established rules. And it needs but a moment's consideration to show how large a section of all that concerns rights to be asserted at sea, or on rivers, or with reference to water boundaries, must be controversial, either as affected by conflicting national pretensions, or as based upon the nicest regard to what is apt to form a shifting and slippery basis, as to facts, and referred to rules which are none the more likely to be intelligible, or readily applicable, for their adaptation to what is naturally erratic and fluctuating.

Messrs. Willcock afford us no indication of the intended scope of their complete work; and it is possible that, in forming an opinion of the present volume as it stands, we give them less credit than they may ultimately prove to deserve.

A Treatise on the Power and Duty of an Arbitrator, and the Law of Submissions and Awards, with an Appendix of Forms; and of the Statutes relating to Arbitration. By Francis Russell, Esq., M.A., Barrister-at-Law. Third Edition. London: Stevens, Sons, & Haynes. 1864.

Mr. Russell's work may now be treated as the book on the Law of Arbitration. Since the publication of the other text books we have on the subject, the obligation and the power to refer to arbitration have been extended to a great variety of matters in litigation, which could formerly only be disposed of at considerable cost to both parties, and rarely with advantage to either. Arbitration, up to a very recent period, only resulted from the voluntary submission of litigants after their differences had arisen. Conveyancers were in the habit of introducing clauses into partnership deeds, providing prospectively for the settlement of disputes by arbitration; and a variety of local and personal acts contained provisions of a similar tendency; but Westminster Hall almost always managed to free the willing litigant from an obligation to refer thus created. At length the Acts of 1845, for consolidating the clauses required to be inserted in a variety of special Acts, contained minute provisions for such compulsory references with respect to disputes as to the taking of land for public purposes, the construction of railways, and the formation of public companies; and the same course was subsequently adopted by the Public Health Act of 1848.

Mr. Russell's book, which first appeared in 1848, dealt not only with the general subject, but with the large field thus opened. By the time the second edition appeared, the common law procedure act of 1854 had provided for compulsory references in the case of a large number of disputes involving matters of account. The new edition just published contains all the decisions relating to this new system of arbitration, and also the provisions of the 22 and 23 Vict., c. 59, which contains a complete code for the regulation of arbitrations in the case of railway disputes; and of the local government Act of 1863, enabling the arbitrator to decide not only as to compensation for works to be carried out, but as to the question whether the works shall be carried out at all.

Mr. Russell's book is well and carefully written.

A Manual for Articled Clerks, containing courses of study, as well in Common Law, Conveyancing, Equity, Bankruptcy, and Crimiual Law, as in Constitutional, Roman Civil, Ecclesiastical, Colonial, and International Law; Medical Jurisprudence, and Book-keeping; a Digest of all the Examination Questions, with the New Statutes, General Rules, Forms of Articles of Clerkship, Notices, Affidavits, &c., and a List of the proper Stamps and Fees: being a comprehensive guide to their successful Examination, Admission, and Practice as Attorneys and Solicitors of the Superior Courts. By J. J. S. Wharton, Esq., M.A. Oxon., Barrister-at-Law: Author of the "Law Lexicon," &c. Ninth Edition, greatly enlarged, and with the addition of Book-keeping by Single and Double Entry, by Charles Henry Anderson, Solicitor of the High Court of Chancery, Senior Prizeman of the Incorporated Law Society, Editor of the *Legal Examiner*, &c., &c. London: Stevens, Sons, & Hayes. 1864.

This Manual has been compiled for the guidance of articled clerks during their preliminary studies. Its value consists chiefly in the practical character of the information it contains. That portion of the work entitled, somewhat quaintly, "inaugural suggestions," together with the preface, may be left unread without much loss to the reader. Indeed, young men would do well to eschew the clumsy, not to say ungrammatical, diction, which renders those pages quite unworthy of the sequel. The manual contains chapters on all the subjects upon which clerks are examined at the final examination :—Common Law, Conveyancing, Equity, Bankruptcy, Criminal Law, Constitutional Law, the Ecclesiastical, Maritime, and Military Laws, Colonial Law, International Law, and the conflict of laws foreign and domestic, Medical Jurisprudence, and Book-keeping. English Composition and English Grammar are omitted, first, because they do not come within the scope of a law book, and, secondly, because they are not in the list of subjects laid down for the final examintaion. The authors have probably acted with some discretion in leaving this branch of the law student's tuition in abler hands. But the pupil may learn a good deal even from the faults and imperfections of his teacher. Let him for example, duly consider the construction of the following sentences, and profit by his reflection. Mr. Anderson states in the preface to the ninth edition,—" I have carefully revised the text of the various subjects, nearly all of which, in consequence of changes in the law, especially bankruptcy, criminal, ecclesiastical, and matrimonial law, required considerable alteration." Mr. Wharton gives the following description of what he calls " the scheme of the work." " It opens with a section containing admonitions as to the method of study, the desirableness of reading upon a plan, and the benefit derivable from a habit of analysis. It debates the comparative advantages of the several means of acquiring knowledge, and suggests a preliminary course of philosophical jurisprudence as profitable for discipline before entering upon the acquirement of technical law." Again, the student is thus warned against the writers of anonymous letters : " These individuals should be avoided by the articled clerk who is desirous of preserving his own intellectability and promoting his own knowledge." Without stopping to speculate as to what the possible meaning of " a preliminary course of philosophical jurisprudence " may be, we shall close our observatious upon the literary character of this portion of the manual with with this unique passage, " But while the rapidity with which Acts of Parliament increase and swell the statute book is great, the dispatch with which reports augment, and pile up tome upon tome, is greater. Happy the man with a memory that can retain even a tithe of the restless changes : lucky he, who possesses the patience to wade through the the chaotic heap to learn the new gloss, and to unlearn the superseded comment. Hitherto, indeed, the comparisons of celerity have been the disengaged rock from the mountain peak, the winged arrow, the swallow's flight, the rushing wind, the lightning's blaze, the thought-flash or the less poetical allusions to an express train, or the electric wire : but they must all—all—yield to the more truthful and striking simile of fast things conveyed by the hey ! presto ! publication of law reports." The articled clerk may safely take it for granted that no questions will be put to him either at the intermediate or final examination, more puzzling or difficult to answer than the following :—

Describe the various means by which an articlod clerk may " preserve his intellectuality ? "

In what respects does this differ from the process of "promoting his own knowledge ?"

What is the text of a subject ?

State briefly what is meant by the "hey ! presto ! publication of law reports ?"

How is "the thought-flash" produced, how long does it last, and describe the various ways of preventing, controlling, and putting out the same ?

Making due allowance for these eccentricities of style, the law student will glean a considerable amount of useful information from the pages of this book. The advice given, the hints thrown out, the programme of study and course of reading prescribed deserve that attention and confidence which is always accorded to those who speak from personal experience and observation. The following is a brief outline of the general plan of the book. Each chapter consists of a general and almost popular dissertation upon a special department of law, in which articled clerks are examined at the final examination ; and is supplemented with a digest of all the examination questions cognate to the subject matter of the chapter extending from 1836 to January 1864. The questions are transcribed from the examination papers, but the answers are not given. To supply the answers would involve a considerable amount of trouble, and give to the book a somewhat catechetical form. But we have no hesitation in saying that the value of this manual would be greatly enhanced if this additional trouble were taken. Even if it should turn out to be impracticable to give the answers at full length, references to the authorities where the answers to each question might be found, would be of the greatest practical use.

The book is divided into three parts : the first consists of separate chapters on the common law, conveyancing, equity, bankruptcy, and criminal law. "Summaries of the most prominent subjects are introduced, and a selection of the books and authorities recommended, for the purpose of working out their details. The second part is devoted to the consideration of constitutional law, the civil and ecclesiastical law, colonial law, and to medical jurisprudence." Speaking of constitutional law, the author recommends its careful study, as being a subject peculiarly demanding the attention of an Englishman in these days of repressive measures and experimental despotism. To "revert to the fundamental principles of our dearly-bought freedom has become essential not only to baffle the insolent efforts of irresponsible authority, but also to keep in remembrance the glorious causes of our prosperity and independence."

The third, and last part of the book, contains two most useful chapters, the one on book-keeping by single entry, the other on book-keeping by double entry. An Appendix concluding the work, shows the career of an articled clerk, from the time of his entering into the chambers or offices of his principal, to the period of his standing within the threshold of his profession, prepared to commence his practical life. Precedents of articles of clerkship, assignments of articles and affidavits to enrol them, are here given ! and also the requisite notices of admission and examination, and the documents to be lodged with the Incorporated Law Society. The regulations for conducting the examination, the practice of being admitted into all the courts, with forms of the necessary affidavits: the mode of obtaining the several commissions, and the issuing of the annual certificate, follows, together with all the necessary stamps, fees, and charges.

A Manual of Times of Procedure in Chancery. Embracing chiefly the provisions of the General Rules and Orders of the Court. By Thomas W. Braithwaite, of the Record and Writ Clerks' Office. London: Edward Cox. 1864.

In a former number of this Magazine we alluded to the uncertainty which existed on the part not only of counsel but of the judges and officers as to the rules and orders of the Court of Chancery before the issue of the consolidated general orders. We also foretold how the probable issue of new general orders from time to time would again confuse and complicate the question, and we called attention to the plan of Mr. Braithwaite, for giving permanent completeness to the code. Mr. Braithwaite has now produced a work which so far as the "times" of chancery proceedings are concerned carries out his scheme. The preface will best explain the arrangement: "The information is arranged under certain leading lexicographical headings, denoting the subjects of practice; and the provisions of the rules of the court governing the times of procedure in relation to such subjects are set forth under sectional divisions and subdivisional articles—and such a typographical arrangement is employed as will greatly assist the practitioner in readily discerning the information applicable to any particular case. . . Numerous cross references are introduced. . . The several parts of a subject are brought together. . . Thus subjects of practice dealt with in separate issues of general orders, and consequently, presented in fragmentary and complex form, are united and simplified." The value of the work is apparent from this description of it, and the close adherence to the language of the Acts and orders makes it reliable. It will be evident too that the arrangement will readily admit of entries under the proper headings of any orders as to "time" hereafter to be made, so that a very little labour will maintain the work as a guide to the law. We can only regret that the author's labour had not been expended in *including* rather than *excluding* many parts of the orders which do not relate to "time." The question of "time" however, is of great importance and of very frequent recurrence in Chancery proceedings, whilst the resources of the most retentive memory cannot enable the practitioner to dispense with a tedious investigation on the subject, and this clearly arranged work will therefore be of great service to the Chancery lawyer.

The Law and Practice Relating to Discovery by Interrogatories under the Common Law Procedure Act, 1854; together with an Appendix of Precedents and a Full Index. By William Corner Petheram, Esq., of the Middle Temple. London: W. Maxwell. 1864.

THIS little work seems to contain an able and discriminating examination of the apparently conflicting divisions of the Common Law Courts on the subject of Discovery. The author shows that most of the leading rules as to discovery in equity are applicable to the same subject at law. We welcome a treatise, the size of which is a result, not of superficial work, but of honest labour of compression and arrangement; and we think with the author, that from a careful perusal of the text and the examples in the appendix, "enough can be gathered to enable the reader to judge, with some approach to certainty, what questions will be allowed," in interrogatories under the Common Law Procedure Act.

The Laws of Marriage, and the Laws of Divorce, of England, as established by Statute and Common Law, arranged in the Form of a Code, for Popular Use. By Alfred Waddilove, D.C.L. London: Longman & Co. 1864.

THIS, although a law book, and the work of one of our most esteemed civilians, may, we think, be described as a well contrived essay for the information and use of almost everybody *but* lawyers. The author indeed tells us that his object is "to meet a wide circulation among the non-professional public," and he therefore withholds in the meanwhile his "authorities and sources," without which, however, not even the work of a juris-consult of such learning, standing, and authority, as Dr. Waddilove, could, with a due regard to the punctilio of forensic literature, be deferred to by the profession. He at the same time admits that "doubtless, it would be more complete with them" (his authorities and sources), "and may in another edition be supplied." We sincerely hope that they may be supplied in the next edition, which, we doubt not, from the very favourable opinion we have formed of the merits of the code, will speedily be called for.

The Revision and Consolidation Act, 26 & 27 Vict. c. 125, appears to have suggested the idea to the learned author, who remarks: "It was said on the introduction of the Bill, that the law of any advanced nation ought ultimately to be reduced to the form of a code." But it was added, "that if the law is in a state of transition it is not fit for that process; in fact, that we must wait for our code until our law, both statute and common, has been revised, expurgated, consolidated, and harmonised. This may be true of the main body of our law, but there are some branches of it in which the principles and positions are now clear and definite. Of these marriage, as far as England alone is concerned . . . may be said to be one." The code, in fact, ought to stimulate the energy of the Government and the legislature, in the too long neglected field of law reform, of which so much is professed and talked, but so little done.

To the public at large, clergy as well as laity, the work will be invaluable ; and, if it is necessary, we beg to assure them that from no member of the bar could they more safely receive and act upon a statement of the law than from Dr. Waddilove.

A Handbook of Bankers' Law. By Henry Robertson, Notary Public, Bank of Scotland. Second Edition. Edinburgh : Bell & Bradfute. 1864.

THE office of notary in Scotland, is, in some respects, a more strictly professional one than in England, and there is therefore not only no impropriety in any gentleman holding it writing and publishing a law book, but such a work is entitled to be received with all the respect due to an author who has publicly and officially proved his legal knowledge in the way Scotch notaries are obliged to do. With this observation, which, in a strictly professional periodical like the LAW MAGAZINE, we have felt it necessary to make, we have no hesitation in recommending Mr. Robertson's modest little book, of the intrinsic merits of which the fact that it has in about eighteen months reached a second edition is perhaps the strongest testimony. Although a handbook of bankers' law, and intended by the author for the more immediate use of those engaged in banking, it might in many particulars successfully compete with more pretentious treatises ; and it may with benefit be consulted by any member of the profession in Scotland or in England. The modesty of the title of the book is so great, indeed, as almost to mislead. The book is in fact a full, and we believe accurate statement of the Scotch law, not only in regard to bankers' law, but in regard to monetary securities and contracts in general, including "diligence" or legal process against defaulters, and the effect of bankruptcy. No doubt, so much legal knowledge on the part of bankers would be very useful to themselves as well as beneficial to the public. But it may be doubted whether they can acquire it ; and even in the best case we think our banking friends would act more wisely in consulting their lawyer than in relying on themselves for professional assistance. The Bank of Scotland, whose Notary Public Mr. Robertson is, seems highly favoured in having an officer so admirably qualified to advise them ; and to all who are in any way concerned with the contents of his book we would say, "Get the book, read it carefully, carry its precepts and rules in your minds, and as a consequence you will be rewarded by having your money well cared for."

Papinian, a Dialogue on State-affairs between a Constitutional Lawyer and a Country Gentleman about to enter public life. By George Atkinson, Serjeant-at-law, B.A. Oxon. London: Longmans & Co. 1864.

MR. SERJEANT ATKINSON is an author well known both in legal and general literature, and in this book he combines his talents in either department. The work belongs to that excellent class of instructive productions, such as the "Legal Studies," by Mr. Samuel Warren, Q.C., and the "Hortensius" of Mr. Forsyth, Q.C., which impart a knowledge of the ways, means, and doctrines of jurisprudence, to the general, as well as the legal, reader, in untechnical and ordinary language and style. Serjeant Atkinson goes even further, for in his anxiety to be as plain and clear as possible, he has adopted the conversational form—a form upon which the famous "Doctor and Student," has put the stamp of ability and success. The Serjeant's work will indeed at once recall its standard predecessor, "The Doctor and Student," and may be fairly termed a most worthy scion of the same stock. Profound learning, perspicuity of thought and expression, playful and ready wit, these are the marked characteristics of the Serjeant's "Papinian." The book is invaluable as an apt and full *exposé* (in a space, perhaps, too brief, for it might well be longer) of our constitutional polity and law; and it has this further merit,—Serjeant Atkinson maintains throughout his teaching a high moral tone and bearing, the influence of which imperceptibly acts upon and elevates the mind of the reader. The British Constitution is a thing of perfect but delicate texture. Its very purity puts it oft in the power of a vulgar enemy to shade it with misconstruction, and even a vulgar friend, in handling the theme of the Constitution roughly, may not bring out all the whiteness of its fame. It should be approached, studied, and explained in an elevated and gentlemanly spirit, and Serjeant Atkinson shows himself to be just the gentleman to thoroughly appreciate and act upon this principle. His work is great in ethics as well as law. All who have their eye to a parliamentary career should make "Papinian" their special study: the forensic and general student will do also well to master its pages. In fine, it is a praiseworthy attempt to popularise the deep and mighty subject of the British Constitution, and deserves to be welcome with us all. From the work itself we must now give a few samples. Serjeant Atkinson thus enlightens us on Parliamentary Committees:—

"SERJEANT.—As the House of Lords consists of 458 Members, and the House of Commons of 656, it stands to reason that they must divide themselves into smaller bodies, for the despatch of business; otherwise little or nothing would be done: for what is everybody's business, as we all know, is nobody's business. Frequently, in our courts of justice, causes are withdrawn from the 12 jurors sworn to try it; because it is found that one of them, or some other person, would be far better for the purpose. Hence arbitrations.

So, likewise, in all bodies, 1, 3, 5, or 7, are better able to transact a given business than 656, even if all or the major part of them could be got together, which is not at all likely. In the Houses of Parliament, for like reasons, a few (say five) are selected by the whole House. For that purpose, they are, generally, armed with all the powers necessary to carry out their object. When done, they make their report to the House; and the House acts accordingly. This is called a select committee as opposed to a committee of the whole House. In one of the latter kind, the Members have an opportunity of speaking more than once on the same subject, which they cannot do while the Speaker is in the chair. On a committee of the whole House, he leaves the chair, and the Members have many advantages. In addition to a committee of the whole House, and a select committee, sometimes there is a mixed committee of both Houses, as recently for examining the different metropolitan railway schemes. The election committees of the House of Commons are constituted under the 11 & 12 Vict., c. 98, for the trial of election petitions. In the first session of every Parliament, and every subsequent session, the Speaker, by his warrant, appoints, subject to the approval of the House, six Members to be a general committee, who make the necessary regulations. Out of an alphabetical list of all the Members of the House, they select, at their discretion, six, eight, ten, or twelve, to serve as chairmen of election committees. These again are formed into a separate panel, called the chairman's panel. After the chairman's panel has been selected, the general committee divide the Members remaining on the list into five panels, and report to the House the division so made. The clerk then divides, by lot, at the table, the order of the panels, as settled by the general committee, and distinguishes each by a number denoting the order in which they were drawn. These panels are then returned to the general committee, and are the panels whence the numbers are chosen to serve as election committees. All election petitions received by the House are forwarded to the general committee for the purpose of choosing select committees. These are chosen according to the order on the list. Their chairman is chosen by the Members on the chairman's panel. The names of the members in the select committee are also reported to the House."

Papinian earnestly impresses the hereditary nature of the British Crown:—

"SERJEANT.—The Crown is now hereditary, though not so absolutely as formerly; and the common stock, or ancestor, from whence the descent is traced, is also different. Formerly, it went to the next heir, without restriction. Since the Act of the Settlement, the inheritance is conditional, being limited to such heirs only, of the body of the Princess Sophia, as are Protestant members of the Church of England, and are married to none but Protestants. Again, the common stock is altered. Formerly, it was King Egbert; then, William the Conqueror; now, it is the Princess Sophia.

"DE VITRY.—The elective seems, *primâ facie*, to have charms about it which the hereditary principle seems to want.

"SERJEANT.—That may be so: but the history of the world gives the most emphatic negation to every appearance of claim to any such advantage. It may be, as some say it is, a prejudice: but it is, as Gibbon says, 'a useful prejudice that establishes a rule of succession, independent of the passions of mankind: and we cheerfully acquiesce in any expedient which deprives the multitude of the dangerous power of giving themselves a master. The superior prerogative of birth, when it has obtained the sanction of time and popular opinion, is the plainest and least invidious of all distinctions among mankind. The acknowledged right extinguishes the hopes of faction, and the conscious security disarms the cruelty of the monarch!'"

Papinian takes no laudatory view of William the Conqueror's merits:—

"DE VITRY.—Well, if it were not at the time of the Conquest that the foundations of our liberties were laid, to what period are we to attribute them?

"SERJEANT.—I will explain. '*Ce beau système trouvé dans les bois*' of Germany remained the same for twenty years after the battle of Hastings. At this time William's conduct is not unlike that of an Egyptian tyrant of our own day. Mehemet Ali, under the pretence of forming an alliance with the Mameluke Beys against the common enemies, the Wahabees in Arabia, invited the whole host of them to a conference at his palace in Cairo. Not suspecting any treachery, they accepted the invitation, and, on the day appointed, entered the palace of the renowned Saladin. The moment they were in the citadel, down went the portcullis, and they were dead men. Only one, Emim Bey, escaped to tell the tale of butchery. Even he is, I suppose, by this time no more; and the 'Dynasty of the Foundlings,' that ruled so long in the land of Pharoah, gone for ever. The Norman despot, like the Pasha of Egypt, invited the English nation to join with him against the Danes. Not suspecting any treachery, they joined his standard, and entered his feudal fortress. No sooner done, than down went the portcullis, and they were all slaves; tied hand and foot, and manacled together in the adamantine chains of the feudal policy. It is true he spared their lives, but on conditions which made life not worth having. When they were fully in his power, he declared himself the universal head and original proprietor of all lands in the kingdom; among his Norman and Breton followers, the ministers of his will, he divided the forfeited estates; lord and vassal were substituted for Saxon and freeman; he depopulated whole regions to make room for beasts of chase, to which the life of a vassal was deemed as nothing; and, as if in mockery of the past, he taunted them with their voluntary submission, and bade the curfew toll the knell of departed liberty."

In conclusion, we may observe that this "Papinian" affords a pleasing proof of how ready and willing lawyers of the present day are to put their learning within the reach of all.

The Law relating to Mines, Minerals, and Quarries in Great Britain and Ireland; with a summary of the Law of Foreign States, and Practical directions for obtaining Government Grants to work Foreign Mines. By Arundel Rogers, Esq., of the Inner Temple, Barrister-at-Law. London: Stevens, Sons, & Haynes. 1864.

THE subject of Mr. Rogers's work is so important in its bearing upon the manufacturing industry of this kingdom, and his treatment of it is so full and exhaustive, that we hope in a future number to be able to deal with it at some length. The treatise contains a summary of the Roman Law, and the modern laws of foreign countries relating to mines, which precedes the main subject of the volume, and Mr. Rogers claims the credit of having first attempted "to bring before the English lawyer the leading principles of foreign mining laws." There can be no doubt that such a summary must prove a useful contribution to the body of our law. In the distribution of the remainder of the work Mr. Rogers seems to have directed attention to every branch of positive law which affects the possession or working of mines, minerals, and quarries, in Great Britain and Ireland. The last chapter contains a number of precedents for licenses and leases.

The Law of Compensations by Arbitration and by Jury, under the Lands and Railways Clauses Acts, with an appendix of Statutes and Forms. By Charles Wordsworth, Esq., Q.C., Counsel to and Associate Member of the Institution of Civil Engineers. London: Shaw & Son. 1863.

Compensation to Landowners; being a Practical Digest of the Law of Compensation. By George V. Yool, M.A., of Lincoln's Inn, Barrister-at-law, and some time Fellow of Trinity College, Cambridge. London; W. Maxwell. 1864.

A Clue to Railway Compensation, the value of Estates and Parochial Assessments. By Thomas Morris. A popular discussion of the subject, illustrated by Tables and Examples. London: Simpkin, Marshall, & Co. 1863.

The demand for books like the foregoing, must have vastly increased of late years, on account of the extraordinary growth of public enterprise in this country. We are all more or less affected in our private rights by the companies that come to treat with us for our property, vested with great parliamentary powers. No landed proprietor—no occupier of any house—can, in these days, feel secure from the designs of some speculative engineer or contractor. It is the duty of every one to know something of his legal rights, with regard to public companies; and such knowledge Mr. Wordsworth and Mr. Yool have undertaken to supply in these works which are now before us.

Mr. Wordsworth, who is Counsel to the Institute of Civil Engineers, and who has had considerable experience as assessor to the Sheriff in compensation cases, brings to bear upon the subject considerable practical knowledge. His work is elaborately prepared, and cannot fail to be of value, not only to the profession, but also to surveyors and engineers. The propositions in the text are authenticated by a copious reference to cases in the notes, and we have in the appendix a reprint of the statutes themselves.

Mr. Yool says that his object has been to explain the subject of compensation to landowners in a manner which shall be as little embarrassing as possible to those who are not engaged in legal pursuits. His work is, in reality, a valuable and clear digest of the law on that branch of the subject to which it relates, written in intelligible and accurate language. He has compressed in forty-five pages the results of great thought and reading. A work of this kind will be of great value, not only to the engineers, for whom Mr. Yool modestly professes to have written it, but also to the student and legal practitioner.

The perusal of these works has awakened in us a feeling of surprise that our most cherished rights have been so interfered with by this branch of legislation. The courts have gone far in protecting Companies in the exercise of their privileges under these and their special Acts. "If," as Mr. Yool says, "it is to be considered as finally established that no compensation is payable for damages from vibration, noise, &c., caused by traffic on the line, the point is one which may merit the attention of the legislature." A man has spent a life and a fortune in providing for himself a retreat of quiet—which has suddenly been destroyed by the advent of a railway to the wall of his study. He is then told that his case does not come within the compensation clauses, because lands, under these, can only be "injuriously affected" when damage is done by the permanent erection of the works. In *Vaughan* v. *Taff Vale Railway Company*, (5 H. & N. 679) the plaintiff sought to recover damages for the destruction of his wood by fire. The wood was combustible, no act of negligence was proved against the Company, and the plaintiff was told that he had himself been to blame because he did not keep his grass more closely shorn, and had not cleared the dry branches out of his wood. Applying the rough rules of natural equity to such a case, one would be disposed to say that a man may keep his grass in what state he please, and that if a neighbour carries on a dangerous trade and does him injury he must pay him for it. However, the law has been laid down "that any act other than the erection of the permanent works, if properly done by the Company in pursuance of the statute, whatever damage it might cause, is considered sufficiently compensated for by the public benefit expected to follow, and is neither a subject of action nor compensation." We can only hope that the vested rights of property will some day receive a more liberal consideration from the legislature and the bench.

Mr. Morris offers certain rules and data for the guidance of persons who may be interested in the sale or valuation of property. Tabular forms are interspersed throughout the work, showing the equivalents of lifehold and leasehold tenures, and showing the present value of estates of a certain rental, for any number of years, when the perpetuity is estimated at so many years purchase. Dealings with companies have been more especially kept in view in these calculations and forms, but the contents of the volume apply, with a few obvious modifications, to ordinary transactions. It is difficult to understand why some of the chapters which have been thrown into the book, were ever written. To understand many of the paragraphs contained in the said chapters is a still more difficult task. We fear that the book will not add much to the fame or profits of the author. Indeed, we must frankly admit that we consider portions of it an intrusion upon our literature.

The Act providing for Superannuation Allowances to Officers of Unions and Parishes (27 & 28 Vict., c. 42.) with Introduction and Notes. By R. Cecil Austin, Esq., of Gray's Inn, Barrister-at-Law. London: Butterworth's; Knight & Co. 1864.

Mr. Austin has lost no time in preparing for the public a well arranged and useful edition of the Statute passed this session, for providing retiring allowances to Officers of Unions and Parishes. The Act, which was passed on the 14th of July, confers a power on Guardians and Trustees, with the consent of the Poor Law Board, to grant superannuation allowances under the following conditions. No officer shall receive an annuity under this Act on the ground of age, unless he shall have completed the full age of sixty years, and served as an officer of some union or parish for twenty years at the least. The allowance may be granted to any officer whose whole time has been devoted to the service of the union or parish, and who shall become incapable of discharging the duties of his office with efficiency, by reason of infirmity of mind or body, or of old age, upon his resigning, or otherwise ceasing to hold his office. The annual allowance shall not in any case exceed two-thirds of the officer's salary at the time of his resignation. Mr. Austin has appended to the sections of this Statute some valuable notes, and it is understood that the second edition which is in course of publication, will contain some recent precedents of considerable importance.

Suggestions for Improving the Law and Practice of Courts Martial. By Captain L. A. Hale, Royal Engineer. London: W. Mitchell. 1864.

This pamphlet has been written by an officer who has evidently bestowed much thought upon our military judicature; and contains many useful suggestions for the amendment of this important portion of the law. The author is a thorough and ardent admirer of his profession, but his reasoning is exceedingly dispassionate. He considers the present system of courts-martial well adapted to the management of an army in times of war, but by no means equal to the proper administration of military law in times of peace. "It does not make sufficient provision for those cases, which, occurring chiefly in times of peace, and not in active service, involve other considerations than a simple breach of military discipline. The fact that the present system requires no alteration when brought into play on active service affords a strong presumption that it is not so well suited to times of peace."

Several cases are cited for the purpose of showing the anomalous functions of the Judge Advocate, and the utter disregard of the laws of evidence which characterise the proceedings upon courts-martial. Another defect strongly animadverted upon in this pamphlet is the lengthy mode of conducting the proceedings, especially the examination of witnesses. Every question is first written down by the party offering it. It is handed to the President, then to the officiating Judge Advocate, who enters it in full. Every occurrence, however minute, connected with the proceedings is likewise recorded. The Mhow court-martial sat twenty-seven days. The Aldershot court-martial sat twenty-two days. The court-martial on the Paymaster of the 35th regiment, occupied no less than sixty-two days. Captain Hale proposes that a higher form of courts-martial should be constituted. The President shall be selected, irrespective of army rank, from a specially trained class of officers : but the members of the court, with regard to rank and number, as in the case of ordinary general courts-martial, dependent on the rank of the prisoner and the station at which the trial takes place.

The duties of the President shall be strictly judicial, and shall be assimilated as nearly as possible to those of the judge of the civil courts. The members of the court shall be the judges of the facts, and they shall decide upon the sentence to be passed. In order that the presiding judges should be fully competent to direct and control their courts, it is suggested that a degree in military law should be conferred upon candidates who shall have gone through a certain course of study and passed successful examination. This branch of our judicature must sooner or later receive the consideration of Parliament, and we have no hesitation in saying that the suggestions of Captain Hale well deserve the thoughtful attention of those who are interested in the amendment of the law.

Mr. Forsyth's learned and highly interesting work on the "Life of Cicero" will be the subject of an article in our next.

A notice of Mr. Serjeant Woolrych's new edition of his "Treatise of the Law of Sewers, including the Drainage Acts" (which came too late for the present number), is unavoidably postponed.

Events of the Quarter.

BAR MEETING ON LAW REPORTING.

A Meeting of the Bar was held, on the 1st ult., in Lincoln's-inn Hall, to consider the report of the committee on law reporting. The Attorney-General presided, and there was a very large attendance of barristers. The report has been already published, and that part containing the scheme of the committee will be found in an article on the subject in the present number.

The Chairman explained that, on the 2nd of December last, a committee was appointed to consider whether some improved plan might not be devised for preparing and publishing law reports. That committee had endeavoured to perform their duty conscientiously, and whatever opinion might be entertained as to the plan recommended, the profession generally must feel indebted to them for the trouble they had taken. It was no part of his (the Attorney-General's) duty to say a word on the report itself, or to prejudice the opinions of any one present on the one way or the other. He should be glad if the meeting could have been held at a later period, so that more time might have been afforded to the profession to consider the report before they were called upon to vote upon it, but there was no option between holding the meeting now and leaving the whole matter to stand over until after the long vacation. Under these circumstances the committee thought it right that the bar should be invited to meet that day to consider the report.

Mr. Amphlett, Q.C. moved the first resolution:—"That the report of the committee appointed at the general meeting of the bar held in Lincoln's-inn Hall on Wednesday, the 2nd day of December, 1863, and the scheme recommended therein, be adopted." He observed that the evils of the existing system were the unnecessary number of cases reported, the unnecessary length, the multiplication of reports of the same cases, the delay in publication, and the great expense entailed upon the profession. The remedy was to establish an organised system of authorised reports, the present system of what was called authorised reporting not having organisation in the proper sense of the term belonging to it. By the proposed scheme the reports would come out at regular intervals, prepared by duly qualified reporters, and carefully edited by properly qualified editors, at a fixed rate of subscription. It was a question whether it would be better to have a system of reporting by reporters and editors appointed and paid by the State—and of course under the control of the State—or whether it would be better to leave the control in the hands of the profession. But as they were not likely to obtain the necessary funds from the government for the purpose, if they decided in favour of an official system it would become a dead letter and be a bar to all improvement. It was therefore necessary to determine in favour of a system organised under the authority of the profession, and in that case he could conceive no better plan than that recommended by the committee, by which the reports would be prepared and edited, as he had stated, by efficient reporters and editors members of the bar, and under the control of a council which would have the power of revising the details of the scheme as occasion might require. The question of salaries had been anxiously considered by the committee, who had been guided in fixing the amount by a desire to secure as far as possible the services of the present staff of authorised reporters in the several courts. It had also been thought advisable to place the reporters and editors in a certain degree independent of the chances of trade, by assuring them one moiety of the salary agreed upon whether the publication succeeded or not, the other moiety to depend upon the commercial success of the undertaking. It would, doubtless, be more agreeable to the reporters if the government would advance the first moiety of the salaries out of the Consolidated Fund, and he did not despair of persuading government to do so, and in that case there would be no difficulty in finding a publisher who would undertake the risk provided they could show a list of subscribers, say to the extent of £10,000, which he thought would cover the entire expense of publication. The only other point was the price at which the reports could be furnished to the members of the profession, and this it was obvious must depend upon the number of subscribers.

Mr. E. James, Q.C., seconded the motion, observing that he did not agree in all the details of the proposed scheme, but on the understanding that it was to be subject from time to time to such modifications as might be necessary for the benefit of the profession, he was induced to recommend the adoption of the report in its entirety.

Mr. Best, who was very indistinctly heard, commented upon that part of the scheme which proposed that editors should be appointed at high salaries to revise the reports, and asked whether they were to have the power of expunging, or whether they were to be merely clerks at a high salary. He moved as an amendment that that part of the recommendation which referred to the supervision by editors be omitted.

Mr. Miller (reporter of Vice-Chancellor Wood's court), who argued that the scheme as proposed would deprive them of all control over their own reports, and put an end to the independence of the reporters, seconded the amendment. He objected to the proposed superintending council, as well as to editors.

Mr. Wordsworth, Q.C., urged that they ought to have more time to consider the report before they were called upon to decide upon it, and moved the adjournment of the discussion to some day in November next, to be fixed by the Attorney-General.

Mr. Malins, Q.C., seconded the motion of adjournment.

Sir H. Cairns thought it very reasonable that the profession should have more time to consider the scheme.

After some remarks from one or two other barristers:

The motion for adjourning the debate, as proposed by Mr. Wordsworth, was agreed to.

DINNER OF THE LAW AMENDMENT SOCIETY.

The Annual Dinner of the Law Amendment Society (with which is now united the Jurisprudence Department of the National Association for Promotion of Social Science) took place at the Ship Tavern, Greenwich, on the 2nd ult. The president of the Association, Lord Brougham, in the chair.

After the usual loyal toasts had been drank, the noble president, in proposing the toast of the evening, namely, the "amendment of the law," said that we owed to the pure administration of justice which distinguished England, if not from all, almost all, other countries, the enjoyment of our rights and liberties under our admirable constitution. No doubt, the law, ancient as it was, and in most respects admirable, had many defects, partly arising from original inherent vices, partly the consequence of time, and the change which time had effected in the circumstances not being met by a change in the law. Therefore, the amendment of the law was a most important object of national desire. Of all social sciences, there was none so important as that of the amendment of the law. He ought to give a summary of the labours of the Law Amendment Society during the past twelve months, but as they would be found detailed in the report, he would only allude to one or two of the latest attempts at law amendment. Their worthy colleague, Sir F. Kelly, had made various attempts to mend and improve our laws, of which his Bill to prevent gross bribery and corruption at elections had been one of the most important. If that Bill, or a considerable portion of it, had been carried before the last general election, we should not have seen those disgusting outrages of all law, as well as of all morals. Another Bill he had introduced was for a court of criminal appeal. His learned friend considered that it was quite impossible that we could go on much longer without a regular reformed method of revising the judgments recorded by juries. He (Lord Brougham) wished the Bill, with the various modifications and additions of which it was susceptible, all possible success. There had also been some important measures propounded by the Lord Chancellor in the House of Lords, and one of those was of very great importance—he meant the County Court Amendment Act Bill. If that Bill, or anything like it, had passed, he would venture to say that it would have shut up the county courts altogether. County courts without the power of commitment were absolutely impossible. The power of commitment was absolutely essential to those courts, but there were parts of the Bill which he considered excellent. He referred especially to the extension of equitable jurisdiction to these courts, which would be a very great improvement. It had been attempted over and over again, but had always failed; still, he hoped the Legislature would be induced to pass a measure with that object. Then there was the subject of the limitation of actions on simple contract debts. He thought that the limitation of six years was a great deal too long. The Bill proposed one year, which, however, was a great deal too short, but the Lord Chancellor admitted that it was too short, and he said he was prepared to adopt two or three years. It was unfortunate that these two excellent provisions were found in bad company, because they suffered accordingly, and the Bill had to be withdrawn. The noble and learned lord, after some further observations, gave the "Law Amendment Society," a toast which met with a most cordial response.

Mr. T. Chambers, the Common Serjeant, in giving "The health of our noble, learned, and venerable President," alluded especially to his great services in the cause of law reform, and observed that those members of the legal profession who were the strongest opponents of the measures he was instrumental in passing, were now the first to acknowledge their great value and usefulness.

The toast was drunk amidst loud cheers.

Lord Brougham, in replying, said he had always considered that our jurisprudence was generally good, and he had only endeavoured moderately to select those parts which were defective, or partially defective, leaving the great body of it untouched. No doubt many of the changes he had been the means of effecting were at first opposed, not only by members of the profession, but by the judges themselves. He would mention only one of the chief instances—the great, and he thought the most beneficial change which had happened in our jurisprudence during the last 50 years, of allowing the parties in a suit to give evidence, and in some cases compelling them to give evidence. This was at first opposed by the whole bench, and every attempt was made by the then Lord Chancellor, his excellent friend Lord Truro, to prevent its becoming law. Lord Truro went to Lord Lyndhurst, and appealed to him whether it were possible to open such a floodgate for perjury as that of allowing parties to give evidence in their own cause. Lord Lyndhurst heard him, but would give no favourable answer, only observing, "You may depend upon it that the measure will be carried, and you must make up your mind to that." As Lord Lyndhurst had foretold, the Bill was passed, and its effect had been salutary. And to do the learned judges who most strenuously opposed the measure justice, he must say that a year afterwards they confessed that it was of the greatest possible use in accomplishing that which was the great object of all trials, namely, ascertaining the truth. After some other toasts, the meeting separated.

THE EIGHTH ANNUAL MEETING OF THE NATIONAL ASSOCIATION FOR THE PROMOTION OF SOCIAL SCIENCE.

This Association will hold its Eighth Annual Meeting in the City of York, from the 22nd to the 29th September, under the presidency of Lord Brougham.

His Grace the Archbishop of York is one of the Vice-Presidents, and also the President of the Education Department.

The Right Hon. Sir James P. Wilde, Judge of the Court of Probate, presides over the Department of Jurisprudence. The other chairs have not yet been filled up. The Council of the Association have found it necessary, owing to the annual pressure of business, to adopt new regulations. In each of the Departments, now reduced to four, three special questions are put, and a day is to be devoted to the discussion of each, the voluntary papers being read and discussed on the remaining days.

In the Department of Jurisprudence and Amendment of the Law, the following are the special questions for discussion :—

1. Are the laws of real property in the three parts of the United Kingdom respectively, in their substance and tendency, suited to the present condition of society ? and if not, how should they be improved ?

2. On what principle should the law deal with questions of responsibility and mental competence in civil and criminal cases respectively ?

3. Whether any, and what, ameliorations can be introduced into the institution and conduct of criminal prosecutions ?

A Section of this Department will deal with the question of General Average, and discuss the draft of a Bill submitted by the International General Average Committee. Voluntary papers are invited under the following heads :—

I. The Principles of Jurisprudence and Legislation. II. Method of Legislation. III. Administration of Justice. IV. Laws relating to Property. V. Laws relating to Personal Rights. VI. Criminal Law, with the treatment of Offenders. VII. International Law.

In the Department of Economy and Trade, the following special subjects will be discussed :—

1. What are the effects upon trade of the existing laws of maritime warfare ?

2. Is the granting of patents for inventions conducive to the interests of trade ?

3. In what respects and to what extent should Government security and supervision be applied to the provident investments of the working classes ?

A Section of this Department will deal with agricultural questions ; such as "statute hirings ;" "sale and transport of cattle," &c. Voluntary papers are invited under the following heads :—

I. Economical Science. II. Conditions of Industrial Success, including the legislative regulation of professions, trades, and employment generally, and of means of supply. III. Condition of the Working Classes, including strikes and combinations; legislative interference with the hours of labour; emigration, especially female; industrial employment of women; and co-operation. IV. Charity and Relief.

APPOINTMENTS.

The Queen has been pleased to appoint Sir James Plaisted Wilde Judge of the Court of Probate to the Honourable Privy Council.

The Queen has been pleased to appoint the Most Noble Duke of Richmond; the Right Hon. Lord Stanley, M.P.; the Right Hon. Stephen Lushington, D.C.L., Judge of Her Majesty's High Court of Admiralty; the Right Hon. Thomas O'Hagan, Attorney-General for Ireland; James Moncrieff, Esq., M.P., Advocate for Scotland; Horatio Waddington, Esq.; John Bright, Esq., M.P.; William Ewart, Esq. M.P.; Gathorne Hardy, Esq., M.P.; George Ward Hunt, Esq., M.P.; and Charles Neate, Esq., M.P., to be Her Majesty's Commissioners to inquire into the provisions and operation of the laws now in force in the United Kingdom under and by virtue of which the punishment of death may be inflicted upon persons convicted of certain crimes, and also into the manner in which capital sentences are carried into execution.

Dr. Lee, of Doctor's Commons, and Mr. J. B. Aspinall of the Middle Temple, and Deputy Recorder of Liverpool, have been appointed Queen's Counsel.

Mr. J. J. Powell, Q.C., M.P., has been appointed Recorder of Wolverhampton.

Mr. Edward Beavan, of the North Wales Circuit, has been appointed Recorder of Chester, in the room of Mr. W. N. Welsby, resigned.

Mr. George Francis, of the Home Circuit, has been appointed Recorder of Faversham.

Mr. Owen Davies Tudor, of the Middle Temple, has been appointed Registrar of the Court of Bankruptcy for the Birmingham district, in the room of Mr. Waterfield, who has retired.

Mr. Cuthbert Ellison, Stipendiary Magistrate of Manchester, has been appointed Metropolitan Police Magistrate at Worship Street, in the room of Mr. Legh, resigned, and Mr. Robinson Fisher, of the Northern Circuit, has been appointed Magistrate in the place of Mr. Ellison.

Mr. J. E. Davis, of the Oxford Circuit, has been appointed Stipendiary Magistrate at Stoke-upon-Trent, in the place of Mr. T. B. Rose.

Mr. J. R. Bulwer and Professor Abdy of the Norfolk Circuit have been appointed Revising Barristers.

Mr. W. Vernon Harcourt, of the Inner Temple, has been appointed Junior Counsel to the Treasury, in the room of Mr. Welsby, deceased.

Mr. J. Mott Maidlow, Fellow of Queen's College, has been elected to the Eldon Law Scholarship.

Mr. J. Lenton Pulling has been awarded the Gold Medal for the degree of Doctor of Laws of the University of London.

Mr. Henry Murray Lane has been appointed to the office of Chester Herald, vacant by the death of Mr. E. S. Dendy.

Mr. P. H. Pepys, Principal Secretary to the Lord Chancellor, has been appointed a Registrar in Bankruptcy, in the place of the Hon. R. Bethell, resigned; Mr. Augustus B. Abraham has succeeded Mr. Pepys as Principal Secretary; and Mr. John Stuart succeeds Mr. Abraham as Secretary of Presentations.

CANADA.—Mr. Albert Norton Richards, Q.C., has been appointed Solicitor-General of Upper Canada.

The Hon. Mr. Hume Blake, late Chancellor of Upper Canada, has been appointed Judge of the Courts of Error and Appeal.

INDIA.—Mr. James Scott, of the Bengal Civil Service, has been appointed to officiate as a Judge of the High Court at Calcutta.

Mr. A. T. Paterson, Barrister-at-Law, has been appointed to officiate until further orders, as a Judge of the High Court of Judicature at Fort William.

Mr. J. Budd Phear, of the Inner Temple, and Senior Fellow and Mathematical Lecturer at Clare Hall, Cambridge, has been appointed Judge of the Supreme Court of Calcutta, vice Mr. Justice Mills, deceased.

The Hon. Mr. Justice Norman has been appointed to officiate as Chief Justice of the High Court of Calcutta, during the absence of Sir Barnes Peacock.

Mr. C. F. Hall, Magistrate of Allygurh, has been appointed Assistant Superintendent to Deyrah Doon. Mr. R. J. Leeds, Assistant Magistrate in the Meerut division, has been transferred to Mooruffernuggur. Mr. C. N. Pochin has been appointed Acting joint Magistrate of Madura; and Mr. W. F. Hathaway, Acting joint Magistrate of North Arcot.

CALLS TO THE BAR.

Easter Term.

LINCOLN'S INN.—Frederick Eden, Esq.; Robert Thomas Boult, Esq.; William Edmeades, Esq.; Albert Osliff Rutson, Esq.; James Johnstone, jun., Esq.; Henry John Bird, Esq.; Sir George Young, Bart.; John Jermyn Cowell, Esq.; William Payne, jun., Esq.; Arthur Charles Humphreys, Esq.; Charles Bowyer, Esq.; Alexander Robert Pratt Barlow, Esq.; John Armstrong, Esq.; Alleck Moodie, Esq.; John Cyprian Thompson, Esq.; and Robert Wilkinson, Esq.

GRAY'S INN.—Robert Edward Francillon, Esq.

INNER TEMPLE.—Ernest Alexander Clendining Schalch, Esq. (holder of the studentship awarded in Hilary Term, 1864); Lazarus Threlfall Baines, Esq.; Joseph Barratt Jacques, Esq.; Ashley Carr Glyn, Esq.; James William Handley, Esq.; Thomas Clarke Tatham, Esq.; Philip Callan, Esq.; Thomas William Gorst, Esq.; and Peter Williams, Esq.

MIDDLE TEMPLE.—G. J. M. Embert, Esq.; and J. E. B. Cox, Esq.

Trinity Term.

INNER TEMPLE.—John Bealey, Esq.; Francis Henry Lascelles, Esq., certificate of honour (first class); Charles Crompton, Esq.; Charles Edwards Ennis Vivian, Esq.; Richard Christian Betts, Esq.; Robert Lewis Lloyd, Esq.; Charles Wentworth Dillon Sturgeon, Esq.; Charles Edmund Palmer, Esq.; Hereford Brooke George, Esq.; Percy Lee, Esq.; Harrison Falkner Blair, Esq.; Joseph Hodge Simpson, Esq.; Clement Cotterill Redfern, Esq., jun.; Gideon Colquhoun Sconce, Esq.; Francis Law Latham, Esq.; Johannes Herapiet Wise Arathoon, Esq.; Edmund Wright Westby, Esq.; Thomas Turner Weightman, Esq.; George John Scurfield, Esq., jun.; George Octavius Wray, Esq.; Rudolph William Henry Erard de Rutzen, Esq.; Ivanoff Lefroigneur, Esq.; Charles John Stone, Esq.; Henry Fraiser Curwen, Esq.; Henry John Trotter, Esq.; Augustus Fennell Danvers, Esq.; James Gibbs, Esq.; and Arthur Donoughmore Grey, Esq.

GRAY'S INN.—Denis MacCarthy O'Leary, Esq.; Frederick William Campin, Esq.; John Miller, Esq.,; and Clement Alexander Middleton, Esq.

LINCOLN'S INN.—Gerard Brown Finch, Esq.; Basil Arthur Cochrane, Esq.; Robert Phillips Dearden Monypenny, Esq.; Arthur Sterry, Esq.; Walter Coode, Esq.; Leicester Colville Shirley, Esq.; Richard Chaffey Baker, Esq.; William Anthony Jones, Esq.; Charles William Tayleur, Esq.; Fitzowen John Skinner, Esq.; Henry Millett, Esq.; James Fortescue-Harrison, Esq.; Thomas John Edwards, Esq.; Joseph Makinson, Esq.; Francis Burthall, Esq., and Ralph Charlton Palmer, Esq.

MIDDLE TEMPLE.—Francis Turner, Esq. (holding the Exhibition awarded by the Council of Legal Education); John Cunningham, Esq. Certificate of Honour, (First Class); John Chester, Esq. Certificate of Honour, (First Class); W. Francis Phillpots, Esq.; James John Turnbull, Esq.; John Macrae Moir, Esq.; John Andrew Shand, Esq.; Edward Thomas Wilson, Esq.; H. W. F. Harrison, Esq.; John S. Will, Esq.; Wallace J. Harding, Esq.; A. J. R. Bainbridge, Esq.; and Alexander Abercrombie, Esq.

BAR EXAMINATIONS.

At the examination of the students of the Inns of Court, held at Lincoln's Inn Hall, on the 19th, 20th, and 21st days of May, the Council of Legal Education awarded to David Lyell, Esq., student of the Inner Temple, a studentship of fifty guineas per annum, to continue for a period of three years; to Francis Turner, Esq., student of the Middle Temple, an exhibition of twenty-five guineas per annum, to continue for a period of three years; and to John Chester, Esq., Maurice F. Farrell, Esq., students of the Middle Temple, and Francis Henry Lascelles, Esq., student of the Inner Temple, Certificates of Honour of the First Class. To Richard Harris, Esq., and C. F. Hammond, Esq., students of the Middle Temple; G. W. Bomford, Esq., R. E. Davies, Esq., R. C. Baker, Esq., and John Hennell, Esq., students of Lincoln's Inn; Hereford Brooke George, Esq., and H. F. Blair, Esq., students of the Inner Temple, certificates that they have satisfactorily passed a public examination.

At the examination on the subjects of the lectures and classes of the Readers of the Inns of Court, held at Lincoln's Inn Hall, on the 4th, 5th, and 6th days of July ult., the Council of Legal Education awarded the following exhibitions to the undermentioned students, of thirty guineas each, to endure for two years:—Constitutional Law and Legal History," Arthur William Trollope Daniel, Esq., student of Lincoln's Inn. "Jurisprudence, Civil and International Law," Thomas Charles Jarvis, Esq., student of the Middle Temple. "Equity," Charles Royle, Esq., student of Lincoln's Inn. "The Common Law," H. Tindal Atkinson, Jun., Esq., student of the Middle Temple. "The Law of Real Property, &c.," John Matthias Spread, Esq., student of Lincoln's Inn. The Council of Legal Education also awarded the following exhibitions of the value of twenty guineas each, to endure for two years, but to merge on the acquisition of a superior exhibition:—"Equity," Alfred C. Curlewis, Esq., student of Lincoln's Inn. "The Common Law," John Ewart, Esq., student of the Middle Temple. "The Law of Real Property, &c.," John Ewart, Esq., student of the Middle Temple.

EXAMINATIONS AT THE INCORPORATED LAW SOCIETY.

Easter Term.

At the examination of candidates this term for admission on the roll of attorneys and solicitors of the superior courts, the examiners recommended the following gentlemen, under the age of 26, as being entitled to honorary distinction:—W. Gregson, jun., aged 21; J. P. Milton, aged 23. The Council of the Incorporated Law Society have accordingly awarded the following prizes of books:—To Mr. Gregson, the prize of the Honourable Society of Clifford's Inn; to Mr. Milton, a prize of the Incorporated Law Society.

The following candidates passed examinations which entitle them to commendation:—William Goode Davies, aged 19; Frederick Elkins, aged 21; Charles John Ffollett, B.C.L., aged 25. The Council have accordingly awarded them certificates of merit. The undermentioned candidate would have been entitled to a certificate of merit if he had been under the age of 26.—George Butler

Kennett, aged 31. Number of candidates examined, 89; passed, 73; postponed, 16.

Trinity Term.

At the examination this term the examiners recommended the following gentlemen under the age of 26 as being entitled to honorary distinction.

Frederic Ferdinand Smallpiece, aged 21. John Mitchell Marshall, aged 21. William Henry Stewart, aged 21. Frank Taylor, aged 25. George Buchanan, aged 21. Frederick Goodman, aged 21. William Bartlett Harris, aged 21. William Hitchins, aged 25. Thomas Rawle, jun., aged 22.

The Council of the Incorporated Law Society have accordingly awarded the following prizes of books:—

To Mr. Smallpiece, the prize of the Honorable Society of Clifford's Inn.

To Mr. Marshall, Mr. Stewart, Mr. Taylor, Mr. Buchanan, Mr. Goodman, Mr. Harris, Mr. Hitchins, and Mr. Rawle, each, one of the prizes of the Incorporated Law Society.

The examiners have also certified that the following candidates under the age of 26, whose names are placed in alphabetical order, passed examinations which entitle them to commendation:—

Francis Adams, aged 24. Charles Royle Allen, aged 21. Cecil Arundell, aged 20. Edward Bull, aged 25. Frederick Marshall Burton, aged 21. Edgar Christmas Harvie, aged 22. Thomas Mylton, aged 20. Horace Montague Ogle, aged 21. William Henry Toller, aged 21.

The council have accordingly awarded them certificates of merit.

The examiners have further announced to the following candidates, whose names are placed in alphabetical order, that their answers to the questions at the examinations were highly satisfactory, and would have entitled them to prizes or certificates of merit if they had not been above the age of 26.

James Cook, jun., Francis Hamilton Masters, George Andrew Rogers, Edmund Smith Wood.

The number of candidates examined in this term was 154, of these 148 passed, and 6 postponed.

Necrology.

April.

24th. LAWRENCE, HENRY, Esq., formerly a Commissioner in Bankruptcy, aged 85.

27th. BATHO W. MORSE, Esq., Solicitor, aged 69.

27th. SLEAP, JONATHAN T., Esq., Solicitor, aged 73.

29th. UPPERTON, JOHN, Esq., Solicitor, aged 57.

30th. MORLEY, T. GREGORY, Esq., Solicitor, aged 39.

May.

3rd. HARRISON, ALBERT, Esq., Solicitor, aged 37.

4th. PHILLIPS, HENRY, Esq., Solicitor, aged 32.

6th. CHAMBERLAIN, J. HARDY, Esq., Solicitor, aged 64.

6th. CHARLTON, ANTHONY, Esq., Solicitor, aged 67.

9th. RENNOLLS, WILLIAM, Esq., Solicitor, aged 57.

12th. BAKER, FREDERICK, Esq., Solicitor, aged 41.

12th. COOPER, FREDERICK, Esq., Solicitor, aged 68.

21st. WHITE, RICHARD, Esq., Solicitor, aged 90.

26th. JONES, JOHN OLIVER, Esq., late Deputy Clerk of Assize, Norfolk Circuit, aged 76.

26th. CHARNOCK, RICHARD, Esq., Barrister, aged 65.

27th. HETHERINGTON, WILLIAM, Esq., Barrister, aged 59.

June.

1st. WELSBY, W. N., Esq., Junior Counsel to the Treasury, aged 61.

4th. CROSSLEY, JOHN, Esq., Barrister, aged 57.

4th. SENIOR, NASSAU W., Esq., late one of the Masters in Chancery, aged 73.

8th. PRINCEP, CHARLES R., Esq., late Advocate-General of Bengal, aged 74.

9th. SWABEY, MAURICE, Esq., Barrister.

11th. Nokes, William, Esq., Solicitor, aged 70.

15th. Townsend, Horatio, Esq., Barrister, aged 61.

22nd. Matthews, William, Esq., Solicitor, aged 42.

July.

5th. Penniger, Broom, Esq., Solicitor, aged 71.

6th. Harnett, Andrew W., Esq., Barrister, aged 47.

9th. Salt, Thomas, Esq., Solicitor.

12th. Baldwin, George Dimsdale, Esq., Deputy Clerk of the Peace, aged 51.

15th. Hudson, George John, Esq., Solicitor, aged 54.

List of New Publications.

Braithwaite.—A Manual of Times of Procedure in Chancery, embracing, chiefly, the Provisions of the General Rules and Orders of the Court. By T. W. Braithwaite. 8vo. 8*s.* cloth.

Cooke.—The Acts for Facilitating the Inclosure of Commons in England and Wales. By G. W. Cooke, Esq., Barrister. Fourth Edition. 12mo. 16*s.* cloth.

Davidson.—Precedents and Forms in Conveyancing. Second Edition. By C. Davidson, T. C. Wright, and J. Waley, Esqrs., Barristers. Vol. V. Part I. Royal 8vo. 21*s.* cloth.

————.—Ditto, ditto. Third Edition. Vol. II. Part I. Royal 8vo. 23*s.* cloth.

Hayes.—The Concise Conveyancer; or, Short Precedents with Practical Remarks. Second Edition, including a Chapter on Composition Deeds under the New Bankruptcy Act. By W. B. Coltman, Esq., Barrister. 8vo. 18*s.* cloth.

Maude and Pollock.—A Compendium of the Law of Merchant Shipping, with an Appendix. By F. P. Maude and C. E. Pollock, Esqrs., Barristers. Third Edition. Royal 8vo. 34*s.* cloth.

Petheram.—The Law and Practice relating to Discovery by Interrogatories under the Common Law Procedure Act, 1854, with an Appendix of Precedents. By W. C. Petheram, Esq., Barrister. Post 8vo. 3*s.* 6*d.* cloth.

Pritchard.—Digest of the Law and Practice of the Court for Divorce and Matrimonial Causes. By R. A. Pritchard, D.C.L., and W. T. Pritchard, Proctor. Second Edition. Royal 8vo. 26*s.* cloth.

Rogers.—Law relating to Mines, Minerals, and Quarries in Great Britain and Ireland. By A. Rogers, Esq., Barrister. 8vo. 30*s.* cloth.

Russell.—A Treatise on the Power and Duty of an Arbitrator, and the Law of Submissions and Awards, with an Appendix of Forms, and of the Statutes relating to Arbitration. By F. Russell, Esq., Barrister. Third Edition. Royal 8vo. 36*s.* cloth.

Smith.—A Manual of Common Law; comprising the Fundamental Principles, and the Points most usually occurring in Daily Life and Practice. By J. W. Smith, Esq., Barrister. Second Edition. 12mo. 12*s.* 6*d.* cloth.

Strange.—A Manual of Hindoo Law as Prevailing in the Presidency of Madras. By the Hon. Mr. Justice Strange. Second Edition. 8vo. 12*s.* cloth.

Wharton.—A Manual for Articled Clerks: containing Courses of Study in Common Law, Equity, Conveyancing, &c., &c. Ninth Edition, greatly enlarged, and with the addition of Book-keeping by Single and Double Entry. By C. H. Anderson, Solictior. Post 8vo. 18*s.* cloth.

Woolrych.—A Treatise of the Law of Sewers, including the Drainage Acts. By H. W. Woolrych, Serjeant-at-Law. Third Edition. 8vo. 12*s.* cloth.

———.—A Practical Treatise of the Law of Ancient and Modern Window Lights. By H. W. Woolrych, Serjeant-at-Law. Second Edition. 12mo. 6*s.* cloth.

CPSIA information can be obtained
at www.ICGtesting.com
Printed in the USA
LVHW040408200422
716646LV00005B/196

9 783752 593068